BILL COLLETT

The Last Mutiny

ABACUS

An *Abacus* Book

First published in Australia by Hudson Publishing 1993
First published in Great Britain by Little, Brown and Company 1994
This edition published by Abacus 1995

A CIP catalogue record for this book
is available from the British Library.

ISBN 0 349 10643 6

Printed in England by Clays Ltd, St Ives plc

Abacus
A Division of
Little, Brown and Company (UK)
Brettenham House
Lancaster Place
London WC2E 7EN

Bill Collett lives in Portland, Victoria. He is a qualified chemist, a keen amateur yachtsman and a competent sailor.

Contents

For Mrs Clarice Hayman,
of "Nirvana"

Nothing can happen to any man which is not human accident, nor to an ox which is not according to the nature of an ox, nor to a vine which is not according to the nature of a vine, nor to a stone which is not proper to a stone.

If there happens to each thing both what is usual and natural, why should'st thou complain?

For the common nature brings nothing which can not be born by thee.

MARCUS AURELIUS,
A.D. 170

Acknowledgements

My thanks are due to the staff of the Glenelg Regional Library at Portland, and especially Miss Jackie Maling, for assistance in locating source material, to my family for their patience, and to my son Richard, for his technical assistance and enthusiasm.

Chapter One

I keep watch for Mr Ffoulkes's geese — my telescope reminds me of an incident on the *Warrior* — I speculate on the source and remediation of my daughter Anne's epilepsy, and recall Fletcher Christian's opinions — I explain to my daughter Elizabeth the importance of the examination of stools — a melancholy survey of my state of health

"I suppose that feller's got his blasted geese on my croquet lawn again." I reached for my telescope.

"Does it matter, Father? Do they occasion any harm?"

"Probably not, my dear, but it's the principle of the thing. Next thing he'll have his horses in our shrubbery."

"But you can't really call it a croquet lawn, a wilderness is more nearly the truth — we've never played on it." Elizabeth, my daughter, picked up my lunch tray and left me to keep watch for Ffoulkes alone.

I concentrated on focussing the telescope. It was a brass one that had seen a deal of service. It wasn't one I'd purchased — it had joined my effects when I had left the old *Warrior*. I'd painted it black so that Frog sharpshooters wouldn't pick it out. Nelson was the only one of us who used to court martyrdom, and of course he got his wish, and his State funeral, just before I sailed for New South Wales. There is a lot of the black paint missing now, and it catches the sunlight, but there, I have little apprehension of Ffoulkes taking a pot shot at me with his fowling piece.

I'd sent him a smart note at Whitsuntide advising quite freely that a man who could afford to pasture a flock of geese could afford to mend his fences. He had had the nerve and gall to send me an estimate from some gang of robbers offering to make good forty yards of fence at nine guineas, and apparently soliciting my paying half the cost. I had a quiet ambition to take a long shot myself at the trespassing fowl, and if I chanced to wing the gooseherd, why, so much the better! The physical difficulties incumbent in the organisation of this neighbourly act had so far defeated me, but it was not a project of which I had entirely despaired. The pusillanimous Ffoulkes was living on a lee shore.

I was making heavy weather of focussing the telescope, and had a sense that I was being watched. Over the mantel hung a large oil painting, a dignified portrait of a short stout balding man, dressed in the uniform of a junior post captain. He gazed sternly, from blue eyes set in a pale face, directly and disapprovingly at the horsehair settee and at me, his older self, sitting on it. Young Bligh would have had Ffoulkes in his sights in a trice.

I looked again at the instrument and its battered coat of paint...

* * * * *

Warrior was punching into the usual easterly as we skirted the shallows south of the Scheldt, so that I had secured the ink-flask to the desk-top. It contained black paint. I dipped my brush carefully, and applied the paint to the gleaming brass surfaces, taking care not to allow the paint to flow into the moving parts. Ships' painters paint everything, so I had determined to paint it myself.

I was just completing the task when I was conscious of a disturbance on deck, Mr Frazier's nasal shout being predominant. There was a stamping and a challenge from Cpl. Amplett, my marine sentry, then a knock preceded the appearance of Mr Samuel Knowles, Midshipman, who was come to announce the sighting of a sail.

"Well off to starboard, and inshore, Sir," he reported, "Mr Johnston sent me directly to inform you, Sir."

"Mr Johnston? Does not Mr Frazier have the watch?"

"Mr Frazier is in the cuddy Sir berating the steward for playing at cards. His leg is very bad this watch, Sir, Mr Frazier's leg is."

"Bad, is it?" I had my own opinion of Mr Frazier's leg. It could serve him well enough, it would seem, but the rogue was hoping for a survey and a discharge on medical grounds, and if it saved him from a winter patrolling the frozen coast of the Low Countries, why, so much the better. I climbed to the poop deck.

"Whereaway, Mr Johnston?"

Johnston replied, but I perforce could not distinguish his words because of Frazier's racketing.

"Frazier, you damned scoundrel!" I bellowed irritably, "hold your blasted tongue Sir or I shall make it the worse for you, you lagabout." I just said it very naturally, and the villain did stop his lament, so I thought no more about it at the time.

Johnston pointed out the sighting, two points abaft the main and working along the coast — a trading lugger apparently by its size. I calculated the angles. "By George, we can have him. Give me a bearing on the point. How much water can we find in close, Mr Keltie?"

He had an answer without consulting the chart.

"Tide is nearly at the full, Sir. We can stand right in there." He busied himself reading off the angles and the deflection to Cape Zeebrogge, which point the lugger must make if it was to reach safety.

I could see with my eye that he was head-reaching on us. That was, do you see, because of his fore-and-aft rig, but he had the more distance to make up. It was going to be a near-run thing.

"Beat the crew to stations, Mr Johnston."

The ship sprang into turmoil like an ant's nest when broken with a stick, but it was a practised bustle, and the likely opposition being inconsiderable we did not swing out all the boats. Only the launch we trailed astern, as it was very likely we should need it to secure our prize.

The wind was freshening as we beat in to the Cape, but a back wind off the cliff was lifting the lugger, which was perceptibly improving its position against us.

"Steer small there, damn you." Mr Frazier gave the helmsman the benefit of his experience. Clutching at handholds where he might, he had dragged himself slowly and pathetically to join us.

"Don't pinch the wind, Honeybone." I countered his direction to the helmsman, "Keep her running."

I was about to direct Johnston to brace the foresail up and

keep the mizzen-stay full, but three years of sailing with me had made him well aware of my proven theories on sailing a square-rigged ship up into the wind. If you are not to sag off down wind, you must keep the vessel running, keep the speed through the water up so that lateral stability is increased. Then your mizzen is your muscle power to give you the thrust, and it cannot give maximum effort without a handsome curve in the throat of the sail. Next, the tack of the foresail and fore-top must be strained forward as flat as it will go and still draw, to lift the vessel upwind and to spill the wind back into the main and mizzen. *Warrior* lay over, the foresail thrumming, the mizzen creaking and straining and successive waves sprayed over the rail so the chase was obscured. My eyes stung from the salt and a stream of water had dripped inside my tarpaulin jacket, but it was sailing, by God she was going!

"We have him, Sir." Mr Keltie had secured a bearing as we emerged from the spray. The Master was not a man given to flights of optimism, his quiet statement spelt doom for the lugger.

"Mr Johnston, we can I believe come up into the wind, directly, and put a shot across his bow. We will need a launch's crew from the larboard people, and they will need to get away smartly or we could yet lose him." Johnston bellowed for Jewell, the boatswain, and I watched narrowly for the point where we could bear off to bring the starboard guns up to bear.

Suddenly a noise foreign to the working of the ship obtruded. A crack overhead, so that for an incredulous moment I thought that the lugger had somehow put a ball into us. There was another crack and a shout, and then chaos as the mizzen-topsail spar shattered into three, and all hell erupted on the poop deck. The canvas ripped across from the larboard peak and tumbled down so that it rained canvas and rope and tackle. The largest section of the spar fell with a splintering crash that shattered the binnacle housing and tore out the larboard railing. The ship, pulled out of trim by the shift in balancing forces and the slack helm, lurched off down wind, and was pressed down by the tightly trimmed foresail.

I was momentarily stunned by the change in our fortunes, but Johnston, his reflexes quick and trained, leaped forward.

"All hands!" he blared into his trumpet, and the gun deck emptied as the hands swarmed up to trim sail. Keltie was wrenching the wheel around to bring the ship's head back into the wind. The helmsman, Honeybone, sat legs awry on the deck, shocked by a splinter that had knifed into his shoulder.

I looked to see Frazier squashed like a beetle under the spar, for he had been clutching the railing, but his reflexes too had been swift, and he had leapt as nimble as a jack rabbit to safety.

I summoned him to the poop. "I congratulate you on your narrow escape, Mr Frazier," I said, "your legs were very lively indeed when disaster threatened."

He seemed rather less chagrined than I had expected, his eyes seeking out my armpit. I was unable to restrain myself from looking down. My hands were black with paint, and the telescope, clamped securely under my arm, had spread large black stains on my jacket...

* * * * *

I was woken from my reverie by a heavy object falling on my foot. It was the telescope, which had slipped from my grasp and was now lying on the Bengali rug at my feet. I picked it up and resumed scanning the horizon for the topsails of Ffoulkes's geese.

"May I see, Papa? May I look?" Not Elizabeth — Anne had entered quietly. She could be a little mouse, and was crouched beside me.

"Have a look by all means, my dear," I put my arm around her thin shoulders, "tell me if that wicked Ffoulkes has driven his blasted geese over into our property."

"Father, for goodness' sake guard your language." It was Elizabeth, making dumb-show of pointing at Anne, and miming clapping a hand across her mouth. It irritated me excessively. Whatever my faults of temper, no one, no one cares for Anne, or frets about her future well-being, more than I do. I suppose in honesty I must admit that my feelings for her fluctuate from the purest love and heartache for this innocent fruit of my loins, to the deepest despair and anger at the ravages her ailment has wreaked on her gentle mind.

Napoleon, Alexander, Byron the poet, they are, or were, all epileptics, and their genius was inflamed and refined by their distemper. Yet Anne, my sweet piteous Anne, her mind is progressively destroyed by the course of the disease; perhaps because she is a woman, a weaker vessel. And yet she of all my daughters holds my heart. I wake still weeping for her in the quiet hours of the night. Of all my misfortunes, some of them most notable as men tell history, this is the one that will go with me to my grave.

A man most values his children, I have thought, up to the age of nine or ten, when the world lays hands on them, when life's sophistication begins to tarnish their innocence.

Not so with my Anne.

She is my child of nine, she is all children in the world, and she will always remain so, and she is thirty-two years old.

"Will you take her, will you care for Anne?" I had examined Elizabeth. "When I am gone, she will have a home with you?"

"It's a question for me to decide with Richard," she shifted, "but Father, don't fret, she will be well looked after."

If I thought that the efficient bitch might send her to Bedlam I'd change my testament and leave it all to Anne, in trust. Let them chew over that bone, if they wanted something to get their teeth in. I must talk to Carter, my solicitor.

Meanwhile Anne was making little mewing sounds as she tried in vain to find a goose in the telescope. Anne had grieved desperately for her mama, and her attacks had increased as a consequence.

"Shut your eye," I prompted her, "no, not that one, this one, now look over there, down a bit, down I said, dammit, not up."

She had obediently moved her end of the telescope down so that the greater lens was scanning the heavens.

"No," I put my arm round and gently pointed the telescope down in the right direction. There were three or four geese

6

plucking at the bottom of the hedgerow. "There, do you see?"

Barnes, our village apothecary, has her taking an infusion of bryony and sweet violet. It does no good that I can see, yet he describes it as a most excellent physic and a tried and proven cure. Seeing my lack of faith in his galenical — she still is taking fits — he suggested that in London they were using a percolate of Artemis Vulgaris.

"What!" I said, "common mugwort? It grows in every ditch."

"You know your botany," he said.

"I once slept with a botanist for forty days and forty nights." I said. "Longer than that really — best part of three years." I was thinking of the voyage with David Nelson, 15,000 miles on the *Bounty*, 4000 miles in the long boat...

* * * * *

Of all men, I had discussed her affliction with Christian, Fletcher Christian, and he had accepted it very easily. He surprised me by his knowledge and concern. Napoleon Bonaparte was once reported in a medical journal to be dependant entirely on Neufchatel powder to control his seizures. He must have needed a bucketful after watching Nelson annihilate his fleet, burning it before his very eyes at the Nile. I asked Christian if he knew where this famous remedy might be obtainable.

"Neufchatel powder!" he scorned it. "You don't know what Neufchatel powder is, Sir, begging your pardon, or you wouldn't hold it in any regard. Why it's nothing but dried and pulverised moles!"

"Moles? You mean the animals?"

"Aye, the beasts, that's what it is. The poor little maid — it is the Manx curse she has got through her mother."

"But Betsy, her mother, is not epileptic."

"Nay. I would not have expected her to be so, Sir, 'tis not the nature of the disease. It likes to jump through a family's generations. One body in fifteen on the Isle of Man has it, Sir. They used to call it the Manx disease."

"The vicar thinks a devil possesses her," I said gloomily, "and he wants to conduct an exorcism service for her. I refused, but I did let him bless her. The damned fellow won't let her take the sacraments unless she is exorcised."

"It's an empty church he would run in some parts of Man, Sir. Why, every family has a son or daughter, or a cousin, afflicted. But you shouldn't fret too much, Sir, it causes them no pain or grief. It be worse for the family, really. Your Miss Anne, she will be happy enough."

"Thank you Christian," I said, "thank you for your concern. That will do now." A strange mixture he was. As far as I knew there was no epilepsy in his family, but that's the way with the Manx, they see themselves as one family. Maybe it is close breeding that accounts for the disease.

It was on Campbell's trading ship, the *Britannia*, that we spoke, where I took him as a student in navigation. He got that post with me by using his Manx connections — the Manx always stick together. That was why, later on, when Christian ran amok, I should have realised Heywood would stick with him.

Better for me really if I'd never set foot on the blasted island.

*****

I returned from my reverie to find that I needed domestic assistance.

I had became aware of a sour stench. I fumbled in the curtain drapes for the tasselled bell pull that hid there, and, finding it, I pulled it vigorously and repeatedly. Sometimes it didn't work, sometimes it worked but Mrs Peebles did not hear it, sometimes she heard it but didn't come. I pulled it repeatedly, and banged my stick on the floor to reinforce the summons, and was rewarded by the sound of steps on the staircase.

The passage door was unceremoniously burst open, and my housekeeper, Mrs Harriet Peebles, was revealed, cheeks flushed and bosom heaving, but whether from exertion or indignation I was not immediately able to determine. She scolded as she entered the room, stately as a three-decker, and bristling from keelson to main-top with armament.

I referred to a flush in her cheeks, but indeed her whole face was lumpy and reddened and craggy, with the characteristic unloveliness of the Manx. She was a large woman, big-boned and tall, her height in no way diminished by the severe black boots she favoured. Her gown was in some burgundy patterned stuff, a large cotton apron serving as badge of office, for in our quiet household she bullied one poor scullery maid, and filled all other offices herself, including that of cook. It is true that we employ a gardener and handy-man, who looks to our two horses, and makes a very occasional sortie into the house, where he brushes his hair and puts on a jacket, and makes some sort of fist of acting as a part-time footman, but our entertaining is so rare, and his disposition so determinedly independent, that Mrs Peebles can establish no sort of domination over him at all. Jackson is his name, and he was with me quite some years back on *Director*.

Mrs Peebles hair had not gone grey in my service. Grey it was, but not all over, some piebald patches defying the advance of age.

She wore it pulled back into a severe bun at the nape of her neck, which did little to soften her image. Her eyes seemed to me to be at times unduly protuberant, as is the case with the goitrous, although at other times they seemed normal enough. Possibly it was a trick of the light, then. Right now they definitely were bulging at me with rancour.

"It's not enough to be preparing the food, I suppose, and cleaning the breakfast room, but how is a body to be coping with traipsing up and down the stairs at everyone's beck and call, when that girl wants watching all the time if anything is to be done?"

I chose not to treat it as a question that needed an answer, nor as an observation that required consideration.

"Mrs Peebles, I would be very much obliged if you would investigate that closet. There is a closeness in the air that suggests to me that the night pan is as yet unemptied."

"This is a grand position," she observed to herself as she removed the offensive bed-pan, "this a regular treat for someone who has been used to having seven beneath her, and what am I doing here I would like to know?"

"You are emptying my bed-pan." I prompted her, crisply, "And I suggest you remind your young assistant to attend to it each morning as I understand she has been instructed to do."

"Why Sir, as to that, Miss Evelyn is a natural, poor thing, and I may as well save my words. This is too big a house to have a poor simple thing underfoot. She is well enough if I set her to a task, she will do it, but as for using her initiative, well, she has no such resource."

She bore the offending utensil to the door, the evidence of her martyrdom, at arm's length. I found myself somewhat offended by her attitude.

"You might decently cover it with a napkin. There is no occasion to parade my motion before everyone's gaze."

"And who will be seeing it, the butler, the footman, the parlour-maid?" She was pleased by her rich irony.

A fresh voice broke into the conversation. "Mrs Peebles, please cover the pan and take it away, now."

"Yes ma'am." All irony and insubordination vanished on the instant.

"The pan is to be removed every morning. Send Miss Evelyn to see me as soon as she has finished the silver." Mrs Peebles departed, and Elizabeth, who had re-entered during our interchange, came efficiently across to check the invalid's progress.

Everything that Elizabeth does is efficient, very much my daughter. Born a boy she would certainly have made her mark in the service. As it is she can look forward to being a very efficient solicitor's wife — that is if she ever gets to marry her Richard. As for now, I could not spare her from her tasks of ordering my household. There is plenty of time for marriage in years to come, and I believe there is a lot of the spinster in Elizabeth. I don't doubt I do Richard a favour in delaying his nuptials.

She plucked the pillow from my back, plumped it into shape, then stuffed it back behind me.

"It was all right as it was." I said ungraciously. She looked at me accusingly.

"The maid tells me that yesterday, when she came to take the pan, you told her to leave it."

"I hadn't finished."

10

"She believes that you had."

"I hadn't examined it medically. A man's spirit can be determined by his bowel. A hearty breakfast followed by a hearty motion, and Nelson was the hero of Copenhagen. An attack of sluggish colic and Hyde Parker stood back saying 'Will I, or won't I?' until the business was done. History recorded him a fool, and yet the essential difference between the two men was no more than a gill of gas."

"But you yourself have always said that Hyde Parker was a fool."

I chose to ignore this sophistry. "Nothing is more instructive of a person's state of health than to examine the stool. Consistency, colour, whether it is black and tarry, or are there undigested gobbets of fat, or is it the pale biscuit colour that means liver."

"Liver?" She was revolted, but curious.

"One of the first signs that your liver has gone," I explained earnestly, "is finding that your stools lack pigment. No bile, you see."

"Are you worried about your liver?"

I pressed my hand into my right side unobtrusively. The lump was still there, I thought. "No, not especially."

"And who taught you all this?"

I had to think. "Why Parkinson originally, the surgeon on *Providence*."

"You mean you have been staring at stools for twenty years?"

"Don't you think a man learns something from a lifetime's study? You know, it really is a privilege of a sort to have a well-informed invalid to care for. You should be grateful to me, and not careless of my feelings." I was half in jest.

"Well," she said thoughtfully, "the house is certainly going to seem empty when you are gone. I was saying to Jane and Frances, yesterday, that it would be silly to keep it on just for the four of us."

I was surprised and hurt, and my face must have shown it, for she gazed at me strangely. I was hurt that she could so readily contemplate, and project herself into, a world without

11

me. I suppose not one of us likes to speculate overly on the world in which we no longer are the reference point, or that we only do so through testamentary concerns. But then I wondered who would get my patent ship bed bottle. Would they know what it was, or would they use it as a kettle? It was a cheerful thought.

"You may have to wait a day or two for me to be gathered to my forefathers. I hope I won't occasion you too much trouble in the meantime."

"Mr Troubridge will be here this afternoon. I shall ask him to speak to you — he will cheer you up."

Troubridge, the vicar at Lower Farningham, is an outstanding ninny.

"Mr Troubridge will certainly exercise his death-bed charm to extort a stained glass window out of me." He would too. It was a telling line, and I punctuated it by breaking wind again. Not that I had meant to, mind you, but it had been building up, and took the opportunity of my leaning forward to elude the haphazard vigilance of my sphincter muscle.

Elizabeth looked pained. "Father, your personal habits have become very careless since mother's death." She went and opened the window. She had a point. It was a great relief to me, with Betsy's disapproval withdrawn, to indulge in comfortable but mildly antisocial vices. A little farting, the scratching of an itching nostril, the digging of wax from an ear were privileges I reckoned to have gained with age.

"Pardon, m'dear, slipped out, I'm sorry." I thought of adding — "Better out than in!" I'd heard Jackson say this to the butcher in the garden one morning, and I was rather taken with it, and so was the butcher, for he clapped Jackson on the shoulder and guffawed. I couldn't see Elizabeth slapping me on the back and guffawing, so I forbore.

Nowadays such a plague of complaints attend me each and every day that I have long since despaired of curing them. I have long accepted that I must learn to live with what I cannot banish. I can't cure but I can alleviate, and so it is that I wear a flannel binding around stomach and back to ease a weakened back that aches in the cold and to support a rupture in my stomach wall. I have all my teeth, bar three, but I often wish that this was not so, and I have to curb their aching by avoiding very hot or very cold foods and liquors, which otherwise have me sending out for laudanum. Anyone who suffers the torment of the toothache can believe very readily in hell. That damned rascal Barnes, the pill roller, or his raddled old mistress who makes his deliveries, never miss the chance to deliver to me a lecture on the perils and evils of opium-taking every time I send out for a bottle.

Then my scalp is falling out all over the place in great snowflakes of skin and dander. I use sulphur mixed with tallow to control it, but the disorder follows a regular cycle. First I get lumps of dry scale cropping up along a six inch patch — and they itch! Not intolerably, but enough. Enough for me to get exquisite pleasure from scratching them out. It relieves the itch. More than that, I feel that if I could just pick and rub the pate down to a smooth finish then that might fix it. The trouble with this line of treatment is that my exertions leave a tell-tale shower of dandruff and quite large flakes of dead scale flour my jacket, and the chair, and even the carpet. Elizabeth is always catching me guiltily brushing the evidence from my shoulders.

"You've been scratching your head again," is a constant chorus. "Leave it alone and it will clear up — you make it worse."

Trouble is, she's right, well, partly right. Leave it alone and it doesn't clear up, but scratching certainly makes it worse. Sometimes I scratch until it bleeds, but always the denuded lesions ooze a serous fluid that dries to a yellow crust, so that next day I look like nothing so much as a cat with mange. Sykes, on *Calcutta*, concluded that it was a ringworm and treated it with some muck called Blue Ointment, a mercury paste, good for almost everything, so he claimed, and plastered it on my scalp. After a while I swear his treatment was giving me head-aches and blearing my vision, and as it didn't stop the scurf I stopped him using it. It was only a couple of patches the size of a farthing then.

The sulphurated tallow seems to take the inflammation out of the scalp, but the same nostrum does nothing for the piles. My blasted swollen rectal veins bleed and itch and ache so that I walk bandy to ease them and stuff rags down my smallclothes to check the bleeding.

"Your father walks like he was still balancing on a quarterdeck." That was the vicar's wife tittering pleasantly to Frances. Frances, I was amused to note, fluttered an anxious glance at me, well aware of the cause of my crablike locomotion, and desperately worried that I would tell the silly ecclesiastical bitch how it really was, or worse even, show her. It's another reason I keep a close watch on my bowels: griping or forcing out your stools, you know, is the worst thing in the world for piles. But then so is a flux of looseness.

Mind you, the Reverend Mrs Troubridge was not entirely wrong. It is a sailor's disease as much as anything. You show me anyone dressed in canvas pants, drenched in sea water, who works his bum back and forth over the stern-sheets of a small boat in a seaway, and I'll show you someone who will suffer with piles. That's what causes piles — sea-water splashing on your bum for days on end. That and horses. Horse riding is bad for it, not that I ride horses. Oh, and buggery too. Horses and buggery, both bad for piles, horses and buggery and sea-water.

You get plenty of the last two in the forecastle. No horses though. Anyway, with me it's sea-water, I haven't had any truck with the other two, horses or buggers.

So that's how I struggle through each day, worrying about my scalp, and my bowels, and my piles, and my aching teeth, and latterly there's a tenderness in my liver that gives me a bit of a pause. I palpate it often enough, to discover any lump or swelling, but the trouble is I can't remember what it used to feel like. Old age is accepting all the failures of your body as something that you will not cure, but must cope with. Death is what happens when you lose the will to cope.

Then there's my hearing. Comes and goes, though I must confess, it mainly goes. I've devised a standard to measure it by. I check it by listening to the clock ticking. I used, not so long back, to hear it clear across the room. Now I have to get up close, within a foot of it, to hear it.

People talking, I can hear them as loud as ever, but I do have trouble in distinguishing what they are saying. I can if they will just talk plainly; the trouble is, these days, there are a whole lot of people who just mumble. There is a great deal of mumbling, and I will tell you of another annoying thing. You mis-hear a couple of words that someone has said and ask them to repeat it, and they will always repeat the part that you heard perfectly well, not the part that they mumbled. Usually it's the start of a sentence that I miss — they gabble it out before you are paying them proper attention.

But I'm not deaf. They were firing cannon over at Gillingham last week, must be all of twenty miles, and I heard them, the only one in the house that did.

"Napoleon," I said, "mark my words, Napoleon's out again. Should have shot the feller while we had the chance."

Jane was convinced that I was imagining it. "Well, if I'm right, and I've heard too many cannon in my time to be mistaken, then we shall hear all about who was right and who was wrong in a few days." I was right of course, not about Napoleon, that fellow is still eating his head off on Saint Helena, courtesy of the British land-holder. Should have shot him, would have saved a power of money. No, they were aiming in a new battery they have sited at Gillingham. Waste of money that, too — shoal water at Gillingham right around. Can't see too many of your precious French marching up that beach. I sometimes think that the Admiralty has better charts of Van Diemen's Land than they have of the British Isles. So, I'm certainly not deaf.

Some mornings, though, it seems too hard to muster the control of one's body necessary to continue through another day. Give up then, give in, don't make the effort, and would the spark of life dim and vanish? We have trees on the estate here, a couple of elms down behind the stables, fine big trees, that just dried out and died last year. There they stand, tall skeletons with everything apparently in good working order, and the spark of life just deserted them. Had a creeper, a pelargonium, covering the side of the terrace outside the drawing room, all its leaves went grey and drooped.

"That be dying, Mister Bligh," said Jackson.

"Nonsense," I said, "you can't kill a geranium." Geranium, pelargonium, same thing, but it was dead in two weeks and Jackson had to pull it out.

It gets too hard, living, and you give in. Then it's all over with you — that's what I believe.

Chapter Two

An interlude with Anne — I canvass the support of Sir Jos. Banks in my forthcoming legal battle with Mr Ffoulkes — contemplations of the many faces of roguery — I have problems with the disposal of ear-wax, and extol the merits of my Sea Captain's Patent Urinal — I recollect my Court Martial, and receive an unwelcome visitor from beyond the grave

I was thinking these morbid thoughts when Anne came running into the room with a scared face.

"Father, don't die!" She buried her face in my lap, "Papa, what would I do without you?" Don't tell me that she doesn't sense things that other people can't fathom.

"Here, my lamb, go and fetch your poor old father his chocolate and he will contrive to hang on for a day or two."

Her sobbing and fright subsided, and she looked up, "I was in the garden and I've bought you some daffodils."

"They're lovely indeed." I took them, and didn't know what to do with them, "Damned thoughtful of you, my dear. Maybe you had better find a vase for them."

But Anne was off on another tack. "Papa, tell me about the geese, Papa."

I leant over and put the daffodils in one of my boots, the only receptacle within arm's reach. They made quite a brave show. "The geese? Why Anne girl, they belong to Ffoulkes, that wretched fellow—"

"No, Papa, I see Mr Ffoulkes's geese. No, Papa, tell me about the geese in the story."

"Geese?"

"In the story."

"The geese that saved Rome?" I was struggling a little.

"No, the geese and the goose girl," and she softly sang—

> Blow breezes blow,
> Let Curdkin's hat go.

It came back to me, or the next line did,

> *Blow breezes blow,*
> *Let him after it go.*

My baritone was still light and pleasant.
"Bravo, Papa," she laughed and clapped and sang,

> *Over hills dales and rocks,*
> *Away be it whirled,*
> *Till the silvery locks*
> *Are all comb'd and curl'd.*

Half-witted or not, she has the most damnable memory for nonsense like that. It came back to me dimly, some tale about a goose girl and a princess, and a talking horse's head, but how it ran was more than I could fathom now.

"Sit down here, by my feet, and I will tell you about the two-headed cannibals who live in the Fidgee islands, and ride about all day on great crabs."

She nestled down beside me and I lied to her most wonderfully until the autumn afternoon faded, and Elizabeth shepherded Evelyn in with our tea.

As the tea trays were cleared away, I caught Frances' eye and she, understanding, gathered her writing materials, paper and ink, a fresh quill and some sand. Frances, twin to Jane, has by far the neatest hand of all our household, and we have formed the habit of letter writing in the evenings. I still run a journal of sorts — nothing like the logs and journals I used to keep in my time at sea, you understand, but it's a useful habit, and one I've kept up for fifty years now. The difficulty is that I am washed up on the beach with very little action to report. Still, I record the passing of the seasons, and the opening of my bowels, and any of the various law suits that I have put in action the last two years. The intrusions and outrages of neighbour Ffoulkes are also recorded, and may very well in their turn provide the basis of action at law.

The thought giving rise to the action, I swung my telescope discreetly around to take a last sweep of the boundaries before the night closed in. I wasn't discreet enough to deceive Elizabeth, who was I gather waiting for some such action to re-open the discussion about the said gentleman.

"Mr Ffoulkes is a very pleasant person, and a most helpful neighbour. When the oak tree at the end of the terrace cracked and fell last week, he sent his man to help Jackson saw it up. I really cannot understand why you are intent on conducting a vendetta against him."

"You find Mr Ffoulkes ffffascinating, do you?" I lisped, but it was lost on Elizabeth, "You do realise that fence is our boundary, do you not? The fellow has no call to be incessantly trespassing."

"Father, I sometimes wonder if you cannot be happy unless you are in dispute with some other person. I am quite sure that Mr Ffoulkes has no intention of trespassing, or of annoying you. Indeed I am sure that he is quite unaware that you feel any bad blood toward him." This was just possible, but a possibility that infuriated me.

"Well miss, I can assure you that he will be in no doubt of his standing when we get this matter of the fence straightened out in court."

"Would it not be easier to pay our share of nine pounds and have the fence fixed? Are we not obliged, at law, to share the cost of boundary fence repairs?"

An excellent lawyer's wife she was going to make if she went around interfering with everyone, and talking them out of litigation.

"It's as plain as a pikestaff," I said heatedly, "that the fellow's geese are breaking down the fence, and that he must assume responsibility for the entire cost of replacing it."

"But Papa, the fence must be thirty or forty years old — the palings are rotten. Why, Jackson sometimes takes them for kindling the fire."

"That's beside the point."

"Would it not be cheaper to pay to get it fixed rather than pay for litigation?"

"It's a matter of principle," I said, getting to the crux of it, "I've always been prepared to make a stand where a principle is involved — that has been my guiding practice right through my life."

"And look what difficulties and ignominies it has brought on your head."

Elizabeth was insolently persistent, and I lost my temper. "There can be no ignominy involved when a man is right, and I tell you now that in those events I presume you refer to I have always been in the right, I have always been right." Elizabeth stared at me flushed, and frustrated. Anne began to cry.

"It's all right, my sweet, it is all right my sweeting." I petted her until she was consoled.

"Are we going to write up your journal?" Frances was eager to ease the situation.

"No. I have some letters to write that can go with Jackson to the inn tomorrow, to catch the Post." I dictated, and she wrote:

Manor House, Farningham,
Kent.
October 10th., 1817

Sir Jos. Banks,
My Dear Sir,

I have reason to reproach myself for my delays in returning thanks for your kind attentions here. Sir Henry and Lady Howly of Leyborne Grange have proved amiable and energetic friends to us all during my late indisposition, and I thank you for recommending me to them.

I am strengthening rapidly in our pure country air, and have little doubt that, with summer's enervating days behind, I shall soon be out and attending to my small estate again.

I am, I believe, singularly unfortunate in my neighbour, a Mr Ffoulkes. The man has some instability and spends his days driving his flock of geese through our fence, where they have turned my croquet lawn into a jungle. I have spoken reasonably to the man, but it seems that nothing short of legal procedures will curb his trespasses. I know you will sympathise, and lend me your support and counsel if this becomes necessary, as you have

*done so generously in the past. I shall advise you further if we are
to go to court.*

*I look to be in London next month consulting Mr Tregenza
about my general health, and I thank you again for my introduc-
tion to him. He has proved to be a most informed practitioner of
his medical discipline, and I have formed great confidence in his
judgement.*

*I trust that this letter finds both yourself and Lady Banks in
good health, and I remain, Sir, your most sincere servant,*

Wm. Bligh.

I carefully inscribed my signature at the foot of the letter, and
folded it. Banks is my only constant friend, and has supported
me through all the conflicts that holding to my principles has
brought upon my head. His faith in me is steadfast, as I have
been shown time after time to be blameless in all but the choice
of the people I have to do with. The Lord must have, I fancy,
some special purpose for the metal of my soul, having tempered
it so diligently in the furnace of my life.

"Your journal, Father?"

"No, a letter to Carter, the solicitor, first I think." I wanted a
copy of the title plans to our manor to establish the precise
boundary, then a smart letter from Carter to Ffoulkes might
bring the fellow to a sense of his neighbourly obligations.

I put it to Carter, and Frances scratched away at the paper.
The expression on her face gave me warning that Ffoulkes had
suborned another of my troops. "And do I see that you side with
your sister, young lady? You, too, have been charmed by Mr
Ffoulkes?"

"Indeed no, Papa, I am indifferent to his charm, but I don't
like to see you excite yourself so."

It shows how much a man has tottered into old age. Can you
picture Duncan at Camperdown signalling — "Don't look now
Bligh, there are a dozen Dutch ships-of-the-line bearing down
on you, but I don't want you exciting yourself." Or Nelson at
Copenhagen telling me — "Bligh, I want you to anchor opposite
the Danish commodore and endeavour to blow him to pieces,
but do try not to get over excited." Can you imagine MacArthur

and Johnston forbearing to march their blasted regiment down O'Connell Street in case it was harmful to my nerves? I have strode all my life through tumult and bloodshed and malice and treachery, and Frances didn't like to see me excite myself!

I bit back a sarcastic reply, and said, "Why, my dear, you're right. I believe I let small rogues upset me more than big ones."

Quite right too, I do. Christian, the Nore mutineers, even MacArthur. I can understand them and their egotistic conceits, and make allowance for them, and handle them, but the petty irritations of your Fryers, your Ramseys, your Fraziers, and your Ffoulkes, I have never had the patience to try to understand their carping and grizzling.

Take Fryer, for instance, I took the fellow in the long-boat on sufferance because the mutineers didn't want him and would probably have slit his throat. I didn't want him either but I could hardly tell him to jump in the ocean and swim. I cajole and cosset and carry them all along so that I bring the whole boatload safe through storm, and coral reefs, and cannibals, over four thousand miles in an open boat from Tofoa to Timor, and when safety is in sight this chicken-livered Fryer has no better gratitude than to foment another mutiny because I had had to ration their provisions to do it!

This same Fryer was, of course, the Master of the *Bounty*, the one man who should have been in a position to foresee and forestall the Mutiny. The truth is that I have never had Cook's luck in my Masters — Cook had me.

Ramsay, Master of the *Director*, I had in front of a court martial for impudence. I told him he wasn't up to doing his job properly, which advice was as fair and constructive a piece of criticism as he was likely to come by. "Why then, try to replace me!" says this saucy villain — a piece of impertinence which he has had some years on the beach to regret.

The other villain who comes to mind was Frazier, off the *Warrior*. His infamous and as far as I know unique offence was to call a court martial on me! What the Admiralty was thinking of to allow the tern's turd to bring it to them I cannot conceive. A fine thing if every jack smarting under a reprimand can hie his commander up before a court to answer a charge of speaking unkindly. Frazier, I have heard, now runs a poor sort of draper's stall in Cheapside. Runs it very badly I have no doubt. I must go and make myself known if I ever get to London again, I'm sure he would take it as a kindness — he can't number too many Admirals of the Blue among his customers, I would think.

My cogitations were accompanied by a vigorous, and vastly relieving, gouging of my left ear, which had set up an intolerable itching. As Frances dutifully presented me with the letter, and offered me the pen to sign it, I became aware that my little finger was encrusted with a small nugget of ear wax. Hastily I waved away the pen with the other hand and said, "Let it lie till morning, I may wish to add to it."

I clasped my hands behind the chair. Elizabeth was frowning over some embroidery, sitting close to the fire, Jane, who had been feeling dull, had left us, Anne was gazing into the flames and her lips were moving, reciting unheard words, probably about goose girls. I wondered if I might wipe my finger on the curtain without Elizabeth noticing, so I clasped my hands pensively before my eyes, which gave me the chance to examine the wax sample. It was a rich amber, almost translucent, but with a dark shadowed core. Just as a man's motions are a barometer of his body's health, so I fancy do his aural exudations give a measure of the lucidity and quality of his cerebral processes.

I don't insist on it, but it does seem logical. I am in truth a man in whom the juices, the secretions, the liquid bodily exhalations are particularly generous. My sweat glands and my ear ducts, my nasal mucus and my gastric excretions are all of astonishing volume, both to my pride and my distress. I am a man of fine taste, but of gross humours. I looked up to find Elizabeth's eyes fixed on me.

"Time to retire, my dear?" I tried to jolly her along.

"Time for everyone else to retire, I think. I shall stay and help you into your bed."

"Yes," I thought about it, "possibly you would fetch me some water, a jug, and I'll wash down that muck of Barnes, so that the taste doesn't accompany me to bed." She turned to the bedside table, and I hastily wiped my finger on the antimacassar at my neck. Each daughter came and saluted me, "Goodnight Papa," and kissed my cheek. Anne pressed her hot little face into mine and I held her for a moment, tight. It was like holding a little quivering bird, and then she was gone, but the quivering stayed for some time, deep inside me. Elizabeth supported me to the bed, and modestly took hold of the garments I passed to her, then helped me into my nightshirt. My trusty howitzer, my sea going copper urinal was handily under the bed, and I rattled it out to hurry her exit. She went to the window and drew the curtains, and then, as I live, she went around each of the chairs and collected the antimacassars.

"These can be laundered tomorrow." She lifted mine from the chair and seemed to give me a long look. I swear she has eyes in the back of her head.

"Goodnight, Father, your water is by the bedside."

"Goodnight, Elizabeth." I took the urinal and applied myself to it, reclining against the bed. It requires some practice, but then, I have been at it for twenty-five years. It resembles a large kettle, no lid, do you see, but an enlarged spout, and very good stability so it cannot tip in a seaway. In my time I have invented a rangefinder for use in navigation and in gunnery, I have also taken a leading role in designing your modern frigates with their sliding keels, but nothing has given me as much personal satisfaction as my invention of the Sea Captain's Patent Urinal. Twenty-five years I have had it, and for twenty-five years it has stimulated the most colourful and unbelievable rumours in the crews of each of my ships.

The stories as to its incredible uses come back to my ears because ships are sounding boards for discreditable rumours, and because a small community is enclosed within a wooden wall with a limitless moat outside, so the stories go round and round gaining in detail on each circuit, until they become unrecognisable on the second or third time of repeating. Now, you might imagine the ship's captain as being remote, aloof from all this, but indeed quite the opposite. No one in the ship has such a vested interest as he in everything that goes on, no one has such a vital concern in the morale of the crew, and in fact no one enjoys such an active spy-ring, such a network of underground informers, as does the captain. The Machiavelli at the centre of this clandestine web is always the captain's steward. He it is who drops rumours about the supreme being into the fertile pit of the mess and galley, and garners and polishes the latest startling gem of information about the crew, or indeed the officers, then delivers it in a hoarse but confidential whisper with the morning coffee or ale.

The darkness of the room was relieved by the small lantern I keep as a night light, and by the embers of the fire glowing dully in the grate. My mind dwelt on the exchanges we had had about Mr Ffoulkes, the neighbour, and I practised some of the legal arguments with which I looked forward to pinioning him in the court of law. I would have made a very fair attorney myself, I fancy, if my father, instead of dropping me as an eight-year-old onto the deck of old H.M.S. *Monmouth*, had signed my indentures and left me on the doorstep of the Old Bailey. I have spent a good deal of time in courts, one way and another.

I dozed, and as the lantern flickered in the draughts of the old house, a sudden rainstorm pelted the window-panes. The elm branches sighed as an easterly blew in with the cooling night, the house leant to the freshening breeze, the room heaved quietly in the familiar and soothing motion, the swinging of the cradle in which my young life had been formed. The way the cabin had swung the day when Frazier had had the blasted effrontery to drag me before a court martial...

* * * * *

The waters swirled past the stern windows, and a gull called discordantly outside. I opened my eyes and was, for a moment, disoriented. I felt myself to be falling sideways, I reached out and finding the arm of a chair I grasped it and pulled myself upright to listen.

Lieutenant Boyack held the floor, but the noise that had disturbed me was formed by the waves tossing on the beach — their surge and the susurration of gravel and pebbles formed a background to the deliberations of the court martial. An easterly was making into Torbay as the morning ripened, and the *San Josef* was pitching steadily to her cable. She was an unseaworthy old tub, not worth her purchase price, but then much the same could be said for Charlie Cotton, the Court President, I thought. Both superannuated out of the battle line. The snivelling cur, Frazier, was at pains to avoid my eye, God rot him in hell! Instead I bent my gaze on Lieutenant Mr Boyack, who flushed, and gathering himself with an effort testified that he had heard me describe him as "a rascal and a scoundrel, God damn me if you aren't". I looked at the President to see what effect this alarming disclosure had had on him, but he gazed back stolidly. It occurred to me that he had gone to sleep with his eyes open, surely. Otherwise, he could scarcely have contained his mirth.

"Further to that he called me a lubber, and a disgrace to the service," thus Boyack defiantly. What are we running, I wondered, a dame's school or a navy? Never was a commander lumbered with such a set of precious blackguards. I started to my feet intending to describe his character to the court more accurately, although he'd done a reasonable job on himself, but Cosway, the advocate, caught my eye and signalled to me to sit down. There may be worse ways to spend a winter's morning than sitting listening to a crew of lily-livered bilge scrapers snivelling and bleating that they had been called Jesuits, and damned villains, all of which was perfectly true, but I resented it keenly. I was keeping the record carefully in my mind. I'll sweat you for this, you pelts of bitches, I thought, wait until I have you safely back on *Warrior*, and see if I don't.

A smell of putrefaction wafted slowly through the room, hanging in the still cold air. "Lying and farting" I said to myself, looking hard at Frazier. His head turned involuntarily to look at me. I smiled pleasantly and knowingly, and he flushed and tore his eyes away.

Marcus Aurelius says —

When thou art offended at any man's fault forthwith turn to thyself and reflect in what like manner thou dost err thyself.

I reflected, but came to the comfortable, but inescapable, conclusion that I had erred not at all. I redoubled the intensity of my pleasant smile, but he kept his eyes averted.

Now it was the turn for Mortimer of the Marines. He started forward with his face set, and determined to do me whatever mischief he might, but he came adrift over his oath, and swore that God would tell the truth, and nothing but, which so discomposed him that his face became as crimson as his jacket. His eyes bulged so that I feared we might have a corpse joining the proceedings. Quade, the surgeon's mate, was waiting without, it being his turn to lie and dissemble next. A providence, I thought, if he should happen to have a leech or two about him to drain this flushed lobster.

The smell of foul air perceptibly thickened, and I wrinkled my nose at Cosway. The lying buggers are full of ill wind, said my look, but no glint of understanding or complicity came back to me. I began to worry. How was it possible that all these reasonable people assembled here were taking this farce, this ludicrous rigmarole, seriously? Surely the president must shortly rise up, wrathful, and drive them out of his court cursing their frivolous nonsense. What was Cosway about? It must be abundantly obvious to him that no case had been established, and that they were making fools of themselves into the bargain. Surely we did not have to condone it by sitting listening with long faces and serious expressions to such gibberish?

I, William Bligh, no stranger to valour, though I admit it myself, valour proved in the engagements at Camperdown and Copenhagen, I was on trial for calling the ship's Master a damned scoundrel! This in a navy where men could be, and were, flogged until they were crippled. Cook, the venerated martyred Cook, he flogged his way around the world to the manifest satisfaction and admiration of all Christendom, but I was being court-martialled for calling a blackguard a blackguard! It passed belief.

My trust in Mr Cosway was fast ebbing, and I gave up trying to catch his eye, and writhed my buttocks so that a painful pile was eased away from the hard oak, and I settled to listen to the gallant marine's colourful inventions.

Mortimer swallowed several times and fixed his gaze on the Jack on the bulkhead behind old Cotton, but although the Court waited with flattering attention for his words, nothing was forthcoming.

As it became apparent that the Captain remained on the silent defensive, Lieutenant Mr Frazier came forward to try him with a few leading questions.

"Mr Mortimer," quoth he, "did you see Captain Bligh attack Mr Jewell and push him down from the poop?"

"Aye."

"And did you hear him abuse Mr Waller, the carpenter, calling him a dastardly, cowardly old man?"

"Yes, yes I did that."

"Would you agree then that Captain Bligh's behaviour to his officers was generally tyrannical and abusive?"

"Yes, I would agree."

This seemed to satisfy Frazier, but I never heard of such a forsworn, led witness. I ignored Cosway and lumbered to my feet.

"Mortimer," I snapped.

"Yes, Sir," he jumped to attention and gazed at me anxiously.

"Mortimer, would you like to describe to the court an example of my being tyrannical towards you?"

"Why, Sir — no, Sir, Captain Bligh, I'd have to say you was always polite and attentive to all the marine officers."

"Thank you, that will do." I sat back well content, while several members of the court made notes on their papers.

"Captain Bligh." It was Admiral Cotton leaning forward, pixie-like and malevolent. He was eighteen years older than me, Charlie Cotton, but he had only been a dozen captains above me on the Navy List. That's what comes of being entered into the service when you are only eight years old. I didn't have too much regard for Charlie.

"Captain Bligh, have you discussed with the last witness what evidence he was about to give? Have you had any commerce with him along these lines in the last few weeks?"

The old buzzard thought then that I had been suborning witnesses. I had, of course, but only the ones I was sure of.

"Certainly not, Admiral," I asserted with pained honesty,

"In truth that seems to me a question that you might better put to Lieutenant Frazier."

"Thank you, Captain Bligh, I shall decide what questions it shall be proper for me to ask, unless you have some objection."

I sat back unabashed, I was in fact becoming strangely elated by the proceedings, a little above myself. I felt an unusual detachment from my surroundings, and my mind seemed to be groping down a dark passage in time fumbling for reality.

We now gave our attention to Lieutenant Robert Russell, fifth officer on the *Warrior*, a milksop and Frazier's cuddymate. He had no slightest trouble with his evidence. He had obviously learnt it by heart and was able to rattle it off pat.

"I recollect one day when Mr Frazier was in charge of the cutter, going from the ship, Captain Bligh hailed him calling out, 'God damn you, why do you not hoist your sail?' Again, off the Black Rocks the Captain damned Mr Johnston several times for not getting the cable paid down more quickly. I heard him call Mr Jewell, the boatswain, a damned vagrant and he said if he ever was to disobey his orders again he would have both his legs in irons and I have often heard him use the most scurrilous language." All this came out in one breath, but as that breath began to run short it turned into a whine. I shook my head at Cosway who frowned back at me. I eased myself again in my chair, my gut was building up a head of wind that was rumbling painfully around its corridors.

The next witness was listed to be Quade the surgeon, whose namby-pamby cosseting of Frazier's malingering had caused the whole business.

* * * * *

At this point in my recollections I must have fallen asleep, for recollection turned to nightmare. I glanced up as Quade entered, blinked at him, then fell back stupefied. I'm damned if I wasn't staring at the brutal features of Matthew Quintal.

Quintal the mutineer! Quintal the murderer of the *Bounty*! It had to be a fantasy! I shut my eyes then stared at him again, there was no mistaking him.

I tried to find my voice to denounce him, to demand his detention but such was my passion that no words could I muster. Did no one else recognise him? Matthew Quintal, dead in the Pacific for sixteen years. The villain began his evidence in tones of measured sincerity.

"Why gentlemen," says he, "it's good of ye to call me to give witness to the be'aviour of the defendant. It's the chance, do yer see, that we've all waited sixteen year for, the chance to tell yer how he drove us to mutiny. It were his shocking intemperant language we could not abide gentlemen. It's hard, it's very hard for you to understand his damning and his violence, his rigadoon bitches and his dastards, his sons of whoremasters and his blaggards. I swear Sirs, it made our lives a misery." Honest sweat and remorse stood out plain on his troubled face as the bold hypocrite faced the court. Was I the only one there who realised he was dead, cold as mutton, long since eaten by the fishes? I made an effort, although I found myself shaking as if I had an ague, and clawed my way to my feet. Sixteen years of hatred focussed my mind on his destruction. I took a deep breath to shout his perfidy, to send him twisting to the gallows.

"Christian," I croaked, "what happened to Christian?"

Chapter Three

Elizabeth displays unwonted weakness, which I counter with strength — a collapse of the guttering reminds me of incidents in the long-boat following the mutiny on the *Bounty* — a nightmare of bloodshot eyes — the death of Norton — my steadfastness in the face of attempts to usurp my authority

The embers no longer glowed in the hearth, and the candle in the lantern had burned down so that the medicine bottle cast a steepling shadow on the wall. Outside the wind had blown itself out and it was a crisp, clear cold. An owl called, and there was a flutter and scurry as something banged against the wall under my window.

I lay soaked in sweat, and my heart was hammering as if it would beat its way out of my breast. I crossed my hands over the pounding organ and pressed while trying to control my breathing. It often works, I find. Breathe in deeply and slowly, counting — one, two, three, four, five, six, seven.... I mean, you count to ten while breathing in, hold your breath while counting again, then breathe out slowly counting to ten before starting the next breath. It works. It works to control the racing of your heart, it works to control fear, but I couldn't quite make it to ten. I breathed in series of sevens until it slowed and then I got the count up to eight.

Soft footsteps hurried along the landing and my door was quietly opened. The draught finished the light which flickered and went out. Soft arms encircled me, and a moist warm face was against mine.

"Anne?"

"Papa, it's me." It was Elizabeth.

"Papa," she was quietly crying on my shoulder. I was mildly surprised. Quietly crying on people's shoulders was not Elizabeth's strong point.

31

"There, it's all right," I patted her shoulder affectionately.

"Papa, Papa, they have hurt you so much, and now they come to torture you in your dreams."

"Dreams?"

"You were calling out 'Christian, Christian!' in your sleep, and here, you are drenched to the skin. I'll get you a dry shirt and change your sheet, and your pillow, your poor pillow."

It was a bit moist.

"Papa, you have suffered so much, and now you need someone to care for you, and I have been cross and short with you."

It was true, she had been.

She held against me still and I felt her body shaking. There were, I suspected, more tears.

"There, there," I tried again, "you're making the poor pillow worse."

"I wish I had gone to New South Wales with you!" She was fierce, "I would have helped you, I would have counselled you." I could believe it.

"The soldiers wouldn't have got in the house if I had been there instead of Mary, you would not have had to hide from them under that bed..."

This was a sore point, a point that I had gone over a great many times with almost anyone who would listen.

"I was not hiding under the bed." I drew a deep breath for it involved a lengthy explanation, but I never shirked it.

" — and you still miss Christian, don't you?"

"Eh?"

"Christian."

"Miss him! What do you mean, miss him? It was Edwards in the *Pandora* who missed him. What I missed was seeing him hang."

"Father," she was looking at me with curiosity, "you didn't really want to see him hang?"

"I would have done my very best at his court martial, supposing they had caught him, to see him dance in a hempen collar. Him, and Heywood too. But I suppose part of me would have died with him. Part of him died when he set me adrift." I reflected, "He tried, really, to kill us both, himself and me."

"You think he is still alive somewhere then?"

"Christian! Still alive! Good Lord no, he's certainly been dead these twenty years. Dead and eaten."

"But why? How can you know? Why could he not be living somewhere like Defoe's Crusoe, on an island with his men, your men, and his black wife?"

"There is nowhere in the world to hide him." I said it with certainty. "Look here — oh well you can't look now, but I'll show you on the globe tomorrow — practically every habitable corner of the world has been discovered and charted; not a small part of the Pacific Ocean by myself, I might truthfully add. A single man might hide himself but not a motley group such as he was leading." I thought about it.

"And then there's the ship. Every civilised navy in the world was keeping an eye out for her. Not an easy thing to hide or disguise, a ship — not unless you sink her or burn her. Again, where would you do that? Only place you could do it without discovery would be on a deserted island. You couldn't do it in the Americas, or in most of Asia, or China. New South Wales and Van Diemen's Land have British penal colonies, as you well know; India and Cape Colony were alerted to look out for them. So they were trapped in the Pacific. We know they tried to set up a colony on an island but had to abandon it because of the hostile natives. They would have been killed and probably eaten, black man and white man, on any inhabited island from Fidgee to Borneo, from Torres Strait to Panama. What chance would they have had of finding an uninhabited island with a temperate climate and hospitable flora and fauna? Precious little — I can think of none, and the Pacific basin now is like Billingsgate on a Friday night. Your missionaries and traders, colonists and whalers running everywhere, and not one report of them in twenty years. No, they must have run on a reef and sunk, or tried for Japan, and been eaten by the savages there. You can forget Christian."

"But you can't."

"Can't I? No, well you are right in a way. But there now, you had better be off. Back to your bed before you take cold, or catch a quinsy." I presumed that the attack of religious guilt, or whatever had brought her weeping on my shoulder, had run its course. Spinsters can be as hard to live with as first lieutenants.

"Father, I will go as soon as you are dry and as soon as you are tucked up in dry bedding. You change your shirt while I change the bedding and the pillow."

We each busied ourself with our allotted task.

"I found no sheet in your closet so I have covered the mattress with a rug, but Father I am sure that your bed is damp. Will you let me just use the warming iron to drive the immediate damp out?"

The clever minx was fencing with me here — I allow no warming pans in my house.

"Certainly not, Elizabeth. You know very well my views about warming pans. Half the house fires in this kingdom are started by people using them, hauling panfuls of red-hot embers up and down stairs and tipping them into beds."

"But, Papa, this is such a cold, damp house."

It was on the tip of my tongue to suggest that if she were not satisfied with the lodging I provided for her, scot-free, then she should go and make her own arrangements. After a little reflection wiser counsel prevailed, and I contented myself with saying, "Run along now, you are shivering. Thank you for rescuing me from my dreams."

"Goodnight, Papa." She stirred the fire and added some coals, then slipped from the room and I heard her quick, light footfalls scurrying back to her own room.

Left to myself I remembered that I had not pursued with Elizabeth the matter of the bed, and that I had not been hiding under it, well, not because I was frightened or craven. I suppose I must have spoken of it to her before, but I find it hard now, sometimes, to remember.

My musings were interrupted by a rattle of hail at the window glass, startling in the intensity of its arrival. Not a gust of wind nor drop of rain had preceded it, or not that I had noticed, but here it was, sudden jags of ice slashing and ricocheting off the panes. The room was charged with a muted drumming from the slates on the roof and then a squall of wind threw a fresh onslaught of hail against the window. I climbed to my feet and supporting myself hand over hand went over until I could see out. To the west the sky was still clear, but directly over the manor-house and to the east it was black, black as the pit, and the storm clouds were poised above me to try the temper of the house. The hail eased, and then squalls of rain bucketed down so that, as I watched, the terrace below turned to a lake. I knew what would happen next, and so it did, almost immediately. The spoutings, blocked by the hail, could not cope with the torrents of water running into them and overflowed, the water cascading down in untidy streams.

There was a tearing noise, and a bang, and a section of the overloaded gutter broke loose, hung swinging for a minute, then tore itself free and fell to the ground. I instinctively ducked. It was for all the world like our jackspar falling across the poop at Copenhagen, but this time I emerged with my collar bone unscathed. The whole sky was now dark, and the rain was heavy and steady. Water running down the wall was leaking in through the window to form a pool on the floorboards. I tried to roll the edge of the mat back but I could not get down, not safely, not so I could get back up. Clutching the chair back I shoved at it with my foot as outside the rain blanketed everything.

I'd seen rain like it, many years before, when Fletcher Christian had set us to find our own way home across the endless Pacific in an open boat ...

* * * * *

I contemplated a waterfall.

Several small streams ran together to meet at an elbow, then diverged and meeting more water formed a torrent that plunged into space to fall splashing into a heaving pool. The pool broke its banks and formed a river of rubbish and dirt and water that ran toward me until checked by a dam wall.

The dam wall was my boot. I lifted my foot and the water surged further down the bilges, then paused, and surged back as the launch nosed down the next sea. Nature in a microcosm. Reluctantly I left off consideration of a world in miniature to tackle the larger problems of survival and existence.

The rain hissed into the sea with such spite that it seemed to deny their common heritage. All feeling had left my arm, and I pulled the tiller back and forwards to reassure myself that I was still holding it. My fingers were locked around it like a vice so that I was going to have trouble straightening them out, and my hands were a dark grey-blue, the very colour of a corpse I had once seen rolling in the Thames, and the similarity was strengthened by the water dripping from them.

As the boat pitched and rolled, a couple of hundred gallons of water seethed from end to end, banging various items of hardware against the thwarts, and tangling rope and canvas round our ankles. Smith and Lebour were taking watch at bailing, steadily working — dip, lift, toss, dip, lift, toss — but their machine-like efforts were barely able to hold their own against the rain and the spray. The exercise was at least keeping them somewhat warmer. They didn't shiver with the same fierce intensity as the rest of us. Linkletter and Thomas Hall were in the bows, pulling at their oars to keep the boat from rounding up into the wind, but we were so heavily laden that we had little freeboard and water was coming in very copiously over the forward quarter. The rain was so heavy and the sky so black that it seemed like night, but it was just approaching six bells.

We were a boatload of clowns, wet clowns, drenched, not to the skin, but a couple of inches inside our skins. When the chill penetrating my back meets the chill in my chest, I thought gloomily, I'm a dead sailor. Water ran down my neck but felt warm against my cold flesh.

I clutched the tiller with both hands and shook the water from my eyes as a larger wave thrust the nose around, but hastily grabbed again at the stern bench as the boat's motion threatened to throw me to the floor boards. I held to a remembered dictum of Marcus Aurelius,

Nothing happens to any man which he has not been formed by nature to bear.

I suppose I am more or less waterproof, but nature had done a poor job in protecting my bottom. It was raw with open ulcerous sores, as indeed was every bottom in the boat. Being constantly wet and being thrown around on the uncompromising benches was tearing the very flesh off us.

Lebour changed his position with a groan and a curse, kneeling into the flood to ease his back as he bailed. His hair was plastered across his face and a stream of water ran from his chin.

"Better this than roasting under the sun," I shouted at him — not that I believed it, but sanity demanded communication. The wind tore the words from my lips and I was blinded by a douche of salt water so I was in doubt if he heard me. I brushed my sleeve over my face and, as focus returned, I found Lebour leaning towards me, his teeth twisted into a snarl. I recoiled, then realised his grimace was a grin.

"Why, Captain Bligh, I be gettin' more'n me ration of rainwater today, and what are you going to be doing about it?"

As jokes go it was fairly flimsy, but in the hell of wind and water that surrounded us it shone like pure gold. He never stopped bailing; he worked without urgency, but with the economy of a machine, and as tirelessly.

"When we share our rations tonight all hands will get a tot of rum," I decided. It was one of the few cards I had left in my pack.

"Better drink it now," said Purcell.

"Why's that?" I asked incautiously.

"Because we mightn't be here by tonight."

I took it as a pleasantry, although that is not how he had meant it. Purcell was a born complainer and troublemaker.

"You and the Master are next watch onto bailing," I said, watching Fryer cautiously. He'd been sitting hunched and immobile for some time without showing any animation at all, but now he lifted his face to me, blank and expressionless.

"There's no point."

"Mr Fryer?"

"Bugger bailing — don't you see, we are all dead men?"

"What is this?"

"Bugger bailing — what's the point of bloody bailing, we're bloody dead men. Why don't you let us die in bloody peace, you bloody bugger?"

I took Lebour's arm with my hand and clamped it on the tiller then lurched down the boat to front Fryer. I held his eyes as I shoved Purcell aside and grabbed the gunwale beside him for support.

"Mr Fryer, you bail, or you are a dead man," I said levelly. His eyes widened as he felt the point of my knife at his ribs. He remained slumped against me, staring at me disbelievingly, which rather dashed me. I'd hoped for a quick resolution. I jabbed the knife forward an inch to quicken his decision, but he reacted in no way at all, just stared at me with frozen eyes. I jerked the knife away and dealt him a buffet on the ear that rolled him against Purcell. "Purcell," I snapped, "look to the Master, he's cut himself. As soon as you've tied it up you can take the buckets from Lebour and Smith."

I resumed my position at the stern and took over the tiller again. I glanced at my blade, it was stained with blood two inches from the point, but the rain skun it off and sluiced it away. Purcell peeled back Fryer's shirt, then turned to look at me shocked. I stared him down, and he busied himself tearing and folding a wad of sodden canvas over the wound. Fryer picked up a bucket.

Incongruously Lebour, relieved of the bailing, favoured me with a wink, or had I imagined it?

His face now was streaming and impassive.

I was cold and wet, I was tired, I was confronted by a literal sea of troubles, but under it all an exhilaration gripped me. It was strange and inappropriate, but it had started as we were cast off from the *Bounty*. A sense of relief if you like, almost a feeling of exaltation — the noise and fury were done, the personal associations that had become so tortuous were severed by the act of mutiny.

I well knew that I had done no wrong, nor committed any error of judgement. The wheels of fate had spun with a velocity beyond my control, so I felt an inward happiness that was unaffected by the trials and depressions of the passing hour.

My ship had been in perfect order, my mission well nigh accomplished. Christian and his fellow pirates had destroyed everything to return to the dissipation of Otaheite.

My task was clear — to bring this launch and its crew, grateful or otherwise, home to Britain, to recount to King and country the criminal actions taken against us, and to see those actions redressed and the mutineers brought to trial. That I might fail never troubled me. I felt confident that I had not weathered so many misfortunes to founder now. The strength of my determination would blunt and defeat the tempests raised against us. By God, I would lead these drownlings, and bend them to my purpose, and save them in spite of themselves.

"Fryer, Purcell, you are to take over the bailing now."

They came forward sullenly but silently, like curs, and started working.

"Better this than broiling in the sun," I shouted, but this time there was no response. I called, then by signs summoned Elphinstone, the Master's mate, to come and take over the tiller. The wind had veered to the south, and as it was six days since I had been able to read a sight of the sun, I was mortal afeard that we might be on a course to be thrown on the reefs and coast of New Guinea, but, as we had not enough freeboard to quarter these seas, our only recourse was to show a square of sail and run with them. As it was, enough water broke in over our stern to keep the men at their bailing.

Each man had his small share of beef and of biscuit as his daily ration. For our supper this night I had nothing better to offer than a little coco-nut flesh to go with half their bread ration, but I served to each man a spoonful of rum, a dessertspoonful, and the wind and seas moderating somewhat, we all stripped off our rags of clothing and wrung the water out of them, which afforded us some little relief.

I looked at my brave crew. You never saw such a drenched woebegone set. Most of them looked half dead, and I truly believe that, were I not there, they would have fallen on the bread and the little food we had saved, and drunk all the rum, and in very truth left it to the Lord to provide for the morrow.

I tried to encourage them with certain proofs that land must be nigh, but after fifteen days of nearly continuous deluge they regarded me, I feared, more as Jonah than Moses, or Noah. I described New Guinea and New Holland to them, giving all the information in my power to set in their minds the relative bearings of each land mass to the other in this western corner of the Pacific, so that, any accident befalling me, they would have some chance of making their way to Timor.

There were times when I felt strongly that the Lord had me under his particular protection, but there were others when I was panicked at the thought that the news of the *Bounty* outrage might be lost to the civilised world by some mischance or oversight of my own. As far as instructing my delinquent jacks in the practice of navigation I feared that I might as well have used my breath in singing of Simon the Pieman.

I stretched myself on the stern lockers so that no man could come at the stores, and fell quickly asleep. We could all sleep like cats, one eye and one ear open for any fresh disaster.

The morning light was lifting over a smoother sea when I was aroused by movement and excited shouting. We had all trailed lines over the side in the hope of varying our diet with some fish, but I never knew such fishless seas. This dawn, however, young Tinkler, the boy, the only one who still tended his line, had hooked a small barracuda-like fish. As he was exultantly pulling it in, a booby had swooped down on it, and swallowing it with three bites was unable to disgorge it, so it found itself in turn pulled to the boat. The shouting and assistance as the lad pulled in his double catch was such that he nearly lost it, but its wings were much tangled in the cord so it came flapping and tumbling into the floor boards, whereupon everyone within reach tried to secure it. At length John Smith, reliable in all, took it in his leather hands and wringing its neck presented both fish and bird to the larder-master, which is to say, to me.

"Land," he said. "It's a sign we are approaching land."

"Never mind that," said Linkletter, snatching at it, "it is our breakfast." He began plucking it frantically.

"Here," said Nelson, abruptly emerging from the trance-like state in which he had wrapped himself for the last several days, "here, don't throw those feathers in the sea, don't throw them in the ocean." A trail of white feathers was laying a furrow across the ocean in our wake. "Let me have them." He passed a sack to Linkletter to receive them. "Fill them into there."

"You going to eat them, are you, Nelson?" It was George Simpson, the quartermaster's mate, and his unpleasant laugh drained any humour out of the situation.

"No," said Nelson seriously, "feathers are soft and water-proof, they will be very handy."

"Going to stick 'em all over yourself like a bird, are yer?" Simpson again.

"No just stick them to his arms and fly home."

Young Fletcher laughed heartily at his jest until, his weakness overcoming him, he fell across the seat still shaking.

"I'll fill this bag, then I've got a cushion to save what's left of my bottom, or a quilt to stave off the cold."

There was a silence while these observations were absorbed, then a burst of activity as further lines were let out in the hope of trapping another bird. Envious eyes were now watching Nelson stuff his sack. Fatigue and exposure were taking a heavy toll on our veneer of civilisation. The good sense demonstrated by Nelson, and the undoubted fact that by his enterprise he had increased his chances of survival, were galling to others who now felt, illogically, that if his chance was increased then so in proportion was theirs decreased.

To break the resentment I said briskly,

"Now then, I'll weigh out our breakfast biscuit, and we'll divide up the duck to portions, then divide them out by the old seamen's method of "Who shall have this?" By this method each man turns his back, and calls out to a friend who nominates what portion he is to receive. It usually works well, but today it nearly occasioned murder, several protesting their portion.

We ate the entrails, beak and feet, and four small mullet from its gut. I got one leg and a foot, and tough nauseous eating it was, but I chewed and worried the foot all day. A brace of flying fish blundered into the boat in the afternoon watch as we sailed and paddled and bailed our tedious way to New Holland. As I had anticipated, the wind was making into a south-easter, which wind is the prevailing pattern up the New Holland coast, another one of my observations for which Cook had modestly taken the credit. By mid-afternoon it had dropped to a whisper.

"It will come up again at sunset."

"How do you fathom that?" It was Fryer, anxious to undermine my authority. I ignored him. His time was coming.

We ran out the sweeps, and pulled our way across a sullen ocean towards the west.

It was Smith, typically, who saw it first. A cloud on the horizon ahead of us.

"It's land," he said quietly.

Everyone turned to gape, Linkletter scrambled to his feet for a clearer view, dropping his oar and clutching at the mast as he fell over Purcell.

"Just a bleeding cloud," he snarled in disgust. He was possibly expecting coco-nut palms and dusky maidens.

Smith looked at me. We both knew it was land.

"Take your oar, Linkletter, and sit down, we'll share a ration while I think what best to do."

I got out my measure and my balance, in this microcosm world the symbols of my authority, the badges of my office, the household gods, the *Lares et Penates* of our aquatic household. I had foreseen early the discontent likely to arise over division of our miserably straitened rations, which could be the seed to grow into disaffection, so I had devised a pair of scales from a rod of brass and two halved coco-nut shells. Old Lebogue having come up with some lead pistol balls from a locker in the launch, I calculated that these ran eighteen to the pound, so that the weight of one ball represented the amount of bread for a man at each meal, a little over two ounces each, per day.

I used a gourd to measure a gill of drinking water and a small leather measure cup for totting out the spirit, so that as I went through the meal time ritual I gave nothing in ceremony to the priest in the Abbey at high mass.

Thirty-four eyes watched me carefully — thirty-three actually since one of Lebogue's clouded orbs was at odds with the other, and perforce they performed alternately. Each man dipped his biscuit cautiously in salt water to soften it and to swell its volume. I ate mine from a shell with a spoon, making myself take such time over the precious crumbs as I might otherwise take over a banquet. Our water beakers had nearly been filled by the rain we had trapped, and I was tempted to increase the daily ration, but a caution held me. Broiling weather and stern work might still very well be ahead of us. I hadn't spoken to the men of it yet, but assuming we got safely inside the reef at New Holland in the next few days, the more hazardous part of our journey was still before us — to find our way to Timor.

Arthur Phillip might be at Botany Bay. He sailed six months before us. He might never have reached it.

He might have reached it and been driven from it, abandoning it to the natives. I didn't trust Botany Bay, and so I had not mentioned it as an alternative destination.

Fryer took the evening watch, and the wind coming up as I had indeed foretold, we hoisted the lug-sail, and thankfully stowed the oars inboard as the launch rolled towards the distant shore. I composed myself in the stern quarters to gain some rest before the business of the morrow.

"The sail comes down at sunset," I cautioned him.

My sleep was fitful and piqued by the consideration of a landfall. I could again feel the boat in the surf, and see Norton clutching, clutching at the stern. His face was a nightmare with the eyes rolled back, and I beat at his grasp to free us as he pulled us back to death.

The boat lurched into a changed motion and I was suddenly awake. Norton had gone but I could still hear the surf. Fryer was a shadow at the tiller, but beyond him the lug-sail still strained at its clew. I burst from the bench, shoving him aside.

"Stow the sail, get that frigging sail down," I wrenched

the tiller into my hands, "God's balls! What do you think you are about? Out with the sweeps, smartly, or we are dead men."

The seas were bigger, and were starting their shoreward roll. I picked my moment as a break of water foamed past us, then pulled up the helm to bring us round. "Easy larboard, pull her round starboard." The boat was clumsy to turn, and the next roller caught us amidships, but somehow we survived and then we were about. "Pull together now. Heave, damn your eyes, pull, get her moving, get your backs into it!"

Slowly the launch gathered way and punched back into the seas, and away from death. Foot by foot we clawed our way off the lee shore and back out to sea, to safety. It was stiff work, but the men persisted until we had sea room. Painful work it was. The oars reaching back for their stroke seemed just to clear the puddle of the last stroke, but there was no help for it as our clumsy sail would not put us up into the wind, no, not by a degree. I changed the oarsmen frequently, although all of them, even Smith, were inclined to grizzle.

"You have Mr Fryer to thank for your labours," I reminded them pleasantly, "Mr Fryer, who decided to look for a gap in the reef by starlight. Explain now Mister, did I not order the sail to be brought down at sunset?" The useless clown was staring at me with a wild look, but could find no explanation or excuse for his behaviour. I looked at him closely; his eyes were staring but there was no intelligence in them. The fellow's deranged, I thought, something has carried adrift up aloft in him. I thought it best to leave him, and that was to prove a mistake, but then if I had the living of my life again there are numerous mistakes I might correct.

We held into the breeze until daybreak, then turned and ran back with it, and by noon we were inside the reef.

* * * * *

I woke shivering, not in a long boat, but in my chair at the window, but my bottom still seemed bruised and cramped from a night in the launch. I pulled together the rugs and covers of the bed, and taking a cushion and a bolster I made myself as easy as I could in my tumbled nest. I yawned massively, and could find myself falling down into sleep.

That was where the eyes found me.

I don't know if there is a pattern to it. It is a recurring dream. Not a dream, a recurring nightmare. It is always the eyes. It starts with a wall of eyes staring at me, bloodshot eyes, staring expressionless; or is there terror in them? or is the terror in me? They move towards me, getting larger as they close, larger and larger until I can only see one pair.

The pupils are red, a dull arterial red, and I gaze at them unable to flee, unable to block them out. If I shut my eyes I can still see them, and as I gaze at them tears slowly trickle from them. Red tears. Tears of blood. The vision continues to increase until I am staring horrified into one glaring enormous pupil. The pupil splits open like a door, and I stumble through.

Then I am running. Then I am wading. Running, stumbling, wading through a sea of blood. Running from sheer horror, fleeing from a terror the more terrifying because I know not what it is. The unspeakable draws nearer and nearer, but my feet are as clumsy and heavy as basalt. As I drag them down a blood red beach I chance a glance over my shoulder, but now the eyes are following me.

"Wait!" It is a very human voice, and familiar. I turn again, and it is John Norton's face — fat, friendly and familiar, but twisting now with effort, sweating in runnels down his nose, his eyes screwed shut as he reaches for me. He reaches out his hand, I reach out my hand. As they touch he opens his eyes wide, and they are blood red.

I recoil and fall back, and as he reaches out again I am slashing at him with a cutlass, slashing and slashing into a tangle of flesh and blood and eyes.

Then I was back in my bedchamber staring at the window opening, breathing hard. It had been a familiar nightmare, it is a familiar nightmare. But my breathing was shallow and my heart pounded. I don't spend too much time now agonising about poor Norton. Did I mean to cut his hand away? It doesn't matter now. But the nightmare comes back.

* * * * *

Norton had been pushing at the stern as Smith and Cole pulled at the oars and Elphinstone in a frenzy swung another pair into the rowlocks. I pushed at the stern quarter until the boat was fairly launched and moving out, then with a last heave tumbled in. Norton, still pushing at the stern, grunted as a stone thudded into his leg. The faces— painted demonic faces leaping and screaming, snarling teeth and hurling rocks. Rocks showering, splintering, bruising, tearing, smashing. God! for a musket, God damn you to hell Quintal, just a musket.

An oar splintered under a chunk of rock the size of a man's head. Norton was still in the surf, still shoving us out as a stone club fell on his shoulder.

I clambered to the stern to cut at his assailants with a cutlass, and a jagged piece of larval rock whistled past my ears and caught Samuels in the midships, laying him out stunned and bleeding in the bottom of the boat. The same rascal who had hurled this missile now laid hands upon the thwart, but whether he meant to check our progress, or to leap in I was unsure. Elphinstone raised his oar to strike at him but managed it so clumsily that the native seized the blade and would have wrenched it from his grasp. Ledward, cool in adversity, rose up with the other cutlass and jabbed it into his throat, so that for a moment the savage hung there, fairly transfixed, clutching at the cutting blade with bloodied fingers.

The despatch of this rascal gave some pause to the rest of the savages, and also to Simpson and Lamb, who sat there goggling at him. "Pull! You boobies!" I screamed, "Pull, or it will be your heads next!"

Norton shouted, and I turned and slashed again at his assailant, but then cutting at a cannibal hand on the gunwale I brought the blade down across Norton's fingers. He fell back in the surf under a flurry of hammering clubs, and was dragged, dead I think, to the shore, where two of the natives continued pounding at his head with stones while

46

another half a dozen struggled to see who would have his clothes.

Several native canoes, crewed by shrieking cannibals, all armed with stones, paddled to cut us off, and although none closed with us, showers of stones fell around us and into the boat, so that all of us were to some degree wounded. One canoe outstripping the others placed itself squarely before us to block our way, but I steered directly at them, and then they learned the strength of English oak and English muscle, for their craft was stove in and overturned. Their compatriots hesitated to come to their succour, and we left them floundering, for their craft burthened with stones had plunged straight to the bottom. One at least of them was taken, I fancy, by a great fish as they struggled in the water, but this gave us no cause for sympathy.

The other canoes took up the pursuit, and I did not well know how to shake them off, as our men were tiring and it could only have had one end, but at Nelson's suggestion I cast some clothing into the sea, which stratagem diverted them into fighting between themselves as to who should claim them.

Darkness was coming down, and we were able to set our lug-sail, and escape to safety. We sat down then, each man, to take stock of our injuries. I broached our brandy cask and served a tot of the spirit for each of us. Nineteen tots it would have been, but John Norton would have no need of his. Brave John. If he had not gone to free the grapnel anchor on the beach we most certainly should all have perished, but it brought his death. Brought his death, aided and abetted by his commander who slashed his hand away from safety. An accident. A thousandth of a second that would persist for years. An accident as I strove to save him. I see his eyes in my nightmare, but then surely they had been closed as he fell back? I poured his measure of brandy, and held it aloft thinking to pour it into the ocean as a libation to his spirit.

"Norton saved us."

"You did your best for him Captain, there's no blame." It was Smith, that sensible able seaman. His words gave some comfort, and prudently I poured the brandy back into the bottle. The whole attack at Tafoa was to me anyway a

47

nightmare relived. It reminded me of the attack at Moraie when Cook was speared and clubbed. King had left me 'to act on the defensive', as he had so wonderfully put it — to guard the ship's sails that had been spread on the beach for repairs, where they were entirely at the mercy of two thousand howling savages. At least there we had had muskets in our hands to keep the stone throwers at a distance, even if King had expressly forbidden us to use them.

Certainly if the launch was to lose a man, then John Norton, good and loyal seaman though he was, was an excellent choice. He was by four or five stone the heaviest in the boat, and his bulk might well have caused us to founder in the storms and wild seas we had yet to face. We had little enough freeboard as it was. I caused Lebogue, the sail maker, to fashion and stitch a canvas screen to heighten our weather side, and give some shelter from the spray and weather, and to keep out the odd rogue wave that came rolling over the side.

I also had him fashion a catchment for rain which we kept in readiness to rig in the event of a shower, for our water kegs would not be sufficient to bring us to land.

The next day we jogged along under our sail, the men resting and dressing their wounds.

I had been thinking of our options, and put it to them that we could seek food and water at Tongatato, but that we risked like dangers. Our alternative was to sail and pull twelve hundred leagues to Portuguese Timor. To get there we might have to live on an ounce of bread and a gill of water a day.

I sent a prayer to the Almighty to bring me through safe so that my account of the Mutiny might reach the Navy Board, that the pirates might be hunted down, and hanged, and that, this boon once granted me, nothing more would I ask for in this life.

I may, from time to time, have suggested in these pages that the cults of Buddha and Krishna are mysteries to equal Christianity once you have travelled east of the Cape. I can assure you now, that on that afternoon in the open boat it would have seemed folly to quibble with the power of the gods of my fathers.

All hands were badly scared, and fearful of landing at any more savage islands. All promised to abide by my rationing, and they all solicited me to bring them back to their home.

"For," they implored me, "without you we are lost indeed."

Indeed they would have been. The sun going down in a welter of red and indigo, I set a course to the west-nor'-west, hoping to lay the Fidgee Isles and thence to the coast of New Holland.

This realistic appraisal of my role in their hopes of survival lasted for several days. Then —

"Why", said Purcell, "I'll take no more bidding from you. I'm as good a man as you are."

We were all hungry and frustrated, I suppose. I'd spent most of the day coasting along the mainland, but when we entered a creek that offered promise of providing a sheltered landing we were driven out by a tribe of a score of natives. They were waving branches at us as, I supposed, a sign of welcome, but they were all armed with spears and some of the gestures were of a truculent nature. I very much wished to establish communication with the indigenous peoples, but we feared canoes, and when a larger body of savages were discerned moving through the wooded area to join our would-be hosts, I hoisted the sail again and ran down the stream back into the waters inside the reef. Two crude bark canoes were pulled up on a sandy spit at the creek entrance, and we pulled in there and Elphinstone splashed over to them and smashed their bottoms with a rock. He brought two spears back into the launch as evidence of their warlike propensity, but they were only fish spears, such as are common in Otaheite.

We had run three leagues up this coral passage and landed on a deserted island which, the day being the Sabbath, I marked in my log as Sunday Island.

"Now I want you to scour the island in pairs, garner anything edible whether it be nuts or fruit, turtles or shellfish. With luck and a little industry we can prepare ourselves our first hot meal in a month. With better luck we can fill our boat with fresh food to carry with us. Mr Fryer will guard the boat, and prepare a fireplace and fuel."

Purcell, his spirits lifted well above himself by our landfall, had been stalking up and down the shingle haranguing himself into a state of mutiny. I had seen it all before. And now he confronted me.

"I'm as good a man as you are!" he boasted.

Purcell apparently had it in mind to celebrate the Sabbath by abstaining from toil. I had it in mind that if all bent their efforts to gathering oysters and clams to the common good, then a nutritious sea stew could be ours to sup.

I watched him carefully, judging my man. He was all puffed up by his insolence, looking from one to another with a boastful grin, seeking their recognition of what a bold independent Jack Tar he was.

I could not see when, or where, this would end, so, taking a deep breath, I resolved to end it right now.

I snatched up two cutlasses from the boat, and stamping up to him I jammed one into his hand. Raising the other one, I called him to come at me, and then we should see who was the better man. He stared at me stupidly, taken aback by my resolution, and the projected violence I had lain on him. Now the Master, Fryer, came up to us, alerted by the disturbance. I readily supposed, as you can imagine, that he came to my support, and to seize the mutinous carpenter. To my astonishment nothing was further from his intention, for he began castigating me and calling to the boatswain to restrain me, and haranguing the others to aid him in effecting my arrest, for, as he put it, 'I had been plotting this long time to kill him!'

It wasn't such a bad idea, and I shortened my grip on the cutlass and turned away from Purcell who had dropped his own weapon. I confronted Fryer with the naked blade an inch from his throat.

"If you ever interfere again, Mr Master, in my orders, and if there be any further tumult, then believe this most sincerely, I shall put you to death instantly, the very first person."

He was craven on the instant, falling to his knees and clutching at my feet, and he blessed me for a judicious and farseeing captain. Indeed, it transpired he had always maintained an enormous regard for me — I should ask the others, had he ever spoken against me, even one word?

"Aye, you did do that," said Nelson succinctly, but without elaborating further.

At this Fryer set up such a fracas, such a volley of excuses and alibis, that I shoved him over in the sand with my foot, sickened by his knavery and his cowardice.

The other boat people were coming to know him for what he was, and even his particular cronies gazed on him askance.

We scoured the island for food, turning up some three score of shellfish, but no turtles or seabirds that we might apprehend. Smith clambered on a reef of rock, and poised himself over a runnel where he thought to spear fish as they swam from pools as the tide ran out. His practice was not good, and he only contributed two small crabs to the kettle.

Fryer, left to build a fire for our cooking, constructed such a bonfire as would signal our presence to every cannibal within six leagues. The man was a danger and a liability, and it seemed very bad luck indeed that he did not elect to play a part in the Mutiny, and confer his invaluable services on Christian. Looking back it was his lack of resolution and poorness of spirit that allowed the Mutiny to kindle and take hold when a bold effort on his part could have had it quelled and put down right at the outset.

The party waxed jovial over our first hot, savoury and adequate meal in what seemed like a year. I determined however that we must push on on the morrow. There was little hope of gathering enough food there to provision the launch, it having taken a day's foraging to provide one day's dinner. Nelson agreed with me. I could not help contrasting these relatively barren islands with the abundance of Otaheite and Oahu, where coco-nuts and breadfruit, bananas and native plums fall into your hands. I set a watch as we settled for the night, but although this insured our safety against savage or alligator, it afforded no protection against swarms of mosquitoes that made a feasting on us.

* * * * *

51

"Papa! Papa!"

I woke with a start, a painful start for an ague seemed to have taken my neck and frozen it askew to starboard.

"I couldn't find you, Father, you weren't in the bed. I looked to see if you were hidden under it."

"I do not make a habit of hiding under beds, I believe I told you —"

She interrupted, "Because you are all tucked up and asleep in your chair by the window."

I looked at her searchingly. Sometimes I'm not sure with Elizabeth. This business about 'hiding under the bed' — she would have known it was an unfortunate choice of phrase. Had she used it purely by chance? More likely, I thought, she was subtly attacking me to compensate for some embarrassment about her emotion of the previous evening, by her lapse into hysteria. Elizabeth likes to create an impression of capability and strength.

"And what about you?" I asked kindly, "Are you all over your little upset last night?"

"Thank you." I was to be met with an armoured politeness on that tack.

"I'll send Mrs Peebles in with your breakfast if you would like to take it now."

"Yes, very well, very well." It was a likely time, it had occurred to me, to run a telescope along the fence line, to check what incursions and depredations might be being undertaken by the enemy. Having formulated the intention I was impatient to be rid of Elizabeth so that I might carry out my survey of the battle field forthwith. I was also in some discomfort and mild embarrassment because of a, what shall I say, a suffusion of blood, a resurgence of vitality in my groin.

I take it to be a common affliction of gentlemen, well, of men in general, this distension of the male organ on first waking. But it was not so common, I would have believed, in gentlemen of my age.

I once heard that ass Troubridge preach a sermon on the sublimation of man's animal nature, and then pray that 'the curse of Adam' might pass from him as the blessings of tranquillity and grace descended upon him.

I doubt that he troubles Mrs Troubridge too much. Probably the enforced years of abstention the service forced upon me left an untapped reservoir of vigour that still, from time to time, seeks expression. A legacy of the sea, if you like, like piles.

I suppose it was what led poor Nelson into making such a fool of himself in that last year. The whole of London and the counties were laughing up their sleeve at the dance he was being led by that fat Hamilton trollop. Not so much up the sleeve either. There were posters and broadsheets being passed around lampooning the 'lovers'. The best thing he ever did for his reputation was stopping that Frog bullet at Trafalgar. Fate working out its strange destinies again, that.

"Bligh," he once said to me, "you and I showed them at Copenhagen, eh? You and I, and the rest of them came up when they saw how the two of us were taking it and giving back better."

It's forgotten a lot now, what I did at Copenhagen. People prefer to talk about beds and bad language. That's the way of it.

But there it was, old Adam's short sword, straining at my pants. I viewed Mrs Peebles, as she presently brought in my tray of breakfast, in a fresh light. Not by any means did I ogle her in a carnal haze of desire, rather I noted that she was strong and useful, and that if you ignored her face she could be described as reasonably handsome. You don't look at the mantelpiece when you are stoking the fire — that's a coarse jest that I heard in Ambrose' coffee shop in London.

To my discomfiture she turned abruptly and catching my eyes at her hips gave me what I read as a look of reproach. I was taken aback, although I have noticed before that women can detect a man's eye fumbling them. Stare at a plump bosom across a hall, give it a little jollying in your mind, and its owner will often as not turn around and give a look of either haughty reproof or frank invitation, depending on the recipient's moral inclinations. Is it possible that desire can be felt as a ray of heat warming the desired convexities?

Mrs Peebles waited, disapproving look still fixed in place. I rallied. I know a thing or two about the Isle of Man, so I gave her a bold enough stare back, and presently she flushed, and picking up her aprons marched off to her domestic kingdom. My thoughts, still dallying along licentious lines, toyed with the girl, Evelyn, briefly as she stooped over the grate brushing the ash, then swam back over all those years to Timor, and the Daughters of the King. Timor, the promised land at the end of our boat odyssey, and thinking of it brought me by a logical progression of thought to the tumults and dreams of the night.

It seemed to me that my life had been divided into two halves — one half before the forty-eight days in purgatory, the other half from then onward.

Did I leave my youth behind then?

No, it wasn't the boat trip, it was the Mutiny. Everything changed from the moment of the Mutiny.

Everything that happened prior to that happened to a different man or in a different world to everything that was to come after. It was as if an umbilical was cut as the launch separated from the *Bounty*, and I was propelled into a new life, one where all my values were upset, one where all my memories were now seen from a different aspect. It was an event of such magnitude that I should measure everything in later life against it, just as Noah's flood divided the history of the world. I dare say Christian's life was similarly severed into two halves, or uneven parts — very uneven I hope.

* * * * *

There was a sense of being reborn, of being purified by the challenge of torment that exalted and excited me as we pulled away from *Bounty*. The stultifying shackles of my old life were snapped away, the frustrations and worry of coping with bonds that had corroded were gone. I was without reproach, ready and required to perform prodigies of valour, excesses of seamanship that would win me a deathless name. The crew of the launch seemed to me, in that first hour of my reborn life, to be my partners and comrades in an undertaking of heroic proportions. This was a gross overrating of their capabilities.

Dear me, even their behaviour on countless occasions during the boat trip had not prepared me for their venality when I delivered them to safety. It was the second night on Java that a deputation waited on me. Elphinstone it was, Master's mate, and Mr Hallett, Midshipman. They represented their comrades in adversity, so they put it to me, and they had found courage in strong drink to come to the point. I had no quarrel with the solace of the strong drink, but it was concern for their fellow crewmen that had dragged them from the tap-room to acquaint me with their problem.

Elphinstone posed it. "Us be wonderin, Sir," he said in his execrable Devon, "us be wonderin, Sir, what about our money? Will it be payed like till we gets home, and what about our kit, do we get money for our kit what we lost on the *Bounty* like?"

I was tired, and I'd had enough.

"For God's sake," I snapped, "It's not my worry, see Mr Christian about it."

It was out before I realised it, and we gaped at each other for a full minute, then I started to laugh.

I laughed, and could not stop. But there was madness in it.

* * * * *

Chapter Four

A worm manifests itself in my stools — mixed feelings on hearing of John MacArthur's return to New South Wales — the Reverend Mr Troubridge celebrates the Battle of Camperdown — I recall the roles of Admiral Duncan, the Almighty and myself in that great victory — reflections on Holy Communion and cannibalism

I gazed in horror at the pan, unbelieving. I was stricken, I couldn't move. The thing raised its eyeless head and stared baldly at me. I felt a chill as of ice start in my brain, small, the size of a thumbnail, but the ice grew and spread. I could feel it numbing my brain, spreading through my skull then down into my vitals, paralysing me. I shivered; it was fear, it was disbelief. I was willing it not to be there.

Worms eating my faeces today?

Worms eating my body next week?

I saw my mortal remains lying in a garden loam and worms writhing through my corpse devouring my tongue, my liver, my eyes, wriggling through my brain. An intense pain gripped my gut. I pushed the pan away and made an effort to grasp reality. It was not an omen, it was an anal worm, common in the squalor of shipboard messing. Worms ate the ship's bottom, and ate the crew's bottoms. Everyone had them, and suffered from them with itching and stomach cramps. The ship's doctor dosed us generously with wormwood and iron, which made all the people shit like seagulls. 'Checking the sprit stay' was the euphemism for a visit to the heads. Some days it seemed that the ship ploughed through a sea of faeces, that an enemy could follow our passage, plain from the black stain we painted across the canvas of the ocean. The sailors thought that the worms got in at their arseholes and sometimes extraordinary measures were taken to prevent their ingress. One extreme prophylactic was the insertion of a length of tallowed rope in the rectum.

"It keeps out they worms and they buggers" said old Carmichael on *Providence*.

Banks agrees with me that they are the larval stage of moths hatched from eggs either consumed in our foods or dropped in our nostrils while we sleep.

Frances coming in fresh with news looked at me with distaste. "Father, for goodness' sake, you poke and pry your nightsoil like Cassandra peering at a pigeons' parts to divine the omens at Delphi."

Cassandra at Delphi? A classical education is, of course, wasted on young ladies, but she should be able to come closer than that. I covered the pan and shoved it in the closet, and called Evelyn to clean it away. I wiped my hands on a towel.

"You have a letter. From Bond, is it?"

"No, Papa, from Captain Tobin. It is for you but there was a note addressed to all of us too."

"Good gracious, what has George Tobin to do with you?"

"Why, it's about MacArthur mainly."

"MacArthur! Is the rascal dead?" I was pleased.

"You're not to excite yourself Papa, but MacArthur is to return to the Colony."

"What, sent back to be tried?"

"I don't know about that, Father — I think as a free man. Captain Tobin will explain it in his letter."

"Yes." I could feel blood rushing to my temples, but I forced myself to be calm. It would be a great pity if MacArthur did for me now. Frances was looking at me with concern. "They are probably going to make him Governor do you suppose?" I got it out with heavy irony, and was reasonably proud with myself. "That's what happens when you have influence in high places."

Frances' sense of humour has always been feeble. "Do you really think they would make him Governor, Papa?" She was wide-eyed with concern.

"Aye, and pay him ten thousand pounds compensation for his exile into the bargain."

"Papa, they wouldn't!"

"No my sweet, I dare say they wouldn't. They should have

stood him up against a wall and shot him, and they didn't do that, either. Now, why don't you give me Tobin's letter and give me some peace to read it?"

"I'll fetch you a drink and your biscuit."

Most of your gentlefolk take a glass of madeira for their refreshment, though some prefer your burgundies, and thin sour stuff it is. Some drink tea or coffee, but I have a long habit that my family respect and she returned presently with a glass of dark rum. I poured a little steaming water into it from the kettle and sipped it with some satisfaction. After a while I remembered the worm. The memory clouded my satisfaction somewhat, but I sent Frances for some nutmegs in their grater, and added a good shake of the powdered spice to my toddy. I remembered Banks saying it was used in the low countries as a vermicide. Anyway I mused, it's not the one that's out you should worry about.

"Pardon, Papa."

"Nothing, my dear. Let me have Tobin's letter."

My dear Bligh — I wasn't his dear Bligh, but that's the style now.

Many unfeigned thanks for your interest in my convalescence. I gather that we are indeed fellow invalids, and trust that even as you receive this you will be well recovered.

I have been reliably informed that Mr John MacArthur has sailed this last month for New South Wales to rejoin his wife and take control of his business interests there. He has had some very earnest work done on his behalf to have Castlereagh's veto withdrawn. I understand Northumberland and Lady Camden have all brought influence to bear at that level so that he has been able to return to Sydney safe from the threat of prosecution. You may very well think this is a miscarriage of justice. However, I believe that the eight years he has been separated from his family and his property have chafed as severely as if he had been convicted and imprisoned. I understand also that his health and spirit have been to some extent broken by his enforced exile, and that intemperance of speech and action have become his familiar habit.

I have received papers from Francis Bond and he wishes me to forward to you his kindest respects and was distressed to learn of your ill health.

Yours most faithfully,

Geo. Tobin

"He'll find his wings clipped out there," I observed with some satisfaction.

"MacArthur?"

"Aye, Peters writes from Baulkan Hills that Macquarie has taken a strict line on rum selling and clamped down on land grants. Of course, he doesn't have the New South Wales regiment to assist his efforts, so he has that much better chance of success. Added to that MacArthur will find that most of the cronies and lickspittles that made up his influence have either left the Colony, or taken advantage of his absence to usurp his perquisites."

Frances was having some difficulty appreciating my summation of antipodean politics, so I took another sip of rum. My mind ran very much on MacArthur in New South Wales, you may be sure. We had both finished up losing, MacArthur and I, that was undeniable. I had been ousted from my job; MacArthur, apart from the eight years involuntary exile, had lost face, and that was most important for 'Jack Bodice', the son of a corset maker.

MacArthur saw himself, I think, as a premier Duke of Australia. One night when Blaxland was in his cups, and they quarrelled, I saw MacArthur's face when Blaxland called him that, 'Jack Bodice'. He literally went a bilious puce with rage, and would I believed have killed Blaxland on the spot if the means had been at hand.

My reflections were interrupted by Elizabeth, who entered wearing her black gown with the velvet collar, a sure indication that she was about to prostrate herself before her Lord.

"Ready for church, m'dear. Has Jackson got the carriage ready for you?"

"Come Father, let me help you into your uniform. You do remember that we must all go to matins this morning."

59

"Why, m'dear, I'm not at all sure that I am strong enough to weather one of the very Reverend Mr Troubridge's short dissertations." The bloody fellow never preaches for less than a half an hour.

"Father, you must come, you agreed. Do you forget what Sunday it is?"

"Sunday?" In all truth I had no idea what she referred to.

"Camperdown Sunday, Father, and the vicar is blessing the Camperdown window that Lady Spencer gave to our church."

"Ahhhh, Camperdown." Of course it was October. It would be, of course, most appropriate for one of the leading participants in that famous victory to be present as the window was dedicated. The ship depicted in that window was undoubtedly the 64-gun *Director*, a palpable tribute to myself.

"Indeed, people would remark if I was not there, Elizabeth It would be very ill to absent myself from such an occasion."

I pulled myself upright, and submitted to their several grooming efforts. Anne fetched my hat.

"Vice Admiral of the Blue, eh?" I found few ceremonial occasions now, and wasn't too put out to don my sash and the jacket with its slashings of gold lace.

"Father, you look so fine," Anne clapped her hands. I took one of those hands and squeezed it affectionately. She was right, of course. My illness had left me a little thin, but my face and bearing were certainly not those of a man in his sixties. I hung my Camperdown medal on its ribbon about my neck, and flanked by a supportive daughter on each side, we made our way down to the side door in the east that gives best access to the driveway.

Jackson opened the door for us — but what was this? It was not the battered tan of the Bligh carriage, but a trimmed grey equipage and two grey horses, useful looking animals. Our own horses were matched if you like, but only in age and decrepitude.

"What's this?"

"Why Father, the bay, Achilles, is lame, and Jackson says he can't put Ajax and the new roan mare in, as they don't work together. Isn't that what you say, Jackson?"

"Yes." Jackson didn't believe in embroidering his opinions nor advancing more than he was asked for.

"So where did this carriage come from?"

"Why, Father, it belongs to Mr Ffoulkes, and he insisted on lending it to us when he heard of our difficulty. Now you're not to be silly."

I felt a cold futile rage.

"I am not going to be beholden to that fellow."

"Do you mean we're all to miss church then?"

"I am not going to ride in that carriage with that fellow, and that is that. You may go. I shall stay."

"But Father, Mr Ffoulkes is not in the carriage. He has lent us his stableman to drive it, but he rode into the village on his hack. He said he didn't wish to impose his presence on you as you might not wish it!"

The man wasn't bereft of sensitivity then.

"You go then. It's good enough of him I suppose, but I won't come."

"But Father, it is Camperdown Sunday."

It was a very well-upholstered and sprung conveyance, and put ours to shame. Even down our rutted lane and through the water courses that fretted over our right of way, it conveyed us smoothly.

"Bang on the shutter, tell him to stop at the corner of the green. We can walk down the pathway to the church."

I didn't want to be driven up to the door in my neighbour's carriage like some poor relation. I thought Elizabeth was going to protest, but she thought better of it. She opened the small round scuttle that allowed speech to the driver on the box and he dutifully brought us to a halt and dropped me down on the stone pathway that skirted the graveyard, and led to the church door.

"Thank you, my man, and I dare say we shall see Mr Ffoulkes inside to convey our proper sentiments to him!"

"No, Sir!"

"No?"

"No, Sir, master bean't church, Sir, master be chapel."

"Chapel, good Lord!"

What you might expect, really. We went in to the polite greeting of Cosgrove, the vicar's warden, and he escorted us down to our pew — the second front row on the left had our name on it. The choir were starting to play some hymn from their loft behind and above us. It was completely unfamiliar to me and it was accompanied by such screeching and sawing and spluttering of the cornets and the fiddles that it was hard to be sure. It could have been the Old Four Hundredth, but they alone (and the vicar, and God, presumably) knew. I conveyed this opinion to Elizabeth, but she looked at me blankly. She liked to work up a religious trance leading towards communion. I would have been the only one in our house that had eaten; she made sure of her sisters fasting so that their sacrament would not be impugned.

The choir lurched into a fanfare, while we pulled ourselves to our feet as the vicar came down the aisle carrying the crucifix. The boy altar server was on the occasion carrying a banner which was rather crudely and tastelessly inscribed with a ship and the legend *Camperdown*. Mr Troubridge, due to the consequent shortage of hands, was carrying both his book of common prayer and the large lit candle which he placed on the altar. The Sexton had been elevated in the proceedings to carry the incense-pot. The procession was completed by the two warden's carrying their staves of office. As a procession it compared poorly with the procession down Whitehall when they celebrated Trafalgar and buried Nelson, but for Leyborne village it was adequate.

"Open thou our lips, oh Lord," Troubridge warbled. Cosgrove dropped heavily into his seat behind me and clinked his wardens stave into the clip on the end of his pew.

"Let us praise the Lord."

"The Lord's name be prais-éd," I bellowed in company with Cosgrove. I liked having him behind me.

The Camperdown window was a small arched window in the transept left of the nave. It was less than decently shrouded by a blue piece of curtaining that I presumed Troubridge would draw open to the wondering gaze of the public as he reached the peroration of his address. I practised a few modest expressions to furnish the occasion as the only member present of the victorious fleet. A dazzling bar of greenish blue light shone forth at the bottom of the inadequate curtain, representing, I supposed, the sea, Britannia's preferred element. Modern stained glass windows are in fact a very poor imitation of their predecessors — a travesty really.

"Lord have mercy upon us," warbled Troubridge.

"Christ have mercy upon us," Cosgrove and I rumbled, warming nicely to our work. There was a great comfort in the familiarity of the Church of England service. The prayers and collects change in a never-ending cycle with the seasons; we pray for God and we pray for the King, and for all those who sit in authority under them. The altar cloth is red or green or white depending upon the ecclesiastical calendar. I was sitting on my kneeling pad, which was an indulgence I considered due to a pious invalid.

I drowsed a little as Troubridge got into the musical complication of the 35th Psalm. His voice trilled and broke and carolled as he rejoiced with David in the defeat of the Lord's enemies. It was, I suppose the most appropriately warlike psalm he'd been able to find.

"Take hold of shield and buckler, and stand up for my help," the vicar intoned dolorously. I wondered if the Dutch had realised they were anti-Christ.

* * * * *

The sea then hadn't been a steely blue, it was grey and lumpy that day with spume blowing from the crest. Nothing to stop the wind, but then it was no better or worse than any one of a hundred other days on blockade in the low countries. I've not to this day known what moved De Winter to bring his ships out on that day to their predictable destruction. Was it madness brought on by months of boredom and inaction and frustration? Did he decide to stake everything on one bold throw? Did he maybe think the Lord Mynheer, God of their Reformist Church, would wreak destruction on their enemies, or did he just think he'd have a nice sail up and down the coast and scurry back home again without being challenged?

Duncan was in no doubt about it. He was on his knees half the third watch thanking his Presbyterian Lord for delivering their common enemy unto him. Duncan was fortunate in that not only had the Lord delivered up the foe, he'd also instructed Duncan on the way to go about beating him. It was Dick Howe's gambit. You must remember Howe's famous victory on June 1st, the Glorious First of June. Howe swapped the hoary and vastly venerated scenario, whereby two opposing fleets approached in line of battle and ran together ship to ship, broadside to broadside. That was how it was done, you see. That was how it had always been done, you see. But Howe ran his ships through the enemy line, raking them fore and aft as he crossed through, and came up on their lee side. He was as successful as the name of the battle suggests, and Duncan was all on fire to emulate him. We had had several meetings in his cabin where he'd explained it to all of us — Howe wasn't mentioned. It had all been worked out between Duncan and the Lord.

"Do any of you gentlemen have any comments or questions?"

He glared around like a hawk. Actually he was as tall as a giraffe, but a great deal more religious.

"A splendid idea, Admiral." I was loath to be the one to quibble but honesty and concern had me on my feet. "A splendid battle plan, but I presume circumstances may dictate whether it is appropriate or not."

He stared at me discouragingly. "Go on."

"For example, Sir, if the Dutch lay trapped on a lee shore and we had the weather helm, then we could destroy them at our leisure. Pound them into wreckage, smash them into the shallows. We would be mad under those circumstances to put ourselves on the shore underneath them."

There was a subdued rumbling of agreement.

"Mr Bligh, you concern yourself unnecessarily. Do you fear that the Lord is going to run His fleet into jeopardy and destruction, to desert us when the trumpets call the advance?

Nay, when the clarion trumpets blow, then will the confusion of the enemy be accomplished and the Lord God of Hosts will lead us down on them to bring to them the fire and the sword."

Duncan was not only as tall as a giraffe, his face was I fancy not unlike the animal also. A large nose reddened and misshapen dominated it, and there was a large wen on his left cheek with a coarse patch of grey bristle protruding from it.

Why does the Lord always animate such ugly protagonists?

His eyes were burning, and I found no reserves in me to prolong the debate. His explanation was not the most lucid but it would have to do me for today.

We had an observation squadron out following them as they sailed from the Texel, and wandered south west. The wind was in the nor'nor'west, and if he was just out for a Sunday stroll to let his men feel their oats he'd have done much better to head into it so he could cut and run home. A cutter, the *Myrmidon*, reached Duncan on October the eighth with news of the Dutch sortie and he hastened to block the hole while the mouse was out. And so we found ourselves back on the black and featureless cape patrolling the approaches to the south of the Texel on the morning of October the eleventh. It was a dark morning with squalls of sleet blowing in from the Arctic. The sea was grey and the depths were black, the spume was pitted by hail and rain.

"There'll be snow before this blow is finished, Mr McTaggart."

The first officer agreed — he had to. We were on a starboard reach with the wind on our quarter and the seas running under our counter, so that we surged and dropped. The odd rogue wave curled over the weather rail and pelted across the waist. Even on the quarter-deck we were wet and cold. Icy salt water was finding the gap between my souwester and the oilskin great-jacket I was huddled into.

As the daylight struggled for recognition there was a hail above from our mast head.

"Sails to the south-west."

At the same moment a string of signals burst out on

Venerable. Duncan was detaching a frigate to investigate but soon I could plainly recognise the frigate *Circe*, from the squadron shadowing the Dutch. She sailed up until she could be sure of us through the mist and haze and as eight bells struck in the second watch she fired a gun and signalled 'Enemy in sight — south by south-west' then 'Sixteen ships-of-the-line'.

This was it, then. There was a pause, as we all watched the *Venerable*. No signals. Duncan, as I learned later, was on his knees for ten minutes communing with his maker, then it was helms up and we turned into line and ran down to the south-west. It seemed to me at the time, we could have run smaller to force De Winter out from the coast, but then I had no divine instruction. I sent Mr Church to see the galley put out a hot breakfast while the chance offered. There was a very poor chance of eating again this day.

I went below to change my stockings. A misplaced notion of vanity? No. Wool carried into a leg wound causes putrefaction, gangrene eventually. Silk is reputed to be safe. All down the fleet officers would be pulling on silk stockings like a parade of Wimbledon whores preparing for an evening of jollification. I crammed my two-pointer hat on my head — you must prepare if you have any aspiration to be a handsome corpse — and stomped back on deck.

The *Director* liked a broad reach, and where she had been shouldering the seas and lurching down the troughs, she now sniffed imminent battle and ran handsomely down hill, down the channel, picking up the waves and running with them.

Two bells of the third watch and the topsails of the Dutch fleet could be seen by our lookouts. The flags raced up *Venerable*'s mast.

'Prepare for battle.'

The galley fires were raked out and tossed overboard, but at least all hands had had a gutful of porridge and pork fat, as they were piped to quarters. It was hard to believe that at last we were preparing for action in good earnest, and indeed might get more action than was enough.

For a year we had practiced for this moment as we patrolled the Texel, drilling the watches to keep the men active in the deadly monotony of blockade duty. I really think the deadliness of the duty contributed as much to the unrest at the Nore as the demands for better pay and conditions. Powder boys were running for cartridges to Stokes in the magazine, who, slipper-clad and in near blackness, would be working like a Trojan.

'Fearnaught' screens of heavy blanketing hung around his explosive lair to stop any flash detonating his powder. The marines were clambering into the tops as the yards were secured with chains, and the boarding nets were roused out.

Birch, the Master, was starting the men with a rope's-end as the nets blew in the squalls, tangling on cleats and belays in their usual infuriating habit. It is the worst job in going to stations, and he was having a hard time of it. They weigh a ton wet, and have to be roused out right along the rail, secured by lashings to the chains, and then when secured all round to lines from the top of the sprit and the yard-arms, the lines are rove through the upper edges of the netting so that hauling on the falls of the tackles would lift them into position. At last he had them stretched out and secured to his satisfaction but not mine. A blind man could see there was a twist in it. I let him have them half way up, then came to his assistance.

"Belay that Mr Birch," I shouted through my trumpet.

"Are you blind or mad, you dog, that you string it up like a mess of washing, you pelt of a bitch? Get it down — I'll have none of your rigadoon slops here." Forceful! It came down quite quickly, and the men under Purdie, the senior midshipman, wrestled with the wet mass.

Thorne, a monstrous rough villain, snarling and grappling with an armful he was turning over, cursed and wrenched his arm out, the thumbnail torn clean off his left hand. That was the first blood on our deck today. Blaguire had the purser and the cook spreading sand on the decks and wetting it to give a footing to the gun crews and making sure their spilt powder would not ignite.

Mr McTaggart was shouting at a party at the pumps who, having filled buckets for the gun crews, were now filling the long boat with water, both to protect it from fire and to give us a reservoir of water to tackle any outbreak. Down in the orlop Smithson, the surgeon, with Revin the steward and my clerk Hughes, would be setting up their operating station with boards set on sea chests, and tubs for severed limbs. Nobody wanted to check how they were getting along.

"Captain, Mr Ireland wants to know how he is to load his first broadsides." A facetious answer came to my lips, but I bit it off, and wondered vaguely if I was showing a touch of derangement.

"Tell him I want the upper deck double-shotted with ball and chain, and ball and grape in the lower battery."

"And the carronades?"

"Grape.

The carronades were our trump card in this as in other engagements. They were short wide-barrelled guns mounted on the quarter-deck and the forecastle. They could throw an enormous weight of iron at the enemy over a short distance. Their accuracy was nothing remarkable at more than a hundred yards, but they equalled the lower deck guns of the first-raters in the size of their charge. The Dutch, like the Frogs, carried only light ordnance on their decks.

"Mr McTaggart."

"Sir?"

"I'll have the guns loaded but not run out; the ports can remain closed until the action is imminent. Open the lee ports on the lower deck and we will have waves sweeping in green."

"Aye, aye, Sir."

"And send Mr Birch to me."

The boarding nets were rigged trimly now, taut and shipshape.

"Mr Birch!"

"Sir?"

"You have the nets taut, so that any monkey of a Dutchman might swarm over them. They are doubly effective if they sag. Please slack them off."

"Sir." He waited with some apprehension but I had no interest in abusing him.

We were running down on the enemy, the *Director* in the

first group of four ships with the *Monarch, Russell,* and *Montague.*

The helmsmen stood to the double wheel with the quartermaster behind them. More often the man to windward does most of the work at the wheel pulling down the spokes to correct the weather helm that I like to trim the ship to. Cook always fussed about shifting ballast and stores to get lee helm under some nonsensical idea that his ships ran faster that way. Even the best of us have our Achilles' heel, but then on the *Resolution* it wouldn't have made too much difference.

Now with the wind coming astern both helmsmen were kept alert for a broach or a falling off. The quartermaster's eyes were constantly patrolling the luff at the sails, the compass needle, and the feather tell-tales streaming forward and out from the standing rigging.

"Flagship, Sir" called Eldridge, midshipman handling the signal lines. "Our number, and 47 — 'form line of battle.'"

Ireland, my third, was squinting through his telescope at the *Russell* which was on our quarter and relaying signals. He snapped his telescope shut, and his silence confirmed the midshipman's reading. Birch, the Master, and McTaggart stole glances at me, expecting an order. I was fairly confused. The *Monarch* was jamming on all sail to come to grips with the enemy first. *Director*, sharpish on the run was holding her own and as near to our designated position as I could estimate. The *Montague* and the *Russell* were astern on our quarter. They were back out of their respective positions in the line of battle.

What the devil did the old fool want me to do about it? Duncan didn't have a line of battle. He had two mobs of vessels lumbering down on the enemy, each at its chosen pace.

A fresh string of signals fluttered up.

"General signal, Sir, 'Close up the fleet!'"

Duncan was giving his signal lieutenant a brisk morning. I examined my telescope while I considered the situation. It was an excellent instrument, an achromatic hand telescope fashioned by Peter Dallond in London. I turned it on the second bunch of ships. No one had swung into line, and we were opening a bigger gap on them as we drummed along under main and topsails.

"We'll reduce to topsails, Mr Birch."

"Topsails, aye Sir." He raised his speaking trumpet and bellowed the orders. Ships go into action under topsails only, so it was useful to shorten sail now rather than when action was imminent.

It's traditional in stories of naval action to describe the encouragement given by the captain to his young midshipmen seeing action for the first time. To reassure them, and charge their confidence. In fact I could have done with someone to charge mine. Not only was I distrustful of Admiral Duncan's command, but it was the first fleet action I had ever been involved in. The only time before was the skirmish at the Dogger Bank in '81 when I was in *Belle Poule*. We were nothing more or less than onlookers in that rout of the Hollanders.

I was tense and nervous that in some regard I should not perform my part, but likewise did not wish to hazard my ship, nor my crew, from any intemperate or ill-judged action.

"Captain! Sir, *Russell* has set t'gansels!" The crew were swarming in the rigging of the *Russell* and over her deck, and she was a marvellous sight as she thundered past us. Just as she drew abreast studding sails were set on the tops, and the gallants.

"Sir!" It was Lieutenant Foote.

"Mr Foote?"

"Do you see the *Russell* Sir? Why, she's flying at the enemy!"

"So she should be, Sir, her place in the line is before us."

"But Sir, should we not run up our top gallants? We don't want to appear shy of the battle."

"Mr Foote, allow me to judge our proper position."

I had no doubts about my ability to sail the ship. I can say honestly, but in all modesty, that I was the most competent sailor in King George's Navy.

"Signal, Sir! Our number."

There was a pause, then —

"Sixty-three, Sir, 'Lead the fleet!' "

"How the devil are we to do that?" I asked in exasperation. "*Monarch* will be in action before we come up with him."

Onslow was charging in the *Monarch* at the gap behind the Dutch Vice Admiral. The *Russell* had broached, carrying away her larboard studs, and we came up to her as her top men scrambled to drop them.

"The tortoise and the hare, Mr Foote," I muttered.

"Sir?" Then "Signal, Sir — 'shorten sail!'"

"Go to the lower gun deck if you please, they can't run the guns out until we close with the enemy."

The Hollanders had the best of us there. Like the French their ships were, rate for rate, rather bigger than ours, so that they provided a more stable gun platform and on more than one occasion, I had heard that they were able to fight their lowest tier of guns in weather that rendered the gun decks of our ships unusable because they were shipping water.

"Signal, Sir! 'Fleet to come to wind together to dress line'."

Then —

"Number thirty-four, Sir. 'Break through the enemy line'."

Belliqueux, apparently losing patience with the string of signals, abruptly turned out of line and steered for the nearest Dutch ship, engaging it yard-arm to yard-arm.

It was 12.40 p.m. and the *Monarch* was enveloped in a cloud of smoke as her first broadside rolled out. The crashing of the cannonade reached my ears some seconds after. The *Monarch* was steering directly at the Vice Admiral's ship, and the whole hostile fleet were lying hove-to, double-shotted no doubt, and waiting for us. The *Jupiter*, Rear Admiral Reyntjes' ship, seeing *Monarch*'s intention, had backed her fore-topsail yards around so that she turned off the wind, presenting her broadside to *Monarch*. As the smoke blew clear I could see that *Monarch* had lost her mizzen-topsail yards in this preliminary exchange, but I could detect no damage on the *Jupiter*.

Ten minutes had passed from the opening shot, and the *Russell* coming again across our bows ranged herself up to the sternmost in the rear squadron, and I brought us along-side the second in the rear and to windward of her at a range of seventy to eighty yards. Our gunners make much better practice than their opponents and this is an advantage we throw away if we come to point-blank range.

There is a popular sentiment that it is manly and in the best traditions of the service to fight an action with ship locked against ship, yard-arm tangled with yard-arm. This is manly, traditional nonsense! These fellows today lived because their commander could think rationally and was not bound by their foolish traditions. Marcus Aurelius came again to my assistance:

> If sailors abused the helmsmen, or the sick the doctor, would they listen to anyone else? or how could the helmsmen secure the safety of the ship, or the doctor his patient?

I was prepared to ignore them, and suffer some degree of criticism that a dozen were not killed to bolster our image!

There was some mismanagement of our first broadside as our gun deck was not run out, so that we used only the carronade and the guns on the main deck. Even so we brought down a spar and she fell out of the line as our carronades swept the quarter-deck, striking down one of the helmsmen.

Her answering salvo was poorly timed, firing as she rolled on the lift, it seemed, for her shot whistled astern and above us, knocking some timbers from the stern but causing no apparent injury.

"Captain Bligh."

"Yes Mr Birch."

"Are we not to close with them, Sir, are we not to fight the gun-deck armament? Are we not cutting through the line?"

"Mr Birch, return to your station."

"But Sir" —

"Go, Mr Birch, and wait for my command."

He went, but a series of bangs and screeching from the starboard side told me the hatches on the main broadside had been raised, apparently on his command.

We had moved past the Dutch ship as general firing broke out all around us. The enemy line was no longer distinguishable as it fell into a general mêlée. Duncan, flying a signal 'Engage the enemy more closely', was hammering yard-arm to yard-arm with De Winter in the *Vryheid*, and the rest of our fleet were into the middle of theirs. A cloud of smoke was enveloping the battle. The only ship I could see was the *Agincourt*, brought to, half a mile to windward of us. I sincerely hoped she made sure of her target if she began firing from there.

A rift in the smoke revealed an ornate gilded stern labelled *Alkmour*.

"Mr Foote, run out, and direct the gun captains to fire as they bear." The ship shook as the cannon rumbled out, and one fool fired immediately into the smoke and haze, his ball splashing uselessly a hundred yards away.

"Get that man's name." One of the boatswain's mates went down with a starter to apply correction. Smoke and the rank smell of powder set me coughing and wheezing as a ragged series of shots rang out, and I saw at least two of them splinter into the *Alkmour* before we were past her.

Topsails loomed ahead — it was the *Montague*. She had also baulked at passing through to the lee of the enemy, and was flying a string of flags at her mizzen telling all and sundry that she had found shallow water. Anyone unaware of the shoaling banks two miles to leeward might have been grateful for this advice. I fancy it was flying as an alibi. I edged the *Director* down to leeward and found we were heading towards Vice Admiral Onslow's ship, the *Monarch*. We got a smart broadside into his opponent but got little credit, as we discovered it had already struck to him. An officer on her quarter-deck ran agitatedly to the rail waving a white flag at us and shouting.

"He's striking to us, Sir."

"No Mr McTaggart, he's struck to Onslow." We stood aft. There was a Dutch ship a hundred yards ahead and I told the quartermaster to let our head fall off so that we ranged down on her within fifty yards. I was pandering to some degree to the local prejudices in favour of a decision reached in mutual cannonade and bloodshed. I glanced at my watch and was astonished to find two hours had passed since we commenced the action.

"Bring the head up to the wind as we come level with her

stern, Mr Robertson. Fire as your guns bear, Mr Foote, pass word to Mr Birch." This time we got a respectable broadside into her, most of our shot piercing her hull, one shattering a launch on her poop. Her response was a ragged fusillade, but some splintering on the main deck brought down two men of our larboard gun crews.

Suddenly a salvo of twelve-pound round shot whistled through our rigging. A hail of chain and rope fell in a tangle from our foremast dislodging one of our marines who fell into the netting then, fortunately on to the deck, relatively unscathed. I swung up my telescope and searched beyond our target and there was the familiar top hamper of a ship-of-the-line, a 74. It was *Adamant*. We had sailed into her broadside.

"Swing onto the wind, smartly," I bellowed. The helmsmen pulled the wheel down and *Director* picking up some seaway slid past the bow of the Dutchman. Our rear carronade fired down into her waist as a passing shot but then with a smash we hooked into her sprit with our stern as it lumbered past. There was a smashing of glass from my great cabin light. The starboard gun of our stern-chasers exploded under my feet and the ball smashed through the bowsprit chains, so that the whole spar fell suddenly to starboard and her furled spritsail tore loose and added a dimension of confusion by flapping like some demented giant ensign. A rasping, tearing noise, and we were free and plunging into the haze.

A Dutch ship-of-the-line was burning and a dense livid yellow smoke was rolling out of her. The *Belliqueux* was unsympathetically circling her and raking her stern, creating I think some appreciable damage to her gun crews. I looked around and was mildly surprised to find the sea ahead of *Belliqueux* empty of ships. Behind lay four ships in a haze of smoke, and I could see the royals of a fifth above the smoke beyond them, but whether friend or foe I could not say. Away four points to starboard, and some distance from us, the five ships of the Dutch van were apparently unengaged.

"Bring her down two more points." I snapped, and the chase was on to come up to them before they made good their northing. The Dutch ships were built to cope with their shoaling channel and tidal mud, and probably drew a fathom less than *Director*, but if they wanted to reach the safety of the Texel they would have to come about to make more sea room, and there we should have them. We were coming down with the wind on our larboard quarter, and I'd eat a clog if we couldn't headreach on them.

I reviewed the last three hours. The main impression was one of confusion.

"Mr Roscow!" I sent the fourth lieutenant to stand down the gun crews, and sent a message to Birch to secure the lower gun ports until we came into action again.

My main impression, as I said, was one of confusion, and Duncan's incompetence. Nowhere the two lines of ships majestically engaging, nowhere the enemy line taken by surprise by the English ships breaking through in Howe's classic gambit. By the time we got into action, the enemy had in no sense formed a line. I wondered if the great tactical battles were all conceived as the admirals wrote up their logs and battle reports in the happy aftermath of a victory.

Whichever way you looked at it, I was uncomfortably sure that *Director*'s efforts had in many respects fallen rather short of heroic. It had proved extremely difficult to find a suitable victim to hammer until he struck, and that was seen to be the object of our efforts. Added to this was the undeniable fact that we had not broken through the enemy line to fight from the lee, indeed not a shot had been fired by our larboard guns. We weren't alone in this of course — *Agincourt*, the *Montague* and *Veteran* all attacked like us from windward, where we enjoyed the advantage of not having a lee shore rapidly shelving under our keels.

"Deck there, ship three points to starboard, about a mile ahead!" Masthead from the main-top had picked it up, and as I focussed in that direction I saw a large Dutch ship-of-the-line, emerge from the haze. She was a 74 second-rater with jury-rigged sails being winched to her fore and mains. Nothing stood above her topsail spars and only the mizzen-top was intact.

"*Vryheid* 74, Sir!"

De Winter, by God, the Dutch Admiral! I could make

nothing of this. The last time I had seen him he was shooting it out gunwale to gunwale with Duncan, and the *Ardent* also had joined with *Venerable* in trying to knock him down. It didn't take too long to see in this happy encounter a chance to wipe out with one stroke, any suggestion of a dereliction in our bellicosity.

"Stand the gun crews to, run the guns out, Mr McTaggart." The mate leapt forward a string of commands bellowing through his hailing trumpet.

"We'll bring her up to the wind under her stern, and rake her into submission."

Vryheid was a sitting duck, but that was our good fortune. De Winter was struggling to make the safety of their coast but now we had him. I could see the gazette already. 'Dutch Admiral in a 74-gun ship-of-the-line captured by Captain William Bligh in a 64-gun fourth-rater!' The captain of the *Vryheid* saw our intention as the Master brought us up under their stern, and put up the helm to swing his guns around, but he simply did not have the canvas to accomplish it. We were sailing ten chain to his one, and that was roughly how it went.

For fifty minutes we tacked across his stern firing alternate batteries. The damage and carnage on his ship was considerable, and after our third pass I doubted that they had two guns fit to answer our fire. His masts were sheered off and carried away by the weight of our iron, and even I, the calmest and most even-tempered of men, felt a blood lust, a fighting lust, so that as his men set to clearing the tangled wreckage with axes we ranged past and discharged both our carronades loaded with grape into them.

Still he did not strike, and I decided on a run down his starboard side to give our larboard battery their chance, and that did it. The hull of the *Vryheid* seemed to shake and fall in on itself as the broadside struck home, and so the battle of Camperdown was ended by the *Director* as Admiral De Winter struck his flag, and a white flag was dropped in its place over the stern netting. Nothing stood above his deck to hoist it on. Her decks were full of dead and wounded men, and none of her boats were whole. I sent the cutter and the launch over to bring off the Admiral. He refused to set foot on my ship, but sent some impudent message back to the effect that he had no wish to meet a butcher. I asked the coxswain to repeat the message. I can tell you, I thoroughly lost my temper then.

"Mr Roscow," I shouted, "we will help him to quell his foibles. Load the carronades with grape. Another broadside or two and I'll warrant he'll not be such a pretty fellow."

"Deck there!" It was the masthead.

"*Venerable* standing up, making our number, Sir!"

Ireland came running from the signal halyard.

"Message to *Director* — 'Cease engagement, and send commander aboard Flag'."

Nelson was to turn a blind eye at Copenhagen and win considerable praise for it. I considered the possibility of putting in the broadside before disengaging. The Second and the Master were looking at me.

"Belay that order, secure the guns."

Venerable coming up, we sent De Winter off to Duncan, who shook his hand and no doubt they each told the other what splendid tacticians they both were. We had a Lieutenant Sillard come to us to offer their submission, the Captain having been killed in our first broadside.

Camperdown from then on was a bustle to secure and clean up before night fell, and before the disabled ships were blown into the shallows. At Duncan's direction, I sent McTaggart into *Vryheid* and we sent Clarke the surgeon across too, and a dozen seamen to help with the repairs. Her own men were able to supply enough watches to keep her pumps running. Twenty of our marines under sergeant Peters transferred too, and a swivel gun was mounted on the poop to reinforce our control.

Again at Duncan's direction we took *Egalite*, a captured 64, in tow to pull her back to Yarmouth Roads. A nice job that was, passing him a line and laying out the main hawser to effect the tow. We laboured until two in the morning to have it secured without pulling out the stump of her foremast.

Around midnight I retired to my cabin to refresh myself. Jacobson had prepared some coffee and biscuit and I was prepared at length to toast our success in the same.

So that was a fleet action. I pondered. Had we played our part? I thought so, but it was not a question I could really answer. One thing I knew. Next time it would be an easier part to play, and I had no doubt that Napoleon would ensure that there would be a next time, somewhere between the Mediterranean, the West Indies, or the Baltic Seas.

As I sipped my coffee I heard shouting and a hail on deck. The officer of the watch unhappily was the disagreeable Lieutenant Foote. He appeared behind my marine sentry to report that Lieutenant Brodie in the cutter *Rose* was sent around the fleet to enquire into the state of each ship, and the number of killed and wounded. He had had the greatest pleasure in telling Brodie that we were as ready to fight as when the battle commenced, and had sustained no damage of any sort.

I thought I would choke with choler.

"How dare you give such an answer, Sir, without my authority? Tell Lieutenant Brodie that the ship is not ready, and tell him the surgeon has not yet made out his report on the number of injured." That was true enough. He was in the *Vryheid*. Foote held his face expressionless. "Aye, Sir — we are not ready, and we don't have the surgeons report." He left the cabin, and left my self doubts renewed. Presumably he and Birch would be happy if we had lost half the ship's company and accomplished the same results.

I cut a quill, and dipping into my inkwell began writing a draft of the day's events for my journal, and for the ship's log. There was no point in underplaying our part, especially in making the Commander-in-Chief strike his flag to us.

Some two hours later I read through my notes. I couldn't help but think they would read well in a Gazette, and the more I thought of it the more comfortable I became in my mind.

Well, there was always next time.

＊＊＊＊＊

I fingered my medal. On one side Britannia disported herself in a diaphanous gown that would have caused a riot in Regent Street. On the reverse was a ship and the words 'Camperdown — for valour.' All the commanders and the first officers were awarded one, even on the *Montague* that titted around fretting about shallow water. Only John Williamson in *Agincourt* didn't get one — they gave him a court martial for cowardice instead. I suppose I should have looked at him and said 'There but by the grace of God...', but he was a coward. His lack of resolution resulted in Cook's death, so it wasn't a miscarriage of justice by any means, just delayed justice. He was not hung, just hung up, put out of the Navy.

So I had a medal to testify to my courage. I weighed it in my hand: it was solid gold.

My attention had wandered, and a meaningful silence drew my eyes to the vicar who was intoning all sorts of nonsense about the battle, and the local hero. God had come to the aid of his legions who were sorely outnumbered by the infidel apparently. I smiled modestly. Actually we'd been a superior fleet, in the windward position and to my mind the only circumstance threatening our victory was our glorious leader's divine inspiration.

Troubridge gave up presently and we prepared our hearts and minds for the communion.

"Firmly I believe and truly," I bellowed,

> God is three and God is one
> and I next acknowledge duly

Duly? Julie?.

"Who's Julie?" I whispered to Elizabeth.

"Hussssh!" She was not to be diverted from the communal exercise of the trans-substantiation miracle.

"The vicar's doxy I suppose," I muttered.

I came up the aisle first to the rail, the Camperdown 'hero'. I knelt and crossed my palms, right over left, thumbs outstanding. I was copying my daughters, for I'd never undergone a formal confirmation — how could I when I was in the Navy at eight years of age! The vicar stooped over me "This is the body of the Lord Jesus Christ" he intoned, pressing an unconvincing scrap of stale wafer into my palm.

I picked it up with my tongue.

The Catholics, well we're all Catholics, of course, I mean the

Papists, they ring a bell, and when the bread hears that it turns into the actual flesh of the Saviour.

In Otaheite they take communion by eating the kidneys of their enemies. It all depends what you're brought up to.

We were filing out now, again 'the hero' and his family taking precedence. The vicar was stationed at the door shaking hands and nodding affably.

"Morning Troubridge."

"Good day Miss Bligh, Miss Frances, Miss Jane, Miss Anne, Captain Bligh!"

"Admiral," I said.

"Aah — Admiral, of course. It will be Sir William soon no doubt."

The dog! He had me. All admirals are knighted as a matter of course — once they flew their pennant. My new blue pennant was never likely to fly anywhere but over Farningham Manor.

"Admiral Bligh!" I said, smiling thinly.

Chapter Five

Intelligence from the Royal Society persuades me to visit London — I evade an assignation with a dowry-seeking lawyer — an unpleasant encounter with an onion-guzzling divine — I demolish a proponent of steam-propelled warships — the events of the Battle of Copenhagen recalled

The letter is short but I find it middling satisfying.

> *To Admiral, the Earl of St. Vincent*
>
> *14th April, 1801*
>
> *Captain Bligh (of the* Glatton, *who commanded the* Director *at Camperdown) has desired my testimony to his good conduct, which, although perfectly unnecessary, I cannot refuse; his behaviour on this occasion can reap no additional credit from my testimony.*
>
> *He was my second, and the moment the action ceased, I sent for him on board the* Elephant *to thank him for his support.*
>
> > *I am, & c.,*
> >
> > *Nelson and Bronte.*

I asked Nelson for a testimony after Copenhagen. It's a good letter. Nelson wondered why I wanted it written as you can see, but in the months subsequent to Camperdown I was continually apprised of calumnies circulating about certain ships and their shy behaviour in that battle. To my great chagrin, *Director* was included in several of the broadsheets that spread the libels, presumably because of the small butcher's bill we presented with only seven casualties and little structural damage. So much for careful and prudent leadership.

I folded the letter into the pigeon hole of my desk. St. Vincent had been civil enough to forward it to me with a note that Nelson's comments verified his own impressions. A man as thorough and tactful as he must surely finish as Prime Minister.

I was looking for a letter from the sergeant of the Royal Society, who had apprised me of some papers that were shortly to be presented. Mr Humphrey Davy was to demonstrate a safety lantern for use in the coal, and one he had singled out for my particular attention was the account of a crossing at the channel by a snow, propelled by a fire-engine driving a paddle-wheel.

One couldn't but think how admirable such a vessel would be as what we called a *cartel*. These were post boats which ran a discreet service crossing the Channel from Nantes to England under licence from the Admiral of the Fleet. Now, the usual understanding of a cartel is an emissary arranging an exchange of prisoners, or of diplomats carrying proposals to the enemy shore, but as Boney forbade any exchange of prisoners these boats ran a more discreet trade. They transhipped newspapers and fashions from the English to their adversaries and back, and a trade in items considered essential in the *beau monde* was carried on, with the tacit approval of officials on each side.

The Royal Society members also availed themselves of the cartels, so that science and natural studies were able to spread and disseminate in spite of a war that disrupted most of the civilised world. Members of learned society could, and did, cross to France to meet with colleagues there, but also not a few passengers travelled both ways whose boat cloaks hid more than a thirst for service. On at least three occasions that I have heard of, accessories were dispatched to despatch — dispatched to despatch, not bad is it? — to assassinate Napoleon. But either they took their silver and kept running or Bonaparte's gendarmerie took them, for I heard no mention of any one of them subsequently.

A splendid cartel she'd make, that had never to want and whistle for a wind. Did she run on wood or coal? And how efficiently?

The Jonathons have been playing with steam-propelled vessels on the Great Lakes, I've read, and a ferry they've named the *Clermont* is running a tentative service along the Hudson River.

That's all very well because she can pull into the bank for fire-wood every few miles. Can't do that on the high seas. Maybe in the Channel, cross-Channel certainly.

I pictured a warship churning into the weather quarter to tackle a foe — an advantage that could make our current fleets redundant! Could it be applied on a ship of a thousand tons? I thought I would like to hear the account of the fire-engine vessel, and have a few pertinent questions. It might be possible to persuade Elizabeth that I should visit Tregenza in Wimpole Street for a consultation, and then I could in all convenience visit the Society and take part in its proceedings this coming week. The question was, was I well enough to visit the doctor? I determined to put a bluff face on it, and astonished the family by fronting the table to break my fast.

The young ladies gazed at me, Anne with delight, Frances and Jane with some astonishment, Elizabeth, I felt, with suspicion. Fortunately, as the meal was to reveal, she had other matters on her mind.

"Some bread loaf, and I'll have a slice of ham." Jane sliced the ham, and Frances buttered me a wedge of cottage loaf, while Anne poured me some coffee. My spirits rose; a man deserves a little pandering in his dotage, and if unmarried daughters are a cause for concern, they are also a source of comfort.

Elizabeth was reading an epistle from her cousin Bligh the attorney, her intended husband. She looked up from her paper and said, "Papa, Richard wishes to pay a formal call on you this Friday. Will you be well enough to see him? How would you wish me to answer?"

There was only one reason he wanted to call on me, no, on reflection two reasons. Firstly he would be pestering me to set a wedding date, and secondly he would be seeking an understanding about her dowry.

"An unpleasant custom," I'd observed to him, "demeaning for a girl I say, what? handed out like a bag of groceries with a hundred pounds or so to seal the bargain." I was honest and jovial.

He was not to be fobbed. "Nonetheless, it is the established practice. I'm sure that you would want to honour Elizabeth's wedding with a suitable expression of your regard for her, and of your gratitude for the care and attention she has lavished on you."

There you are, a man is expected to pay for filial love and devotion these days.

"Well, well, we shall have to give it some thought, we shall have to give it some thought. No urgency is there, I suppose? We shall have to consider her sisters situations too, do you see?"

"You must surely be contemplating finalising your estates in New South Wales, Sir?" Greedy dog!

"Certainly there's no hurry about that. They will be worth a very great deal of money one day, you know. A great pity to throw them away now."

That exchange had occurred some months past. Now I gazed sincerely at my bacon rind.

"Nothing would give me greater pleasure than to have Richard call on me. He is always welcome, Elizabeth, you know that." A thought occurred to me. "Possibly he might care to advance an opinion on the actions I propose to curb our neighbour's trespass."

Three faces gave me reproachful looks. My crustiness regarding friend Ffoulkes was putting a satisfying weight of grape through their rigging. "However I have written to fix an appointment with Tregenza in Wimpole Street."

"But you are not well enough to travel."

"Too ill to visit a doctor of medicine? Come now, miss."

"You know very well that you cannot travel to London unaccompanied. Why it is five weeks since you set foot outside the house."

"I intend setting these feet outside this very morning."

"Father you're just doing this to avoid meeting with Richard."

I began to boil. I believe that I know when authority is flouted beyond reasonable limits.

"Elizabeth, I tell you that my intention to visit the surgeon was formed several days since. As you have just told me of

Richard's visit it should be painfully obvious to everyone possessing a brain that no state of cause and effect can obtain."

"Why have you not mentioned it before?"

I lost my temper. It was intolerable to be defied by one's own children.

"Be silent," I thundered. "I have told you that you are wrong, and I will brook no further discussion as to that whey-faced, puking writmonger of yours. He may see me at my convenience, and not otherwise." She got up white faced and slipped out of the room. There was an uncomfortable silence. I rather wished I hadn't delivered a broadside when a shot across the bows might have sufficed.

"Would you pass me some bread." I tried to restore the normality of the meal. Jane passed me the bread but she was staring at me.

"And the honey if you please." It was near my left hand, and I reached out for the crock. To my considerable annoyance the honey was fouled with several curls of melted butter. To my mind half the appeal of honey is in the crystal amber lucidity of the product. The aroma and the flavour, yes, but the appearance too. All that charm is gone if you find it contaminated with butter and crumbs. I expressed my annoyance.

"I believe I have many times stated that only clean teaspoons are to be used in the honey jar?"

There was no answer.

"This jar has been ruined. Some one of you, if not all of you, have been taking honey from the pot with unclean spoons, or indeed knives." I flashed an accusing look around the table, but no one met my eye.

"Very well then." I seized the offending pot, and marching to the window, I threw it into the garden, then returning to my seat I went on with my breakfast.

Jane was still staring at me.

I looked up from the butter and met her eyes.

"Well, miss?"

"Why are you seeing the surgeon? Why is it urgent — are you unwell again?"

I was concerned about a stiff mass I could sometimes find above my liver, but decided against mentioning it.

"Just so he can palpate my chest, my dear, to ensure the lung inflammation has not left an abiding weakness."

"Oh." She looked down.

Anne had left the room after Elizabeth, and now she came back in distress.

"Father, Elizabeth is crying!"

I felt even more uncomfortable.

"What's she crying about?"

It's damned hard, coming from a world of men to the confines of a nunnery. Leaving Lieutenant Frazier aside, I can't say I ever had a seaman burst into tears when I shouted at him.

"Father, it's because you were so cross and shouted at her." Anne, simple creature, wrinkled her face like a small monkey, and pressed moist eyes into my waistcoat.

"Well, look here, ask her to dry her eyes and step back in here, and we'll make arrangements for Richard to call on me." Her face lighted up, and she skipped out on her mission of diplomacy from the fond father.

Fond I say, in its more classical rendering, as foolish. I lose my temper, I readily admit, when I encounter insubordination, foolishness, or incompetence, but I don't hold a grudge, nor stay in a black mood, but having administered the rebuke I am very ready to resume a normal, non-rancorous relationship. I see it as a strength in me. More short-sighted people often see it as a weakness, and it has caused me a fair amount of inconvenience from time to time. I could instance the *Bounty* mutiny there I suppose, and Christian's carrying on like a sulky child because I reprimanded him for pilfering my coco-nuts. One thing I've not told that arrogant apologist for his criminal brother, Edward Christian, is that Fletcher was crying as he set us adrift. The fellow was mad, a complete lunatic, that's my honest opinion.

Anne came back looking bedraggled and woebegone. She does it very well, but I hardened my heart.

"Well?"

"She won't come."

"What did she say?"

"She isn't feeling well." She was dissembling.

"What did she say?"

Anne burst into tears, and Frances gave a sniff. I pushed away from the table, my irritation returning.

"This is like a mad house." My table napkin fell to the floor, where I not only left it, but stood all over it with some petty satisfaction.

"Jane, as you seem to be the only sensible person here this morning. I'll ask you to step into the library and pencil a note for Jackson to take. He can reserve a place for me on Friday morning's coach, inside, and a seat for himself on the boot."

"How will you go?"

"Maidstone over Swanley."

"But Papa, why not go by the turnpike, it is so much smoother and more direct?"

"A waste of money."

"It costs only a little more."

"I have no intention of paying turnpike tolls. Their tollgates are an iniquitous tax on the travelling public. Englishmen should be free to travel on English roads without hindrance wherever they choose. It's most surely a basic freedom." I really believed that.

"But they spend the toll money to improve the roads, and to give better horses."

"They use the money to line their pockets, you mean. Not ten per cent of that money goes back on the roads. Well, they're not lining their pockets with my money."

The grooms were handling and shoving two extra horses into long traces outside the Sparrow at Wrotham Head, to lumber the coach up the long haul towards Farningham, Wrotham Hill — some hill, we should be the best part of three quarters of an hour climbing it. Steam was rising in the lamplight as I came from the snug, buttoning my waistcoat. I have a woollen scarf from Frances, my gift from her last yuletide, and I wound it around my face and over my head, as the night was sharp with a degree of frost. Steam smoking from the horses' nostrils, steam hanging in a cloud over a gully pipe where water from the scullery was gurgling down, steam blown from the top of his mug of cocoa by the guard.

Strong brutes they backed in, bottoms like elephants, nostrils steaming, brass ornaments swinging as they stamped and plunged back. No Derby runners here, but Shire horses, geldings, destined for the plough as their youth stretched into the plateau of age. Their winter coats, coarse and shaggy, had been clipped back to a line running down the quarter of the rump, where the clipped hair was shiny and a darker brown than on the flank. They stamped, and one of them made dung largely. The ammoniac smell of the dung mixed with the steam from the cocoa and caused a queasiness in my stomach, and I clenched my teeth as a sick hollow pain griped my liver. I would have fallen but Jackson caught my arm, and supported me to the coach.

"There you are, up you go, Admiral." He was enjoying mothering me, in return for several years in the service when I had given him my best care, although it is doubtful if he'd always appreciated it. I'd arranged a short meeting with the cat for him in Cape Town and again at Madeira, both times for storing up his grog, and getting beastly drunk. He projected me into the gloom of the coach where I tangled with a travelling rug and a pair of pudgy legs stretched across between the seats.

A pair of small dark eyes half buried in a fat chapped face stared at me with utter disfavour. An ecclesiastic I thought, for the commodious skull was topped by a shovel of a hat redolent of sanctity.

"Beg your pardon," I said brusquely. If, as it seemed, we were to take the next stage together, then I was not inclined to provoke garrulous confidences by being too outgoing. But he said nothing, only withdrew his feet somewhat so that I could get past him. He had, annoyingly, appropriated the starboard seat facing the stern.

"There you are, Admiral." Jackson handed in a rug, and a basket with a hot brick for my feet. He rarely addressed me by my rank, and I took it that he wished to yield nothing to the ecclesiastical person in matter of rank. The west wind would be on the larboard quarter as we tackled the rise, so I took that corner of the seat and made myself comfortable. I consoled myself that I now enjoyed the traditional captain's prerogative of occupying the windward side of the quarter-deck. Jackson, smothered in his old tarpaulin, climbed to his perch behind, and I did not envy him, I confess. A few shouted transactions between mine host and our driver and with a clack of iron on rock we were off.

"A raw night, Sir." Some little extra effort at communication seemed to be called for, but I kept my guard raised. He acknowledged my politeness by the fleeting rise of an eyebrow, and the barest of nods.

"And likely to get worse." It was my closing effort. I had extended courtesy far enough and it was time to put up the shutters.

The coach swung out of the cobbled High Street, and onto the gravel and ruts of the post road.

"'The Lord makes his pavilion of dark waters and thick clouds, he thundereth in the heaven, hail stones and coals of fire are his lightenings'; Psalm 93."

"Yes, yes; 'Everything exists for some end, a horse, a vine. Why dost wonder even the sun and the rain will say I am for some purpose'."

"Yes — St. Paul?"

"Marcus Aurelius, Meditations!"

"A pagan philosopher!"

He closed the dialogue abruptly, turning to gaze out the window.

The gaiters above his boots were now crossed with ecclesiastical chasteness. It is I suppose part of the human condition to view with rank suspicion any other body forced by circumstance to obtrude within our ambit.

I had already formed a passive disliking, and two courses of behaviour appealed to me. Firstly, to hold to an aristocratic reserve and disregard of his presence that would demonstrate my disdain, alternatively, to lure him into a discussion of his worth, in the course of which I would shatter his pretensions.

The coachman was hoarsely bellowing at his charges, and I heard the outside passengers clamber down and add their shoulders to the common effort to breast the rise. A thin leather blind swayed inside the larboard glass and I pulled it aside and looked out. The guard, bare-headed, and divested of his musket, was shouting to them to concentrate their muscle on the wheel spokes. His eye met mine. He was goggled-eyed like a lamprey, and stared at me brazenly. I let the blind fall back into place, and turned my gaze back to my fellow traveller. He was earnestly unpacking a basket, folding back linen towels to get at its secrets. A richness of aroma proclaimed its kernel to be some baked comestible, and presently to his great apparent satisfaction he drew out a pasty and began gnawing at it in the most common fashion. A sharpening of the flavour caused by his breaking the crust revealed its principles to be in the main onions.

I scratched my head, quietly turning over cutting and apt comments that would send home to him the unacceptability of his gustation. He chewed noisily. I scratched. I've had a rash on my scalp as I think I have mentioned, and now I had located a crusty mound of dead keratic scale just above the hair line. I got a finger nail under it and it lifted after a decent show of resistance. I pulled my nail down and inspected the detritus. I hadn't got it all, and a large flake, or flakes, was escaped into my hair, I combed and brushed at it with my finger, and a lump of dander fell to my shoulder in a shower of lesser flakes. I ran my finger along my left incisor to clean the flakes out of it, but looking up I found the bishop's eyes gazing frostily at me.

I shifted my feet onto my hot brick; it was going to be a long journey. The coach was making better time now — the creak and sway assumed a rhythm as we skirted the northern downs and headed towards Swanley. My scalp was itching intolerably now, from the mere imposition of my resolve to not touch it. I ran my finger tips through it, in the abstracted manner of a man of the world straightening a stray lock. There seemed a rash of flaky lumps. I ran my fingers again through my hair, slower, and with a nail burrowing the scales my nail captured a pea-sized crust which from habit I flicked into my mouth. Elizabeth carries on if she finds tell-tale flakes on the antimacassar.

"Really Sir, a public conveyance is hardly the place to practise cannibalism."

I was mortified.

"Nor is it the place to guzzle at onions."

At this exchange the temperature inside shrank several degrees. We each avoided looking at the other, but we each suspended those activities which had drawn criticism. The horses jingled through the night.

The coach swayed and rocked.

I dozed, shook awake, then dozed again... The seat was hard and a hand was gripping my arm above the elbow. I shook it off.

"Huhummmmmm?"

"Steady, Admiral."

It was Banks. I struggled my eyelids open and gazed owlishly at him, confused as to where I was.

"You dozed off. Davy's getting some ticklish questioning!" I gazed at the platform. A fellow I vaguely thought familiar was glaring at the audience from the partial security of a lectern. He had spiky hair that stood up straight from his scalp, and was dressed in a sober suit of black enlivened by a mustard paisley wool shirt.

"Fella looks like a farmer."

"That's Humphrey Davy. That's his famous lantern on the table." A gentleman, who I gathered from his line of reasoning to be a mine owner, was actively questioning its worth. Davy by the look of him was taking the criticism poorly.

"You say it's coal gas, mine damp, which being ignited by the mine's lanterns causes explosions."

"Aye."

"Have you ever actually seen this happen?"

"Aye."

"Would not a spark cause the same effect?"

"Aye, it might."

"And are there not sparks a plenty in a mine, caused by the wheels of the trolleys and barrows, and indeed by the picks of the miners striking the rock?"

"Aye, these might ignite it too, but that's no reason for carrying a naked flame deliberately. They mainly use wooden rails for their trolleys now to keep your sparks away."

"And do they use wooden picks, then?"

"Nay, they don't. But look now, I'm telling you, if you are a mine operator, the best and safest thing you can do is to use a steam engine driving a bellows to pump air through the mine to the coal face, to waft the gas away and dilute it. That's the best thing, but a pretty handful of coppers it will cost you to do that. So I'm telling you and showing you that this safety lantern will save lives, and save you money."

His tormentor fell silent, and presently Davy returned to the safety of the front benches, while Jackway was called up to discourse on his feat of crossing the Channel in a boat propelled by a fire-engine.

I listened closely to his account. It was a lively and informed one, but he didn't discount his difficulties.

"Fuel?", he said, "Why, we used timber, and we restocked our bunker as ballast."

"Not practical then for a longer voyage?"

"It should be possible to tow a barge or a lighter with a reserve of fuel, but I feel that the future lies in coal, or coke, to fire the furnace. It could be carried as ballast."

"Pity if you needed the ballast when you'd burnt it all."

"Well now, I'm not a sailor, but surely water could be pumped in — not that it would need pumping to flood the lower tanks — and act as ballast when the coal was burnt."

"That's a lot of nonsense. It stands to reason that water is no use whatever as ballast as it weighs precisely the same as the liquid element around it. You may discount it because it only displaces its own weight."

"Sir, you misapply your Archimedes, I tell you that a ton of water is just as effective as a ton of lead, or a ton of feathers for that matter, in acting as ballast."

This was a contentious consideration and a lot of shouting and halloo-ing and bally-hooing took place until the chairman, old Brandon, took control and thanked the speaker. "As most of you know we will have a little wine, and some refreshments, in the supper room if you should choose to adjoin, and I'm certain Mr Jackway will be happy to continue the discussion across the table."

This was what I was waiting for; not the supper — that never reached memorable culinary heights — but the chance to tackle Jackway. Speaking of the supper reminds me of the night I actually took along a dish prepared of breadfruit. How I came by them was that I sent a couple of plants from the Cape home to Kew on an Indiaman I picked up there, on the second and successful attempt to take them to the West Indies. They did so well under glass there that they were able to let me have a couple to astonish the Royal Society. The kitchen had served them up in a made dish with lamb or kid, and spices, something they termed a native jumbalayer or some suchlike. It tasted absolutely dreadful, but the people there ate it without much more than the usual grumbles, which shows what standard of food they have come to expect. Incidentally, I learned a little while back that the plants thrived famously in Jamaica, and also on the central American continent, but that the slaves refused to eat it. I think it was Tressigan here at the society told me that. Half apprehensive he was about how I'd receive the news. Their husbanding had, after all, caused me some pains.

I had laughed heartily.

"They might be slaves", I'd said "But they're not stupid."

It was a nicely ironic conclusion to a fine idea which turned to fiasco.

"What, do you look for Jackway, Admiral? He's over by the committee room."

I set sail toward him and brought up abaft of him as he was demonstrating some critical aspect of his fire-engine to Ralinson, the Secretary, by a visual demonstration employing spoons, salt cellar, and several lumps of crystallised sugar.

"The exhausted steam condenses here in a chamber at atmospheric pressure, do you see, and is collected, pre-heated, and pumped manually back into the boiler to be used again, so that your net loss of water may be kept as low as fifteen to twenty per cent, and that makes the economies of steam propulsion much more viable. You don't, in essence, have to cart a great tank of fresh water about with you, taking up what should be your paying cargo space."

"One of the factors I came to discuss with you, Jackway —"

"I should have said fluid, not necessarily water, because now you see, if you can imagine such an engine operating on a fluid that boiled and vaporised at a lower temperature than water, then again economies of energy are introduced that will reduce the amount of fuel needed."

He'd completely ignored my polite opening gambit. I put it down to the eccentricities of genius and tried again.

"Does such a fluid exist?"

"No, not yet, but it will."

I waited for further enlightenment, but it didn't come. He was away into theoretical discussions about 'super-heating' the steam by running it through pipes over the fire.

"This will give it a greater expansion, and again render the fire-engine more powerful, and more efficient. Stephenson's engine, his locomotive engine. Do you know its efficiency?" He paused, and I presumed I was to answer.

"Eighty per cent?"

"Seventeen and a half. What did you say your name was?"

"Bligh, William Bligh."

"Bligh," he thought about it, "I've heard of you."

"Yes?"

"The Stanhope committee, you were one of the committee that designed that shallow draft frigate. Four masts, sixty guns, length five times the breadth, keel boards."

"Seventy-four guns, actually. But they didn't build her."

"Just as well, your idea of three sliding keels was daft. It would not have worked at all."

I like people to speak frankly, but within reason, and this

gentleman appeared to claim expertise in every subject that was raised. I looked at him more coolly.

"And I suppose you see your steam-propelled vessels revolutionising commerce."

I had a cunning list of figures to confound him whichever tack he took here, I'd been doing a lot of thinking about it, and a little research in the Society library. The library was considerably better than the Society kitchen.

"Not as things stand, no," he disappointed me, "but you surprise me, Bligh — a fighting man are you not?"

I didn't know how to take this remark, and my hackles creaked up, ready to defend ancient actions.

"What do you mean?"

"Well Sir," he cleared his throat of a salmon patty "as a prominent Navy Officer, I would have expected you to pursue the military advantages at my craft.

"The advantages are obvious, but so then are the disadvantages."

"I have explained that a coal-fired boiler can operate for four hours on a ton of coal."

"And then."

"Well then, your ships can carry a great weight of coal."

The fellow knew nothing about naval warfare.

"Do you know what the British Navy spends most of its time doing?"

"How do you mean? Sitting in port I should imagine."

I was not diverted.

"In time of warfare."

"Destroying the enemy I should hope, and what a bonny advantage if you could just sail in rings around them."

"Convoying and blockading, Sir, is the answer I was looking for. Convoying fleets of merchant shipping through dangerous waters, and blockading the French and the Dutch and the Spanish to lock them in their ports. A ship of war needs to be able to stay at sea for months at a time and that is patently impossible for your steam-propelled vessel."

"I've already alluded to the factor of refuelling. While you couldn't send a fire-engined vessel to the West Indies you could perfectly well deploy a fleet of them in the Channel."

"And when you did come into battle with your steam kettle, you see it as unbeatable."

"It's been my understanding that the ship that holds the weather beam controls the battle."

"Yes, but then Hood and Nelson would always cut the enemy line to get to leeward to stop the enemy escaping."

"No sailing ship could escape from a steam-impelled vessel. You could rake her through from the stern."

"And what do you suppose the enemy would be aiming at while you were steaming into position. He would shatter your paddle wheels and then where would your advantage lie?"

"They could be housed to protect them."

"From a twenty-four-pound ball? One of those can plough through two feet of oak. That's your Achilles' heel, your paddle-wheel."

"Aye well, I don't think paddle wheels, in their present shape, are the answer. I grant you that. They are vulnerable, and awkward in a sea, but I look to improve these points, possibly with a series of smaller wheels, or an Archimedes screw."

"And then there's the risk of fire aboard ship."

"Your fire's in a steel box, there's no risk there."

"And do you not open the door for lengthy periods to stack fuel in?"

"Well of course you do, but there isn't risk of it escaping."

"I don't believe you can be cognisant of the strenuous efforts which must be made on a man-of-war which is preparing for an action. Every fire is quenched, every spark is stifled. A ship is a natural fire hazard, made of dry timbers, and hemp and canvas, liberally coated with tar, and with gunpowder being constantly conveyed between decks. Add to this the studied malevolence of possible action and you have a veritable tinderbox. And you, Sir, desire to introduce into this tinder box a furnace!"

My hand went to my head histrionically, but my finger tips took the opportunity to check my scalp for dander. It was smooth and hot, but as I brought my hand down I pulled a

96

single hair from my nape. Such a hair, it was four to five inches long, coarse and crinkled, like, why for all the world like a pubic hair. Its shaft was grossly thickened and dull, and it was a deep autumn in colour. I looked at it in some surprise. If I were going to lose my fine natural hair, and finish with a scalp full of pubic hair, I should have to go and live in Fidgee.

"Ah" said my erudite companion, "Fibrosus Gerontosis, the coarse hair common to idiots, and to the aged. A sign, do you understand, that the grey matter, the corpus mentis, the cortex of your brain is rotting, so that its roots enjoy poor nourishment."

"A freak — one hair, an aberration, that's why I pulled it out."

"The hair will coarsen first, then the mind."

"Your ship, Sir, in its present form would be more danger to her crew than to the enemy." I wasn't getting anywhere debating my physical failings with him.

"On the contrary, Admiral, cast your mind back to some of the actions in which you have been engaged. I'll warrant that, if you are honest, you will find that a vessel capable of directing broadsides into the stern of any adversary at will could overcome a whole fleet."

"Danish pastry," I had the perfect answer. He was lost.

"I wish you might have been aboard when Hyde Parker, Nelson and I paid our respects to the Prince of Denmark."

"Copenhagen?"

"Copenhagen. Your vessel would have been worse than useless at Copenhagen."

*****

Hyde Parker was in an invidious situation, we could all see that. He sat at the head of the table in his great cabin and stared at the map at the Cattegot as if the secret of success was written there if he could only read it.

Nelson stared at him, then looked across at me, his face expressionless. Nelson's eagerness was a goad to Parker, who saw himself taking the blame for a mistake, a reverse, while Nelson would win all the glory for a victory. It was no easy thing to have the victor of the Nile as one's subordinate. Parker thought him an egotist, and had treated him with disdain up to now, but time was running against him. The ice was melting in the Baltic, and in a matter of weeks or possibly days the Russian ships might be unlocked.

"It's not just the Danes," Hyde Parker said at last, "we must make provision for the possibility of meeting the Swedes and the Russians in a combined fleet action."

"That's precisely why we should take action immediately, Sir. They can only get stronger while we get weaker. We must strike now while the odds are in our favour."

The truth was that Nelson had no great opinion of the Russian Navy. "They may have a formidable number of ships in commission," he had said to me earlier, privately, "but have you ever been on one of their ships? I swear on the Sta. Katerina they had an icon on the bridge instead of a binnacle. And you can't make sailors of slaves. They use dismounted cavalry, Cossacks and the like, to serve their guns."

"Even so, if they outnumber us two to one —."

"I could wish there were twice as many. They have no idea of a fleet action, and their very numbers encumber their efforts."

However, this argument would not have advanced his cause on this occasion, so he took a different tack.

"Sir, Denmark has expelled our diplomats, we are at war. Make no mistake about that. If we attack them and level their capital within a week of their declaring war, do you not think Russia and Sweden will take pause to consider. The 'armed neutrality' will end there and then."

"But you have the map of their defences that Sir James brought out with him. They are formidable. The northern end of their line, with this great fixed battery, the Trekroner, is impregnable."

"Ha, give me ten ships at the line and I'll take them from the south, and reduce them in twelve hours — this I can promise you."

Hyde Parker looked at us for help.

Groves, the other subordinate Admiral, came up with a question. He didn't approve of Nelson's plan I would judge.

"What of the wind — you count on it backing?"

"It will back to south or sou'sou'east which will be ideal for us to steal in past the middle ground shoal."

"If it stays in the west?"

"We keep going and attack Russia."

That was it. Statesmanship by the simplest of statements. Hyde Parker chewed his lip, then decided to cover himself with some insurance.

"Very well — you take twelve ships-of-the-line and the frigates and sloops and attack the southern defences. The three-deckers draw too much to come to grips there — I will bring them down on the Northern end to bottle up the ships in the channel."

"They won't come out."

"They won't if we're there to stop them."

"They won't anyway."

"I must make it clear, Nelson, that I am leaving the details of this assault entirely to you. It is your responsibility."

"Then Sir, I must beg to be excused. Bligh, a word with you."

I was flattered and surprised. I followed him up a deck where his third lieutenant, Grosvener, hastily fell in the boats crew. He came to the point brusquely.

"Bligh, you're no fool, and I understand you are the best man in the King's navy to chart a shoal."

He was right of course, and I didn't argue with his judgement, but listened carefully as he gave his orders.

"And you must have this work done by daybreak. You can break your fast with me."

Two hours later I was shivering bitterly, trying to stop my blasted teeth chattering, to read a compass and transfer bearings to a chart, and gauge the tide, all at the same time.

We were in the *Glatton*'s gig, and Merrydue the boatswain was in the bows taking soundings.

Astern of us our launch was backing her oars to keep station behind us. She had a swivel gun mounted and her men had six muskets aboard, as I feared the Danes might be running patrol boats along the channel.

They should have been, but we seemed to have the wintry night to ourselves. Our oars were muffled and our progress slow as I tried to chart an edge to the channel we were going to have to sail down to be in a position to attack. It was a sand and mud bottom, but the bottom shelved up and down, and there were shallow outcrops so that it was becoming fairly clear we wouldn't finish in a night. The launch was dropping casks anchored by round shot at the spots I indicated. Lomond, pulling stroke oar, was gazing at the lights of Copenhagen, and he missed his stroke, splashing badly, then getting his blade stuck he crabbed and showered us with water. Nelson was right — the ice was melting.

"I'll see you before me in the morning, mister!" I growled, and he continued, stroking now with elaborate care. The tidal water smelt stale and brackish, and I imagine the Danes discharge sewage into it, for a variety of rubbish of all sorts was keeping us company.

I called Merrydue back and sent Button, the Master's mate, forward to take over the soundings.

Merrydue was soaked and nearly paralysed with cold. I handed him a towel, and teeth chattering loudly he rubbed at himself, then tucked it in around his collar.

The Danes had removed all their buoys and marks along the middle ground, and Nelson had no reliable charts he could lay hands on.

I had a sketch plan I had taken from a coaster, but could not trust it. It showed a spur projecting roughly half way along the shoal, and we should have been approaching it now. We had charted an island of sand only a fathom below the surface, but with a channel between it and the main shoal — not however such that ship could pass through it, and we'd had to go back and lift our marks and move them out around it. The moon was in its last quarter and sailing in and out of cloud, and there was a nasty chop where the water piled up against the shallows, so that it was no very easy task at all. I was working by a shaded candle to the compass, and marking my chart with a needle through vellum. It was no night to be blotting ink. We had four miles to buoy to bring the squadron down past the Trekroner Battery and along past the old city wall to an anchorage where we could group to tackle the southern defences.

"Piling ahead of us, Captain" — it was Big Jones. The *Glatton* furnished me with Big Jones, Little Jones, and Jones the Cooper. A twisted timber stood ahead of us, crusted with mussels and barnacles, and white with the sea birds' shit. A cormorant perched astride its top, and viewed our approach with some concern. It changed its tooting, and stretching its neck, bobbed its head up and down convulsively, as if it had a herring stuck in its craw.

"As like as not that was a beacon that was too solid for them to demolish" I said, and we took a sounding around it. There was plenty of water to starboard of it, and I was cheered to have my work confirmed by the sighting of it.

"Look sharp there, you'll have us into it." The tide was taking us down now and the gig was sliding sideways towards the ancient timber. It cut through a swelling of brown water that eddied and gurgled behind it.

The cormorant gave a harsh despondent cry, and launched itself into the air. The thin cold breeze seemed too insubstantial to support it, and it fell dangerously close to the waves before its wildly thrashing wings gripped enough air to propel it forward and up. It circled above, then flew off to acquaint Hamlet with our trespass.

Lomond pulled a prodigious stroke that swung us clear of the pile, atoning somewhat for his earlier clumsiness.

The Trekroner Battery at the northern end of the defences was helpfully showing a light and I took a bearing from the pile across to it.

"Water's shoaling ahead, Sir," called Button, casting busily.

"Veer her, two points to starboard," I called in a low voice. Voices carry over the water, and I had no wish to have Trekroner dropping cannon balls around me. The channel ran out to starboard for three hundred yards. This was certainly a spur sticking out, as shown on my chart. I took a bearing just in time, as the piling was swept away by a haze of fine rain. My feet were wet in their boots, as we had several inches of water swilling around the floor boards. I pulled out my watch and snapped it open, jamming it against the compass light. An hour and a half to day break. I thought about it. Nelson wouldn't like a job half done.

I turned to the Boatswain.

"Merrydue — signal the launch to come alongside. I'll transfer myself and my charts to her and we'll keep working right through to the anchorage. You can take the gig back and report to the commander that we are still completing the job. The flag is transferred to the *Elephant*. Then take the boat back to the *Glatton* and tell Cameron to take his orders from the Vice Admiral."

I paused for thought. Then —

"Merrydue, you are to run back a cable from the buoys we have placed, and take soundings every quarter mile as you go, in case we have missed a separated outcrop."

This was the best plan. The truly awkward bit was transferring from one small boat to another not much bigger in the chop that was pitching us about.

"Here we go now, Captain."

With a shout the launch was scraping our gunwale, and I half jumped, half fell across and into her. I got wet and I got winded and I got the most appalling bang in my cods that sent a wave of nausea paralysing me. I was all atop their second bow oar who had caught at me, and fallen under me. Figgins, it was, a lump of a Cornish miner, who now gazed at me reproachfully, but I couldn't move. "Help me up, you dolt," I grunted at him through clenched teeth. Honey, the *Glatton's* Master, was at the helm of the launch, and as I came to a sitting position he began to pass my mapping paraphernalia to me.

"Hang on to it, can't you see I'm not prepared?"

I was too proud to rub the damaged glands, then I did rub them after all. It was impossible not to. I was the first casualty of Copenhagen.

We buckled ourselves down to the task, and continued sounding the perimeter of the sand bank. There was about a mile left to particularise, and it was complicated by the tide which was now ebbing strongly. Our soundings were in fact comparative, but given that there was a definite channel that should prove sufficient. The problem areas were those where the bottom shelved up to seven or eight fathoms. At low tide the ships-of-the-line were not going to get through, so it was a matter of taking a line of bearings out across the channel to divine the safest passage. We were laying casks out as buoys, but buoys can move or be moved, and I wanted bearings all down the line, so that each Captain on the morrow would have a copy on his binnacle. I'd devised a system of needle holes in my working chart to indicate the time of the sounding so that the flow of tide could be calculated exactly. I had a 'Baltic Pilot' I'd appropriated some ten years before, but I had Cameron on the *Glatton* taking soundings at their anchorage as the night time flood and ebb lifted and dropped them.

Daylight found us level with the southern gate of the city wall, and the channel had broadened out here and deepened to form what I felt to be a good holding ground. Nelson would, I judged, sail his fleet through as soon as he saw the marks were in place. Dawn was lighting at the eastern horizon, the sea seemed luminous but the sky still lowered dark and cloudy, and we dropped a grapnel on a thin grass rope to hold as the morning took shape.

"Two coastal pinks coming down on us, Sir." Figgins pointed silently. Two darker shadows could almost be detected right at the edge of perception.

"They'll be cod drifters, long-lining."

It could have been the whole damned Danish Navy as far as I was concerned. His night vision must be aided by pisky second sight, but he was right, as the fishing boats edged from shadows to substance. The leading pink caught sight of us and for a moment I anticipated they were going to sail us down, but veering away at the last moment they vanished with the morning haze, still busy with their lines.

Men going about their honest trade are wise to avoid strangers who intrude on their pitch. Strangers with a swivel gun. The second boat turned away sharper and a small patched lug sail struggled up his mizzen as he ran across the channel towards Copenhagen.

"Nothing we can do about him, not much he can do about us."

Early shafts of a wintry sun picked out our line of marks crooked like a horses leg. The seas had gone down somewhat and the wind had backed to the south east. There was not a ship in sight. We raised the mast and gaff, hoisted the mainsail on the launch and ran down toward the fleet. Honey was steering small, letting the tideway balance the leeway, and we crabbed down the five miles odd in two hours to find them all swinging peacefully at anchor.

"Run down on *Elephant*, and secure to her chains." I sent Honey up to report, and to beg a meeting with the Vice Admiral. To my astonishment he came back with a message from the flag lieutenant that Nelson was occupied, and could not see me.

"*Glatton!*" I snapped, and they took me home. Back on *Glatton* it was time for dry clothing, coffee, and a chance to stretch my limbs.

A chart had to be prepared, or half the night's work was forfeit. I laid out my mapping table with dividers and parallel rulers, and sent for a copy of the soundings. It took me three hours and by the time it was done I could not focus my eyes on the paper without a conscious effort, but I was happy with my efforts. Soundings, bearings, time and velocity of tidal race were all shown and the broad outlines of the sand bank were sketched in, together with the position of our buoys. I made a careful copy, then sent the map over to *Elephant* in our gig. Nelson, I guessed, would have every draftsman in the fleet copying it within the hour, and a copy to each ship before we made a move. And so it was.

Agamemnon, *Bellona*, and *Russell* presumably tossed their copies over the side, judging by their navigation during the subsequent action.

April the second found the wind still at sou'sou'west, and at eight o'clock in the morning the drums began to beat through the fleet as we upped anchor and sailed down on the enemy line. Now I intimated this to be a special battle, and so it was. Brother Dane was waiting for us and their ships-of-the-line were moored fore and aft with springs on all. Ships alternated with hulks and floating batteries reinforced by shore batteries and the Trekroner battery at the northern end of their line. Their floating batteries were a particular problem as they stood only eight feet above the waterline and were hard to hit. They also had a constant stream of small boats recharging them with men, powder and shot.

Nelson's plan was the essence of simplicity, indeed he had been working on it until midnight, which may say something about him, or may not. We were to anchor, each in our appointed spot, springs on our anchors, and hammer the boat opposite us into submission. It reminded me of an account I had read of a joust that had taken place in Sussex. Two pugilists had consented to have their right hands bound together, and then had endeavoured to beat each other into insensibility with their left hands and with head butting. I might have expected the 'Victor of the Nile' to come up with some more subtle stratagem. A dash behind the fortifications, for instance, to seize Copenhagen harbour. All Nelson's victories really were gained by direct violence which cowed the enemy into submission.

We were Nelson's second-in-line and, myself checking the bearings, we swung sideways into our station not twenty yards from his stern, with such adroitness that our anchor splashed into the bay at the same instant as his. The *Edgar* and the *Ardent* had led the line in, but now things began going very wrong indeed. *Agamemnon*, scheduled fifth in line, hit on the very middle ground we had charted and stuck fast. Nelson signalled *Polyphemus* to take her place, but as she manoeuvred in, *Bellona*, coming around her stern to pass down to her position, also found a shoal and grounded.

Bellona opened fire on the enemy from where she stood and succeeded in knocking a spar away from *Polyphemus'* gallants. The firing spread along the line and the *Russell*, coming up in the smoke, followed *Bellona* on to the middle ground shoals. Of Nelson's twelve ships-of-the-line, three were not able to take their place, but our four frigates ran down to the northern end of the battle and engaged the floating defences there.

We, on *Glatton*, found ourselves tied in our duel to the death with the Danish Commanding Officer on the *Dannebrog*, a well-found 74, and no mean opponent. We also came under fire from a floating gun platform moored astern of him. And so began a long, long day. I often wonder if anyone who took part in that battle escaped without causing loss and damage to his hearing. The thunder of the guns was unbearably loud and unceasing and went on for so many hours that the very reverberation dulled your senses and made logical thinking damned near impossible. Not that much thought was called for, it was just a case of British Bulldog. Hang on grimly and punish until your opponent cried "Enough!"

The breeze dropped to nothing so that the cloud of gun smoke hung over us grey and bilious yellow, acrid and choking. Men were gasping for breath and on the gun deck our people all had kerchiefs soaked in water and vinegar tied over their mouths, and this seemed to give some relief. No relief however for our eyes, and after a couple of hours of our cannonade everybody was streaming tears and their lids red raw. The sulphur tore at my throat, which was a particular personal hardship: I find in a battle I like to do a lot of shouting at people. It gives them heart to hear me because this has always been my procedure during gunnery practices, when I threaten dire punishments for inept handling, but today it was a croak that came out as I strove to make myself heard.

This was a simple battle for me. No worry about signals, no indecision about tactics, no jockeying for the windward position. Nelson had usurped to himself the blame, or the praise; we just had to stand and shoot. Persistence was the true mark of valour at Copenhagen. Persistence and luck. I strutted the deck in my best uniform, fool to do so when there might be a fore-top full of marine sharpshooters to aim at one, but here it was a duel of the long cannon, so if luck was to forsake me then a handsome and well-found corpse was well in order.

We were suffering a great deal from the *Dannebrog*'s iron —indeed I think no other ship that day caught it near as hot as us. We lost our fore-topmast shot away and bringing down with it a great tangle of rigging. The mainmast was split and indeed, by the end of the action all our lower masts had to be double fished, and our spars and sails were cut to ribbons. No question of us deserting our station — we couldn't sail a league in the condition we were in. At noon we suffered further loss as a storm of ball came ringing in on our top deck. Two of our guns and one of our carronades were immediately overturned. Mr Johns commanding the firing from our top battery was hit and nearly disembowelled by a vicious splinter that flew from the gunwales.

"Get sand on the deck there," I plunged down to take command as our main armament was in disarray. A fresh broadside smashed into the hull below us, and a crash and screaming told of loss below.

Our carronades, squat, fat cannon, not dissimilar to a mortar, were ranged on the *Dannebrog* and had been wounding him grievously with their gigantic forty-pound balls. We only had three of the five left firing and I was anxious to get them back into action. A mist of blue smoke was wreathing our opponent now and I thought he might have been hit hard, might have his death in him, but a howl of shot and a splintering crash saw two more guns on the top deck knocked out of the action. As a fifty-gun boat we could only bring twenty-two guns into action on the larboard battery, as against thirty-four of those on the enemy. Our firing rate was still excellent, and the people's discipline and spirit was exemplary.

I counted the flashes along the *Dannebrog*'s side, trying to determine how many guns he was still fighting. They say if you see the speck of a cannon ball in the flash of a cannon, then you are a dead man, the ball will hit you. Well, I must have been several kinds of a dead man this day as the Danish guns flashed and winked.

There was about a cable between the ships. I shouted in triumph as I saw flames torching out at *Dannebrog*'s stern cabin, but my triumph was dented by two more shots that screeched in, dismounting our forward carronade and a brass bow-chaser that we had dragged around to bear. It didn't fire a shot. "Clear those bodies away." The starboard battery had been seconding their shipmates, filling the gaps and lending muscle. I took four as a burial squad, and they heaved eight bodies over from the shattered guns' crews.

Johnson, midshipman, came to report from the gun deck. "Mr Patterson's compliments, Captain" he gabbled, "we have nine dead down there, and two guns broken, but he has filled the gaps from the starbowlines."

Nine guns gone. We were being reduced to an unarmed

hull. "I'll get a detail down to clear the bodies," I croaked, "Tell Mr Patterson to keep his machines firing — the action is by no means finished."

"If you please, Sir, we have put the bodies out the gun ports, Sir." His eyes were big. "Carry on, Mr Johnson." A rumbling from below told me that Patterson was running guns from the starboard side across to fill the gaps.

"Mr Neville" I croaked. The acting Master scrambled to my side through a tangle of tarred line he had had the young gentlemen cutting away.

"Aye, Sir."

"Will you take my compliments down to Mr Patterson on the job he's doing, and exercise yourself in trimming ship." With all our cannon on the larboard side the ship was definitely starting to heel. The strange thing to my mind was that no one else seemed aware of it. Single-mindedness I suppose. Your job is to work a gun, you load cartridge and ball and aim and pull the long cord. Actually all the guns on the main deck seemed to be using slow match. Lanyards are fine when they work. Slow match always works.

A shout of warning and I flinched and ducked as a wooden block came tumbling from the mizzen-tops. It was brought to, a yard above me, by the halyard which had fouled the spanker boom.

"Signal, Captain, number 39."

"From Nelson?" I was incredulous.

"No, Sir, Commander in chief."

Thirty-nine was "Discontinue the engagement."

"*Elephant* Sir, repeating 39, but flying 16 above it."

Sixteen was to engage for closer action.

Holy Hades! Was one to obey Nelson or Hyde Parker?

I looked down the line, but could see nothing for the smoke.

"Get a man aloft with a glass, Mr Aders."

Aders, the third lieutenant, made his way with some caution up to the mizzen-top.

"Deck, there!"

"Carry on."

"Frigates discontinuing the action, Sir."

The four frigates were, of course, clear up to the north end of the battle, and right under Hyde Parker's eye.

"Deck — *Defiance* flying number 16."

That was Graves, the other Rear Admiral, taking Nelson's lead. Our course of action had in fact been decided for us — we had no means of discontinuing the action. It was going to take two days work before *Glatton* was going anywhere under her own rigging. I turned my attention back on the *Dannebrog*. She was well ablaze now and drifting down on the *Crontory*, which had also ceased firing and was undoubtedly watching the approach of her flaming consort with marked apprehension.

I was shaken out of my reverie by a splintering crash from under my feet as a ball from the floating battery ploughed through my cabin.

"Load carronades with grape and aim down to clear the deck of that gun platform."

At this range the carronade was deadly. The forward carronade fired and I screwed my eyes to my telescope to observe the full shot. I could see nothing. Another crash and a splinter flew from our rudder.

"You're firing over, bring it down a notch." A simple system of wedges and notches controlled the elevation of our carronades.

The aft carronade went off with a thunder and two seconds later the gun platform was obliterated. Not a man was standing.

"Shall we hold our fire, Sir?"

"Keep hitting them with grape until they hoist a white flag."

Both carronades had the range now and we hit them twice more with canisters and grape.

Our gun deck had fallen silent, I sent down to see why. Patterson appeared helpless, dirty, and clutching an arm.

"Sir?"

"Have you been given an order to stop firing, Mr Patterson?"

"But Sir, they have ceased firing."

"You have better eyes than I to see their white flag."

"Sir, there can be no one alive to hoist the surrender."

I looked at the wreck of my ship and a cold malevolence

seethed through me.

"You will cease firing when I order you to cease firing and not before, Mr Patterson." He stared at me, then turned. He went below, and I heard the guns being run out again, grudgingly, I thought, although they were tired enough I imagine.

"Deck there!" Mr Aders, was still at the mizzen-top.

"*Elephant* signalling Sir — discontinue action."

One of the gun-deck cannons roared out a second later.

"Pass the word to cease firing" I said. It was over. A boat under a flag of truce was leaving *Elephant* and making to the Danish line. Nelson would be offering a truce.

There was another splintering crash in the rigging, then a sickening thud. I had ducked, expecting a shower of rope and splinters, but it was Mr Aders arriving on the deck rather more speedily then was good for him. His right leg stuck out at an odd angle. He looked at me speechlessly for a moment then fell forward with blood trickling from his mouth. I went forward to Hastings, the gun captain on the aft carronade, "One more shot, Mr Hastings, to square the account for Mr Aders."

The avalanche of grape hit the gun platform squarely and there was a ragged cheering from the gun crews on *Glatton* as it slowly, very slowly but inexorably tilted then settled under the sea. A report to our right made me spin around. Nelson had fired a gun to reinforce his signal to discontinue the action. The flag was flying over our pennant. "Acknowledge the signal" I said, and looked across with some satisfaction at the gap we'd blasted in the Danish defence, and the floating wreckage that had been a gun platform five minutes since.

"This," said Nelson, "is a madeira that I saved up to drink after a victory. How many bottles have we left, Hardy?"

"Two dozen, Sir, after we drink this lot."

There were only Hardy, Nelson and I, and a dozen bottles of the hero's madeira winking at us.

I drank a generous mouthful and slowly swilled the sticky brown draught around my goblet.

"Are we expecting some reinforcements, then?"

"Graves will be in directly," said Hardy, "Foley, Parker, and Riou. You'll have to play the man with your bottle."
I find it ridiculous that a man was thought less of if he didn't empty a bottle.

"Riou won't be in," I said flatly, "He was cut in half by one of the last shots they fired."

"Talking of last shots fired, Bligh," Nelson was frowning, "that was a damned bad business, raking that battery after we'd sent in the flag of truce."

"They knocked my third lieutenant out of the rigging, Sir, with a shot fired after the flag had gone in, and we returned the compliment. Not the only signal that was ignored today."

He looked at me hard, wondering how to take it. Joy in his victory swamped his sternness, and he filled his glass, swinging it around, so that half of the wine splashed on the canvas flooring.

Victory and fame were to him intoxicating and aphrodisiac. It would not be long, I know, before he began lyricising his domestic paradise with the beautiful Lady H. and their bastard child Horatia.

"A total surrender!" he gloated. "Now we can sail up and rub the Russian's faces in it. Confusion to the enemy!" We drained our glasses. Nelson was sparkling and gyrating, so that every one else among us appeared sober and staid.

"The Crown Prince tells me they had more than fifteen hundred men killed and wounded. We must have had fewer."

"They fought sternly and well, Sir."

"How many did you lose, Bligh? What was your butcher's bill?"

"We had over fifty casualties, Sir, indeed I think our ship was hit by more shot than any other."

He clapped me on the shoulder in delight.

"You're my brother in arms — we took it smoking hot and gave it back with interest."

It was ironic, I thought. At Camperdown I lost only six wounded and had the Admiral's ship strike to me, by fighting with prudent seamanship, making best use of our advantages, yet some there accounted me a coward. Here I sat still and got shot to pieces, and everyone acclaimed me a hero.

I thought best to get it in writing, not tonight, but a eulogy from Nelson could do me no harm.

* * * * *

"So please understand this: while your vessel has undeniable advantages in belching its way across the channel, in this one battle I've described it would have been useless."

"Well that's debatable."

"Not at all, the battle was a set piece, the advantage was in weight, in ponderability. Your craft would have only represented a danger to its neighbours.

"These boats you spoke of that ran aground, was that because of faults, errors in your charting?"

"Certainly not! *Agamemnon* started to leeward and was so lubberly handled she could not get far enough to windward to weather the middle-ground shoals."

"But a steam-propelled vessel knows no leeward or windward."

I made my excuses and came away. The fellow knew nothing of naval affairs.

Chapter Six

My London surgeon prescribes an aphrodisiac — the Reverend Mr Troubridge preaches on carnal desires — Midshipman Bligh joins the brotherhood of man — my daughter Jane proposes to farm turkeys

You were asking me about Fletcher Christian — weren't you? I thought you were. Everybody does. Wants to know what I really thought of him, how we got on together, before, you know. Well I've already told you, I think the fellow was stark raving mad! Just took me a long time to ferret it out. Too long, you could say — I'd accept that.

Before I start on Christian, I'd better sketch in the details of my appointment with Tregenza. I did make an appointment with him, and I must confess to feeling my usual lowness of spirits as I was shown into his parlour or waiting room. It was an old and dark granite house, built right on the street, and you surmounted stone steps over an area where some depressed shrubs languished in stone pots.

A ruby glass in the door was illuminated by light from within to declare that this was the door of a surgeon. The door was opened, not by a housemaid, but by Cardus, his butler. Cardus was a long, lugubrious gentleman's gentleman, who would don a leather apron and serve as surgeon's assistant when the work warranted. A small coal fire was burning in a grate and faded velveteen curtains in a drab shade of brown shielded the medical mysteries of twenty-nine Wimpole Street from the cheerful afternoon sunshine outside.

I sat fairly gingerly on a leather settee, and looked without great interest at a volume of steel engravings of somebody's travels in Italy. Cardus came back bearing a salver with a glass of madeira for my approval, which was damned civil of him, but suggested to me that my wait was likely to be a longish one.

The room was furnished with surgical impedimenta — instruments, charts, and species jars in a manner possibly calculated to buoy the expectations of the patient. Glass in hand, I wandered over to inspect the case of instruments. They must have been a set he had used, and retired, for they were, in general, cheerfully stained in a manner to excite the imagination.

There were pruning saws, and coping saws, gimlets and blades, tweezers and probes, augers, scissors and what looked like button hooks, all in blackened steel. Dominating the lot was an enormous brass syringe with a brutal nozzle. It would be a hard man who could look at that syringe and not cross his legs, and feel his anus flinch. Before the case of implements, a tank of green water was home to a school of leech. Tregenza was still a disciple of Broussais, at the Paris school, who considered that inflammation played a major role in all distemper and disease. Dieting, blood letting and leeching were his counters to inflammation, and if they failed, then — he cut it off.

Over the fireplace hung a human image, but what an image! It was a full length human body depicted, sans skin, and with the blood vessels coloured red, and the nerves flayed open and brought to our attention by their bilious green coloration. 'Fyfe's System of Anatomy 1800' said the caption. The mouth was twisted into a companionable grin, but I rejected its invitation to complicity, and looked away. Hanging over the mantel like that, one expected a portrait of Tregenza's grandfather, or some other forebear, so that it provided something of an affront to decency when your eye took in its detail. I can't be sure, of course, that it wasn't Tregenza's grandfather.

A case of bottles, each carefully labelled, stood between the windows, and each bottle contained a dissection of the human anatomy performed presumably by my skilled surgeon.

Mrs Colecatch, a widow in our village at Farningham, keeps in her pantry a row of glass bottles each containing a pickled pudding. They are black gelatinous lumps floating in a poisonous looking yellow liquid. I believe her, that they are pickled puddings, but to my eye, they appear very much like aborted

114

foetuses. This may be my mind playing tricks, as she has also the reputation of being the county abortionist. So be it, but Tregenza's graveyard of metastased malignancies reminded me of her pickled puddings. I leant closer to scrutinise what appeared to be a scrofulous nose, but recoiled in fright as I found an eyeball, the size of a walnut, gazing at me unblinkingly. A further bottle drew my attention as it was apparently a diseased liver. It was a livid grey, but whether as a result of disease or immersion in spirit I was not to know.

Furtively, I reached my fingers up under my waistcoat and gently probed my own liver. For a moment I felt nothing abnormal and a great feeling of relief swept me up. Then I followed the rib cage down, and — there it was. An unyielding mass. I looked at the bottle and felt bile in my throat. I swallowed it back, then jumped as Cardus appeared at my elbow.

"Mr Tregenza will see you now, Admiral." He was smiling knowingly. I collected my hat and gloves and was ushered into the 'holy of holies'.

"And now Admiral, this is the area of your concern?"

"I said it was my liver."

"Quite," he obviously thought I didn't know the difference between a liver and a lung, because he'd spent some considerable time percussing my chest with a small hammer while listening with a small wooden tube pressed between his ear and the chest wall. I'd done so much heavy breathing at his direction that I was feeling quite dizzy.

"There's a lump" I said, tentatively. I wanted him to tell me that there wasn't.

"Is that tender?" My stomach muscles tightened involuntarily as he plunged his fingers into the affected area.

"No," I grunted between clenched teeth.

"Just relax your stomach muscles."

He probed his fingers in again.

"I can't."

He pushed and squeezed and measured.

"There is some swelling. Do you drink a lot?"

"No, no, nothing at all."

"Bottle a night?"

"I was at a dinner last evening, but no, as a general rule just a glass of burgundy with my meal."

"Hmmmm."

I don't know if he believed me or not.

"Well," he said. "There is, as I say, some swelling. Likely there is some morbidity. Spirits can do it to your liver, of course" — he waited for me to confess to a cupboard dipsomania — "but as you tell me you don't drink then we must look for some other cause. Did you bring a motion with you?"

"Good lord, no. Should I have?"

"Aye, well, it's a great facility to have a motion to study when it's the liver you are considering. The texture and the colour, do you see?"

I nodded wisely — this I understood.

"Have your stools changed over the last few months?"

They had, as a matter of fact. Elizabeth has introduced Scots porridge at our breakfast table and I took something of a fancy to it. With honey. Makes your stools float, but I didn't know how to tell him this, so I shook my head.

"Then we must consider either a tumour, or some liverish humour causing inflammation."

I could see my fate inexorably closing in on me. Any minute now he'd have Cardus in, and they'd have my liver out.

"You're not suffering pain?"

"A little wind."

"Where does it catch you?"

I showed him.

"I take some heart then, that it may be a liver flux. We shall try you on some willow-bark."

I took a bit of heart myself.

"I've been eating liver, thought it must be a good thing, couldn't but help."

He ignored me but scribbled on a scrap of paper.

"There you are, Cardus will give you a bottle of willow-bark extract, but that fellow in Farningham, the apothecary, he'll be

116

able to make some more up for you. Give him my note."

I've been drinking willow-bark for two weeks now, and its made me as horny as a cormorant. They should market that stuff as an aphrodisiac: 'Liquid extract of Salix Alba, one teaspoonful to be taken before bed. Caution. Too much may be dangerous!'

That damned ninny Troubridge was turning his goat's eyes up to heaven last Sunday and eulogising married love, and what do you think its purpose is? Procreation! I nearly stood up in the pew to denounce him as a damned hypocrite.

"Marriage is not to be entered upon lightly, unadvisedly, or just to satisfy physical desires," he intoned, "but it was ordained by God for the procreation of children."

"Now look here, vicar," he likes to be called Father but I don't give him the satisfaction. I'd caught up with him in the porch, "what about the marriage service, doesn't it say that marriage is to hallow and direct a man's lusts and to keep him from fornication, words very much to that effect?"

"Why yes, Bligh."

He becomes defensive when challenged in his own sphere, but then I was something of an expert myself. I read church services once a week right around the globe. Not many marriages, mind you, but a power of burials.

"Well there you are then, the object of marriage is to keep a man happily occupied rogering his wife, instead of spreading it around the neighbourhood."

"That is one interpretation."

"An interpretation that most husbands might prefer, and one or two wives I'll be bound."

"The ladies of the Anglican Women's League asked me to give that sermon to celebrate the sacrament of Christian Marriage. I must satisfy all my parishioners you know." He was being reasonable.

"I hope you satisfy Mrs Troubridge, then."

I left with the honours of the last word.

I've never heard such nonsense really. "It's a man's world," they say — well so it is. Couldn't be any other way, could it?

would be going against nature. Is the cock not the king of the fowl yard? Does the stallion master his mares? and mount them at his will? And so it is with man and woman. A woman is physically, emotionally, and mentally unsuited to many of the tasks of a man. Can she plough, or drive a coach? Can you imagine a woman as a doctor, or a barrister, or indeed a captain of a ship?

Can you imagine the country if Westminster was run by women? Parliament would divide along lines of intuition, rather than party. The prosecution of the war with France would be suspended during the season. You might even have women voting, or holding cabinet office. The House of Lords would become the House of Ladies! But one can't imagine them all behaving like ladies! Parliament would no longer go into recess for the grouse season, but would stop for the *débutantes* coming out. I could go on in this amusing strain for some time, but the idea is ludicrous.

No. A woman is built for man's pleasure, and to rear his family. She is the antithesis of the perils and hard knocks a man experiences in running a country, or a ship, or a business. Her business is to foster to her mate, and to give him those comforts that a man desires. God has designed her to this end.

I sometimes think that I am a very carnal man, but then the privations, and deprivations, of a seafarer can cause an imbalance. I'm aware of this, and unhappily, Mrs Bligh was rather of the vicar's persuasion. She did not take the joy in it that was there. There was a love between us, there was even passion, at the beginning, on the Isle of Man at Douglas in '81 when we courted and wed, but so trammelled about with convention and modesty had we become, so much inhibition and stultifying counsel was passed from mother to daughter, that the way of a man with a woman was degraded into a sterile ritual.

After our first months of marriage, my Elizabeth could find no animation in surrender, only a grim sense of self-sacrifice, duty duly done. Indeed, although we consummated the marriage at regular intervals, with a view to procreation, I never saw her unclothed after this time, and yet I have seen the simple natives on Otaheite, indeed on all the islands celebrate the beauty of their couplings with dance and drum. Riding through the wain trail behind our wood, I surprised a yeoman and his nancy hard at it in the bluebells, indeed I heard their shouts of merriment as I approached. A blanket of despondency descended over me as I contrasted their pleasure in life with the civilised and constrained behaviour of their betters. 'Poor William — poor Elizabeth.'

Elizabeth was constrained by the sorority of suffering womankind, as exemplified by her mother, and the weight of her precautions about proper modesty, and the insatiable lusts of man. My sexual education had been all gleaned in the forecastle and quarter-deck of a man of war where morality and expediency tend to be blurred. But an eight year old on H.M.S. *Monmouth*, learnt quickly or went under. I learnt so quickly on that voyage that eighteen months later and paid off, I cut a swathe of wicked worldliness through Plymouth Free Grammar School.

***** *

In the gun room of H.M.S. *Monmouth* I learnt spelling and mathematics, and cyphering, but I also was initiated into the wonderful brotherhood of man. Young ladies, as you might imagine, were very scarce on the decks of *Monmouth*, though dockside ladies of a coarser kind were no rarity, some taking up residence with their lawful spouses while the ship was in Plymouth, some others plying their trade as professional enchantresses. I remember one burly lady with chests like melons, (I had no slightest idea of the function of the female breast), one lady of pleasure who I picture now, dressed in a soiled pink robe and a tousled mob cap, one of her aforementioned breasts escaping largely the confines of her bodice, who bedded with half the crew, the common seamen that is, although she went also with Peters, the Master's mate, a warrant officer.

Pengilly, also aboard as captain's servant, and my schoolmate in the Captain's cabin, was of a like age to myself, and with two such worldly rakes the discussion often would turn to the women one had known. I had, even at this age, strong interest in the private particulars of the opposite sex and had discovered even then the pleasurable impulses which were occasioned by fondling my own organ. What I took with me aboard *Monmouth* was a guilt, a terrific sense of shame that I took such pleasure in thoughts of which, I was very sure, my mother would strongly disapprove. In my second week aboard ship we were visited on the Sunday by Captain Stewart's family, his wife, Lady Stewart, and her two daughters. One of these attractive young ladies, Sarah the younger, set herself to tease the young gentlemen. She was a bonny attractive young person, all coquettish grace and mischief, swirling her skirts and flashing her pantaloons at Pengilly and me as she pretended to climb the rigging, or to steer the ship with the great wheel. At last she cried, "Dear me, has the cat taken your tongues, David and William, what boring company you are to be sure." She was certainly a provoking young minx, but the Captain, disturbing us on the quarter-deck, put an end to her frolic, and bore her off.

"I say Bligh," Pengilly lowered his voice, "I wouldn't mind seeing what was under those pantaloons."

"What!"

I couldn't believe I was hearing it right, and I made him repeat it twice before I let myself go with the pleasure of meeting a man with parallel interests in vice. A great light dawned upon me: all men were the same, I was not a depraved miscreant. My relief ran away with my tongue as we compared and shared our limited sexual experiences.

"And were you bathed with your sister?" I was intrigued by the intimacies of family living. I had experienced very little of it. "And did you look at her bottom?"

Suddenly he was reserved. "Yes, of course," he said, "but that doesn't count, it was different."

I couldn't see why. I had no brothers or sisters and my mind had become choked with a carnal voluptuousness. My best dreams were peopled with unclothed female bottoms.

"Mr Bligh!" I leapt guiltily, then ran for the deck, fantasies banished in the urgency of being at my station when the First Lieutenant reached the quarter-deck. Pengilly vanished below to claim our hammock. We messed with the midshipmen, but in such mean style that there was only space for one hammock between us. One tumbled out to go on watch, one tumbled in to snatch his sleep. Never have I slept as I did on that voyage. Physical exhaustion plagued me, and the minute my head hit the canvas cushion that served as pillow, my eyes would latch tight. As a Master it was always my practice to organise three watches. It makes for a more content crew. Watch and watch four hours on four hours off is an exhausting routine that takes its toll on the human spirit as well as the human body. Mind you, sailors on watch and watch are too tired to worry about plotting mutinies.

Sea air and harsh exercise take their toll of a growing body. I grew three inches on that cruise. Rogers the senior midshipman, made us stand against the bulkhead in the mess and marked our height, indifferently nicking my scalp as he jammed his dirk into the plank. That was one of his amiable tricks. One of his disagreeable tricks was to suddenly stick his dirk into the beam over the mess table during a meal. The junior midshipmen and boys were then compelled to race to the deck, and he would seize the laggard and beat him with his belt. Training us in alertness he called it. Edwards the third caught him at it one afternoon and Rogers told him this tremendous cock and bull story about sharpening up our alertness, and how it was very traditional. If there is one thing the British Navy runs on, it is tradition — and bullying. He was an objectionable lout, Rogers, but I prayed for his promotion. However, his brutish stupidity has kept him a lieutenant to this very day. "Cutlass in the beam, cutlass in the beam," we would yelp in terror as we fought each other not to be the last. It wasn't a cutlass of course, just a dirk, because he wasn't a commissioned officer.

Rogers sharpened his personal animosity to a special pitch for me, because of the progress I was making in using the navigational tables.

It was, I think, the very most fortunate thing that happened to me, to be instructed in the elements of navigation by Captain Stewart. He instructed us each day in the forenoon watch, and busily we would scratch at our slates on the trestle in his cabin, or labour for a sight of the horizon as the deck pitched and fell under our feet. We studied the celestial charts, and learnt the use of sun and star tables. Dead reckoning, chart reading and correction, the taking of magnetic bearings, and the use of backstaff and quadrant to measure the shadow of the sun. The backstaff is still used by some merchantmen who calculate their latitude by means of it, run down to the appropriate latitude and then run down the easting or westing until they make a landfall. The reflecting quadrant superseded it and is refined now into the more universally used sextant. It can measure the transit of the planets, or the sun, always provided that one enjoys, (and understands the use of) a set of planetary tables from the Royal Observatory.

Rogers was as one of the brutes in the field when confronted with planetary tables. Captain Stewart had a Harrison chronometer so that longitudinal calculations were also within our compass (an unintentional pun, but an amusing one that I will repeat to Sir J.B.). His principles of instruction, which I find it hard to better, relied upon confronting us right from the start with calculations in spherical trigonometry, for, as he said, we sail on a globe, so it is a needless complication to learn plain trigonometry, and then have to unlearn it. He had rigged a regular galaxy of spheres from the roof of his cabin to demonstrate to us the movement of the planets in relation to our own planet earth. His whole self radiated pleasure in sharing his knowledge and instructing us in the usage of it, and I think he took no little pleasure in my own quick and intelligent grasp of his lectures. He was unfortunately lost while in his prime, not as a result of enemy action, or not directly, being lost from his ship during a blockade of Toulon. There was an inquiry into the circumstances, but I never heard that the details had come to light.

We peered through our quadrants, we passed tables between us, we scratched our heads and scratched our slates. We were all finished, and indeed I had time to compare my result with that of noon yesterday, with bearings I had prudently scratched on the reverse of my slate, but the midshipman Rogers with a look of owlish industry was still deep in his figuring.

"Mr Rogers, would you favour us with your conclusions."

He looked up unhappily and gave us:

"13° 51' N, 32° 30' E, Sir."

There was a silence during which each of us looked hastily again at our calculations."

"And Mr Bligh, do you concur with Mr Rogers?"

I did not, and vastly daring, I said, "Mr Rogers appears to have discovered the source of the Blue Nile, Sir."

There was a shriek of laughter at this, but I only laughed moderately. I knew I should pay for my levity.

"Mr Rogers," said the Captain, kindly enough, "I believe you have made an error. As Mr Bligh points out, you seem to have the ship in the middle of Africa."

Rogers took my good shirt that evening, and tore the sleeves out, saying he needed them for kerchiefs. I wondered at the time at the latitude he was allowed in his bullying, but conclude now that Captain Stewart was wise not to interfere with a system that prepared us for the harshness and injustices that were all an entrenched part of the vast family that was His Majesty's Royal Navy.

"I say, Bligh."

"Pengilly?"

"Has Rogers tried to touch you?"

"Touch me?"

"You know!"

He hadn't, but I wasn't sure what Pengilly meant.

"Has he touched you?" Did I know what he meant?

It was something that wasn't spelt out, it was something that I had not even sorted out in my mind, but a dark and erotic tangle of suspicions fascinated, and repelled me. I was anxious to have him confide in me.

"Has he touched you then?"

Pengilly looked pale — not titillated, worried.

"He tried to."

"What happened?"

"We were down on the mess deck and he came over and showed me his prick. It was enormous, you know."

I knew — we had compared our erections in brotherly

pride.

"It was inflamed, almost purple, I think he had been rubbing it." This was also familiar to us both.

"He asked me if I wanted to touch it, and then he tried to get me to come into his bunk."

"Did you?"

"I was scared of him."

"Did you?"

"I took my dirk and told him I'd stick it in his belly if he came near me."

I was incredulous.

"You did! What did he say?"

"He was furious, but he was scared too. He was scared. He was scared that I'd do it. His prick shrivelled right down, right then, when I showed him the dirk."

"What did he say?"

"He got dressed, he put his pants on, and then he said that I'd threatened a senior officer, and that he'd have me lashed."

"He won't. He won't dare say what he did."

But Pengilly was crying. "I'd jump overboard rather than be lashed."

Lashing happened to the men. They were strapped to a frame and the skin and flesh flogged off their backs.

"I'd rather die myself."

"He won't."

"He said he knew what we do with each other. I said we don't do anything, but he said he'd seen us rubbing our penises, and he was going to tell the Captain."

I needed some time to consider this — suddenly I was involved. I discounted the threat but you never could be sure with Rogers. We had compared our erections.

"He won't do anything."

Strangely that was the end of our trouble with him. Rogers didn't speak to either of us for the rest of that cruise, and in fact both he and I left the ship in Plymouth. Pengilly stayed on for two more years, at least, but I never saw him again.

* * * * *

124

"Father!" It was Jane.

"Yes my dear."

"Father, you know we don't farm this estate."

"Farm it?"

"Yes."

"But there are only twenty acres with the manor house."

"I know that Father."

"Well, you can't farm twenty acres, can you? Take out the four acres of house and you could only pasture half a dozen cattle."

"Poultry, Father. I thought I should like to raise turkeys."

"Turkeys, what do you know about turkeys?"

"Well nothing practically, I suppose, but I know all about the theory of it. See my book."

I'm dashed if she didn't produce a small bound volume with some kind of fowl embossed on its cloth cover. "What's this?" I turned it over. "'The Poultry Farmer's Vade-mecum'!"

"It's very clean and easy to do Father, and Jackson could help me, and it is immensely profitable."

God help me, she was serious it seemed.

"And what would you house your turkeys in?"

"Why, I would have some sheds built for them just next to the kitchen garden." She opened her book, and turned to a well-thumbed page.

"'The shed, for turkey, should be light and well ventilated. Clean straw should be placed on the floor and a series of suitable perches arranged at length of no more than three feet above the ground. Separate nesting sheds will be needed, as other turkeys will peck at the shells, and in some cases eat the eggs before they are hatched. Some farmers, indeed, abandon the natural mother, and hatch their eggs in baskets adjacent to their stoves.'"

"Yes, well, it would have to be built by a tradesman, carpenter, I suppose!"

"But Father, there would be mechanics in the village who could be entrusted with it."

"At my expense."

"Oh, but Father, you would have it all back, and tenfold."

"Hmmmm." I tried another tack. "And do you think it an appropriate occupation for a young lady?"

"Well, Father, I see no company down here, but my sisters. I don't care for riding, even if we kept a stable. You must admit my embroidery is very average." She was right there — she'd embroidered an antimacassar for my chair for my birthday. It was a shade lumpy and distorted."

"I must have an interest here, or I will go mad with boredom. Frances likes gardening, but I have nothing."

"Raising turkeys is not valued highly in a young woman's list of attractive accomplishments," I persisted.

Jane looked at me frankly, her eyes were large and very clear.

"Father you must know that Frances and I are unlikely to wed. Our figures are unfashionable, and our faces are pleasant but plain." She looked at me with a twist to her mouth. Was she wanting me to convince her otherwise, was she waiting cynically for the hasty disjoiner a parent should make? She was too perceptive for an easy and insincere response, but the thing was that what she had said was not, to my eyes, true. The twins were both short and solid, not conforming to the taste of the age for tall willowy women with swan-like necks. Her hair was short and curly, her face brown from walking through the summer fields, her eyes large and brown and intelligent.

"There is a popular prejudice," I thought carefully and chose my words, "a prejudice in favour of long necks, tiny waists, and turned up noses. All these things are very well in their way, but not when allied, as they usually are, with vapid smiles and childlike minds incapable of sustaining an intelligent adult conversation. You and your sister, thank heaven, are not so formed. To my mind your intelligence lights your faces and shines from your eyes, and any man worth winning would be of a similar mind to myself."

She looked at me in silence for a moment, then reached forward and took my forearm and squeezed it.

"As long as this perceptive squire comes courting on a dark night with a new moon, I might get by then?"

126

She knew I was answering honestly, and she was pleased, although still defensive.

"Whether or not your swain would see you in a fairer light with feathers in your hair is a matter for conjecture, however," I said.

"Then I may proceed with my plans?"

I gazed at the window for inspiration. It did its best. The glass was an old moulding, poured in small sheets, and it distorted the world outside, bending perimeters and dusting images with a rainbow border.

A goose with an aura of gold and orange was standing on the stone pathway, emptying its bowel. Its motions complete, it advanced into the garden bed opposite and rooting out some ranunculus corns it ate them with every expression of satisfaction.

"Look at that. I suppose we will have geese and turkeys scratching everywhere like fleas on a dog."

"Why Father, maybe we could train them to go into Mr Ffoulkes's garden and scratch there."

I looked at her suspiciously.

She gazed back with a transparently guileless face, then the corner of her mouth twitched in spite of herself, and then we roared laughing together. Her humour was as rare as it was delicious — like an iced sherbet on a summer's day, it was worth waiting for.

"I'll get an estimate from John Constable in the village, he has been fixing up the vicar's poultry run."

"Well go ahead then, and do that and I'll consider it. You'll need to get three estimates from different tradesmen." This was a prudent idea that had just occurred to me. It would take her some time to find three of our people in the village able to give her an estimate. "Always buy time," old Jarvie used to say, "and when that's used up, buy some more." That had been the Navy's policy with Napoleon's invasion fleets for a decade.

Jane saw through the stratagem immediately — my daughters are no man's fools — but retired gracefully to consolidate her immediate gains.

I looked out the window to check if the golden goose had, perchance, left a golden egg, but it had scratched out of sight.

Chapter Seven

An incident with a cat recalls an encounter with a Prince — my
impressions of the Dutch administration of Timor — I am invited to
visit to the Soultain's palace — grisly memories of a cock-fight — my
encounter with a Daughter of the Soultain — I carry home a dismal
souvenir

I was seated in the window nook of our downstairs parlour. It
was a comfortable room, not grand, not a dining-room, and I
was at a loss to think what its original use or designation might
have been. We used it sometimes in winter as a breakfast-room.
It had a small cosy fire with an iron grate that burned almost all
the time, three hundred and sixty-five days a year, and generally it provided the centre for our family living. As you might
imagine the furniture was, not shabby, but comfortable. Most of
it we had acquired with the house, presumably because it was
not grand enough to warrant a change of air to Curzon Street.

I had a corduroy club chair which was a favourite piece of
furniture, not only with me but also with Anne's family of
kittens. One of them arrived now to dispute its title with me.
There was a scratching and tearing of fabric at the back, as Mr
Stripey sharpened his claws, then with flattened ears and bared
teeth he scrambled up with a rush to promenade precariously
across the backrest. Reaching my neck he suddenly pushed
against it, purring like a ratchet-mill, and tried to snuggle into
the gap between my head and the cushion. Mr Stripey was a
young cat, maybe two months, three months old — I really
cannot remember — and picking him up by the scruff of his
neck I swung him in front of me, eyeball to eyeball.

"Who's a good moggy then?" I inquired. The cat said nothing, so I stretched him on my knee and began to tickle his fat
kitten belly. His back legs began moving in involuntary rhythm
with my scratching.

"Is that a lovely tiger then, is that just what the tiger likes?"

I dropped him abruptly to the floor and pushed him away with my foot.

"Damned animal," I was muttering as Anne came into the room.

"Don't kick him, Papa! Mr Stripey!" She swooped on him. The cat disconcerted by the rapid changes in its fortunes, fell to licking its bottom clean.

"Naughty Mr Stripey, you know the Admiral can't abide cats. You know you mustn't scratch his chair."

Apparently the animal answered her on some pitch audible only to Anne, for a conversation now ensued as she squatted and knelt on the floor and entered the kitten's world.

Two of his siblings joined in the charade.

"Mr Stripey is not Mr Stripey, an Englishman. He is a prince of Madagascar. Miss Bonnett is his princess and Tarbottle is his gentleman usher." An Asian court convened on the parlour floor, with Anne assuming the roll of court reporter. Her prince was attired, reluctantly, in a lace kerchief and his *fiancée* gloried in a scrap of satin.

"There is to be a wedding." The court reporter had all the details, "Mr Stripey is wearing his wedding cloak, and will come riding on an elephant. He has a whole wardrobe of wonderful clothes, lace, satin, cloth of gold. All his buttons are pearls, you know, real pearls, and big, bigger than a pea — big as a cherry, and he has diamonds on his shoe buckles — do you know what Papa?"

"No, my precious."

"One of his shoe buckles is cut from a single diamond!"

"Fancy — what did they cut it with?"

"With a diamond cutter, of course."

"A diamond cutter?"

"Yes, a diamond cutter. Mr Phelps the glass cutter had one when he came to mend the scullery window."

"Ahhh — a diamond cutter!" I don't fancy Phelps cut too many diamonds.

"The Princess Eglantine is waiting. She is quite shy because she has only seen him once, but she worships him. It is a very busy time for M'sieur Tarbottle who has charge of all the wedding arrangements — there are to be a thousand guests." Anne's counting is unreliable once she gets past ten.

"And is a thousand guests a large number?"

"Oh yes indeed," she said, earnestly, "a very great number, it is the biggest wedding ever held in Madagascar."

"Are all the guests cats?"

"Oh no, of course not. Jane and Frances, and Mary and Harriet if they are able to come, and of course, the King of Madagascar, and all of the prince's other wives will be there to welcome his new bride."

I have a very fair knowledge of the weaker sex, and I would have disputed this last statement if the whole thing hadn't been nonsense anyway. I introduced a scientific note into the romance.

"One thing wrong with the scenario, my goose, is that your hero, your prince, is a girl kitten, not a boy kitten, a princess not a prince.

"He's not, he is a prince — why do you say that — why do you tease me so?"

"No, no, I assure you it's a fact, all tortoise-shell cats are female — it's a sexual characteristic, do you see."

She didn't. "Sexual?"

"A tortoise-shell cat is always female."

"What is a sexual characteristic?"

I thought.

"Men have moustaches, ladies don't, that is a characteristic of their sex.

She smiled wickedly, and I am sure was about to remark on her aunt Godolpha Bond, a lady of somewhat hirsute features; however, a disturbance in the wedding party drew her attention.

"He is a prince, a tortoise-shell prince. Tortoise-shells may not be men cats, but they can be princes."

"Anything is possible in the east, I suppose."

I sighed. Actually I had a fair working knowledge of Eastern

Princes. That is, if you can accept the son of a Malayan Soultain being a prince.

The one I met in Coupang had very few inhibitions at all.

*****

"I have a golden cock" said the prince conversationally, leaning towards me to be heard over the throbbing drums. I turned to look at him and was astonished to find that the unpleasant youth was actually anointing his balls with butter, at the dining table, if you please! His penis was encased in a sheath of beaten gold, about the size of a Devon carrot, suspended by a golden cord from his waist.

"Very nice," I murmured, "yes, so you have, very nice indeed."

The music was clashing louder and faster now, reaching, I supposed, its climax, although its complete lack of any structure or melody discernible to my ear made this a matter of conjecture.

The leader of the orchestra, or as such I took him to be, was pummelling frantically at a sort of xylophone.

"Gambongs," said the prince, "like a xylophone. We call it gambongs."

"And the gentlemen with the guitars?" I pointed to the musicians plucking at two stringed instruments, shaped something like the style of Madrid.

"Rebols."

"Gambongs and rebols?"

"Yahh. That is correct."

Some sort of brass pipe was wailing, a hundred small bells were being struck with little hammers, and the wooden drums were being pounded faster and faster by the bare hands of the drummers. No member of this chamber ensemble had any written music sheet so that one might suppose they began and stopped and improvised as their whim dictated. Maybe they were all playing some traditional part, certainly the beat of the drums set the rhythm and the pace.

The dancers shimmered and swung in the uneven lights cast by the torches. They must have been feeling it, by God, for the heat seemed more oppressive now the sun had gone down. I mopped my brow as a trickle of sweat stung my eye.

"They are trained to do it from childhood."

"Eh?" I came out of my mildly erotic absorption in the dancing with a guilty start as my mentor, Mr Wanjon, leant forward pointing to the dancers.

"The dances are traditional, each movement is ritualised. They tell a story of a great love."

I'd thought that was what it was about.

They were young girls naked from the waist upwards, their skin oiled so that it shone with a warm cinnamon lustre in the torch lights.

Each face was covered by a devilish mask, and necklets and bangles swayed in a circle as if they had a life of their own.

I had wanted to observe Malayan practices and customs, it being my habit to record them in my log at any port of interest, and the Governor, Van Este, had kindly arranged a trip for me to the Royal Palace at Omar.

Mr Van Este was suffering grievously from a kind of low fever, which is endemic in that country, the Dutch having made very poor choice in the siting of their settlement. I was in some trouble in my mind considering the likely danger to the health of my crew. Cruel stroke indeed to escape the travails and perils of ocean and savage only to be laid low by the neglect of civilised man, just when danger appeared at an end! All of us landed in such a low state of robustness that the danger of a fatal flux was immeasurably increased. My fears were realised when, on the July 20th, Mr Nelson had died of an inflammatory fever. He was the last, the very last I would have lost, for in this little botanist and horticulturist duty and integrity went hand in hand. He too had been with Cook.

We buried him with all the crew present, and to my gratification all the Dutch garrison, and nearly all of the trades people here attended the funeral. They behaved most handsomely, and a volley was fired over the grave. It weighed on me that no stone was found to mark his resting place, but I spoke.

"David Nelson," I said, "accomplished with diligence and hard work what he was sent out to do. He gathered and nurtured the breadfruit plants, and propagated them ready for their transport. I, William Bligh, will see the pirates who vandalised his endeavours brought to their justice, I will see them hanged, and I will return to this ocean and I will gather breadfruit again. This time no man shall thwart me."

That for his epitaph.

I did it, too.

I had some conversation with the Governor, the Opperhoofd, as they call him in their coarse Hollands dialect, as to the progress of his settlement. The Dutch had been in occupancy for one hundred and fifty years, he told me, and I thought it a fair question to ask why they had made so little advance in all this time. When one looks at what has been done in the Americas, and in the sub-continent under the John Company, one sees the fundaments of law and order established, trade and commerce encouraged and ordered, missions spreading the Christian message, and above all, drains and clean water for the European settlements. Here, all was the chaos and neglect of 150 years imposed upon the chaos and neglect of five thousand years. (The Soultain told me his family had held the island for five thousand years, dispossessing an aboriginal people — whom they enslaved, these wretches dying out after a thousand years of abuse. And he showed me an ornate tapestry which purported to depict the true history of his Kampang Dynasty. His great, great, great grandfather had been the son of a dragon. Certainly the tapestry depicted a paler-skinned inferior race performing menial tasks.

We traversed the coastal swamps and climbed into the foothills following a trodden path to the Soultain's stronghold of Omar.

I was going to write 'The Royal City', but it was a poor city, indeed it would scarcely be the size of an English market town. I travelled in luxury in a sort of bamboo palanquin with a roof of leaves of the pandanus to secure me from the sun.

July was their coolest month, but enjoyed average temperature of 80 deg. F in the shade. Out in the sun it would have been 110 deg., and the humidity was certainly very high. I wasn't going to spoil their protocol by insisting on walking. In spite of the humidity, no significant rainfall was in sight.

This south eastern corner of the Malay Archipelago, the Sundra islands, of which Timor is the largest, come under the influence of two monsoonal cycles. The south-easterly monsoon brings a prolonged dry season from April to October, while the north-easterly monsoon, which sets in from November to March, brings most of the rain, the 'wet' season. 'Wet' is no mere polite term as they get (as I have read in a Portuguese Pilot) an average of six foot six inches of rain in a season, twenty inches of rain falling in January alone. The mountains we headed towards were shrouded with a blanket of cloud.

The Deputy Governor shared my conveyance to point out the highlights of the trip as they unfolded.

"There is no road? Do you not have other settlements on the island?"

"Why yes, there is a settlement, a small town, on the Northern shore, Atapupu, but the only access is by sailing vessel."

"And you've been here, what, one hundred and fifty years?"

"One hundred and fifty," he flushed at my implied criticism, "but we have no resources, no money."

"Is it a Port, Atapupu?"

"A fishing port for the native prahus, but the coast up there is more difficult than here — it is all shallow, do you understand? It is part of the Chinese continental shelf."

"China." I was startled but it would have been impolite to correct my host's improbable geography.

The pathway had climbed out of the fetid mangrove swamp with its feverish clouds of insects, and we were traversing a savanna of grasslands with some fine trees, casuarinas, and what looked like the eucalypts of Van Diemen's land.

Strands of the ubiquitous bamboo were to be seen following small gullies and depressions which I presume would turn to foaming torrents in the wet season.

I made notes to the Royal Society, some time later, on my return, suggesting the strong possibility that the dry monsoon winds beating in from the south-east had been engendered and parched in the crucible of a large desert in Terra Australis, the uncharted great southland. I am confident I was correct.

"One expects sandalwood and teak, Mr Wanjon, but I see none growing."

"They are both to be found in the foothills, Captain Bligh. Some of the land you will see around us is cleared to planting of sugar and coffee."

We were passing the boundary of a sugar plantation that covered maybe fifty acres. It was poorly cultivated, with weeds sprouting higher in some places than the canes. Sudden rustlings and small disturbances suggested to my mind the passage of rats or snakes out of our path into the shady security of the undergrowth.

An enormous frog, or toad, yellow and green, gazed at me with unwinking eyes. Suddenly there was a disturbance at the front of our small procession, and two of our guards came trotting forward, teeth and cutlasses flashing. I craned my neck.

"What is it?"

There was a crashing of the cane as a large beast lumbered off the path, a flash of grey hide.

"A rhinoceros, a small elephant? Surely not."

"A tapir, Captain Bligh. Member of the pig family."

"Oh — I've not seen one. Is that the biggest animal loose on the island?"

"The planters swear there is a family of tigers still prowling the foothills, but I've never seen one. Don't want to. The official line is that they've been extinct for fifty years."

"What makes the planters think they're still here. Have they seen one?"

"Hard to get a reliable report, but there was a woman from one of the kampongs killed and half eaten by something last month, which seems to indicate a carnivore. Mightn't be a cat of course. The wild pigs are not beyond chewing up a corpse. Still, you've got to wonder what killed her."

I put my hand on the reassuring hilt of my sword.

The plantations were soon behind and we were into the

native gardens now. Rice patches, mainly, straggly rice and not above two acres in a plot. The country was becoming broken as we came close to the mountain range that stretched along the spine of the island, small plateaux and fertile valleys each housing a village, a kampong, as they termed them. Here and there, buffalo were grazing, or harnessed to wooden ploughs turning up the land for sweet potatoes. A small thatched shrine had a brass jar of grain offered to a painted deity, but I could not determine whether 'church' or 'chapel'.

"What are they here, Buddhists?"

"No, the majority of the villagers are Hindu, but the ruling cast are in the main Mohammedans. The aboriginal Timorese still worship animals, monkey gods, snakes. Tigers are popular now they've supposedly disappeared."

"But no Buddhists?"

"A few of the Chinese in the town perhaps. The whole country was taken by a Hindu tribe called Madjaparits in the sixteenth century, and they ran a nominal Empire until the spread of Islam brought it down. We took over the ruins at the start of last century, although we were in Batavia back in 1619."

"So our host is not the last of a centuries-old line of soultains?"

"Probably not the great, great, great grandson of a dragon, no — more likely his grandsire was a Muslim trader."

We had come to a muddy slow moving stream, and the bearers had fanned out in a nervous arc, lashing at the water with long staves.

"What now?"

"This is a bad crossing for caymans. An old mugger has been here for as long as I can remember. He takes an occasional horse."

"Alligator?"

"Crocodile, I believe!"

The crossing accomplished without incident, we splashed through the irrigated rice paddy, where simple mud terracing was used to direct and restrain the waters.

The path wound along a spur of the mountain, Pradkah Ganung, explained the Deputy Governor.

"What does 'ganung' mean?" It had appeared before in his explanations.

"Mountain."

"Ahhh."

Crossing the mountain spur had brought us into a green valley, a noisy mob of black mynahs flapped overhead disturbed by our passage. High up near the mountain peaks, two kites were riding the thermal up-currents, sitting at ease on the wind as they scoured the floor of the valley for a movement. A huddle of houses, some brick, clinging to the slopes, some bamboo and timber, crazy on stilts, announced that we had arrived at our destination.

"Omar," confirmed Mr Wanjon.

Some cultivated trees filled in the background and among them stood a larger house, or a fortress, clearly the home of a person of consequence. A tasselled silk banner in gold and burgundy dropped from a horizontal pole at the gate.

"Somebody's home then."

Timotheus Wanjon gave me a surprised look.

Not much sense of humour, the Dutch.

"The Soultain's palace!" he explained.

It appeared to be whitewashed, or the stones were a white calciferous rock, but its charm dissipated rapidly as we drew closer.

It had been originally surrounded by a solid wall of a defensive character, but gaps had crumbled in the stonework and one of the metal gates was off its hinges. The building was fronted by a gravel court in the centre of which a bronze fountain stood in a moon shaped pool, but the pool was full of dried mud and the fountain was still. At first I thought it was heavily corroded and stained but a closer inspection showed that some well-meaning modern had endeavoured to coat it with green paint. Can't be done of course, unless you key it first with spirits of salts. The problems of lacquering brass and bronze are familiar to any seafarer. The building itself appeared larger as we approached it close up, but the same proximity revealed a plastered stucco, which was cracking off, and in a very sad way.

The front door was imposing — a ten foot slab of brass

beaten into various heathenish designs. It opened with some scraping and banging as we approached and a butler, in a clean enough dhoti-like garment, bowed us in and welcomed us into the home of his master. We were in a square room hung with dusty tapestries. A door on one side led to a passage; opposite it to our left a wooden staircase climbed to the second storey. There were no windows but there was an open door opposite the main entrance, which led to an atrium or internal courtyard which looked cool and green.

We were ushered through and found ourselves in a cloistered area surrounded apparently by the main living areas. The smell of cooking and the smells of inadequate hygiene were opposed by the smell of sandalwood and musk from a small brazier. It was very reminiscent of one of Byrne's woodcuts from the 'Arabian Nights' story.

An unearthly shriek made me spin around, but it was only the discordant rasping of a peahen which seemed to have formed an attachment to Mr Wanjon. Some sort of a garden followed a pathway down the middle of the court-yard but it was dry and dusty and bore only a few straggling shrubs which looked to my eye like members of the ubiquitous pelargonium family. Two bantams were scratching dust into their feathers and an Asian cat of some brown variety crouched beneath the shrubs watching the fowl with crossed but unblinking eyes.

A fat dark gentleman sat on a bench by a green crusted pool, supported by a servant, his eyes, the master's eyes, firmly shut. It was hard to determine if he were ruminating, asleep or indeed dead. I hesitated, then the urbane Mr Wanjon stepped ahead and saluted a younger man who had come forward to greet us.

"Your sacred excellency, may I greet you again, and assure you that my heart overflows with the keen pleasure of being in your presence. May I introduce Captain Bligh, an English mariner cast in some distress on our shores, Mr Bligh — Prince Eluiprez Khan."

Damned foreigner. In a hog's eye I was cast in distress on his shore! I'd sailed four thousand miles by my own efforts to call on him, that's what I'd done. I bowed.

"I am privileged, m'lord!"

My impressions of the rest of that afternoon all blurred — heat, dust, smell, sticky sweet-meats that were damned inappropriate and most unwelcome, overpowering thirst, and toilet arrangements that were primitive in the extreme. The Soultain did not stir. Prince Eluiprez Khan apologised for his father's absence.

"He is meditating. He is a god."

"A god?"

"Oh yes, I too shall be a god when he is killed."

"You mean, when he dies?"

"Yes, when he dies."

The prince was a fleshy youth of some thirty summers. His face, which might have been handsome in his earlier years, was disappearing beneath jowls of lard. He was clean shaven, although the shave was not notably clean, and this confused me as I believed it forbidden to Muslims to cut their facial or cranial hair.

"No, no" said Wanjon later, when I quizzed him about it, "the man is a Hajji. He has been to Mecca, and there are dispensations."

"He's been to Mecca?" I was surprised — he looked to me like a greasy sort of cock that had never left his own dung hill.

"Of course, did you not notice the colour of his turban."

I thought back, I had heard something of this. Pink was the elite colour, I recalled.

"If he has not been personally to Mecca, then he has sent someone on his behalf."

"And that counts?"

"Of course."

I gave up. Half these Dutch fellows in the colonies become as superstitious and ignorant as the natives.

We were ushered to the domiciliary part of the building where rooms had been allotted to us. An ewer of water was welcome, but I hesitated to drink it for fear of a flux. Smith asked Wanjon's valet Van Durelij, who said his master mixed it with spirits and then drank it without ill effect. I had some medicinal brandy in my flask, and I mixed it with half a tumbler of the water. The guest room, if that was its function, was a square room about eight yards wide, furnished simply with a bed of cushions on a dais, some cotton drapes, an ancient and dusty portrait of some prince of Orange, and a brass chamber pot. The afternoon grew hotter, and very humid, and I hoped that evening would bring a breeze.

Instead it brought a summons from the Crown Prince. We were graciously commanded to attend a sporting event. I was curious to know what passed for sport in this distant corner of the Dutch Empire, and Mr Wanjon, Mr Hayward and I found ourselves led to an enclosed court at the rear of the main building. There were two rows of wooden seating around a small pit in the ground. I've seen a similar arrangement in Cheapside. "Hullo," I said to myself, "Are we to see terriers taking rats?" The pit was rather too small for rat baiting. Present were a motley crowd of ruffians, all turbans and teeth and musk.

'The Prince Regent and his courtiers' I surmised. Two lower caste fellows climbed up in front carrying each a bucket, or bamboo cage, holding some sort of fowl.

Cock fighting! I'd never seen it done and leant forward curious. The first rooster was freed into the pit, and some grain was sprinkled before him. A sort of master of ceremonies then led off into a chant, and a chorus of responses came back to him from the audience. It was dashed like the vicar at Lambeth leading the congregation "Oh God make speed to say—ave us."

He was a remarkable looking gentleman, wearing, to my great surprise, a pair of gloves. His earlobes were distorted and stretched enormously with pewter hoops swaying down to his shoulders. The lobes were, without a word of a lie, bigger than the rest of the ear. He had a wispy beard pulled into two plaits. He held up his hands to gain our attention, standing in a stylised pose which is *de rigeur* in these parts, hands at right angles to his forearms, one pointing up, one pointing down, palms outward, and if you think that is easy, then I suggest you try it yourself. They all seem to be double jointed. I saw his hands more clearly now and realised that the 'gloves' were in fact, tattoos that covered the hands right up past the wrists.

141

He threw some more grain.

"Why the wheat, why the chanting?"

Mr Wanjon was an aficionado apparently.

"The chanting is to invoke the good spirits in the winning cock to vanquish the evil spirits in the losing cock."

"They know which one is to lose?"

"The spirits do, we mortals don't." I wasn't so sure about that.

"And what about the wheat?"

"The fowl must be made to assume, what would you call it, a proprietorship, he must have something of value to defend, the wheat. They don't always use it, but I've seen two gamecocks sit and brood on opposite sides of the pit, and never come to holts. They sometimes have to hit them with sticks to start the contest." The cock was strutting, and scratching and gobbling.

"If he eats any more of that he'll be foundered, and no use."

"Hush, they have us here on sufferance."

It was gloomy in the pit and when the second bird was released it did not at first see the original incumbent. It squatted and blinked rapidly turning its head from side to side. A stray grain of wheat was in front of it, and a dip of its head snapped it up. It was advancing on the wheat in the middle of the arena when it saw the other cock. It ruffled its feathers and stretched its neck upward, increasing its apparent size by half and raking the ground with its talons.

The other bird had been running through its preliminaries of ruffling and raking, and neck craning, and now it came at the invader like a feathered thunderbolt. Then there was such a riot of wing flapping and fluttering, of bounding up and foot-raking, such a cacophony of raucous cries, and hissing like geese, that I flinched back from the fury of action. Feathers and dust, the yells of the onlookers, one could imagine there were three or four birds fighting to create such a maelstrom. One fowl crouched, its comb bloodied and half detached, the other rose in the air and came down hard upon it, and I saw now a steel spur reeking on its leg. The merciless steel struck down piercing an eye and blood sprayed onto the dirt floor. The stricken fowl hunched further into itself, one leg spasmodically raking at the dust. A great shout came from the onlookers.

"Carna!, Carna!" — blood, I suppose, or death, or victory.

"Come on! Finish him now, finish him, hit, again hit!" I found myself huzza-ing the bellicose victor. Half the crowd were very happy with the outcome. The trainer of the cock secured his triumphant gladiator, and packaged him back into his basket. A bluebottle landed on the ruined eye, a gleeful prince was receiving gold from a less than enthusiastic crony.

"Three times out of five, the first cock in the ring will win." It was my knowledgeable friend.

"Do you have a flask with you?"

He passed me a small tumbler of neat brandy, and I formed another nostalgic image of a group of sporting gentlemen taking a pre-dinner cup in the billiards room of an English country house prior to dinner.

To the heat and the dust and the poor sanitation there was now added a rank smell from the blood of the slaughtered cock. Mr Wanjon dabbed his nostrils with a kerchief splashed with musk cologne. Mr Hayward lurched awkwardly but desperately down the back of the seating and was noisily sick on the tiles.

The candles flickered as a sultry breeze from the punkahs wafted over the remains of our banquet. The dancers departed with ritualistic obeisance, and I turned my attention to what should have been pudding. My neck sweated and prickled. I ran a finger, easing the serge of my jacket from the flesh, but it was inflamed, moist and swollen. We had been regaled with a battery of curried fish dishes, octopus, shrimps, some sort of blasted seaweed with rice and mushrooms, and a very indifferent made dish which Wanjon told me later was monkey brain, crabs and plantain, a sort of banana. Now the final dish appeared — a chilled custard, or sherbet, I hoped, even a blancmange. To my disappointment and considerable surprise it was a garlic chicken soup with large golden heads of melted butter floating on its surface.

The prince had finished tidying up his private parts and

wolfed it down with relish. I took a polite sip but my stomach lurched into a spasm of painful rejection, and I thought for a moment I was to emulate the hapless Hayward.

I pushed the bowl aside and announced my intention of retiring. "A warm night for it" said Wanjon smiling.

She came as I sat on the end of my bed, bathing my neck. She was still attired in the gauzy drapes and veils of the dance. It was, I think, the left hand girl from the second row, although the masked faces had all been similar in the flickering lights. I stood in some disarray and confusion.

"Er, good evening."

She made no reply, but coming to the sleeping dais she arranged the pillows and cushions into an enticing nest.

Ah, I thought, the chamber maid. The pot was full and I'd discreetly put it into the corner alcove behind the screen. But, although veiled, its presence was not entirely a secret. Get her to empty the pot while she's here!

She came and knelt before me — I was at a bit of a loss.

"Do you speak English, young Lady?"

"I am one of the daughters of the king", she said, but it came out as a formula, and I was still unsure as to her ability to converse with me.

"The king's daughter?" This was a surprising honour.

"Are you the king's daughter?"

"I am one of the daughters of the king. The revered one has sent me to you."

"Did he by Jove!" I thought about her correcting the phrase to 'one of the king's daughters', some trick of the tense or of declination I supposed. I can assure you my member had become so tense that no thought of decline was entertained.

That's a joke — a play on words.

Quite a good one actually, but I didn't bother explaining it to her.

"So, the Soultain has sent me his handmaiden to pleasure me." It seems silly, but I really was at a bit of a loss as to how to proceed. I mean, I was all for rogering her, but not sure quite where to begin the business.

We stared at each other, then she slid her arms from her

neck to her waist and her garments fell to the floor leaving her only half a dozen silver bracelets to satisfy her modesty. Not that that would cause her any harm. It was a hot night, my own shirt was unbuttoned half down my chest. My eye was taken by her pubic mound which was as innocent of hair as a pre-pubescent child. An individual aberration, or a racial custom to shave it? Whatever the answer, I found it alien, and rather off-putting. She sank back on the bed raising her arms and her knees. I loosened my belt and removed my boots while I gave the matter some thought.

When Mrs Bligh and I made love she had always modestly contrived to achieve congress without removing any of her clothing, and moreover she would always go on her knees beside the bed and pray before the exercise began. I had come to associate this pious ritual with the mechanics of the performance so much that now, with this gleaming natural princess sliding into my bed, my reaction was twofold: firstly, some uneasiness as to my capabilities in the situation; secondly, a twitch in my knees as I began to slide down beside the bed for a brief, a very brief prayer. I checked myself. 'Muslim', I expect, I thought to myself and I reached out a tentative hand. Her bald *mons veneris* was, I calculated, facing Mecca.

I remember Christian was much amused when the topic had come up between us in the days gone by, in the days of our intimacy. I had spoken of Mrs Bligh's preliminaries.

"What" he had scoffed, "like saying grace before a meal."

"Nothing of the sort, I believe her intentions were genuinely pious, and that she prayed for a fruitful outcome to our consummation."

"More likely she was praying that, just once, she might be satisfied." His coarse laughter was an affront, and I regretted my candour. I moved to the windward rail, traditional Captain territory, where he could not follow, to demonstrate my displeasure. It was clear, even then, that I let him presume too much from our association.

The following night I had young Heywood to sup with me, and left Christian to lord it in the mess. Even so, as I asked the Lord to bless and sanctify our sea biscuit and salt mutton, I fancied I caught a sardonic gleam in Heywood's eye, and it occurred to me that Christian had betrayed my confidence right around the quarter-deck.

A brown hand reached out and embraced me in the groin. Far from increasing my ardour, my natural reserve made me recoil modestly. I found her forwardness brazen and rather common. I could feel my arousal subsiding. It seemed time to get things onto a more formal basis. I pointed to myself "Bligh", "Bligh", I repeated it several times then pointed to her. 'Karpoal' she said nodding her head very vigorously.

"You Karpoal." She nodded her head again.

"Well, Miss Karpoal, shall we begin some jiggery pokery."

She began softly kissing and fondling my organ again, this time to such effect that an erotic shiver began there and then, so that I became apprehensive the proceedings might be over, as it were, before they began. I caught her hand away, and she plunged like a horse, over onto her face, and was grinding her small brown bottom into my stomach. Now I had seen the Oahu belles go to it like this, and I was having none of it.

"Stop your heathenish tricks," I rolled her on her back and clambered aboard.

Then, as I mounted her, the strangeness, the vulnerable eroticism of her nudity and her availability gripped me in the pit of my stomach with an urgency to express my domination. I was a stallion! I was a bull! I was a cock! I was her master!

"There, there, there," I grunted, "There, there, just like an English lady, there and there." My shirt was impeding my efforts, and I paused briefly to hitch it out of the way before resuming the rogering.

She may have been bounced like an Englishwoman but I'm dashed if her hand didn't come up between my legs and fondle my testicles, and before I could protest at her unseemly lewdness, a sharp finger nail jabbed into my anus and my thrusts abruptly climaxed in a flurry of pain and passion.

The jade was still hard at her work, clutching at my body with her double jointed legs, and rutting like a baboon.

I tried to disengage, then caught her a small buffet on the ear that suspended her activity. She retreated sobbing to the corner of the dais where she hugged herself, while I caught my breath.

What I chiefly wanted was to lie still and shut my eyes and let my mind catch up with its impressions. It had been too rich a day, a day full of colours and odours, of movements and flavours, but all alien. I'd have swapped all the octopus and monkey brains for a plate of Lincolnshire roast lamb. I'd have swapped the coffee coloured nudity of my neighbour for a pair of pink and white legs in pantaloons.

Or would I?

I wondered how she must feel, this young woman, treated by the Soultain as a sexual chattel to be lent to visitors for their pleasuring. My train of thought was arousing my desires, my groin twitched with renewed vigour. I rolled over to look at her. For the night I was a harem master, and she my slave to gratify my desires. A man would need to be a saint to waste such an offering.

She sensed my returning interest — it wasn't, I expect, too difficult to see, and began rubbing her cheeks against my ankles. I bent down and catching a hand between her buttocks I pulled her on top of me.

"Karpoal!" said Wanjon with a smile, "Karpoal wasn't her name, that's a name for what you did to her."

A gentleman does not, of course, speak of his transactions with a lady, especially one of royal blood, but Wanjon had inquired with a knowing smile as to how I had slept.

Hayward, the weak-gutted boobie, had slept through the night, but I was certain that Wanjon had consumed a night cap similar to my own.

"Karpoal, Karpoal," I said musingly, "more musical than the Anglo-Saxon word, so we don't know her name. She was, or so she told me, a princess."

"A princess!" There was a world of disbelief.

"The king's daughter, that's what she said."

"Yes."

Mr Wanjon coughed, then chose his words carefully.

"If she was the king's daughter, then I congratulate you.

The King, the Soultain, does keep a harem of young ladies who have became known as 'the daughters of the king'. They are in effect the court prostitutes and their services are enjoyed by many visitors to the court."

We travelled in silence for a space, while I digested this piece of information.

> *How ridiculous and a stranger he is, who is surprised at anything which happens in life,*

says my mentor Aurelius.

> *One should remember purity goes with nudity, for there is no veil over a star.*

"Daughters of the King," I heard myself mutter.

In the end I decided it made little difference, I had enjoyed a night with Scheherazade, and whether she was a blood relation of a shabby monarch or a dancing girl from the market place, she had served me a lovely time.

*****

At least, that is how I remember it. Perhaps recollection has added some details which the event lacked — who knows? Brandy, in my experience, stimulates an exaggerated but vivid memory of pleasure, so that in the end the dream is more real than the event.

That something of the sort did indeed occur is, however, scarcely in doubt. It was at the Cape of Good Hope that a discomfort in my urinary tract took me to the surgeon.

"Gonorrhoea" he said, swabbing a bead of pus from my penis. "Bismuth will fix it up inside six months."

"My God." I thought in a panic, "Six months!"

"Mercury will cure it in three, but it might send you mad."

And so we came back to England, with continent Captain William Bligh R.N. the only returning member of his crew to have the clap.

Chapter Eight

I receive an account of the death of Fletcher Christian, and recall the voyage to Otaheite — a lesson in spherical trigonometry is interrupted by a drunken surgeon — ceremonial at Otaheite — Mr Christian displays his weakness — heathen practices of the natives — Mr Christian tattoos his buttocks

The letter was from the Admiralty, and Mrs Peebles brought it to the dining-room where I sat with Anne. Mrs Peebles had arrayed herself in a new gown, a rich dark blue with white cuffs of lace. I looked at her in some astonishment, she looked quite different with the sun shining in her hair, quite presentable. As she stooped over the table my eyes scuttled down the extreme cleavage of her bodice.

"Is there anything wrong, Sir?"

I was staring at her, I realised.

"No, no, Mrs Peebles, you have a new gown, you look very well."

"Indeed, Sir." A little colour dusted her cheek and she was gone.

"A letter Papa?"

Anne took the letter and spelt out the inscription. She was not a famous reader.

"Admiral Billy Bligh."

"William Bligh, miss, William. Where do you get hold of the Billy?" I took the packet and sounded it out, "Wuh-ill-yum."

"But I heard from Mr Ffoulkes' gardener that William and Billy are the same."

"Not the same at all, miss, not the same at all — a gentleman is called William, a very common fellow might be called Billy."

"But I like Billy better."

"Not in this house. My name is 'William', but 'Papa' will do very well."

"Open your letter. What will it say?"

"Now how could I possibly know that? Probably to tell me my pension is to be discontinued or reduced."

I couldn't imagine anything of cheer coming in an official letter from the Admiralty. The days when my exertions were directed by their correspondence were long over. I opened it.

William Bligh Esq., Admiral of the Blue

Dear Bligh,

I am commanded by their lordships to acquaint you with a despatch presently received from His Majesty's ship Tagus, *currently returned from the Pacific Ocean. As the last commander of the armed transport* Bounty *you will be interested to know that the fate of that unfortunate vessel has at last been determined.*

You may have heard an unconfirmed report some years ago from an American whaler which reported an English colony on Pitcairn Island.

Capt. Pipon of the Tagus *has called at Pitcairn Island and I enclose a copy of his letter.*

I turned the letter over in my hand. Twenty-six years. A generation had grown from infancy. A generation had gone to the grave. I had come from my prime to my dotage.

I was loathe to open it.

Anne crept to my chair and sat quietly against me. She was perceptive of vibrations that other people's senses could not detect.

Christian, Christian.

I unfolded the letter.

Tagus, Valparaiso

18th October 1814

I have the honour to inform you, that, on my passage from the Marquesas Islands to this port, on the morning of the 17th Sept., I fell in with an island where none is laid down in the Admiralty or other charts — I, therefore, hove to until daylight, and then closed to ascertain whether it was inhabited — which I soon discovered it to be, and to my great astonishment found that every individual on the island (forty in number) spoke very good English, as well as Otaheitian. They proved to be descendants of the deluded crew of the Bounty.

The island must, undoubtedly, be that called Pitcairn although erroneously laid down in the Admiralty charts. The first man who came aboard was named Christian …

I looked over the letter at Anne, but the mists were closing around me. I clutched the edge of the table, and it was my sole anchorage, the line holding me to the dining-room in Kent. A brown annular ring spread from the margin of my eyes constricting my vision to a porthole, there was a hammering in my temple, and I hung to the table with both hands.

"Papa! Papa!"

Someone was calling, but I could not focus. I stared at the table and gradually my hand took form, then colour. My knuckles were blanched and the letter crushed against the oak.

The mists receded, and the waves of pressure pounding in my skull were stilled. I could see the window as a white patch, a source of light that gradually gave definition to the room.

Anne was clutching me. I attempted a smile, but it gave her no reassurance.

"Shall I fetch Elizabeth?"

"Don't leave me."

I clung to the table and put an arm around Anne. My heart beat violently, my arms were cold with sweat, trembling, my mouth was dry.

"A little water."

Presently I felt better in control of myself.

I flattened out the letter.

… The first man who came aboard was named Christian, Thursday October Christian, son of Fletcher Christian by an Otaheite woman; he was the first born upon the island (which must have been soon after their arrival and settling in it) and was called Thursday October in consequence of his being born on that day and in that month.

I come next to the interesting narrative of Fletcher Christian.

151

It appears that this ill-fated young man was never happy after the rash and inconsiderate step he had taken, but was always sullen and morose, a circumstance which will surprise no one; this moroseness, however, led him to many acts of cruelty and inhumanity which soon was the cause of his incurring the hatred and detestation of his companions here. One cannot avoid expressing astonishment that the very crime he was then guilty of towards his companions (who assisted him in the Mutiny) was the very same they so loudly accused their Captain Bligh of. This miserable young man sailed from Otaheite to Toobouai, one of the Friendly Islands, but finding it unsuitable returned to Otaheite with a feigned story, which the islanders readily gave ear to, of having met Captain Cook, who had sent him for provisions. Having filled the Bounty with hogs and such provisions as he thought necessary, he sailed away for the last time on Sept. 22nd 1789.

Sixteen of the crew elected to leave him. His object was to find an uninhabited island, where he could establish a settlement, and here at Pitcairn he at last arrived. Finding no anchorage he ran the ship against the rocks, and having cleared her of everything he thought necessary, he set her on fire.

The fate of Fletcher Christian himself was such as one might have expected from his cruelty and extraordinary unfeeling behaviour: from what we could learn he was shot by a black man whilst digging in his field and almost instantly expired. This happened about eleven months after they were settled in the island, but the exact dates I could not learn. The black, or Otaheite man that thus murdered him, was himself immediately assassinated. A circumstance had arisen that had inflamed the Otaheite men, and aroused their fury to a degree not to be pacified. Christian's wife had paid the debt of nature, and, as we have every reason to suppose that sensuality and a passion for the females of Otaheite chiefly instigated him to the rash step he had taken, so it is to be believed that he would not live long on the island without a female companion. Consequently he seized on one belonging to one of the Otaheite men and took her to live with him. This exasperated them to a degree of madness, open war was

*declared and every opportunity taken to seek his life. Thus
terminated the miserable existence of this deluded young man
whose connections in Westmorland were extremely respectable,
and who did not want talents and capacity to have become an
ornament to his profession had he adopted another line of conduct. We could not learn precisely the number of blacks and
whites who were killed whilst this kind of warfare continued,
however many must have perished by the hands of each other,
and only John Adams remains of the men that landed on the
island with Christian.*

John Pipon

I watched my hands with clinical detachment as I folded the
letter. There was nothing new; I'd known he was dead.

* * * * *

"Is it better to die for love, or live without knowing it?"
The speaker was young Heywood.
Christian drained his wine with a bumptious assurance
that underlined his immaturity, although that had not been,
of course, his intent. "Sordid lust beats unrequited love all
hands down, every time."
He liked to adopt a sardonic man of the world attitude to
Heywood. I looked forward with interest to see if the bare
chested belles of Otaheite would disturb his sang-froid.
I looked at them both with a paternal indulgence. We all,
I fancy, enjoyed these dinners together much more than the
plain fare would suggest.
Christian was banging his ship's biscuit on the table to
dislodge the weevils. He did it by long habit, as did we all.
We were five weeks out of Cape Town and fresh provisions
were only a memory. Smith had stewed some onions and
some dried celery into our salt beef, but it was not a great
dish. I had lost my last sheep a week ago when a wicked
green sea spilled across our waist, tearing loose its crate. It
was going to be the best part of a year before I secured
another one, I calculated, though there was some chance of
a hog or a goat at Otaheite if we were well received.
Heywood must have noticed my thoughtful gaze upon
my plate for he cut into my train of thought. "Captain, shall

153

we make a landfall in Queen Charlotte's Sound? Do you plan to seek fresh meat and fruit there?"

No, I did not. "We shall make a landfall at Cape Henry in Van Diemen's Land for wood and water. If the winds are favourable we may call at Dusky Bay in north-west New Zealand to collect some flax plants. If not, we'll make well to the south of New Zealand and make our next landing in the Society Islands.

"Why go south?" Christian was not disputatious — he wanted to know. I saw it as my duty to train these young men in seamanship and navigation, much as I had hoped to do with Cook. As it turned out, of course, Cook on his last voyage was part of the time an invalid, part of the time an irascible incompetent, and it devolved on me to do his navigating. Most of the charting too, that he had such credit for. Still he had been a good man, the best sailor of his day. His understanding of the natives and his treating with them were, of course, deplorable. That led directly to his death. History may do me more justice for my ability to understand and manage other people.

"We go south to pursue a new track which will be of use to future navigators, and make this in very fact a voyage of discovery."

"But is it not empty ocean?"

"Empty apart from about two hundred islands and reefs."

"If we call at New Zealand should we not get celery and scurvy grass?"

"We can last until Otaheite. We have some essence of malt and the surgeon can issue that."

"Mr Huggan says we have three cases of scurvy now."

"Did he, indeed? And who were these unfortunates?"

"Mills and Brown, and McIntosh, Captain."

"McIntosh has rheumatism, Mills and Brown have the usual prickly heat, nothing more, I don't have scurvy on my ships!"

"Mr Huggan is very certain."

"Fetch him."

They looked at each other."

"Now?"

"Fetch him now."

154

Christian shrugged and nodded. Heywood got up and went out, passing a word to Quintal, who was acting as sentry at my door — a luxury I will have to dispense with when the great cabin fills with pot plants.

"I thought to demonstrate to you my approach to spherical geometry." It was the method of Old Captain Stewart on *Monmouth*, of course. What he advocated was not trying to bend plane geometry and trigonometry, nor to discipline the map of the world with Mercator's projection.

"What you must do is consider it as an exercise on a sphere right from the beginning. Now let's take this globe and work out some triangular bearings. Tell me — does the theorem of Pythagoras still hold true on a spherical surface?"

"Well of course it must." Christian pondered for a moment. "Each side would be increased."

"Don't worry about the lengths, what concerns us is the relationships between the sides and the angles."

"Yes, the linear relationship must hold. The arcs would simply increase, each in proportion!"

"So you say, but is a right angle still a right angle on a sphere?"

Christian was saved by a shuffling, and a muttered curse in the companion way. The medical man was with us.

Heywood knocked, then entered backwards, half supporting, half dragging his companion, who was lending him a few thoughts on the mess arrangements.

"Doan' mesh with the bloody Captain, do I? Mesh with the Master. Good man the Master, put down by Bligh you know, no gennelman" — he trailed off. Heywood looked horrified, Christian looked serious, Quintal was bringing up the rear grinning like Punch, and the surgeon grinned vacantly in response.

"Mr Huggan!"

He tried to focus, but came close to losing his balance.

"Mr Huggan!"

He located me.

"Cap'n."

"Mr Huggan, stand up! What state is this we find you in?"

He grinned again, and slid to his knees.

"Every night, Mr Christian?"

"Aye, Sir, and half the day."

"So how much reliance can you place on his diagnosis?"

"None, Sir."

"He'll be lucky to see Otaheite."

"If a surgeon be any good he won't by choice be on a boat like this, indeed he probably won't be on a ship at all. You're better off to make sure you have an experienced surgeon's mate on board."

"All the same, Captain —"

"Yes Heywood."

"All the same, I still think Brown might have scurvy."

"He has prickly heat."

"Two of his teeth fell out at mess last night when I was on duty."

"Quintal."

"Aye, Captain."

"Support Mr Huggan back to his bunk and wedge him in. Make sure he has a bucket."

That dealt with that.

"So, Mr Heywood" I said, "can you have a right angle on a spherical surface? If so, what table do we use to predict the length of the hypotenuse?"

They drew close to me as I got out a tape and a pair of dividers. We had spent many similar nights examining and discussing my concepts of charting and navigation. Since accurate time-pieces have become available, thanks to Mr John Harrison and his chronometer, it is now possible to calculate longitude, and with latitude more easily calculable by means of Hadly's reflecting quadrant, accurate astronomical measurements are able to be taken from the pitching deck of a ship at sea.

It was of course one thing to measure the sun's declivity, another one to understand the principles involved, and this is where Christian and Heywood's aptitude and intelligence flourished under the fountain of instruction I was able to supply. Any capable navigator should now be able to ascertain his position on a clear day to ten miles of his true bearing.

My own special proclivity had been, with some help from Cook, in mapping and measuring angles along strange and uncharted coasts. It is no boast to say I am the best in the Royal Navy at this exercise — which means best in the world. I showed Heywood a device I had invented for reading the bearing on two points of the coast, so that an intersection might be marked.

It comprises two arms bolted together with a sighting lens attached to each and a calibrated curved scale between them, a bit like the old backstaff, but adapted for horizontal use. I have demonstrated it at the Admiralty and Reye's instruments are to make them a copy. It was my second marine invention. The first was the spill-proof bed-pan which I think I may have mentioned. Not a bed-pan, but a steel urinal shaped like a kettle. It is a boon in rough conditions and I would not be without it. Samuel, who has the job of bringing my cocoa and rum in at night, has cast one or two awe-stricken gazes upon it. To him I believe I can attribute the story which has gone around the lower deck that I have a tin kettle that I roger each night for amorous relief. The 'iron maiden' waited demurely in my closet. The triangulator lay on my desk as I demonstrated to them its advantages.

"Mr Christian, Mr Heywood, let us draw an apparent right angle with the apex at the North Pole. Follow then each side of the angle down to the equator and then turn a right angle, one to the east, one to the west. What will happen? What figure does it form?"

They considered it with some interest as I knew they would. It is a fairly well-known paradox.

"Why Captain, you have a triangle with three right angles in it."

"And three hypotenuses," added Heywood, "so Pythagoras goes out the window."

"Precisely. It is the extreme illustration that concepts of plane geometry can not be transferred to a sphere. Let us now consider that axiom of Euclid, which refers to the shortest distance between two points."

I led them through the calculation of courses employing great circle lines. It is difficult to grasp until you realise the

157

corollary — that charts, maps, can never be accurate, but only a compromise, that you cannot transfer spherical geometry to a plane surface.

I thoroughly enjoyed my role as guide and instructor because of the quality of my disciples. Christian was engrossed in tackling the concept. He had a good quick mind and with a little steadiness, I thought, he would make a very able commander. But Heywood — Heywood was quicksilver, his mind danced ahead of the instructor, probing, asking, teasing. His thought processes worked in intuitive leaps and flashes, and his mind used our slower wits as a foil for its brilliance. It was hard to remember he was really just a boy! The night was far advanced, and Christian's watch was almost upon him, before we put the charts and pilots away.

There was a good will grown up between us that we had all come to hold dear. I relished having young agile minds to instruct — they valued that instruction. Really, I could think of no more pleasant time in my life then the hours we had spent together on this cruise. Heywood and Christian were both on *Bounty* at my personal invitation, Christian had sailed with me twice before and I knew his worth. His quick and lively turn of mind and his affectionate good nature compensated for a certain degree of easiness in his diligence in day-to-day shipboard matters, and he confessed himself a fool where the opposite sex were concerned.

Hayward it was next day, Thomas Hayward, not Peter Heywood, who sighted the Mewstone, a high bold rock about 15 miles to the south-east of the south-west cape of Van Diemen's Land.

He actually identified it as a whale, but I was unfussed as I had been expecting its appearance that hour past, such is the science of navigation now. I must confess it still gave me great pleasure to make an accurate landfall after the run from the Cape of Good Hope.

It was one thing to sight Van Diemen's Land, another to reach it, for the wind turned foul and we beat backward and forward for two days before anchoring. The men dragged a seine net to try to supplement their diet but caught not two score of a mean flat-headed fish. Mills, who has been a fisherman, identified them as 'foxes', a fish he had caught in Flemish waters. There was but poor eating in them.

We anchored in the very spot where Cook had anchored in 1777, where I knew there to be a gully where we could fill our water casks, and they only had to be rolled sixty yards. Brown, the gardener, wandering along the coast in search of botanical curiosities, fell in with some of the miserable inhabitants, and indeed a party of about twenty of them came out of the wood and approached to where we sat at anchor in the ship's launch. We threw gifts tied up in paper, mirrors and nails, and various gewgaws, but while we watched they would not unwrap them. They made a prodigious chatter with their speech. Mr Nelson recognised one among them, most curiously deformed, having met with him in his visit with Cook. This would suggest a regular residence by them in this vicinity. Cook inferred that they slept in hollowed tree trunks, but this I take leave to doubt, as we discerned crude shelters, in the form of wigwams containing beds of bark and leaves.

Mr Nelson rejoined us at noon on September 4th, bursting with good spirits and enthusiasm, and with no less than seventy plant specimens of new varieties.

"Mr Christian," I said, "we shall have more in common as this voyage proceeds."

"Indeed Sir," he was puzzled.

"Yes indeed, Sir. My cabin shall be host to the breadfruit plants, your cabin shall be host to Mr Nelson's collection. We shall wake and sleep as natural scientists!"

He was less than enthusiastic about the honour, but Heywood and Hayward were radiant. They had supposed them consigned to the midshipmen's berth.

Hayward was raucously triumphant. "Ha ha ha" he shouted. "Mr Mate, you'll have more trees than a pissful dog in a wood."

Christian rolled up his eyes. It was beyond him to cope with this insubordination. Heywood caught my eye, suppressed a sympathetic grin, and turned away.

Hayward's banal vulgarness is a penance for us all.

I was talking of him to Heywood and Christian on our

first night at anchor in Otaheite. We dined on the deck beside the companion way, a board being set on trestles. It was a fine warm night, and quite light, which was an advantage as our lantern quietly became choked with moths and mosquitoes, whose bites were an extreme irritation. At the head of our table sat a portrait of Captain Cook.

Otoo, chief of Matovai, had had it sent over saying that 'Tooke', his word for Cook, had desired it to be brought to any English ship as a sign of friendship. We toasted him, but it was a particularly dour painting, and our levity did little to soften his expression. I am resolved the savages must not be acquainted with the manner of Cook's death, or we might expect all sorts of mischief to develop. The crew have been solemnly warned of this.

Otoo, Paramount Chief, came to pay us a call the next day. He is a great brute of a man, well over six feet in height and proportionally stout. He might tip the scale at twenty stone, and it didn't happen by chance. As chief, he cannot feed himself but is fed by an attendant who sits by him, and is kept in constant employment.

His wife Iddeah was also statuesque, and they were a very imposing couple. We lowered a seat rove from the foremast yard to hoist him aboard.

"Drop him in the ocean, Mr Churchill," I pleasantly observed, "and before he sinks, I shall have you strung by your neck in his place."

It went without incident, and we came to very agreeable terms about the purchase of breadfruit. The only problem was one of time. The plants must finish fruiting before we moved them. Mr Brown assured me it would be a good three months before we started transplanting in earnest. I had to give some thought to setting up a shore station to superintend the packing and potting. Christian, who had eyes for nothing but the half naked wenches in the canoes, had volunteered — a little eagerly I should say — for the honour of occupying this position. I didn't propose to deny myself the pleasure of his company at my table for three months. On the morrow we would explore a site for our plantation — or transplantation.

Point Venus was the name given by Cook to the position on which we established our camp. It could hardly have been baptised more appropriately.

The conduct of the men, and the handling of their liberty ashore, was a topic at our dinner table the night we had just sighted Otaheite. Christian raised the matter.

"Captain, how do you propose to control the men when we are at anchorage, and while the plants are being collected?"

I had decided the matter well in advance. I had been through it all with Cook nine years ago.

"These are a different people, Christian. They have few inhibitions, and unmarried women copulate freely with whomsoever they fancy. Poor Jack Tar with his canvas jacket and uncouth speech comes among them as Prince Charming. It is idle to suppose we can prevent him from lying with the ladies. What we must do is ensure that no troubles are aroused with them that may prejudice our success."

"They just sleep with anyone?" Heywood looked at Christian. He was a virgin, I know for a fact. He had told Christian and me one night, blushing like a turkey cock.

"The next thing is to see that the work of the ship does not suffer. We will scale down to two watches on board, Mr Christian, a daily working party and a reduced night watch, just an anchor watch. We shall have a working party with a base on the island, under a petty officer, and at the direction of Brown, to gather plants.

"Liberty boats will take those not on watch to shore, but woe betide any man who is late for his duty, or unfit to perform it."

"And the officers?"

"I will expect the officers to set an example."

Heywood's face fell.

"I expect we will be invited to attend banquets arranged in our honour. They take their royal house seriously you know."

"Anything else, Sir?" Christian was matter of fact, a man of the world. Heywood was ready to skip with excitement.

"Two things more, Mr Christian — no natives are to come

on the ship, except Royal visitors and their entourage. Even then, keep a close watch on them. That's where Cook got into so much trouble — he let them clamber all over the ship, and let the men bring their wahines aboard. They pilfered everything that wasn't nailed down.

"Wahines?"

"Native young ladies of generous virtue!"

"And they stole things?"

"He lost the very astrolabe he came to measure the transit of Venus with. Muskets, clothing, the bower anchor, rope, nails. It's a wonder the ship didn't fall apart. No natives on board."

"And the second thing?"

"Mr Huggan is to act the pox doctor. I want every last member of the crew inspected for venereal disease. Any man infected will be confined to the ship."

Otaheite floated in the night sea like a dark blue mountain garlanded with a necklace of white surf. A gentle breeze wafted offshore bringing the noise of that surf and the smell of the land. A perfume compounded of smoke, seaweed, and the faint corruption of rotting tropical vegetation.

The three of us stood in silence for a while.

"Captain," it was Heywood, "possibly only the three of us on this ship appreciate the beauty of this scene. Where are all the rest?"

"In their hammocks, checking their equipment," said Christian coarsely. I thought he was embarrassed by Heywood's sentiment.

It had been a rather exclusive banquet, possibly a rather subdued banquet, as Otaheitan banquets go. We were bade to dine with Tinah, chieftain of the Matovai, and his plump jolly wife Iddeah. I was surprised to hear him called Tinah, as last time I had met him, with Cook, he had been named Otoo. His young son now bore this name, and I believe it to be their custom, that when a son and heir is born to the paramount chief he succeeds his father at birth, the father acting as regent until the son achieves his majority. A state of affairs, it occurred to me, which might possess some advantages for the British system.

As well as the family of the paramount chief, we were privileged to dine with the members of the Arreoy society, a warrior priest caste. These gentlemen sat aloof from the general levity of the banquet, and received with great equanimity gifts of the choicest morsels of food.

For our part, *Bounty* was represented by myself, Mr Christian, Mr Heywood, Mr Stewart and Mr Hayward. Mr Fryer was left in charge of the watch. Heywood's lurid hopes of a night of sensuous delights was rather flattened by Tinah's presenting of a twenty minute speech, all of which was in short disjointed phrases, and I can assure you, completely incomprehensible to us. Whether it was comprehensible to the recipients, the Arreoy society gentlemen, was also a matter for conjecture, as they received it with stolid indifference.

We dined well, being offered fish baked in the coals of a great fire, all wrapped in leaves to save their charring. Also we were given great pieces of sucking pig, which beasts turned and dripped over the flames on a kind of spit. The chieftain's *towtows*, his servants that is to say, conducted a yava ceremony, at which their intoxicating liquor is prepared.

The yava root is chewed by the towtows to the semblance of a cud, and the juices spat into a gourd, where it is a grey evil looking mess. Coco-nut milk is mixed with it, and each man taking his coco-nut shell and solemnly pronouncing "Yow", it is a matter of 'pass the jug' and let laughter reign supreme.

It was, as you can well imagine, something of a trial to partake of the preparation, but it was equally impossible to decline to do so without arousing the reproach of our hosts.

The concoction was pungent, astringent and — in Hayward's case — emetic. I looked anxiously at Tinah for his reaction. To my surprise he was in no way put down by Hayward's crassness, but smiled and referred to him as a praulite, which I gather is a term of mockery for a callow youth.

The yava caused, almost immediately, a deadening of the tongue and cheeks. I blanch to think of its action on the stomach lining.

"Mr Huggan will be grieved to have missed this ceremony," Christian observed, holding his draught. He then fell to smacking mosquitoes, for a string of the insects had joined the festivities. The women did not dine with the men — I gather this is a taboo.

I made a short speech, acquainting the savages with the particular regard in which they were held by King George, and on behalf of my monarch I presented Tinah with such royal gifts as hatchets, saws, looking glasses and shirts. To Iddeah, I gave earrings and necklaces, and a quantity of red feathers. This proved to be a very popular segment in the evenings proceedings.

Tinah anxiously took council with me as to what gift would be suitable for 'Georgie no Brittainy.'

"Breadfruit" I said earnestly. "We would like some breadfruit."

"Three plants, five plants, ten plants?" he presented his fingers to me.

"A thousand plants would be a fine gift." I didn't have a thousand fingers, but any such a gift was a better bargain than the one I had struck with Otoo.

As we had finished eating, and as the yava was beginning to bite, we were now treated to a dancing 'heiva'. This is a lewd performance, in this case three women and six men being the performers, when in time to the throbbing of wooden drums the couples perform wanton gestures and motions, suggestive of sexual congress, to the very great excitement and satisfaction of the onlookers. The dancing lasts for about a half an hour, at which time the suggestiveness has communicated itself, and recommended a certain course of action to many of the ring of spectators.

With some amusement I saw Christian and Heywood drawn into the dancers by interested young ladies. Heywood looked so self-conscious that I should not have been surprised had he burst into tears.

Christian loved it, and danced with a lewd agility that provoked mirthful admiration from his audience. He subsided into the shadows at the conclusion of his performance, his head in the lap of one of his dusky admirers, his hands busy I can scarcely say where.

164

The immorality of the natives is a sad feature of their society, and I deprecate it the more in that their community has otherwise so much to offer us in their simple sharing of the bounties that nature has supplied. I dare say the gentle-men of the London Missionary Society will reach here one day in the near future, and then will Tinah and my friends cover their nakedness with trousers and Eden will be lost again. Too heavy a price to pay, yet I could wish they might have distinguished between a coco-nut and a maidenhead as commodities.

Heywood accompanied me back on the launch to *Bounty*, and the picket boat pulled into shore to collect the rest of the celebrators.

"Come to my cabin and take some madeira to banish the taste of the yava," I said. I looked forward to a gentle colloquy about the very topic I have been mentioning, as we took a 'night-cap'. Heywood saw the boat back and secured in the davits. I didn't think the Otaheitians would steal such a large and traceable item but I must confess that I was not over-confident of this.

He came into my cabin rubbing his arms, and shaking his hat.

"Is it raining?"

"Rain, Sir, no, but there is a devilish cold mist settled over the bay." I glanced from the stern windows, and it was so. I could no longer distinguish the fires in the native village.

"Did you ask Mr Christian to join us?"

Heywood looked at me carefully.

"Mr Christian did not come back on board, Sir."

We had a short drink, and then I dismissed him.

That night as I lay in my bunk I could not keep my thoughts from the fleshly pleasures I pictured Christian enjoying. My groin ached and throbbed. I ran my hand over my straining organ, but relief was not to be had. The Cap-tain must be above passion.

In the morning Christian was back aboard — how I can only guess. One of the natives must have paddled him out in a canoe. He served his watch, and offered no comment on his absence.

Two bells in the afternoon watch found Christian and me walking along a beach two bays east of our anchorage. We were looking for a suitable site for our breadfruit nursery.

Our requirements were fourfold: access to the parent plants, a clear landing for the boats to ferry the pot plants to the ship, shelter from the south-westerly winds that bedevil the islands during the months January to March, and a stream of fresh water.

I proposed to erect a stockade and two huts to shelter the land party. An officer, the botanist and four of the ratings should, I imagined, be adequate during the preparatory stages.

"We shall have a look at a roster of the officers. It won't, I'm afraid, be a very popular posting, out here, virtually alone, and with no shipboard comforts."

"No Sir, possibly not, although it will give whoever has the job an excellent opportunity to study the natives and learn their language and customs."

He glanced at me, gauging my mood.

"Venus speaks all languages, Sir."

"Hmmmm."

We ploughed across into the edging undergrowth to clear the landward end of a large rocky outcrop that leant into the sea. Black basalt.

"What's that?"

There was a rustling in the bushes, and a grunting.

"It may be an animal, Sir."

We advanced slowly, my hand to the hilt of my sword, Christian, slightly in my van, clutching a cutlass. He peered cautiously around the bole of a palm tree, then stopped, a large grin creasing his face. I looked at him perplexed, then strode forward to view whatever was diverting him.

There, blatantly beaming at me, was the bare backside of James Morrison, Boatswain's mate. He was certainly threshing the undergrowth down, and entirely oblivious to our presence as he thrust with all main and might into the accommodating and shapely rear of a young native lady. They were coupling like dogs, grunting and panting and writhing around in their unnatural engagement. I had seen the natives go at it before in this fashion, man on maid, and indeed, man on man, but it was a different thing to see a white man hard at it.

I leapt forward lashing at them indiscriminately with my stick, and calling out my disgust. I got in some shrewd blows and with a bellow, Morrison had disengaged and swung around snarling and threatening. I raised my stick to strike him down, but he was disconcerted to find himself fronting Captain and Mate. With a change of heart he turned and plunged into the undergrowth in the path of his paramour, who had scuttled away.

"Stand, stand!" I shouted, but he was away and a crashing in the lantana signalled his progress at some distance.

I found myself panting with emotion, my heart was hammering in my chest, threatening to choke me.

Christian was dismayed. "Why?" he asked. "Why did you do that?"

"You saw them," I panted. "Good Lord, you saw them yourself going at it. They were committing beastliness, they were defiling the bodies God gave them, they were committing a crime against God and against nature, they were committing sodomy."

"But, they love it," said Christian. "Begging your pardon, Sir, but they see nothing wrong with it. All the natives do it."

"That's no sort of argument at all. They all get drunk and fall in the fire, they all sacrifice first born babies to their foul gods — that's no argument for us doing the same."

"But it does no harm, Sir."

"You are judging with your loins, Christian, not with your head. Anything that lowers us to their primitive savagery is harmful."

I was unpleasantly aware of a treacherous pressure in my own loins. I was aroused but disgusted, disgusted but aroused too. It was eleven months since I was with my wife. I waited until our passions had cooled before I returned to the topic. Christian swung the attack.

"Captain, you could have your choice of the native girls. The King would count it an honour."

"Do you make that proposition seriously? You have a very poor conception of the position and behaviour appropriate to the position of a naval commander, Mr Christian."

My traitorous groin swelled again, but my indignation bore it down.

"Be very certain that I shall do nothing to besmirch my commission from His Majesty; and I count on my officers to set an example too."

"You forbid us to have commerce with the natives."

"I say that I expect you to remember that you are British naval officers and gentlemen, and so must behave as such."

This engendered a long silence.

We selected the first adequate camp site we came to and marked it by cutting blaze marks in the pines. We made our way back in silence, apart from necessary directions, and cautions.

"We have a camp, and a name for it," said Christian in answer to Heywood as we climbed back to the deck. "Point Venus!" He gave me a quizzical look. My laughter released some tension in him and we enjoyed an evening of good high spirits and enhanced companionship. I was glad.

Three nights later Christian had a native girl in his bunk. There is a foolish side to him, a strong decisive man, but weakened with a foolishness for the opposite sex. He had set me a puzzle, for discipline was to be maintained. I could disrate him, I could clap him in irons and give him a few weeks to cool his blood. I was loath to do so, as he was popular with the crew, and if he chose to set an example he could certainly be of immense value. It was a difficult situation, maintaining a tight ship, while all the crew on liberty were wallowing like pigs in a swill of sensual satiety. I summoned him before me.

"Mr Christian, you have chosen to defy my positive command that no natives were to be entertained on board this ship. You also have chosen to disregard the hope I had expressed, that you might set an example of gentility and control.

"I think it best that you be removed from the ship for a period to reconsider your behaviour.

"You will, please, organise a detachment of four of the men and proceed to erect the stockade and depot on shore. You will then remain in command of that garrison."

I knew how he had valued our shared intimacy, and had decided that for a sensitive person, such as he had shown himself, this period of banishment from our presence might best bring home my disappointment with his behaviour. I thought he may have begged my pardon, asked to stay on board. I should have refused. He did neither. He looked at me impassively, then saluted and turned away.

Within the hour the detachment was pulling to shore on their way to Point Venus.

"Heywood," I said, "this is the best bottle of madeira we have broached. I give you — very good health, and the successful conclusion of our expedition."

"Aye, and we have that well in hand." Nelson, our botanist and gardener, had joined the Captain's circle for supper, and along with the rest of us, his gastric juices were gurgling around a stomach full of pig and sweet potato.

Nelson had regaled us with a full, very complete description of his methods of propagating the breadfruit plant. I had mooted the possibility of just transporting a bunch of seeds across the ocean to Jamaica. Nelson discountenanced the idea. The seedlings are unreliable, he opined, and breed bastard plants. Moreover, many of them are sterile and will not reproduce. No indeed, it was plants we must take, and then we enjoyed, more or less, a discourse on the relative virtues of stem cuttings against layered plants, of aerial layering against grafting and I know not what else.

Now, six hundred plants, or a very few less, were propagated into pots and ready for transhipment. This was very satisfactory, really very satisfactory, and I foresaw us leaving some weeks earlier than I had feared.

If we didn't leave soon the natives would have stolen the masts out of the ship! I was rendered very disappointed and cross, for knowing as we all did the unfortunate proclivity of these Indians for stealing anything they fancy, it necessarily argued that the blame lay with my officers and petty officers for their laxness which made it possible. I really believed that no commander had ever been saddled with such a set of useless rascals, of weak untrustworthy self-servers, as constituted the officers on this vessel, *Bounty*. We had that very week lost two axes, a water cask, a compass, and from the stockade the bedroll out of Mr Peckover's hammock, and a musket from a seaman standing sentry. As regards the first derelictions, they were facilitated by Mr Hayward, who was found to have been asleep on his watch. I had the rascal put in irons. The matter of the musket I viewed most seriously, and sent an armed party to Tinah, and threatening the direct retribution, and in fact to burn the village. We were successful in having the gun returned to us within the hour. The sentry I sentenced to twenty lashes, and the native produced by Tinah as the culprit was given one hundred. Only the last cuts broke his skin, which was much swollen. All the natives moaned and cried as the punishment proceeded, yet apparently regarded it as just retribution. Hayward I left in irons until we sailed.

I spoke to the company in my cabin, that is Nelson, Heywood and Stewart, of the fact that the cat had not cut the native's back.

"It would seem that as well as being pigmented so much more heavily than ours, their skin is actually more leathery."

"It may be that the tattooing which covered so much of his back has toughened it." That was Heywood's explanation.

"But then," I said "Jack Tar is often tattooed as heavily as these gentlemen, yet he bleeds most effusively when the cat scratches him."

"They use different dyes, and their method of tattooing is quite different," said Nelson. "Also their patterns. You must have seen the warrior bucks with their buttocks tattooed so they appear to be wearing short pants."

"That's not a sign of a warrior" said Heywood "it's the symbol of a married man. The head of a household."

"Mr Christian has just submitted to having his bottom tattooed," said Stewart.

"Christian! — surely you are jesting!"

"Yes, he has."

"Heywood, what is all this? Has he taken leave of his senses?"

170

"Why, Sir, he told me that his tyo, Isabella, had asked him to do it. She believes she is carrying his child."

"You mean in these few weeks ashore he has set up a domestic establishment?"

"Something of that sort, Sir."

"And has he a bone through his nose?"

"I believe he is behaving honourably towards her."

"He was sent ashore to pot breadfruit, not impregnate half the female population."

"He hasn't done that, Sir."

"And you too want to go ashore and set up a harem?"

"No Sir — I do have a friend now, Ohataya. I call her Maria!"

"And you are rogering the wench stupid every time I turn my back are you?"

"Sir, no, we are friends." He coloured famously.

"Does that mean you don't have to give her a nail, or some beads every time she rolls over?"

"Please, Sir, I thought you would understand!"

"I understand you all right. I understand you both. I was wasting my time teaching you to take sights. Damn me for a fool, the only sight you were interested in was under a grass skirt!"

Heywood stood gaping at me, the poor booby, his mouth open. His inarticulateness aroused a cruel rage in me.

For three months it had been like some lewd farce with every man jack of the crew, even blind Byrne the fiddler, deep in his doxy every night he could escape the ship. I verily thought I was the only celibate person on the entire island. I gave thanks to God for my strength, but I was sadly let down by Christian and then Heywood.

An irresistible desire to hurt him was nearly choking me. He was so stupidly vulnerable.

"And will you be bringing your nigger bride home to meet the family on Man? Will you be married in the Cathedral? Or will you be dead of venereal disease by then? Don't tell me she's clean. Who do you think she might be jiggering with the nights when you are on the ship? her cousins, her brother? Half the population, perhaps."

A sullen stupidity had enfolded him now, very like dumb insolence, it occurred to me.

"Get out" I blared, "And you are confined to the ship, Mr Heywood."

Making a fool of me, and laughing together at me.

"Will you excuse me, Captain?"

It was Nelson making his escape.

"And I suppose you have a black bitch too, on heat for you!"

He followed Heywood out, and I had the cabin to myself. The cabin and the last bottle of madeira. I poured a glass and took a mouthful. It was warm and sweet and sticky. A sudden fury took hold of me again, and seizing the bottle by the neck I smashed it on the arms chest.

"Samuels!" I bellowed, "come and clean up this mess."

* * * * *

"Papa, here is Mrs Peebles with our dinner."

I looked at the letter, and resisted the urge to open it and read it again.

"Thank you, Anne, m'dear, I was not asleep, just going through a few old memories."

Chapter Nine

My poor dear sweet Anne, how could I share these events with her?

I had, indeed, only shared a small part of it with any of my family, not even with Mrs Bligh. While she was well aware that the citizens of Sodom and Gomorrah had displeased the Lord mightily, it had not, I believe, occurred to her to determine precisely how they had incurred His wrath.

Elizabeth? Elizabeth would disapprove of the messenger rather than the message. She is of the school of Dr Thomas Bowdler, who is, I hear, publishing an edition of the works of William Shakespeare from which the grosser passages have been removed. His argument is that Shakespeare's coarseness is the source of the moral decay of our young people, who would otherwise remain innocent. Yet the young people of Otaheite seem to learn their decadence very effectively without the help of Shakespeare. I hope for Elizabeth's sake that her beloved attorney is better briefed on such matters than she.

Could I talk with Frances? The answer, I regret, is "No". At least, I could talk, but she would simply say "Yes, Papa" whatever I said. Hers is a clear but not a questioning mind. She is like the gentlemen of the Naval Commissariat, who demanded that accounts of expenditures should add up correctly but did not demand that the individual items bore any relationship to reality.

But Jane? Though Frances's twin, she has of all my daughters the least prudish sensibilities. I am not saying that she would happily share the ribaldry of the quarter-deck, but she constantly surprises me with her awareness of the world. Considering that she has hardly seen anything beyond the confines of our little village, this is most unusual. Of course, she reads a great deal. She has read all the books in my own library, and has on occasions come to me with the most searching questions about matters of navigation and astronomy. Perhaps I could share with her some account of Otaheite, though it is less easy to find the occasion to do so..

As for Mary and my first-born, Harriet Maria, they might also understand. But neither Harriet nor Mary is, of course, a member of our little company. So I am alone with my recollections.

* * * * *

Twenty-three weeks we were on Otaheite, and on every night but the last the fires blazed on shore and were the loci of dancing and mirth. We had got all the plants stowed aboard by All Fool's Day, one thousand and fifteen breadfruits, and we had a boat laden besides with hogs and goats, coco-nuts, yams, fruits and vegetables of all kinds.

We but wanted an offshore breeze to carry us out of the bay at Oparre. As is common in these places, an offshore breeze blew each evening as the land mass cooled down, but I preferred to sail in daylight, although we had buoyed the reef.

The westerly backing north on April 3rd, I determined that we should up anchor on the morrow, and a farewell dinner was held on our decks on that evening.

I had Tinah, and all his relatives, and as every man jack of the crew had his 'tyo', or friend, the ship was crowded with natives. I took some pleasure, you may be sure, in the lugubrious countenances worn by Mr Heywood and Mr Christian. I looked with some gratifying anticipation to buckling them back into the harness of ship-board discipline.

I made final presentations to Tinah, and to those Indians whose assistance had especially helped our breadfruit enterprise, but as the time came for them to leave their grief became voluble and alarming. Several of them took shark's teeth or other sharp instruments and began slashing their faces in token of their despair. A fine man, Teppatoo, one of their chieftains, and a particular friend, disfigured his eyeball by this means.

Christian neglected my table, and was, as I suppose, whispering fond intimacies to his extremely pregnant lady friend. As it was time to be quit of our visitors, I summoned him to his duty.

"Mr Christian, get your tattooed arse up here on deck!"

He appeared looking sullen and reproachful. He also looked ill-shaven and disordered.

"Sir!"

"Mister, I expect you to jump when I shout. You are a naval officer back on a naval ship, no longer a savage in a native bordello. Is that clear?"

I was shouting. I'd meant to tighten the screws of discipline quietly on my erstwhile disciple, but I went on shouting.

"Mr Christian?"

"Aye, Sir," and off he went.

He did pull himself back together as far as appearances went, and as the cycle of watches and the routine of working the ship reasserted itself, he began to fill again his niche in the chain of command. Young Heywood followed his lead — he had a better wit than Christian, but the older man had established a predominance.

There was a brooding distemper in Christian now, a discontent that seemed ever present under the surface. I searched out the sore spots, and flicked them for amusement. I was making him pay for twenty-three weeks of desertion.

We all settled into a routine.

Nelson and Brown watered the plants, and turned them, and carried them up in a regular roster, to bask in the sunlight each day. They reminded me of ants in an ant nursery as they laboured like foster parents carting their children about. Christian and Heywood dined with me on occasion but I had Nelson and Stewart to complete the company. I intended to restore our former intimacy, but only after a suitable period of deprivation and penance. I was not pleased with their behaviour, even making allowances for the passions of youth.

The ship was like a bum boat, with vegetables and fruits stacked everywhere, to the impediment of navigation.

Each man — master, mate or jack — had his share of coconuts put aside against harder times. I had a basket of them wedged between the stern-chasers, but noticed to my displeasure that they were sensibly diminishing as the voyage progressed. I determined it was a point on which to make issue. I summoned the officers, and asked for an explanation.

"Why, Sir," said Christian, offhand, as if the matter were beneath him. "I have not seen a man touch them."

I quizzed each in turn, but the answer was the same.

"Then," I said, "if it be not the men, it must be the officers. Mr Elphinstone, be good enough to have all the coco-nut stores brought here to the quarter-deck. Mr Samuel, you shall take account of them. I shall come to the bottom of this affair."

You might think this was petty, but I tell you it's a fine line between discipline and anarchy, and you cannot make exceptions and concessions. I questioned each of them carefully and tallied the result until I came to Mr Christian.

"Well mister, so we come to you, and how many coconuts do you have aboard."

"I don't know, Sir, but I hope you don't think me so mean as to be guilty of stealing yours."

He looked so hangdog that pity and rage disputed in my breast. Rage won.

"Yes, you damned hound, I do. You must have taken them or you would be running this enquiry for me. You are all in this together, you blaggards, you're a set of thieving scoundrels. You'll be taking the yams next. I'll sweat you for it, I'll have half of you jump overboard before we get through the Endeavour Straits, may God damn me if I don't."

No one said anything. No one caught my eye.

Heywood had gone very red in the face.

"Mr Samuel, no grog will be served this day, and tomorrow's yam ration is to be halved."

I left them to it. I could hear them murmuring among

themselves, but I knew that firmness was necessary with a class of rascals like them to keep their respect.

I called Samuel, my clerk, and gave him the particulars to organise a special dinner for this evening. We had a fish, and some young pork, and fresh fruit besides, "And open the last of the Cape wine." I would surprise them both. It had appealed to me as the occasion on which to re-establish the intimacy of our trio. This may seem strange to you, to be considerate above usual after a dressing down, a punishment, but it's my way. The iron fist in the velvet glove, or something like that. There is a time for punishment, and a time for civility, and I wanted to demonstrate that having judged, and punished, that I was not the man to hold a grudge. I think I understand my fellow man better than most. When Christian and Heywood cooled down then they would realise that I put my authority on with my jacket, but that I could slip it from my shoulders and be the best of good companions privately to the wretch I'd just pilloried publicly.

Heywood was glad of the invitation. His eye lightened, and he blurted out, "and Fletcher — you are inviting Christian, are you Sir?"

I found Christian by the quarter-deck, and taking a turn with him I quietly and civilly asked him to join us for the evening meal.

He had been pacing with great suppressed energy, and on my words he sprung around, like a released steel coil.

"Don't ask me," he shouted, "I'm in torment do you hear, in torment. Don't play your hot and cold games with me."

He flung himself down in the waist and vanished below. I was too taken aback to move in time to check him, so I shrugged my shoulders and said, "We'll see, mister, we'll see who is playing games." I confidently expected that he would accept the invitation. A captain's request is a royal command in the ships of His Majesty's Navy.

Heywood turned up late, which was unusual for him. He looked around rather wildly, and I expected him to comment on the table I'd set out with the spheres and mathematical tables for four figure calculations. Natural logarithms were a field I had long wanted to share with them

177

both. The crisp economy of calculations carried out in the world of logarithms fascinated me — it was a doorway into a world of mathematics that most people did not know existed. I had taught myself their use, but I was eager to carry it further. Logarithmic values to a base ten can, I believe, be comprehended most easily, but what about the use of a binary base, or what arcs of computation could be charted with a logarithmic table based on pi?

"Good evening, Mr Heywood," I poured him some sherry. "And is our mutual friend accompanying you?"

"Sir, you must see him, there is something very wrong."

"Indeed, and I have invited him to come and see me."

"Sir, there was talk..."

"Talk of Mr Christian making a raft, Sir."

"A raft!"

"They say he was planning to leave the ship and paddle to the nearest island."

"And then catch a ferry back to Otaheite? What nonsense!"

Heywood looked at me unhappily. "There was timber and rope, Sir, in the quarter-deck, concealed, and no one could answer my questions as to how it came there."

I considered this matter.

"You had best go and find him, Mr Heywood, and direct him to join us. As to the other matter, you could come and look at this."

I drew him to the stern windows of the great cabin — with some difficulty as the breadfruit pots filled the floor space.

"Look there."

The waters bubbled black and furrowed behind the ship, great rolls of ebony glass heaved up, rolled out and sank back into the all. A darker black shape slipped through the fluid shadows of the wake. Its outline sparkled occasionally with phosphorescence, but mainly it was just a darker black on black. A leviathan of the deep, it followed the ship relentlessly. It looked as bulky as an elephant.

"A shark!"

"Yes, a great shark."

"How did you know it was there?"

"It has followed us for three days. It is supposed to be a sign of death. You might like to mention it to your headstrong friend. It isn't a nice night for boating."

He looked again, then shuddered.

"Go and look for him."

Christian was in his bunk. Heywood reported him as sick.

"Then I shall invite him for tomorrow night. Come let us acquaint ourselves with the marvels of logarithmic mathematics while we taste our sherry."

Wanted for piracy of his Majesty's Barq. Bounty.

Fletcher Christian, 24 years of age of a dark complexion, about 5'9" in height, strong made and rather bow-legged, extensively tattooed and tattooed on the buttocks, subject to violent perspirations, particularly in the hands, so that he soils anything he handles.

The hand that grasped my shoulder was sodden with perspiration. This alerted me to Christian's presence. There was a heavy fetid odour — the breath of a sick man? The hand pulled at my shoulder importunately.

"Samuel, is that you?"

Christian's hand, but only Mr Samuel would take the liberty of disturbing me. I found it hard to wake; waking, I couldn't hold my thoughts in line.

There was steel glinting dully, sharp-edged and threatening, yet I could not fathom what was happening. The threat of steel took form as a cutlass in Christian's hand, tearing unceremoniously at my blanket. The light flickered, and came and went, and flickered again. There was a lantern held by an unknown arm, and shadows, elongated and threatening swayed over the bed.

A bayonet jabbed into my breast and I was speechless with disbelief.

Christian's face flared with the light, his eyes blazing. My head swam as he rolled me over, harsh and rough, and a cord cut into my wrists.

He'd lost his reason, he must have lost his reason. There

was something wrong with this explanation, but my head was too muzzy to pinpoint it. Then I had it. Christian had lost his mind — but who was holding the lantern?

I rolled back as the cord jerked me to the floor. I hit my head on the edge of the bunk, but my vision cleared and I identified the lantern holder — it was Burkitt!

"Burkitt", I gasped. "Christian! He's lost his mind!"

Steel again, point tearing against skin. "One word, say one word, make a sound and I'll run it through your gizzard." Christian glared maniacally but was silent. Eyes watched from the shadows across the deck outside the great cabin. "Mr Fryer!" I bellowed

"Piracy, Mr Fryer!" The eyes convulsively vanished and a door banged shut.

"Elphinstone!"

My head jerked back as Churchill slipped from the shadows and hit me in the mouth.

"Another sound and you're dead."

Bayonets everywhere combing the officers quarters. Elphinstone was thrown to the floor trussed in his hammock, his head making a sick dead thud as it hit the deck. He moaned then lay still.

Christians' eyes — his hand with the cutlass ranged, and pointed and slashed, he still said nothing, but his eyes were tormented. I hunted for them with my own.

I had only to meet them and hold them, and everything would be all right again, but they glared everywhere but into mine. I knew I had only to speak to him to bring him to his senses.

"Christian — Fletcher!"

Churchill must have doubted his resolve too, for he shoved between us.

"I warned you."

He wanted to bayonet me — I could see it in him — but he lacked the resolve, just lacked the resolve. The Master had two loaded pistols in his cabin. I had forgotten them. They were kept to fire the guns in an emergency. A sound from his cabin, and the door creaked open an inch. Quintal took position to one side of it, musket raised, ready to crash the butt on the skull of who ever came out.

"Watch for yourself," I shouted urgently — and the Master came out. He was on his knees, and before any could take action he fell on his belly writhing and squirming for mercy. Quintal stepped contemptuously over him and stepping into the cabin came out with the pistols, one of which he stuffed into his belt.

"Give it here, Matthew!" Christian's voice was hoarse and strained as he took the other pistol. Jamming it in my ribs most painfully, he pushed me through to the deck abaft the mizzen-mast and set a guard on me. Smith it was — how many were in it?

"What do you mean by this, you damned villain?"

"Not a word Captain, not a word or you are dead."

There was a disturbance forward, and Hayward come stumbling aft, a musket at his throat. He had had the watch with Christian. Last time he had fallen asleep on watch it had cost us an axe and a water cask. This time we had lost the whole ship.

I had been watching Churchill closely, and Christian, and adjudging neither of them have the stomach to despatch me in cold blood I made an effort to rally the crew.

"Mr Hallett, Morrison, Martin, Ellison, Purcell, rally to me, do you want to swing for this, and rot in hell?"

Purcell was lounging back with an impudent sly look on his face. I really think I despise Purcell and Fryer more than any for their parts in the performance. Too craven to stand with me, too scared to declare themselves with the mutineers, where their weak evil inclinations would have had them, they skulked and would not meet my eye.

Quintal came up and drawing back his bayonet looked to Christian, who moved him away.

"We have the ship, Matthew. Run out the cutter and bundle them into it."

"Finish him now, here" said Quintal. "If we don't finish him now he'll finish us."

The Boatswain and other loyal members of the crew were now set to hoisting out the cutter, but they set up such an outcry — the craft was so leaky that certain death would accompany it — that Christian told them to pull it back in.

"Get them into the launch then, give them a cask of water

and shove them down into it."

Hallett and Hayward and Samuels were ordered down into it, but Mr Samuels, the best man there, staunchly refused to go, but went to my cabin and returned with trousers and a boat cloak for me. The dawn had come up while these events were unfolding and the ship with backed topsails was floating in a glassy ocean. Away to the west the peak of Tofoa swam upside down over the horizon — twice its relative size, a not uncommon mirage in the tropics.

Where all this time were my friends and companions, the people in the vessel who should have been supporting me? Heywood and Stewart were of the opposite party. Stewart, excited like a child playing out an adventure, was strutting the deck armed with a knife he must have purloined from the galley.

"I'll finish him off, dammed if I don't, just let me at him and I'll take his coco-nuts for him."

Heywood was apparently completely under Christian's spell, and was facilitating the loading of the launch. I called to him but only achieved a snarl and a cuff from Quintal, who was very unhappy to leave my breath in my body. Tom Ellison also was party to the Mutiny so that I had great cause to curse the day I ever knew a Christian or a Heywood or indeed any Manx man. It seemed incredible that the very young men I had taken an interest in, and rendered service to every day, had turned villain and chosen a life of shame.

Mr Samuels now fronted Christian and Quintal, and demanded what was needed in the launch.

"Come, Sirs, you intend no murder I think, so we must have some pork and biscuit and more water, and muskets and maps and a sextant and cloths for our protection from the elements."

Then there came a great shouting from the mutineers, with some calling out to 'throw the dogs over' and such like, and honest shouts of indignation from the true crewmen who were being herded into the boat.

In the midst of the shouting and acrimony an odd note obtruded, for Matthew Byrne, poor blind Matthew, who had little idea of what was taking place and was upset by the shouting, to everyone's surprise put his fiddle to his chin and started playing "Come round pretty Jenny." He had only sawed out a bar or two when Churchill with an oath dashed the fiddle to the deck smashing it. Byrne stood there, dropping the bow, his face twisted, and crying with great tears rolling down his cheek, all six feet six of him swaying with misery. Everything stopped, everyone hushed. Then, after a pause, Quintal started laughing, a brutal savage laugh, and one by one, or two, the rest of the mutineers picked it up so that they were all mocking poor Byrne. And that was the cruellest sound I heard all day.

Samuels came back on deck and came straight to me. Christian still had my arms secured with the cord, and twisted up behind my back cruelly, so that I could do nothing to assist myself. Samuels was all indignation, and actually pushed Christian aside so that he could assist me don the clothing he had brought on deck. Quintal took the opportunity to secure Christian's ear and from the dark looks he directed toward me I had little doubt what he was proposing. As it happens, Quintal was quite correct, for I very much doubt that without me the other crew members would ever have survived, or found their way to Timor to relate the sad history of that day's piracy.

"No, no." Christian, although he was still appearing dazed and scarcely coherent, sent Quintal to re-hoist the cutter inboard.

The Boatswain and seamen who were to go in the boat had collected canvas, twine, lines, sails and cordage, and an extra cask of water. Samuels asked me quietly what was required for our navigation.

"Quadrant, sextant and compass, a log, and a chart, and a timekeeper. If you can lay hands on the chronometer so much the better."

He reappeared, laden down. As he hastened across to the rail, Quintal shouted an oath, "What have you there? Lay that down, Sir!" We were stripped of our chronometer, the sextant and the charts that the faithful Samuels had secured. He was allowed to take a quadrant and a small hand compass with him, and he had secured my log book and my commission, which I was most happy to have.

The mutineers were now hurrying every one into the boat as the sun rose higher. Its warmth was frugal but grateful to my bones. I had been confined on deck in my nightshirt for over an hour, and I was most loath to shiver lest it be taken as a want of courage, but my treacherous limbs were hard put to stay still in the early morning chill. Samuels, who was working like a Trojan, in contrast to every other soul aboard, clambered down into the boat with a handsome basket of bread and some wine and rum. Christian, benighted soul, with some poor idea of ceremony, directed Musprat to broach the cask and serve a dram to each of his misguided crew.

A new dispute now arose as to who was to go in the launch. The carpenter's mates and the armourer were all there wanting to go in the launch, but Christian foresaw their future usefulness, and would not countenance their leaving. Poor Coleman was vastly downcast and afraid at being forced, albeit against his will to stay with the mutineers.

"Never mind," I said, "you can't go with me but your faithfulness shall be recorded in my log and you will find justice in England."

In truth, I was glad to be quit of them and of a few more, for the boat was grossly overloaded and boasted only seven to eight inches of freeboard.

"Mr Fryer shall stay with you."

"Never, the useless dog, he can whine after you."

Neither side wanted the wretched Master, but of course, in these circumstances, Christian's will had to prevail, and so he joined us in the launch, as much to his displeasure as to ours.

Now it was my turn.

Christian cast the cord from my wrists and forced me to the railing, and I met his eyes.

"Is this a proper return for all the friendship I have shown you?"

"That Captain, is the thing; I am in hell, I am in hell — in hell."

"Let it go now, let's have done with this nonsense, I'll swear to you we'll fix it up, and it will be taken no further."

His eyes were wild, and his lips twisting. I felt some hope, but Quintal, who had been watching him with concern, bustled over and said, "Send him down now, Mr Christian, send him down one way or the other, don't trust the bugger, he'll have us."

And so I quit the *Bounty*.

Heywood steadied the top of the ladder. I looked at him.

"Why did you do it?" he asked. "Why did you force me to choose between you?" His face was pale.

"Me force you?" I was incredulous.

"How could you make him do it?"

He wasn't worth arguing with.

I climbed into the launch and took the tiller, and we were cast adrift. I took a few minutes to arrange the stowage, and some weighty items had to be thrown over to improve our trim.

There was a splash beside the boat, but I could not see what had caused it. I was shading my eyes and looking up when a crash at my feet made me start aside. There was a howl of mirth from the pirates lining the rail of the *Bounty*, and looking down I saw a smashed pot and a broken breadfruit plant lying in a confusion of earth at my feet.

After this the missiles came in a steady shower, splashing and breaking around us, to the accompaniment of a chorus of derision.

"Give way there!" We had little wind and we pulled raggedly down, and out of range of the agricultural bombardment.

When we were sixty or seventy yards off, there was a ringing report, and a musket was discharged in our direction. The ball hit the seat besides Purcell, and then sang into the ocean. I had no way of knowing if it were meant for me, but I had no idea of cowering. I stood up straight and steered us from the stern, but my flesh had tensed involuntarily, expecting at any second to be ploughed to my death.

There were, however no further shots, and within an hour the *Bounty* was hull down and heading west-nor'-west. West-nor'-west was not going to bring them to Otaheite, but then she was commanded by a raving lunatic.

* * * * *

I laid the letter down beside my plate, pulled a kerchief from my cuff and blew my nose explosively, seizing the opportunity to flick from my cheeks two mutinous tears which threatened to betray me.

Chapter Ten

"It's official," I said "Christian is dead. One of the natives put him out of his lunatic misery."

I said it with a hard cynical smile, and it came out all right but I felt the tears once again prickling at my eyes.

"Father," Anne had her arms around me, I beat down a sob with such an effort that my throat ached. I held her for a few minutes, and then it was gone.

It meant nothing.

"He was a mad dog, and he died like one," and I took the marmalade and finished my breakfast.

There had been two other letters on the tray, but I had forgotten about them in the emotion of the Admiralty missive. I took them up now. One was from Coutts and Company, my bank men, the other one was a printed notice from the Royal Society, begging to acquaint me with the fact that a Mr Michael Faraday would be giving a discourse on electro-magnetic induction, whatever that might prove to be. I have heard something of his experiments but paid little attention. I had an idea he was something in the way of a disciple of that fellow Mesmer, who of course was a charlatan. If it had been anything in my line I am confident Sir Joseph would have written under separate cover to bring it to my attention.

I sighed and opened the seal on Mr Coutts's statement of my affairs. I expected little joy there. It was all going out these days and precious little coming in.

I said as much, something to that effect. That's one effect of loneliness, you see, confiding in yourself. Somebody described marriage as just being 'sharing bad temper during the day — sharing bad smells at night!' Some modicum of trust, but it is agreeable to have someone whose duty it is to listen to your opinions and complaints.

"Is it bad news, Sir?"

Anne had left us. Mrs Peebles was standing beside me, quite close.

"No — I don't know yet." I was unfolding the bank instrument, and I held it at arms length. I find I need to squint a little to read small print or hand writing nowadays, or hold it at arm's length. This was damned crabbed writing, but very even. It was a list of my assets in New South Wales that I had lodged with the bank for collateral at one stage when I was looking at purchasing a mining property in Cornwall. Coutts had sent a list of rents and rates, and an estimate of realisable market values. Some of their estimates were fairly startling.

"It's a list of my property and income in New South Wales."

She found an invitation in my voice and stooping looked at the list.

"Do you intend going back there, Sir, to do business?"

"Good Lord no, they kicked me out, didn't they? But looking at the value of this land on the Hunter, well, I might have the last laugh."

I had absent-mindedly put my hand on her waist as we looked at the paper. It was unpremeditated — a spontaneous gesture that I had often done with Betsy. I was a little alarmed to find it there but as no protest was elicited I left it there.

"Miss Jane says it was outrageous what they did to you, Admiral, rebelling like that. Two mutinies, you might say, you've had to put up with."

"Two mutinies? Four!"

"Four?"

"Four mutinies — well, three official ones anyway."

"Never — where were the others?"

Her concern and disbelief were all the spur a lonely old bore like myself needed to start resurrecting his past.

"The Nore. You will remember the disturbances at the Nore. I was at the Nore in '97."

"When all the ships mutinied, and wanted to go over to the French!"

"Nearly all the ships in the anchorage mutinied, but there was no real talk of going over to the French. Only the leaders and the delegates talked of taking a cutter, and escaping to France. They knew what would happen to them if they didn't, of course. In fact some of them vanished and may have got there."

"And did your crew mutiny — did they harm you?"

I slid my hand from her waist to her haunch and gave it a friendly squeeze. She was obviously worried about my dangerous past.

"I had *Director* then, a sixty-four. She was actually the last ship to mutiny. The trouble started at Spithead in the middle of that April, but the people at the Nore, although there was quite a lot of disobedience, the people at the Nore didn't raise the red flag until the twelfth of May."

* * * * *

Murrack was on the books as a boatswain's mate. He was a boatswain's mate, no better, no worse than any other boatswain's mate, but he had a talent with rope. Knots and splices, whippings and seizings were his meat and drink, and much of his time was devoted to the running rigging and to assisting the sailmaker.

Three two-foot lengths of three-inch rope lay beside him, whipped with tarred twine at one end, unlaid at the other. He was busy splicing braided cords, quarter inch in diameter and two foot six long, into the unlaid rope ends. He had three cats to make, nine tails to each cat, for we were calling all hands to witness punishment today.

There was a murmur in the crew, but none watched him overtly at his splicing. If you want value for your flagellation then you set your boatswain in the middle of the deck to make the cats. You lash a hatchway grating to the bulwark twenty-four hours in advance. It's in the mind, isn't it. It's a deterrent — not a vengeance.

The Naval regulations specify that floggings shall not be carried out for twenty-four hours after sentencing. That's sensible too. I'm not a flogging captain, not compared to some. Twelve or twenty-four stripes is my usual sentence, but again I mix compassion with sternness. Lash a man one day, and indulge him the next, I'm never the man to carry a grudge, and the men appreciate my tolerance. I have made something of a study of managing people. I think I shall, some day, publish a pamphlet with my conclusions.

The rain slanted down at us, which was a little unkind. It was nearly the end of April, and we were tied up in the Thames, home from the wintry Texel, where the fog only lifted to make way for wind and rain.

Mr Purdie, midshipman, bustled about the waist organising a party of sulky seamen who were lashing a grating to the bulwark.

Mr Murrack, covered grudgingly with a tarpaulin, was splicing ropes in the prominence afforded by the main hatchway. Patiently he went about his work.

Patience is the main requirement for rope work, patience and strong fingers.

I folded the paper and pocketed it in my jacket and nodded to McTaggart. The drums rolled as Norton was strapped to the grating, and a leather pad strapped over his kidneys. My mouth was dry, and I had had trouble reading the articles of war. I think a lot of people are affected physically by watching corporal punishment. A tenseness gripped my gut, and as his shirt was torn away and the kidney pad strapped on, my own back bridled under my jacket. Anticipation and a cruel sort of pleasure excites the onlooker. I tightened my stomach muscles as a cramp threatened my bowels.

The lash rose and fell, and a livid weal was cut across the back. "One," called McTaggart. I let out my breath, I hadn't realised I had been holding it. "Two," "Three," and now he was feeling it, a stain of dark red spread across his ribs.

"Blood" I muttered. Jenkins looked at me curiously. The boatswain combed the blood-stained strands with his fingers.

"Twenty-three," counted McTaggart.

190

McDougall was lashed up in his turn, and then William Roland. I felt myself purged and renewed when it was done, almost as if it I were being scourged of the evil in me.

My shirt was rank and cold at the armpits, and I felt a moistness in my small clothes at the groin, as I stepped forward and took their attention, then I read to them the 'Proclamation of the addition to Seamen's wages'. Five and sixpence a month extra for every man jack of them!

It was I think a most satisfying mornings work. The stick and the carrot, and unless Jack is an ass then that should stifle the malcontents.

I hung on for a week after the other ships. Mind you the villains wouldn't take the ship to sea, but it wasn't until the nineteenth that the delegates came back from the shore and said quite apologetically, "Captain Bligh, on behalf of the ship's company of *Director*, we must ask you to go ashore, Sir, and Lieutenant McTaggart is to take over if you please Sir." They were much more polite than Mr Christian, I can assure you. They brought around two boats to take my belongings to land, and the boatswain was ready to give three huzzahs for me as I went over the side, but in the event Mr Parker, the delegate, said it wouldn't be fitting.

* * * * *

"And the villains, they did it for greed?"

"Not villains I think, Mrs Peebles, although certainly some of them were bad men, and some were foolish men, but they had real grievances you know, and indeed, showed real forbearance and patriotism, and the Admiralty responded to a great many of the considerations they raised."

"It was a strange sort of mutiny."

"It was a very strange sort of mutiny. Parker and the other delegates used to march with their committees through the streets of Sheerness each morning with a brass band at their head, and the people cheering. Admiral Lord Keith came down with an infantry battalion, and put a stop to that. Then I remember on May the thirtieth waking to the rumble of gunfire, and thinking 'that's it now, they intend to fight their way down the Thames to the Channel,' but do you know what was going on.

Every ship in the fleet had hoisted colours and was firing a nineteen-gun salute to mark the anniversary of the restoration of King Charles. They did the same in June for the King's birthday — twenty-one guns for the King of course."

I released Mrs Peebles, with an admonishing pat, and folded my papers into order while she took my tray from the table.

I hadn't thought about Parker in many a year.

* * * * *

Parker was a bold fellow. He knew he was going to be hanged, and a naval hanging is not a nice hanging. You didn't know there were degrees in hanging? Well there certainly are, and not for him the quick drop at Tyburn and a broken neck. No, he would be pinioned, arms and legs, and hoisted to the yard-arm to choke his life out.

He was brave, he scorned to run and hide. Instead, after his shipmates voted to return to duty, he handed over the keys to the magazine and led the three cheers that signified the Mutiny was over. A week later he was hoisted to the fore yard-arm.

'Admiral of the floating republic' bold Richard styled himself, and he said to me at the end, "Bligh," he said, "you should never make yourself the busybody of the lower classes. The one they glorify one moment as their leader, they'll cheer for next week on the gallows."

He was a florid orator, and — most dangerous for an orator — he became intoxicated by the magic of his own eloquence, so that he misjudged his moment, he misjudged the temper of the Admiralty and he misjudged, at the last, the will of his fellows. Three fatal errors.

After I was beached, not unceremoniously, from *Director*, I hastened, as you might imagine, to offer my services to their lordships of the Admiralty. You don't, after all, get a great many men experienced in the business of mutineer's victim.

Nepean sent me with a secret letter to Admiral Duncan directing him to prepare to attack the mutineers and suppress the Mutiny. At the same time the garrison at Sheerness was reinforced with redcoats and supplies to the fleet were stopped.

What would have happened if the North Sea fleet had sailed in to tackle them I don't know, for before Duncan had talked to God about it word reached England that the Dutch at the Texel had embarked and were only awaiting a favourable wind to sail with their invasion force.

Duncan was ordered to sea, but as is now common knowledge, the bulk of the North sea fleet mutinied and turned back to join the red flaggers at the Nore. Only *Venerable* and *Adamant* remained loyal. This was England's blackest hour. Some of the captains, including myself, were then employed touring the batteries and the dockyard, and any of the ships that would have us on board, urging the men to accept a pardon and return to duty. There was no pardon available for the ringleaders and so they not unnaturally resented our efforts very strongly.

Some little danger was incurred to our persons. The Earl of Northesk, Captain of the *Monmouth* and myself were aboard that ship, pointing out the hopelessness of their situation, when a group of these same gentlemen seized us and used us very roughly indeed. Their first proposal was to pitch us over the side, and with the tide way running, and my poor prowess at natation, that might very well have been my death sentence, but then an even less attractive line of action was proposed.

"String em up, says I," quoth one Fidge, a delegate to their council, "For if we was taken by them, that's what'll happen to us."

This was received with a deal of noisy approval by his followers, and hustled we were under the yard-arm. I stood firm, but I fear my face was grown pale and white, for it is a cowardly death, and I felt quite unmanned.

"Lash their hands" was the call, but then there was a pause, as a lank fellow in an officer's coat pushed aft through the throng.

"Are you mad?" he said, not shouting, but his voice increasing in intensity as they paused to listen. "Are you mad? Are you mad? Shall we, who have at last found ourselves as free men, shall we act like animals? Shall we, having bested oppression and degradation in our masters, show the same cruelty now we are the masters? Are not these men, Bligh and Northesk, come bravely to convey our negotiations to their lordships? Have you not eyes to see the smoke on the shore? They are heating red-hot shot in the batteries, and the guns are aimed at you. Free me these men and we shall send them to my Lord Spencer with our ultimatum. Hang them and we are all dead men!"

We had a glass of wine with him before we left — I had a very dry mouth, I can swear to it — and, damned if they did not cheer us over the side. I said Parker had misjudged his timing, he missed the tide completely that had brought the Spithead mutineers through to an amicable agreement, and if the Government had acceded to the demands at the Nore, then mutiny would have achieved respectability as a means of social protest.

They had to be subdued and a decent number of them had to be hanged. Twenty-eight were swung up, but of these only two of my people.

The Government, once the decision was taken, blocked the channels and removed all navigation buoys, ringed the anchorage with cannon, some indeed with heated shot, and proceeded to starve the mutineers out. Once the desperateness of their situation became apparent the worst fellows turned to drunkenness and piracy, so that they lost the support of the public, and then of their own people. One by one the ships companies overcame the core of mutineers and pulled down the red flag.

The first to go was *Leopard*, which occasioned me great satisfaction as I had expended much time with the seamen, recalling them to their duty, and so the great Mutiny at the Nore spluttered and fizzed out.

It was a black mark in the history of the Navy, but I have a letter from Nepean congratulating me on the success of my efforts as an intermediary.

*　*　*　*　*

There was a disturbance outside, and putting down my mail, I looked out at the sullen day. The bottom of the croquet lawn was bordered by three gaunt poplars. Little suggestion, here, of the avenues of Lombardy. One, cut off and stunted in its growth, had formed an ill-shaped lump atop the main stem, from which a half dozen bare sticks poked into the sky like a witches broomstick. The other two pushed bristles upwards, darker grey and ugly against the lowering steel of the wintry sky. They reminded me of something somewhere — I thought about it, and then I had it. They were very reminiscent of the patch of bristles starting from Admiral Duncan's face the night before Camperdown. I looked with a warming pleasure at the pussy willows by my carriageway. They flamed a golden apricot, the very branches and twigs of the trees touched by Midas. The colour of winter, the relief from the drab leafless trees. It seems strange to me that the poet, Coleridge it was, he knows his English winter countryside, and praises the ash and the elm, the walnut and the lime tree, but not a passing word for the pussy willow. They lifted my spirits, a peace and unusual tranquillity, a sympathy with the countryside in its season stayed my limbs.

Suddenly with a fearful scratching, and an impact that must surely have come close to shattering the pane, a turkey was scrabbling at the window.

I started back, then —

"Jane!" I bellowed.

Mrs Peebles hurried in wiping her hands on her apron.

"Admiral?"

"A blasted turkey!"

She goggled at me, uncomprehending.

"There's a blasted turkey!" I moved to the window and peered down. The glass was spattered with mud, and in the crocus bed below there was not a single turkey but a brace of them scratching and scouring the earth apparently in quest of the bulbs.

"The blasted park is full of blasted turkeys!"

"Oh dear. Miss Jane said that Conkey from the village had fixed up a run and that the birds were to arrive next week."

"Get her."

"Yes, Sir." She bobbed briefly, and hurried out. I took up the missive from Coutts again, and soothed myself by scanning the figures in the indenture relating to my holdings in New South Wales. The biggest were a thousand acres in the upper Nelson river district and a hundred and five acres at Parramatta, on the road running out of the main settlement. There is a township growing around a cluster of grog shops there, and I calculate this land may be ultimately divided into town blocks. Then there were two farms at the Hawkesbury with tenant farmers, and a further two hundred and forty acres on the Parramatta Road which is not cleared. Camperdown and Copenhagen I named my largest properties. Prudence would dictate the early disposal of these holdings in the Antipodes, particularly as I have some reservations as to the honesty of my agent in Sydney. Honest and competent clerks just cannot be found in that penal colony. However, what I take I like to hold, and I believe it may double in value as the ever-increasing number of settlers crowd into that narrow coastal plain.

My mind turned to the criminal MacArthur on his voyage back. It is not a trip to be undertaken lightly, a fact that the unpleasant villain Short can testify to.

* * * * *

Captain Joseph Short was Captain of the *Porpoise* when I went out to New South Wales as Governor, but a more self-opinionated villain it was never my ill luck to chance upon. Captain of the *Porpoise*, convoying us out in the *Lady Sinclair*, and as it happened he was also planning to take up a land grant in Port Jackson. For this purpose his wife and seven children accompanied him aboard *Porpoise*. I might add that *Porpoise* was quite illegally burthened by a great quantity of farm implements, together with general merchandise that the opportunistic Captain Short intended to sell at a great profit on his arrival in the Colony.

We were no sooner at sea than he started the most monstrous efforts to usurp my authority.

Now, we were quite a small convoy, the *Lady Sinclair*, carrying passengers and goods out, the *Justiana* with sale goods, two convict ships, the *Fortune* and the *Alexander*, and the *Elizabeth*, a whaling ship. Convoying them all was *Porpoise*, twenty-eight guns only, but then there had been no reports of the French being at strength anywhere in the Indian Ocean.

Every report suggested that my posting to the Governorship was a very good posting indeed, and Banks told me it was good for three thousand pounds per annum at least. As I was assured of retaining my seniority in the Navy lists, I looked to return with a comfortable nest egg, and to find an appointment as Admiral to greet my return. There had been much speculation round the service that the Admiralty would re-create the position at Admiral of the Red — this position had formerly been appointed as an order of admirals of the third rank. The French wars and Nile and Trafalgar in particular had thrown up so many heroes to honour.

This, however, was all for the future. For the present I had invited Short across to dine with me, and proposed taking the occasion to confirm our route and ports of call, and to set down rendezvous in the event of bad weather disrupting the convoy, for we were sailing into the southern winter.

Next thing, to my astonishment, a cutter rowed across with a note, a very short note, that because of the exigencies of getting the squadron under way he would be unable to join me that night, but would welcome the chance to dine with me on the morrow, and thought it more suitable that I should join with him on *Porpoise*. This was a very impudent move. Quite apart from the fact that I was the Governor going out to take up my appointment in the Colony, I was the senior naval officer in the fleet. I had no doubt his first move when he got the appointment to the convoy was to check his Captain's list. I was thirty-three places above him on the list, four years seniority at least.

"Oh ho!" I thought, "that's to be the way of it, is it?"

The difficulty was, of course, that I carried no commodore's flag, and so it could, I stress could, be asserted that I enjoyed only the status of a passenger being convoyed. That was not the way it was going to be, of course. Back I sent the message smartly that I expected him the next evening to dine with me on the *Lady Sinclair*, and I settled down with interest to see what the morrow would bring.

He must have baulked at a deliberate affront to me, for over he came, smooth as silk, merry as a cricket.

"Glad to meet you Bligh," said he, all cordiality. "Took the liberty of bringing a bottle of madeira across, though one can look forward to picking up some splendid cases of hermitage at the Cape."

"Splendid wine, as you say, but whether I decide to call at the Cape will depend of course on the weather conditions." That laid it on the line for him, best to spell it out clearly, I thought.

"Naturally we want to get the new Governor to New South Wales as soon as possible so he may establish his authority."

I looked at him narrowly — he looked at me narrowly.

"You are leaving the service to take up land in the Colony I believe?"

"Yes Sir," he fumbled in his jacket, "I have with me a letter which I am pleased to present to you covering a grant of land I have been promised by Lord Camden."

I took the letter, and read it carefully.

"It is, I see, from Mr Cooke, Lord Camden's agent."

"Yes, Sir — it would be, wouldn't it, he transacts all his Lordship's business."

The letter stated that it was Lord Camden's intention to instruct Governor Bligh to grant Short six hundred acres of land, together with sufficient convicts to clear and cultivate it.

"You will be very well set up with six hundred acres," I said folding the letter and handing it back to him.

"Indeed it is not unlikely we shall both do very well in the Colony Captain." The slimy villain; I decided to puncture his *bonhomie*.

"I shall look forward to receiving Lord Camden's instructions in the matter so that I may proceed with your grant." He looked pained.

"But the letter I have given you is very clear."

"The letter I have given you back in fact only gives me a second-hand account of Lord Camden's intention. I will naturally require official confirmation."

He pursued the matter no further, but his eyes had become small and beady, and I knew that the matter would be raised again. I determined to pursue my advantage.

"You will realise that I am the senior naval officer in this squadron, so I am glad we shall have this opportunity to determine our route, and establish both our course, and a series of rendezvous in case we are separated by a storm."

"Certainly it is something which must be done, but I must point out that my orders from the Admiralty instruct me to take charge of the convoy, but to put myself under your command when we reach New South Wales."

"And I would remind you that because I am your senior I have been appointed first captain of the *Porpoise*, even though I am taking passage in the *Lady Sinclair*."

It was mutiny again, insubordination and mutiny, no doubt about that. I took refuge in Marcus Aurelius — he doesn't let me down.

> *Everything which happens is as familiar and well-known as the rose in spring and the fruit in summer; for such is disease, and death, and calumny, and treachery, and whatever else delights fools or vexes them.*

He had some tribulations in his time, and it shows. I also have had some tribulations.

"I am sure, Captain Bligh, that we shall work together very well."

We ate our dinner with a polite animosity, but the main topic of discord, the areas of seniority and command, were not alluded to again.

After our pudding, a refined plum dowdy with syrup and dates that my mess man had put together, we drew forth the charts and set down our objectives and our rendezvous. This wasn't too difficult as most ships rounding the Cape of Good Hope run down the Atlantic to Tenerife, Cape Du Verde, Rio and so to the Cape. I like a more southerly route to use the great westerlies which sweep the Southern Ocean at this season. Short advocated a higher latitude, because, as is my guess, he is shy of the ice.

And so our voyage began. For me it was softened and warmed by the presence of my daughter Mary, now Mrs Putland, on board the *Lady Sinclair* with me. Her husband, Lieutenant Putland, was third Lieutenant on *Porpoise*, and on arrival in New South Wales was to take up his duties as my Lieutenant and aide. Mary is a famous letter writer, and took upon herself all the duties of correspondent, so that I had a very easy time of it.

Putland, Mary and I had a day ashore together in Tenerife, and a splendid day it was. The sun blazed on us from an orange sky and by ten the morning clouds had vanished in the mysterious way they do most days in the tropics.

"Mary, your skin is not made for this harsh light."

I bartered at a barrow stall for a palm frond hat. I wasn't sure she would wear it, but she pulled it on and laughed coquettishly, making enormous eyes at the negro hat-seller. She is a remarkably attractive young miss, and Putland is a lucky fellow. I'm not sure that he knows this — maybe he stands in awe of me, but he is always very dignified. Then to my delight he seized a banana palm hat for himself, although his face is burnt bronze from his years at sea, and taking Mary by the hand he marched down the gravel strand between the stalls proclaiming they were Tobias and Maria, the leading sambos in Santa Cruz.

The climate here in the Canary Islands is delightful, not humid and unhealthy as it would be in the corresponding latitude on the African coast, but almost Mediterranean. This is because of a cooler current, the so called 'Canary current', that bathes the coast of the islands. One feature they do have from the Cape is the use of small wheeled shays pulled by one or two of the blacks — rickshaws they call them — and we hired a likely vehicle with a strong steed. He shone his teeth at us but baulked at taking the party, so he presently hailed a friend and off we set in two carts, Mary and I in one, Putland and the lunch box in the other.

"I have the best of the bargain," he called. "You must take care not to be separated from me."

Off we set at a spanking trot through the canefields and along gravelled paths by a green stream that ran through grassy banks for all the world like a Devon brook. The peak of Mount Tenerife was towering above us, crowned with a rocky escarpment. Twelve thousand and two hundred feet it reached, and most useful it is in triangulating a position at sea if you are anywhere within twenty miles of it. Not that it was any use to us today, but that was because we were too close to it, do you see?

Lunchtime was in the shade of a clump of tobacco plants

grown to a ludicrous height. We had biscuit, and some cold fowl, a smoked tongue, and a thin bottle of local wine. Mary, who had never eaten a banana, tried one, at my suggestion. Putland pulled two ripe yellow stalks from a plantation palm, but as he wrestled with them he gave a sudden shout of alarm and leapt back as a large hairy brown spider scuttled out of the clump across his wrist. It amused me to see a hero of the Nile, who had not flinched at a storm of shot, so disconcerted by an insect. Mary could not eat the fruit, declaring it greasy and nauseous, and delicately spitting it out, but I ate four as I think them excellent. They are more floury than ones I had eaten previously, the kind which they refer to as plantain bananas. The natives cook them with rice. Would they, I wondered, fruit in New South Wales?

The next day we were at sea again, not wasting a mile of the precious northerly that the morning watch had brought. Stowed carefully in a tub in the after hold of *Lady Sinclair* were a dozen banana palms, their roots packed with wet sand, their fronds cropped short.

"Just a chance," I had pointed out, "but if they thrive in New South Wales, what a useful plant they will be and a bonanza for the planter."

We ran down into the South Atlantic with the winds kindly all the way. No more than three days did we idle with flapping sails. On March the 7th we 'crossed the line' and the hands kept up their usual sports. King Neptune holding court was the occasion of much mirth, and some rather rude handling of the younger sailors. Nor were the passengers confined to just watching, but the lusty monarch bestowed signs of his favour on all of them, the ladies being garlanded with fronds of seaweed and wrack, which attention they greeted with much amusement, but some dismay when the weed was found to carry a somewhat old-fashioned odour.

Mrs Putland, my Mary, was invited to be Queen to Neptune's King, but scarcely knowing how to refuse such honour, she donated to the merry tyrant a necklace of sea shells, and returned prettily flushed, with but a royal kiss on her hand.

Sterner weather closed in as we made our southing, and the passengers were less to be seen on the deck. I favoured a tarpaulin to defeat the wind, a jacket of close woven cotton impervious to the weather.

But now instead of defeating the invading cold it seemed to hug the chill to me, to wrap the frost amongst my bones and quaking skin, and grudge to let it out.

"I'm getting old," I told Mary.

The seas were rolling larger, but that had not brought us down to the true westerly latitude, so that I was unhappy with our progress. One morning it came to a head.

"Mr Johanssen," I said to my Master on the *Sinclair*, "we should stand further southward to find the steady westerlies. Mr Short is erring in his judgement. I believe we will show him the lead." I had him bring the ship around onto the starboard run, at the same time signalling for the fleet to change tack and follow.

That brought *Porpoise* quartering down on us at a great rate, hoisting gallants on his fore and main, so that she laid over in fine style and shouldered the seas aside. Johanssen watched her approach with some concern. I calculated that he meant to run within hailing distance and dispute my orders.

"We shall ignore the fellow," I said to Johanssen. "Hold to your course, he will have to follow."

"Oh, Aye," he said, watching the frigate come abreast of us."

"Signal, Sir," Johanssen's first officer had seen service with the King, for he rattled off the signal as soon as the hoist was clear.

"Rejoin convoy on larboard tack."

"His guns are run out, by God," the first officer looked rattled.

"I assure you, Mr Johanssen, he is bluffing!"

The blasted words were not clear of my mouth when there was a puff of smoke at his side followed two seconds later by the crack of a gun. A shot splashed across our path and vanished into the sea a quarter mile to larboard.

Johanssen looked at me.

"Hold your course."

There was another billow of smoke from *Porpoise*'s gun deck and this time a ball skipped over the water a scant fifty yards astern of us.

"Port your helm, ready about! Starbowlines to the braces."

The crew were galvanised and leapt to their tasks. There was a crack that made me flinch as the spanker boom crashed across. The yards were chattering as the officers called the watches to haul them around.

"Mr Johanssen!" I was choked with rage. Mutiny seemed to make me its caged bird. "My last command to you was to maintain your course."

"Mr Bligh," he stopped to shout at his mate who had neglected a larboard runner, "understand this, whichever of ye is in command of *Porpoise*, I am the Master of this vessel. Master, and part owner, for I have taken up two parts of her and I have taken a charter to convoy you to New Holland, but I have taken no agreement to be a target for His Majesty's Royal Navy."

"Make a signal to *Porpoise* — 'Commander to repair aboard flag'."

The signal was ignored. I could feel the rage beating in my head, waves of pain and pressure felt as if they were forcing my eyes from my skull, and my stock was choking me. There was nothing however I could do but plan Short's eventual discomfort, so after another menacing stare at the frigate, I stamped into my cabin.

Next day a letter came across from Short. He sent Putland over with it but I deferred the pleasure of opening it. My Mary, Mrs Putland, came to me in great distress when he returned to *Porpoise*.

"Oh Papa!" was all she could sob on my shoulder for some minutes, and then she spoke with feeling, and many a sob, of what Putland had conveyed to her.

"Putland could scarcely speak when he met me, on the subject of the shots that were fired at us. Captain Short had the brutality to make him fire them, for he was officer of the watch. Oh Papa! and he made him prepare a third shot which was to be fired right into us if we did not bear about."

Here she succumbed again to her agitation and fairly shook with sobs. "Surely no one could ever do such an inhuman thing as to order a man to fire at his wife and father."

The nearer we got to New South Wales the more apologetic Short became in his epistles, for I had refused to see him at Cape Town, and so for fifty days I had to endure not only being storm tossed but also such appeals to sweet reason as

> ...*I am sure that you will be the last person to hold rancour against a commander who discharges his duty with energy and decision*...

and again,

> *... having weathered our differences, and reached agreement on our separate duties, it is with good hopes that I look to our mutual future in the Colony.*

The craven rogue! I made very certain in my mind that it would be a long and discouraging wait before he took possession of any land grant from me. He used the stratagem of sending Mrs Short across to visit Mrs Putland, 'so that they will not land, friendless in the outpost of civilisation', but Mary found her to be a very common vulgar sort of person, and not at all a gentlewoman, and did nothing to encourage her pretensions.

It was early August when we anchored off Sydney Town. Winter had sailed around the globe with us, but apart from the rain it was not a severe cold in New South Wales, and we quickly were cheered by two frosty mornings that had rime coating the deck, making it treacherous, but which turned into glorious golden days. Golden was the impression of the woodland, for every headland was crowned with the golden flowers of the wattle trees.

Governor King, ex-Governor King, had wisely waited to sight our topsails before planning our official reception, so that I was greeted with a projected delay of four days before I was to be welcomed ashore as the incoming Governor.

"And is it supposed that I shall sit on my bunk for these next four days while every single body on this ship has sought the relief of the shore?"

"Indeed no, Sir." Lieutenant Astbury, King's aide-de-camp, was the bearer of a note from his employer. "Indeed no, Sir, I am to invite you and your party to land this day, and to be received informally at the Government House."

And so it was that I was rowed ashore to my first impressions of New South Wales.

I must confess to a certain disappointment, as I calculated that twenty years had elapsed since settlement, so one might have expected a regular small town to be laid out with public buildings and offices of some size established, but in the scattered village that met my eye no order of any sort was apparent. A rude stone quay had been formed where deep water ran in under a headland to our right, but not of a size to take larger vessels, which perforce must swing to their cables offshore. The central aspect was dominated by a stone barracks, and a poorly constructed prison compound largely fabricated of similar stones. I was to learn that the convicts, apart from those doubly convicted, were largely housed in sheds or shanties, ten or a dozen to each, with one female convict to care for each shanty. The unfortunate doubly-convicted felons were housed on Goat Island, a small rock in the harbour whereon they subsisted more or less as animals.

It was steadily raining as I moved onshore and a dozen clay coloured streams ran down from the heights above us. They looked like sewage, and they smelt like sewage. With the worst will in the world I paddled through them.

"Governor King did not send his carriage as this is an informal visit, Captain Bligh," said Astbury, anxiously.

"And I am to be drenched then, am I?" I had no brief to be pleasant to Astbury under the circumstances.

"No, Sir, the Governor has sent his umbrella," and he unfolded this dignified instrument and held it over my head. We climbed up a well-cut set of stone steps and I paused at their head to take stock.

A crowd of idlers in all sorts of rough dress were sheltering under a timber verandah outside a bond store or warehouse. A commercial enterprise, I presumed, as I observed some trade taking place and a horse dray being loaded in a courtyard. The crowd were motley in the extreme, dressed in rags of corduroy and hessian, but one large rough was arrayed to my astonishment in flounces and furbelows, and his coarse cheeks were scarlet with rouge. He was being clutched fondly by a gentleman, some six inches shorter than he, who was dressed as something of a dandy, in that he affected a billycock hat, and wore a pair of boots, the only man in that company to do so.

A drab young lady lifted her skirts and relieved herself in a doorway.

"Mr Astbury, what are those?"

"Convicts, Sir."

"Convicts? Then why are they not at useful tasks?"

"Why Sir, lacking sufficient wardens and superintendents it is very difficult."

"I will countenance none of this idleness."

"No Sir, however, it is very difficult."

He was a poor sort of fellow, I concluded. I determined to be rid of him as soon as I decently could arrange it.

We came past the barracks and crossed the barracks square. A roughly-formed road ran past what seemed to be a market area. This was their 'High Street', but we didn't follow it, but turned along a lane called Pitt's Row which was ornamented by a gallows-tree, and so into 'O'Connell Street' which led to the glories of Government House. This to my disappointment was a verandahed cottage of two storeys, of mean proportions. I looked at it glumly, but haste was indicated as rain was trickling down my neck. I pushed aside a wooden gate and strode up a dirt path to the main entrance, and so I came, more or less like a thief in the night, to my vice-regal residence.

Governor King invited myself and Mary and Putland to stay at the Government House for the four days before I was to officially 'land' and taking over the reins, assume the government of the Colony, and it was at his dining table that he raised a very agreeable topic indeed.

"Bligh," said he, "I have it in mind to make a gift to you, to honour your elevation to the rank of Governor."

"Indeed, Governor King?" He had my attention.

"A grant of land, Sir, commensurate with your position in the community, of course, and thereby giving you a home, a private residence, here in your Colony, and a status that will carry weight here."

"Would this not be open to questions of propriety?"

"Well, I should think not. Indeed, it is largely by the size of his land holding that the settlers judge a man's merit, so that to be pre-eminent in this vulgar society you must be at least their equal. Of course if you have a positive objection —"

"Indeed no, no objection," I said hastily, while my mind looked at the proposition from all sides. It was, indeed, hard to find an objection.

"Do you mean to give me a house block?"

"Well yes, certainly a house block, here on the Parramatta Road, but a thousand acres on the Hawkesbury would let you greet the 'landed gentry' of our town on equal terms."

"And you have this land at your giving?"

"Certainly, and so shall you. A wise man would not, of course, appropriate grants to himself or his family, and I have not an acre of land to myself, apart from a town property of some fifty acres."

An appropriate gesture in return was becoming, quite obviously, a necessary part of my rejoinder.

"There would be nothing improper in a new Governor granting lands to the man he replaced?"

"Far from improper, it is quite the case here. The usual practice, by way of compensating the departing incumbent for his labours on behalf of the state."

We settled down to it the next day, and with the help of some military scale maps of the settlement we found mutual agreement. In fact I gave nothing to King, in case of imputed scandal, but Mrs Anna King, wife of Governor King, did very nicely, becoming the owner of eight hundred acres of sheep country in the Evan district. I, in return, became squire of two hundred acres adjacent to the township, and a thousand acres at Rouse Hill, on the Hawkesbury road. I wasn't to set eyes on it for some months as the 'roads' here are no turnpikes, not even country lanes, but rutted bullock tracks, and the rain which fell constantly for fourteen days turned them into rivers. I called my new property 'Copenhagen' to perpetuate my claim on history. Mrs King called her new property 'Thanks', which was simply courting ill-informed criticism.

A deputation had waited upon me, to signify their pleasure at my assuming the Governorship, and I took the opportunity to quiz King about its members.

"You may be quite sure," said he, "that the people who greet you with the greatest celerity, and the greatest fawning, are the rogues who have the most to lose if your favours cannot be won."

"Rogues? But surely not!"

"Let me see then if I cannot pick the composition of your welcoming committee. There would have been Atkins, and Johnston, and Blaxland, and MacArthur, of course — MacArthur."

"Who is this MacArthur? He represented himself to me as a gentleman farmer."

"A gentleman farmer! Understand this Bligh — for your governorship will depend on it — there are no gentlemen in this benighted colony. No, not a one. MacArthur is a jumped up corset-maker who bought a commission in the New South Wales Corps and has been a thorn in the side of every Governor from Phillip to myself. You'll do well to grant him little licence for he'll take what he wants soon enough. Jack Bodice is not shy when money or property is involved."

"Jack Bodice?"

"Call him that if you want to earn his undying enmity, but I would suggest you take him cautiously as he commands a great deal of influence."

The next thing was a delegation of townspeople and a yet larger group representing the settlers in the Hunter Valley.

"The last person to represent us" they said, more or less in chorus, "is the rascal MacArthur, for he holds his meat from the market to force up prices, and is a creature of greed and dishonesty."

"Yes," I said. "Dear me, I shall look into it."

My next deputation was not entirely unexpected. Captain Short had been, very visibly, a bundle of energy since our arrival, transporting his stores from the ship into a shed on the wharf and executing numerous domestic as well as commercial transactions.

An ex-clergyman, Lewisham, a transported felon, had so recommended himself to me by his scholarly abilities that I have impressed him as my clerk now the business of government began. It was he, knocking tactfully at my study door, who announced the arrival of Captain Short.

"Bring him in."

He appeared, all affability, smiling and positioning himself abaft a chair for me to invite him to sit. I left him standing.

"What can I do for you, Mr Short?"

"Why Governor, you will not be surprised when I present you with the direction from Lord Camden that I am to be granted 600 acres of land."

"Indeed, and has a ship arrived with fresh mail? I am surprised I am not informed."

His eyes were wary, his mouth was smiling easily but his eyes were wary.

"I offer you the same letter as I have previously tendered, Mr Bligh. I think if you read it again you will find it unambiguous. You are directed to grant me six hundred acres of land."

"It will be my pleasure to do so — when the official notice arrives."

"You hold a grudge against me!"

"There may be excellent reason for me to do so, but no, I will administer my Colony without fear or favour, so you may take comfort that your extraordinary behaviour will in no way prejudice your grant, if and when it is confirmed."

He took up his letter, and turned to go. While he was putting his mind to an appropriate parting salvo I passed him a document I had sitting on the desk awaiting dispatch.

"Seeing you have been kind enough to call in you have saved me a messenger."

He took the paper and broke the seal. I watched with some interest as he digested the contents.

His face turned white, then flamed a dark crimson. I was interested as it is a phenomenon one reads of in fictional accounts.

* * * * *

"And was it bad news for him, Sir?"

"Well yes, it was rather, Mrs Peebles. I served him with

papers committing him to a court martial. He went back to London for his trial, so that was the end of his grant."

"And was he found guilty Sir?"

"No," I said regretfully, "but he had to sell off his goods there in Sydney for somewhat less than he expected to make for them, so that chastened him somewhat. Oh, and his wife died on the trip back."

"Oh no, Admiral, but then you mustn't reproach yourself for that. That would not be your fault, would it?"

I was a little taken aback. It had never occurred to me that I should reproach myself.

"Well," I said, after some consideration of the point, "as a matter of fact, Mrs Peebles, I don't believe she was a great loss to him."

Chapter Eleven

Further recollections of New South Wales — my vain attempt to treat
MacArthur as a man of integrity — an unfortunate lapse with Mrs
Peebles — my attempt to discipline MacArthur frustrated by the New
South Wales Corps — the Corps rises in open rebellion — I am placed
under house arrest! — bad dreams, and recovery

Ah, conscience! Lucky indeed is the man without a conscience!
It was certainly not my fault that Captain Short lost his wife —
Mrs Peeble's consolations, though well-meant, were unnecessary — and I find it hard to remember any circumstances in
which I acted shamefully or improperly. But conscience, or shall
we say vile memory, pursues me yet.

John Norton, he of the blood-red eyes, found me in Port
Jackson. The cloak of vice-regal dignity had done nothing to
save me from his nightmare pursuit. I had woken shivering...

* * * * *

Daylight was rising in the East as I came to the window and
pulling a shawl around me, for it was chilly though a fine
day promised, I sat a small while to recover my composure.
Six o'clock, or daybreak was the usual time I arose, and the
spring of 1807 being upon us it was usually light enough to
ride out at six on my tour of the works.

Jubb rode daily with me, and Lewisham came a few times
in early days, but the man was not fit to be seated on the
poorest nag without a leading rein, so that he still rose early,
but opened our office, and sought to impose some order on
the petitioners who waited upon me each morning.

A great reputation for wisdom could be gained by a little
foreknowledge of the character or circumstances accompanying each grievance. Thus, I might look into a dispute
about the breaking of a contract to supply bricks, to find
pencilled at the foot of my brief, in Lewisham's precise
copperplate writing, notes to the effect that Rogers, the

plaintiff, was generally considered a rogue, and he was still defaulting on a payment to the Government Store for meat supplied during last year's distress.

Lewisham was so invaluable as a clerk that I readily accepted his disabilities on a horse.

The Sydney Town I gazed down on as the sky lightened was already vastly improved from the squalid camp I had squelched through fourteen months before.

The public buildings, the fort which had only been half built, the granary, and the church were all either finished, or well under construction. Drainage had been my first priority, for you cannot build a town in a cess pit, and now even after a week of rain the principle roads were all firm and passable, though a stain of yellow clay spread half across Sydney Cove. The stench of open sewage lying in pools the previous summer had been such that even my stomach was revolted by it. Privy pits, and our new drains, rebuilt entirely in accordance with the usual demands of gravity, were destined to make this summer vastly less noisome — and make us all a great deal less likely to succumb to cholera.

I had particular reason to attend to the drains, since the cholera had brought a great grief to my daughter Mary. Putland, her husband, had contracted this vile disease, and died in her arms. I had thoughtfully arranged a number of domestic duties for Mary, which served to lessen her sense of loss, besides providing additional support for myself.

Presently, hearing movement in the office — and so commodious and spacious was the Governor's residence that I swear I could hear Lewisham sharpening his quill! — hearing movement I say, I donned a jacket over my nightshirt and went down to confront him with the fruit of my disturbed sleep.

"Lewisham."

"Good morning your Excellency."

"Have a look at this? Tell me what you think." I handed him a sheet of paper.

What disturbed me was the lack of a yeomanry class in New South Wales, that and the lack of women, apart from the convict women, and they were pretty well picked over by my gallant military you may be sure.

Lewisham laid the paper down on his bench and frowned over it. I write a regular hand and he was familiar with it, but I had been writing on a tablet held on my knee at the window, and it was a hurried effort.

"It is meant as a proclamation?"

"An advertisement, do you see? To circulate through the counties at home. Ireland and Scotland too, maybe. There is a lot of unemployment and it could do very well."

He read in silence.

Notice
To All Unemployed Mechanics And Artisans
Free Migration
Is Offered To Married Couples Wishing
To Find Employment And Opportunity
In
The Crown Colony Of New South Wales

Those applying must have a trade such as stonemason, carpenter, farrier, millhand, wheelwright, smith, or have experience as shepherd, bullock driver, or other useful agricultural skills.

Unmarried sisters may accompany the couple if they possess skills in house service.

Application should be made in the first instance to:

> *Geo. Beckridge and Partners*
> *Agents and Providers*
> *Chesburrow Lane; London*

"Very well set out," he said cautiously.

"And...?"

"You'll attract every gypsy and vagabond in the kingdom."

"Attract them yes, but we have no need to accept them."

"Geo. Beckridge and Partners will be busy."

"We need somebody to assess the applicants, and to reserve the berths."

"And who will be paying the passage money?"

"Aah, yes, that's the point I wish to discuss with you."

"You do realise, Sir, begging your pardon, but the Crown has in place a policy of discouraging free settlers."

"New South Wales will never progress as long as it remains a penal colony."

"With respect, Sir, I wonder if the Colonial office wishes it to progress? The American colonies took our convicts for thirty years, but then progress shut the door on transportation. Lord Castlereagh will be very wary of the same situation developing here."

I got down to my second concern.

"Whatever his lordship's policies, it is perfectly clear that we must have farmers or we shall starve, and we must have masons or we shall perish in the winters. My mandate was to make the Colony self-sufficient in all respects. One doesn't have to stretch that direction too far to include the need for marriageable females to restore a balance. The sodomy that goes on here passes belief, and it's completely open, as if it were the most natural state in all the world. Raddled old hags parading in grubby finery with painted faces, and the fate of some of the youths thrown into the stews of the barracks doesn't bear thinking of. We had two suicides last month, as you are aware."

"Can Sir Joseph Banks do anything for us, Sir?"

"I'm pinning my hopes on his influence, and no one has more say in the affairs of the Colony. He tends to treat it as his own pet fief."

"If any success is to be gained then recruiting centres will be needed in the main towns and boroughs. The class of immigrant you are looking for will probably never have been to London in his life."

"That's very true." This problem had bothered me, too.

"So we need official approval that our net be cast wide through town officials and we can then leave it to your agent to co-ordinate the passages."

"Make a fair copy and I'll forward it to Banks in the next parcel of reports and requisitions, and a copy can go to Camden, with a covering letter establishing the need."

"Camden, Sir, I understand is very much in Captain MacArthur's pocket — that is the common understanding."

"So much the better, then. MacArthur will see reason in the campaign for free settlers. More customers for his produce, more grist for his mill."

"You will not have forgotten that the Captain has an appointment with you at noon?"

I had forgotten. "What does he want?"

"The matter of his land grant, Sir, a very generous grant of nearly five thousand acres."

"And is that not enough? I understand it contains some of the finest land in the country?"

"He wants ten thousand acres."

"He won't get it! Ten thousand acres, Lewisham, for a corset-maker! No man should hold ten thousand acres, it's immoral!"

"He claims a promise of a further five thousand acres when his scheme to grow fine wool here has been proven successful."

"He was at odds with Sir Joseph Banks over importing the sheep, was he not? He'll work a long time before I take his part against Sir Joseph."

"How many copies then, Sir?"

"Just do one for Banks, and one for our records. I must use my greatest tact to gain MacArthur's support for the ideas."

We were walking in the garden — not the cottage garden that struggles before, but on the lawns behind. Not Versailles, you know, but a gravelled walk, with a stone wall for shelter and privacy.

" ... and so, if you see virtue in the idea, I will welcome your support, for we will need all the influence we can bring to bear on the people at home to endorse our emigration scheme."

I'd put it to him fair and square, "We've had our differences," I'd said, "but I know we both want the same thing — a successful thriving Colony."

"What bothers me" he said in his unpleasant high-pitched voice, "what bothers me is how I am to depasture five thousand sheep on a little over four thousand miserable acres?"

He carelessly crushed my manifesto into his waistcoat pocket. The damned fellow hadn't listened to a word I'd said.

"Five thousand acres," I said "and some of the best grazing country in the Colony. Why, I'm told you could run a sheep on each and every single acre."

"Over a thousand acres is heavily wooded, and where am I to find men to clear it? You have taken all the convicts labouring on my property."

"Half of them, true, but you still have more assigned convicts than any other two men in the Colony. The best thing I can do for you colonial landed gentry" —I didn't plan it as a sneer, but it sounded a little suspect even to my ears — "the very best policy I can pursue is to arrange a supply of shepherds, smiths, ploughmen, servants, all Sir, available to be hired by you, all mouths to eat your mutton."

"It is perfectly tiresome," said my fine gentleman, "how every person in this Colony regards a sheep as being a bag full of cutlets. My sheep are bred for fine wool, and with that, if you can take a longer view than your dinner table, then you will see it as our best chance to establish a pastoral industry."

His impertinence was truly astounding.

"What are your blasted flocks to me, Sir?"

"I should expect a sailor to have no knowledge at all of the demands of an agricultural settlement."

"I will bid you good day, Captain."

"Do I get my lands?"

"Certainly not."

"Governor," his whining voice was now clearly intending a sneer, "I shall then convey my requests direct to Lord Camden."

"Mr MacArthur, sail too close to the wind and you may be caught in stays."

He gave me a hard look. I'd thought it pretty neat — 'caught in stays' do you see, for a corset-maker — a pretty play on words. MacArthur was certainly overly defensive of his background for he took my *double entendre* at once.

"You will regret that, Sir," and he turned on his heel.

* * * * *

"Will you take some chocolate or coffee, Sir?"

"Brandy and hot water."

"But Sir, Miss Elizabeth has said you are not..."

"Brandy and hot water!"

Mrs Peebles flushed and went quickly out of the room.

Elizabeth knows that it irks me to be treated as an invalid. The shrew was paying me in kind for my hasty remarks about her blasted *fiancé*.

I pulled my mind back from the mud and dust. 'Mud *and* dust?' I hear you say. Yes, mud and dust, and sometimes on the same day in Sydney Town. The only thing that never changed was the rancour.

There was no doubt, if I sold now I would make a good return on my colonial holdings, but give it five years, or ten, and they could fetch anything. There's a shortage of good land between the coast and the ranges, and even though Blaxland boasted of his 'road' across the mountains, it's a week or ten days from the markets.

I was feeling affable as Mrs Peebles returned with my jorum of brandy, and kettle. I drank the brandy, then rang for another. To my surprise she brought it without demur, and as I sipped it my affability grew in proportion.

It may have been the effect of the brandy, or the willow-bark, but as she stood beside me in the sunlight I was taken by the need for physical comfort in a way that has not gripped me for some years. I pulled her towards me and although she looked deep and strangely into my eyes, she said no word at all, nor did she resist my embrace.

It felt very good, very warm and necessary to hold a living person. I felt my strength rise in me and my virility stirred as I pressed her body to mine.

I felt an urge to talk, to communicate, to make promises and commitments, but though a man's groin may stay young, his head will grow old, so I held my tongue.

She had continued looking into my eyes, but now she moved a half step closer. Her hair brushed my cheek and her head was at my shoulder.

Freed from her gaze my eyes took inventory of her body, and my ardour died somewhat. The back of her neck presented for my inspection was wrinkled, and some detached grey hairs, coarse and bristly, were to be found. Her bosom was full and fine as it pressed against my chest, and I moved my hand to grapple with its abundance, but as I did I caught a whiff in my nostrils, of her body odour, and I tell you, she smelt like an old woman. Like an old woman.

Suddenly I felt foolish, and I was urgent to be quit of her. I unwound my arms, and taking her by the shoulders I put her aside, gently, not roughly, but too gently.

She was inclined to stay, and I suspected ready to reveal her emotions.

I quailed.

"Very well, Mrs Peebles," was all I found to say.

"Admiral Bligh?"

"Very well, Mrs Peebles, very well, we shall talk of this another time."

Her gaze was soft, not forward, but definitely soft.

"I think you had better go now."

She looked at me again, and smiled, then collecting the tray she smiled again and left the room. It seemed to me that her air as she left the room had changed indefinably. She came in as the housekeeper. What did she see herself as, as she withdrew? It was a consideration that made me uneasy.

My heart was pounding unpleasantly, and my head began to ache.

What had led me into behaving like that? Was it some weakness in my mind? The fumes of brandy had blown away leaving my mind cold and thin — and appalled. What was I to do with her?

Did she see me as a foolish old buffoon? It didn't really matter what she saw me as, that was what I saw myself as, and it hurt. Also, I had a very good idea of how Elizabeth would view the matter. I imagined her scorn, and flinched at the thought of her sarcasm. I wanted another brandy, but would not call her back.

I retired to bed, and my thoughts returned to New South Wales...

* * * * *

"It's Constable Oakes to see you Sir."

"What hour is it?"

"Three in the morning."

I pulled on a robe and struggled downstairs.

"Now Jubb, where is your constable?"

"He is waiting in the pantry Sir."

"In the pantry!"

"The butler's pantry Sir."

There was a small alcove in the hallway, designated to hold silver and glassware, and concealed by a screen. We termed it the butler's pantry, but it often served as an office for humble interviews.

"Bring him into the parlour, and blow some life into the fire."

The fire was damped down, but consisting of a basket of tree roots it still held its heat.

"Now, Constable?"

"Sir, I have a communication, a note from Captain MacArthur."

"Why at this hour? Where have you been at?"

"Mr Atkins, Sir, sent me with a warrant to Captain MacArthur. I didn't arrive at Parramatta until eleven o'clock last night, Sir."

"And did you serve your warrant?"

"Sir, I did, but the Captain gave me this letter to bring back."

I read the letter with tightened lips. MacArthur and Atkins were of course at each other's throats, but this time MacArthur had pushed it too far. It appeared to be the opportunity that I had been waiting for.

Since my little talk with him about his blasted sheep, the damned fellow had been probing and seeking how far he could go in disobedience and law breaking. He appeared to think himself the very devil of a fellow, and his toadying cronies in the regiment had encouraged his belief that he was above the law.

Firstly he had imported an illegal still, against my very explicit ban on such equipment, and he refused to surrender it to the officers I had sent to confiscate it. He and I then had a further run in over a trading vessel of his which had put to sea with two runaway convicts stowed away. The sheriff had nailed a proclamation to the mast impounding the vessel on its return, but I was deuced if the fellow had not had it sail away in defiance of the court order. He was apparently set on a showdown.

He may have bluffed Phillip, and Hunter and poor King, but he will find I am little impressed by bravado. I agreed with Atkins that the best place for this puffed up pantaloon would be in Court.

Mr Oakes, said the letter,

> *You will inform the persons who sent you here with the warrant you have now shown me and given me a copy of, that I never will submit to the horrid tyranny that is attempted, until I am forced; that I receive it with scorn and contempt, as I consider the persons who have directed it to be executed.*

J. MacArthur

"And have you shown this reply to Mr Atkins?"

"Yes Sir, he sent me straight over here to you Sir."

"I shall assemble a court in the morning."

I scribbled a note.

"Here Jubb!" I called down the passage, and when that worthy appeared I sent him to seal the letter with wax. It directed Atkins to assemble a civil court to pursue the matter of MacArthur's defiance. I particularly told him to include Colonel George Johnston on the bench. If MacArthur was going to defy the court I wanted the military involved on the side of the angels; then I sent Mr Oakes off with the letter to re-disturb Atkins. I had thought to send Jubb, but Oakes had spent all that night riding from pillar to post, so one more trip was not going to hurt him.

Then I went back to bed, and slept soundly with the comforting thought that MacArthur had overstepped himself, and that the problem was going to resolve itself.

It was a rather grim dinner party.

"It's a damned conspiracy." I said. "The officers mess are in it up to their necks. They had a mess dinner the night before the trial, and they rehearsed their villainy there."

What hurt me most was that while planning this villainy they drank a pipe of South African claret I had donated to the mess.

"Grimes was there, and the two Blaxlands, and the MacArthur puppy, and Blaxcell, MacArthur's cousin."

Gore was my provost-marshal, a sound old stick.

"Was Johnston there?"

"No Sir, he found occasion to seclude himself in his home at Annandale."

I poked at my mutton. It was greasy and congealing but my heart was hot, and my brain was busy to come at the damned conspirators.

"And Mr Gore, do you tell me that the members of the court actually formed a military guard to shield MacArthur from arrest by the constables?"

"Aye, they did that."

"I'll have them all cashiered for this."

It was the damnedest thing. The only military force within 5,000 miles of this benighted Colony represented the very forces of evil and corruption that I was trying to stamp out.

"Sir," Lewisham was at my shoulder with a salver bearing a letter.

"What's this?" I ran my knife under the seal, substituting a smear of gravy for the wax. The writing was damnable, the sentiments weren't much better.

"Here's a demand from those treacherous curs of officers. They demand that I appoint a new Judge Advocate to the court. Then they will consider the case."

"But indeed, Sir" — Lewisham was anxious to advise me.

"I have no doubt that Mr Lewisham wishes to point out that I have absolutely no powers to interfere with the judiciary."

It was true, I had no power to replace Atkins as Judge Advocate, any more than I could interfere with a judge sitting at the county assizes in Devon.

A legal dispute having taken the minds and voices of my distinguished dinner companions, I took the opportunity to seek Lewisham's opinion of the communication he had delivered.

"Now what?" His opinion was usually sound.

"What we need now is a regiment of grenadier guards to back up the proper legislative, Sir."

It was a wonderful idea, but it was not, alas, very practicable.

"*Quis custodiat ipses custodes*?" I asked — a little Latin tag I had picked up.

"*Ipsos custodes*" he corrected, "Who shall be in charge of those who are set in charge?"

I banged on the table, and everyone turned to look at me.

"*Ipsos custodes*." Lewisham and Crossley looked at me expectantly. The rest of them seemed to think I was announcing custard for dessert.

"*Ipsos custodes* includes Major George Johnston. I want him here, and I want him before me first thing tomorrow. I want every magistrate in this Colony who is not associated with this damned set of military rascals to sit as a court tomorrow, I want Atkins there, and I want him stone cold sober."

I took a breath, and a moment to consider, then completed my inventory.

"I want all the papers produced in that court today impounded, and I want Mr MacArthur back in jail. We'll see who is running this blasted Colony."

"Do you propose to try MacArthur again tomorrow, Governor?"

"Mr Gore, I propose to have him rot in gaol for the rest of this year. Tomorrow's court is to arraign these treacherous officers and send them home to face trial."

"To England for trial?"

"To England, for trial for sedition!"

There was a thoughtful silence, broken at length by Crossley rising with a glass of burgundy in his hands.

"A toast!" he called. "His Excellency, and confusion to his enemies."

It was rather in this spirit that we concluded the evening,

to await the tumultuous event of the morrow. Lewisham was waiting with a candle as I collected my effects.

"Sir?"

"Yes Lewisham."

"There is I believe a naval vessel due within the week."

His voice was low, and he was not making small talk. I looked at him narrowly to divine the thrust of his thoughts.

"H.M.S. *Porpoise* is due, yes."

"With a complement of Naval Officers, and no doubt a marine detachment?"

"Undoubtedly." I took his line and the more I thought about it the better I liked it.

"You have commanded Colonel Johnston to attend here in the morning?"

"But you do not think the senior military commander may be relied upon to arrive in the morning."

"I have considerable doubts."

"But the senior naval officer in the southern hemisphere is here present."

"That is unquestioned."

"A naval court."

"They will do their duty."

"You can rely on it — a guard of marines for the court-house."

"They will be yours to command."

"And a battery of eighteen pounders commanding the barracks."

"Almost the equal of a regiment of grenadiers, Sir."

He was right, but the damned ship was not here yet.

"You must temporise, Sir, you must delay a showdown until the naval vessel is at anchor."

He was right. The damnable thing was I had put things in motion for the morrow. MacArthur would be back in prison, six officers in court.

I pointed this out.

"Mr Atkins may be ill, Sir?"

Lewisham had a truly Machiavellian streak, there was no question about it. "Is he not fond of rum?"

"He will drink it, when he can't procure whisky or brandy."

"I believe we have a case of brandy in our cellar."

"I shall see to it, Sir," said my admirable clerk, and I wished him good-night and retired feeling rather more cheerful at the prospects of the next few weeks.

The next day, the twenty-sixth of January, was one of the hot gusty days, with a dry wind from the interior parching the very dust we were breathing.

I had the gardener, a convict called Partridge — most apt of names, for he had joined our brave colony of adventurers as a direct result of poaching his very namesake — I had him watering the paths, but his endeavour was so wanting that he made no impact at all, the nearer end of the carriageway being desiccated before he made good the further.

A haze hung around the horizon, and I had little doubt that a bank of cloud would block out the afternoon as precursor to the wind backing right around to the south-east.

I was in the office early to arrange the day's business. Griffin, my bookkeeper, was despatched before 10 o'clock to prompt Mr Gore to arrest MacArthur, and he left full of importance, and haste, and armed with a warrant from the Judge Advocate and signed by my three tame magistrates.

About an hour before noon, Carrock, clerk of the courts, sent me a note to the effect that the six officers had gathered at the courthouse and reconstituted the court with a view to restoring MacArthur to his previous bail.

I thought it best to ignore their written requests for the Judge Advocate to be replaced, so after some short consideration, I gave them no answer at all.

"Let them sit till they rot." I said to Crossley. "They will then have time to reflect on their treachery."

I understand they sat in impatient judicial indignation and apprehension until about three o'clock, when they returned to their barracks, undoubtedly to foment mischief!

I decided to put them out of their misery and had a note conveyed to each, directing his attendance before me the next morning to explain their conduct.

This initiative was approved by Campbell and Palmer and Williamson at the dinner that night — not that we dwelt upon the judicial strife overly much. The change in the weather had not blown in, and in spite of a mechanical fan overhead our enjoyment of dinner was diminished by the heat and the large number of flying insects that defeated the muslin window cloths, and dashed at our candles.

One could not take a quaff of wine without taking in one or more besotted beetles!

We had turned to some limp goat's milk cheese and a dish of fruit when Atkins came bursting in, his neckcloth all ends up, and his eyes bulging out of his head with fright.

"Governor!" he gasped out, without any formality of greeting. "There is a great movement in Barrack Square, and the military are all under arms."

I drained my glass, spat out a beetle, and looked at him steadily until he collected his wits.

"And do you believe that they intend to attack my person?"

"I have no doubt but that they will."

I filled my glass again, and stepped into the window that looked down O'Connell St. There were certainly torches flickering but I could discern no movement. The curtains billowed in with a breath of cooler air, and my ear picked up the beat of a drum.

'The British Grenadiers' it was picking out, as I presently could make out the pipes. There could be little doubt that it was the regimental band — no one could mistake the quality of their rendition of almost any unfortunate tune that fell to their mercies

"A toast to King George," I said, steadily enough, "and then gentlemen I think it in your interests to retire while I dress in a suitable uniform to receive this military deputation."

Campbell had gone very white about his mouth, but said, staunchly enough, "Nay Governor, I shall stay and support you."

"And what damnation good will that do, do you think? No, be off with you. I have no doubt their nerve will fail them before they actually commit a mutiny against the Crown."

Dunn was waiting at the head of the stair.

"What shall us do, Governor, shall us bar the windies?"

"No, you fool, you will get out my dress tunic, and I shall make a thrust to outface the rogues."

He scurried to the press and handed out my uniform, his hands shaking so badly that I dispensed with his further help and sent him packing.

I had a little trouble with the buttoning. My blasted eyes work very well at six feet or at 6 inches, but matters in between do tend to blur, but it was done and I came to the glass to fix my Camperdown medal to my breast. By now the rattle of the music was drawing distinctly close, and I heard some coarse cheering and some muffled commands. The shutters were drawn across the window and I moved forward and peered down through the crack.

Surely enough, they were marching to Government House. I looked in disbelief. The entire regiment were armed and advancing in a ragged column with the band at their head. With wry amusement I saw Lieutenant Compton, in charge of the Government House Guard, running this way and that, beside himself with indecision as to the part assigned to him in the charade that was taking place. Discretion, I felt, would win the day, and so it proved, but as the head of the heroic column swung into the carriageway they were challenged and brought to a halt.

At first I could not make out what was taking place, and then I saw.

It was Mary, Mary, my daughter, my brave daughter. Mary placed herself in the gateway, defying the bayonets, and her voice floated back to me.

"You traitors, you rebels, you shall not enter! You have just walked over the grave of my husband, and now you come to murder my father! You shall not enter!"

Nor would she be put aside, but fought off restraining hands, and continued to shout defiance. Her courage brought a lump to my throat, but came also strangely close to unmanning me.

"... to murder my father," she had said. Was that what they planned? The possibility of personal harm had not occurred to me in planning to oppose the ruffians. But none had gainsaid it. I felt a wave of revulsion weaken my knees so that I staggered and nearly fell. A wave of bayonets had swept past Mary, who was restrained by a burly sergeant, but continued to defy them. I suppose I have an unreasoning fear of the cold steel of a clumsy bayonet in the hands of an undisciplined oaf. I took a deep breath, and walked steadily enough to the stairhead to confront Johnston, who I presumed had arrived belatedly and belligerently to my summons.

As I reached the stair-head the first of the rascals poured into the hallway, and like a pack of cur dogs began ransacking it, ripping their bayonets through tapestry hangings and throwing furniture down. It looked, for all the world like a Robespierrian mob, no officer restraining their violence.

All thought of confronting them vanished and keeping to the shadows I hastened back down the passageway. Gaining time was of the essence. Given time the ordinary farmers would rise in my support, given time I could still slip away and find refuge in the Hawkesbury district, where the free settlers saw me as their champion against the Regiment. Given time, please God, *Porpoise* might round the heads and drop anchor in the bay. There was a thunder of boots on the stair and I darted into a servants' bedroom, and across to the window. A short drop to the kitchen roof and thence to the stables. But it was not to be, a line of sentinels ringed the house.

I was sobbing with fear and frustration now as the coarse shouts and the ring of steel came closer.

"Search well you dogs, and do your duty" it was the coarse shout of Sergeant Sutherland.

"I'll have your tripes for garters you bastard," I thought, "if I come out of this." There was a bed in the alcove and I wormed underneath, then by bracing legs and arms against the bedposts I lifted my body up into the bottom of the mattress so that a casual searcher looking under the bedstead would not descry me.

The door banged open and a number of the searchers tumbled into the room. The press was pulled down, and then I flinched as a bayoneted rifle swept back and forward across the floor.

"Not under here."

"He's gone to ground somewhere, we'll have him."

My arms were trembling with the effort to hold me up, but my fear had been washed away by rage. They tramped from the room, and with enormous relief I let myself down.

Now I had a new fear, that I would be discovered in a position that could sully my reputation.

I scrambled out, brushing feathers from my jacket and was thus engaged when the door banged open again and I was forced back against the bed with a bayonet at my throat.

"Don't kill me!" I said urgently.

Down we went in jubilant and noisy procession to the drawing-room, which was crowded with military wretches all to my eye affected by liquor and all bristling with bayonets. I looked for Johnston, but Lieutenant Moore approached me with a letter.

Addressed in very formal terms, it required me to resign my authority and submit to arrest. I thought to tear it into pieces but, on a second thought I realised its importance as material evidence of the wretched treachery. I folded it carefully and put it in my pocket.

"Well?" It was Moore, the impudent puppy.

"Well what, Sirrah?"

He looked disconcerted. "What am I to tell the Colonel?"

"You address me as Your Excellency, and you ask my permission to speak, you damned whipsnotting blaggard."

After a belligerent pause, he correctly decided that he was considerably out of his depth, and with a sign I was pushed and pulled into the adjoining study, where I found the gallant Colonel, somewhat red of face, and to my mind looking twice as scared as his victim. He was accompanied by Jameson, Blaxcell, and two Blaxlands and Edward MacArthur, in short every thug and villain in Port Jackson, except one.

Johnston began bleating and blustering as soon as he saw me, in an effort, I imagine, to bolster his courage and confidence.

I heard out his calumnies and excuses without a word, which seemed to shake him the more.

"Have you finished?" He had explained that he acted in

the public interest in relieving me of my duties, and to prevent a public insurrection.

"Why then" I said "let us dispense with the services of your corrupt regiment and take our case to the people."

I quoted Marcus Aurelius to him.

> *Thou hast enclosed infinite troubles through not being content with thy ruling capacity when it does the things which it is constituted by nature to do.*

Fairly apt, I thought, but his flushed gaze demonstrated all the intelligence of a Cape baboon.

"You have been deposed, and that is fact," he shouted. "What do you have to say to that?"

There was a murmur of support from the jackals around him.

"You address me as Excellency, Johnston," I said, provoking a barrage of abuse from the rabble, "and I have this to say — on the twenty-ninth of October, 1792, I was at Portsmouth Harbour to see Ellison, Birkett, and Millward hanged by their necks until they were dead. You may have forgotten their names but they were all mutineers off the *Bounty*. I look forward to the day when I return to Portsmouth to see you hang in chains."

I looked around carefully.

"I assure you, gentlemen, I shall remember everyone in this room, and one other who is too craven to appear."

There was an angry murmur from all of them, and I believe that if left to the Blaxlands' mercy I should have been despatched on the spot.

As it eventuated, I was left under guard in Government House with just Mrs Putland, my Mary and Lewisham, and the cook. House arrest it was, close confinement, and twelve months of it to follow, though of course I did not know that then.

* * * * *

I knew when I awoke that the bronchitis had my lungs again. My mouth was bone dry and my forehead was burning, my breathing was short and laboured as if a ton weight pressed on my chest. I coughed to seek relief from the congestion that was strangling me, but my wind passages burnt as if they were red raw, so that I was scared to cough again. There was a pain in my head it seemed at the roots of my eyelids. My body was hot and sweating, and I struggled to a half sitting position against the pillows and bolster. My teeth felt loose and tender, which I have noticed is always a sign of high fever in myself.

I reached for a glass tumbler of water, but in my sudden weakness I could only swallow a mouthful, and some I spilt down my bedding. The water set me coughing again, and the pain made a red mist that blocked out everything. My nose ran clear fluid and tears started from my eyes.

When I could see, I reached out for a bell, a small bell that I kept at my bedside, and rang it as loudly as I could manage.

No one came, and I threw it with a feeble bad temper against the wall.

Presently I heard footsteps coming.

"Jane?" I croaked, but it was Mrs Peebles.

"Why Sir? — Good Lord!" She took stock of my distressed condition and came to me in alarm. Her reactions were sure and comfortable. I imagine it is an inbuilt facility in women, to care for invalids. I was straightened against my pillows, my fore-head mopped with a cooling towel, the bell and the tumbler picked up.

"Medicine — mixture." I whispered to her.

She put her head close to hear, and I saw again the coarse grey hairs. Then like a fool she began preparing me a draught of the willow-bark.

"No!"

What I wanted was the squill syrup with camphor that eases my breathing, paregoric it has in it, or laudanum, and it is sovereign against the rawness of bronchitis. Fortunately Jane came in, and she well knew what I needed.

"No, Mrs Peebles, not the black draught, but this brown linctus."

"Papa, Papa, how are you? Is it bad again — there, don't answer." Jane can nurse me, I have confidence, but it was Mrs Peebles who gave me the linctus, grating the spoon against my teeth.

There was nothing overt she did or said, nothing that Jane noticed, but I was conscious of a change in her attitude. There was a degree of possessiveness, or was I being overly sensitive, was the fever in my veins inflaming my sensitivities?"

"He must rest now." There it was, she found herself in a position to give the commands, and to regulate my life. I did not like it. I turned my head to look at Jane, with some effort, as my muscles were aching, but she had apparently noticed nothing. They tiptoed out, leaving me to my reflections.

Gloomy enough they were. Complications seemed to encompass me, and I needed my vigour to guide my little domestic ship between the perils of material threat to my daughters security, and emotional threats that might break us asunder. The mixture was giving me some relief, and presently Anne came, mouselike, to peep and see if I could take some nourishment. She had an eggnog, beaten with some honey, and thought it might soothe my throat. I thought so too, and sipped it. It tasted dreadful.

"You mustn't pull such a face, Papa, you must drink it all, if you can, because Jane says it will be good for you."

"Did Jane prepare it?"

"Oh no, Mrs Peebles beat it up. She thought it was what you needed, too."

I put the cup down on the bedside table, nor would her entreaty make me reconsider.

"I do very well thank you, but now I must rest."

"Oh yes — I will go." A world of worry and disappointment.

"Will you not stay? You might sew — you will not disturb me, but no one else must come in."

Her face lighted, poor child, and she settled to her vigil, her face so close to her embroidery that I worried she might run a needle in her eye.

All was peaceful, and the laudanum had reached my veins so that I drowsed. It was a disturbed fretful drowsing, so that images came before me and I scarcely knew what was dream, and what was actually taking place...

Elizabeth came before me with her Richard, and he placed his arm around her, and thanked me for blessing their union, and she was dressed all in lavender, and looked not unlike my dear wife, but he placed a ring on her finger and she smiled at him, and there was a severance of the bond between us. I felt it snap like a band of elastic, and she was no longer my daughter to command, no longer my daughter to run my household, no longer my daughter to nurse me in my infirmity, no longer my daughter.

"No!" I called, "you mustn't!" But they waved and smiled, as if they could not hear my protest, and then they began to diminish. They did not walk away, they just diminished in size, small, then smaller, as if dwarfs, then to a speck, a moth in the sunlight that fell through my fingers and vanished.

I called out in grief, and Elizabeth's hand was holding me, and bathing my brow with water.

"You came back to me."

"Papa!" It was Anne. "I haven't left you, I haven't left you."

I clutched her hand, and held it, and weakness laid my head back on the pillows, and my thoughts swirled and wandered again. The window was a bright oblong, divided by a lattice frame, and it took my attention so that I could discern naught else. It seemed to grow larger, then smaller, or was it just the degree of brightness intensifying? I tried to fasten it into reality by calculating the area of each pane, as a proportion of the whole. If it was five feet by two feet, then it had an area of ten square feet. Good. Now count the panes. There were seven, therefore each pane was a seventh of ten square feet, which must be one thousand four hundred and forty square inches — but say, there was something wrong, for the panes were arranged in an even pattern, so how could there be seven? I squinted to see it, but the brightness waxed so that I must look away. I shut my eyes but the image persisted green against the inside of my lids. It floated across my lids, changing in colour to a dull mustard, but I could not focus on it to order the panes, and presently it turned to a crimson, and was lost to my sight. That is to say, it was still there but lost to my sight.

Anne leant against me, cradling my head, and I thought to caution her, for I hold that the sick carry a miasma, that can infect the healthy. But as I held her hand I was too late, for her breath became hoarse and her skin went dry, and to my distress, as I looked at her soft, slender, vulnerable neck, the silken hairs thickened into coarse grey stubble, and I was conscious of the rank odour of her body. I pushed her away in alarm and revulsion, and then I knew it had been Mrs Peebles all along, pretending to be Anne. I lay still, sweating and grasping the iron frame of the bed with my hand, clutching it for reality. It anchored me to the present, but the window was clawing at my lids, desperate to find my attention, and it shone right through the skin of my closed lids, and I could see a drumbeat vibrating through it. It was a familiar picture, but my mind could not find its precedent. Then a whole shaft of drumbeats fell into the light and shook into order, like iron filings scattered over a magnet, and the order that was formed turned a chaos of percussion into a regimental marching tune.

This time I was ready for him, and I met him at the top of the steps, and set him at defiance.

"Where is that poltroon who sent you?" It was a maddening detail, I had had the name on my tongue as I started to speak, but it was gone when I needed it, nor would it come back as long as I searched for it.

But my words were enough, for Johnston shouted back and his face was ashen, and he hung his head.

"Did you expect me to take flight? Did you expect me to cower and hide from you? Nelson commended me at Copenhagen."

"Why did you fire at them when they surrendered?"

"I turned a blind eye"

"MacArthur," the name had come to me. But it was wrong because I was talking to Nelson surely?

"A blind eye," I persisted, but I could not turn a blind eye for the window image was floating in front of me again. I put my hands to my eyes, but the light on my lids was still there.

It changed shape to an oval. I was suddenly terrified it was going to change into the head of John Norton. I forced my eyes open, and Anne was staring down at me.

"Anne — you must get rid of your turkeys."

"Papa, they are not my turkeys."

"They must go, they must go."

"Papa, they are Jane's turkeys."

I gazed at her in incomprehension, and then Frances was there with Elizabeth, back again but as I tried to look at them they floated away, and were gone.

A bell was ringing, and each clap sent a spurt of flame through my eyes, and the flame rasped into my brain with an ice-cold pain.

The bed was rolling slightly but my body accommodated to the motion easily, not so pleasant was the shower of spray that came aft every time it dug its nose into a wave. My face was dripping but my lips were dry and cracked. I have thought of something that had best be done at once, if it were to be done at all, but now I could not bring it to mind, and a sense of panic was close. I shouted at him in the bow.

"We must turn her, mister, take an oar," — but when he turned, it was not Fryer, in the dim light and the haze I could not at once place him.

"You've got water, Captain." He held out his hand.

"No more than your ration — drink it and it's gone."

I fumbled for my coco-nut shell, but it was lost. He came down the launch holding out his hand to me, and with a shout I realised it was him.

"A long time, Captain."

"A long time, Christian." My voice came from I knew not where.

"Did you think I would leave you?"

"I knew you would come back!" I had, I knew it.

It was a madness, but it passed, and then I thought I would go mad.

"So you came back!"

"Came back, captain?" The voice grated and whined.

I stared at him, it was not Christian, it was Elphinstone.

234

"Elphinstone!"

"Captain?" I felt foolish, I felt desolate, then I remembered.

"Spray screens. We must rig spray screens, or we shall surely founder."

He sank down at the end of the bed.

I found I could sleep now that I had made good my oversight, but for a long time I dozed. I knew where I was, but the bed was tossing in an empty ocean, and then I was in the boat, in my bedroom.

A night came and went.

The morning light was soft through the panes, but with the glare gone I could easily distinguish and count the ten panes, — a hundred and forty-four square inches in each. My throat was sore, not burning, but the glands in my neck were swollen and it was painful to swallow, but the fever had left my body and my head was clear.

Jane was sitting at the window writing in a book.

"Jane." She started up, and come to me.

"Papa, are you better?"

"Where is Anne?"

"Anne?"

"She was sitting with me, did she tire of her vigil?"

She looked at me strangely.

"Papa, you have been sick for a week?"

I sank back on my elbow. A week? I found it hard to believe.

"Papa, can I get you something?"

"My linctus," — it would salve my throat — "water, and I think a little breakfast."

"Will you take beef tea?"

It wasn't my first choice of breakfast, but I was very hungry, too hungry to quibble.

"Beef tea with barley?"

"Barley, yes." She measured the linctus.

"Yes, that will be fine."

I finished the linctus and she passed me some water.

"What are you writing?"

"My accounts, Papa. It is going very well. I have a good market, and we have had no setbacks."

I couldn't imagine what she was talking about, and said so.

"My turkeys, Papa. My venture is prospering. I have a clucky hen on a clutch of eggs, and a ready market for the birds and the eggs.

I frowned. It was not what I wanted to hear.

"You must get rid of them."

"What? What do you mean?"

Her crassness and stupidity irritated me.

"You must get rid of the turkeys, I said that plain enough. I won't have them." Her face was a picture of dismay, something inside me wanted to reach out to her, to pander to her whims, to say I spoke in jest to calm and comfort her. A turkey called from the shrubbery, and I hardened my heart.

"You may keep and fatten one for Christmas."

"But Papa —"

She stopped, unsure what line to argue.

"Is Elizabeth at home?"

"No Papa."

"Not home?"

"No, she has gone driving with Richard."

Something, a shadow of a nightmare touched me.

"Could she not stay at home when I was unwell?"

"Indeed Father, she has been with you right through last night. She and Richard had little time together, and they are to marry."

"Marry! What? Nonsense, I have given no permission."

"Mrs Peebles told Elizabeth to go, and that you would be all right in her care."

"The devil she did!" The blasted woman was taking over the running of my house.

There was a crunching of gravel and the sound of a horse.

"They are home now. I shall fetch her."

She slipped hastily from the room, her wretched 'account books' under her arm, and after a short while I heard Elizabeth's firm tread on the stair. There were low voices talking on the landing, and I was amused to hear her say in some exasperation, "Leave me now, and wait in the parlour, there is a fire and we shall take lunch. No, don't come in now until I see how he is."

There was some mumbling in response to this, then I heard her reply crisply, "I can handle him."

"Can you, miss?" I thought. "Can you?"

The bedroom door opened, and she came in brisk but slightly breathless.

"Father, you look so much better!" She pummelled my pillows into shape, "Jane told me you were your old self…"

"Did she so?"

"And thinking of breakfast."

I could win an easy wager that was not all Jane had told her.

"You have Richard with you?"

She hesitated, "Yes, he is in the parlour — he is to take his lunch with us."

"I feel very much recovered. I shall sit out in a chair today, and tomorrow I may come downstairs. Shall we arrange for Richard to call on me the day after that, which will be Thursday?"

"Yes, yes, I'm sure he will be able to. To call on you, you say."

"Elizabeth, there are some matters I must settle with him regarding his betrothal to you, and your setting of a marriage date."

She was taken aback — possibly she had underestimated her ability to 'manage' me.

Chapter Twelve

A happy family luncheon — I recall the outcome of the Rum Rebellion, and the importance of good timing — a timely disclosure of my plans for the solution to our domestic problems — I am met by resistance from the very fruit of my loins! — robbed of victory by being taken ill

The weather was mild for November, and my condition improved remarkably. I was most gratified by the way my tough old body had shaken off the distemper. There couldn't, I reasoned, be too much wrong with my liver if it could do that.

It is fairly common now, to ascribe to the liver the power of overcoming illnesses and distempers. It traps the bilious humours and expels them as a dark slime through the bowels. Thus the looseness of bowels often experienced during such attacks is not to be abhorred nor treated with physics, but rather should be welcomed as a harbinger of better health.

We made quite a cheerful family party on Thursday at luncheon, Richard and Elizabeth sitting together to my right, and her sisters sat opposite. Beside me on the left I had — a rare treat — my first-born child, Harriet Maria, now Mrs Henry Barker, who was visiting the South of England and spent the day with us, and was to stay until the Sunday.

I welcomed her support, for, she was always very sensible, and I was sure she would appreciate my problems. It was a pretty fair table we had set for our guests. I do subscribe to the theory that, if you make your main meal in the middle of the day, then you owe it to your stomach to present it with some serious endeavour, and so it was that we enjoyed a choice of baked meats. There was a saddle of mutton, which should never be despised, for if parboiled before the oven, then you have a joint that is fit for a king, as tender as any meat. Parsnips and artichokes we had with it, which are my especial favourites, and an onion sauce. As well we had a dish of knuckles of pork, which we had looked at the night before, but it was basted and reheated, and it came up again a very pleasant dish.

Our conversation ranged over matters both political and scientific. Canning had replaced Castlereagh in charge of the colonies, and Richard suggested that I should make fresh representations for a pension, as my colonial posting had certainly entitled me to one.

Castlereagh had, of course, taken a partisan line strongly for MacArthur in that rascal's rebellion, and kept the hemp noose from his hairy neck. I did not expect any favours from that direction, for myself. Nor did it seem that Banks had any influence over him.

A missive had arrived, conveyed to me by Harriet Maria, which was from the Royal Society, and concerned the experiments in galvanism performed by Michael Faraday. Harriet had recalled my earlier interest in electricity, and the properties of electrical currents, and so she was assured that I should be interested, and fascinating work it was. Certainly I had been misinformed previously — he was no charlatan.

He had re-demonstrated the experiment of running a current of electricity through a wire beside a compass needle, and measuring its displacement. His next experiment was concerned with using this interesting phenomenon to build a meter to measure the magnitude of the current. But further to all of this familiar work he had demonstrated that he could generate electricity by spinning a magnet inside a coil of wire. This seemed to me to be an interesting novelty but of no established practical value, but this is such an era of scientific discovery that I by no means discounted the possibility that new developments and discoveries would result from it in allied fields.

From science it was back to politics, with Harriet telling of her visit to Paris. I suppose for all Englishmen of my generation, so long at war with the French, it seems very strange indeed for normal intercourse between the two nations to resume. I had been to France myself during my days with the Campbell Line, but only to Calais and then only to load spirits from the bond store, so I could hardly be counted a native of the country. Young Bligh then spoke of establishing contacts with exporters, mainly, I gathered, for spirits and for cotton goods, but to my mind the country is far from politically stable; I should not hazard any great monies there, even if the profits seem irresistible. Sup there with a long spoon.

Mrs Peebles came in with the tea-making equipment, and Harriet greeted her kindly and with interest. To my very great annoyance Elizabeth then invited her to sit in the room. I signalled to Elizabeth, and conveyed my displeasure, but she seemed oblivious. Only Richard caught my scowl, which rendered him extremely uncomfortable, not knowing whether to attract Elizabeth's attention, or to nod sympathetically to me to indicate his understanding of my feelings. I fancy Elizabeth is going to rule their household very thoroughly indeed, when that time comes — when that institution has been ordained and blessed.

I had brought forward two splendid bottles of burgundy which were from a case I had had from young Tobin, who had secured a consignment of it in the course of his Majesty's Customs and Excise service. It grieves me to broach wine which is doing very well in the cellar, but I had lately come to consider the undue benevolence of departing this life and leaving a cellar of first class wines and rum for the gratification of my sons-in-law.

Success in life is not just a matter of doing the right thing, but of doing it at the right time. In Sydney Town, a few days of prevarication might have saved my authority, but it was not in my nature to prevaricate. I stood my ground, and I was at first undone. However, I learnt from the experience: prevarication, even a whiff of duplicity, are necessary allies if right is to triumph. Then, when the right moment is come, nail the colours of righteousness to the mast!

* * * * *

"You will find it a comfortable enough billet," said precious Mr Lieutenant Finucane, "Why, I consider them the best quarters in Sydney."

"Like enough you do," I said shortly. "Like enough you do."

The 'best quarters in Sydney' consisted of two small rooms, one furnished with a bed and a small chest, one with a sofa and an 'easy' chair, which comfortable appurtenance appeared to be having some difficulty in retaining its springs.

It was, in short, a typical subaltern's barrack. There were no concessions made to completing one's toilet, except for a scrap of mirror on a mantel, and no provision for the preparation of food or the decent serving of same.

"How long" I asked, "am I to be confined in this miserable cell?"

Lieutenant Finucane looked pained.

"Major Johnston will tell you of that presently."

Indeed, while he spoke Johnston came into the outer chamber, to gloat over his prisoner, I presumed.

"You Sir, and your precious Mr Paterson and Mr Foveaux, must be as presumptuous a set of rebels as ever existed."

Johnston looked down his nose.

"Mr Bligh," he emphasised the 'mister', but I looked steadily at him until he was out of countenance. "Sir, I am directed by his Honour to inform you that you are to hold yourself in readiness to embark on board the *Estramina*, schooner, when she arrives."

"Where am I to go then?"

"I really cannot say." He obviously did not know what was planned, but he tried to sound all-powerful and threatening. He didn't succeed. He sounded like a jackass, and I told him so. He had no idea, either, as to how long I was to be confined in this close arrest.

Then began seven days of torment — twenty-two feet by ten feet was the size of my reduced kingdom. I had been confined for twelve months inside the walls at Government House, with inebriated sentinels posted back and front, but that was the height of space and luxury compared to this, and I had fretted at that confinement.

"Everything is relative" I reminded myself, "next week I may find myself in a six foot dungeon without a window, and I shall look back on this apartment with regret for its amenity."

I had recourse to Marcus Aurelius.

> *Thou canst remove out of thy way many things which disturb thee, for they lie entirely in thy opinion; and thou wilt then gain for thyself ample space by considering the whole universe in thy mind.*

Marcus Aurelius was, of course, never held in captivity. I read further:

> *Wipe out imagination; check desire; extinguish appetite; keep the ruling faculty in its power!*

Again, Marcus Aurelius never went hungry that I had heard of, but his maxim to keep the ruling faculty in its power was a fairly good description of my position. I was the ruling faculty as far as the *Porpoise* was concerned, and from neither of these positions did I intend to withdraw by one inch.

Foveaux and Paterson were desperate to be quit of me from the Colony. Not that my presence quelled their villainy and rapaciousness by a jot. It is a matter of recorded scandal that they have bestowed freely on themselves, and on every one of the jackals and creatures who support them, vast grants of land. More land has been given away this last twelve month than had been given during all the years since Phillip established the Colony.

But they saw me as a continuing threat, and they were right to do so. I was sure that if I could gain my freedom by any stratagem then the common people would rally to my support.

Foveaux was particularly threatening.

"I was appointed by His Majesty to this position, and I cannot see how any officer can quit his post until he receives permission from his Sovereign, not withstanding that a set of rebels have deprived him of all power of conforming thereto, Colonel Foveaux."

"Then, Sir," he spluttered at me, "we shall have to see what means we shall employ to be rid of you."

I wondered, vaguely, if they would poison my food, but I apprehended that it was more likely I should be bound and forcibly delivered aboard a ship taking me from Port Jackson.

The next day, to my surprise, I had a visit from Lieutenant William Kent, the acting commander of H.M.S. *Porpoise*.

Mr Kent and I had had a difficult year of it since the *Porpoise* had returned from Norfolk Island last year. She came in some months too late to influence the outrageous events of January's insurrection, but you may be very sure that I wasted no time in establishing communications with her. I was indeed, you will realise, the senior naval officer on the station, a position I was not going to abdicate — a position that could be in no wise altered by Johnston or MacArthur no matter how much they might huff or puff.

I had put it to Kent in my letter.

I wanted a detachment of marines and armed seamen to land and free me from my illegal detention so that I might assume control of *Porpoise*, and of the harbour. I awaited his early advice as to when I might expect this attempt to take place so that I might have my family and our effects ready.

A week went past without any reply and then I was thunderstruck to be told by Mary, Mrs Putland, that *Porpoise* had departed her berth and was supposed to have sailed to Hobart on some errand for my captors. "You mean," I spluttered, "this damned puppy Kent has sailed a British naval ship, my ship, out of the port, flying my broad pennant, and carrying out the orders of this mutinous rabble of soldiers?"

"Mr Lewisham said that your pennant was not being flown, Father."

"Mr Kent has pulled down his commanding officer's pennant, and disregarded his orders! It is clear mutiny. Mary, I'll have the poxy cub before a court-martial for this. Mr Kent will repent his double-dealing."

I had a very good idea where our precious Mr Kent was heading, and on what mission. He would have been despatched to summon Colonel Paterson, the Lieutenant Governor, to Sydney Town to lend some appearance of legitimacy to the governance of the Colony. Paterson was languishing in the settlement at Port Dalrymple all innocent of the great and infamous events taking place to his north. I had some hopes, not strong, but some hopes of order being restored if he had arrived at my bidding. Now it had appeared that he would be strongly influenced by the military before I ever saw him.

In the event he proved to be the weakest of reeds, and dominated by Johnston and his co-conspirators.

So now I had Mr Kent before me.

"What do you have to say for yourself?" I rumbled at him.

"Sir?"

"Mr Kent, I have prepared papers here charging you with three counts of dereliction of duty. I propose to lodge them as soon as I am free to return to London and the Admiralty. Do you have anything to say?"

"Sir, I have always done my duty."

"My duty, you blaggard, is your duty. Do you argue that I am not the senior naval officer on this station? Do you pretend to have supported me?"

"Sir, I had no orders directly from you, and was compelled to accept the direction of the Acting Governor."

"So if they had told you to shoot me you would have done that?"

"Indeed no sir, but to bring Colonel Paterson here seemed to be in the best interest of everyone."

"But you did not bring him to me, did you? you brought him to join his mutinous cronies."

"Sir, you were under detention. It was a very difficult situation."

"A difficult situation was it? I shall put you in a difficult situation, Mr Kent, difficult and dangerous to you — a meeting with a hemp rope."

I paused then smiled benignly. "So, what do you want with me?"

"Major Abbott has asked me to offer you passage home on the *Gambier*. He also asks for you to authorise the *Porpoise* to make its way home independently."

"What, give you leave to cringe home and make your whining excuses to Admiral Pellew before I get there?"

"Captain Porteous is assuming command of *Porpoise*, Sir. I shall continue as First Lieutenant."

I dismissed him like the mutinous cur he undoubtedly was, but the seed of an idea had been sown.

Seven days of torment, I said, and that was what it was

about—to make my life so opprobrious that transportation would be embraced willingly. Uncomfortable enough it was. The summer sun streamed down on the barracks which stood without shade. Trees had indeed been planted around the parade ground, and to provide relief to the front of the building from the burning sun of January and February, but so poorly had they been tended that only two miserable saplings survived, and they with scorched and crumpled leaves. Elm trees they had chosen, all out of season, and I comprehend that a better solution, though not so appealing to homesick eyes, would have been to transplant some of the native eucalypts or mimosas which grew like weeds with the very slightest of nurture or care.

The footings were of cut stone but the walls were lined with timber planks and no breeze penetrated the corridor, so that it was an oven I was confined in. I took pains to dress each day in my uniform, and that included my tunic coat, but I had no chance to remove it between visitors as my outer door was kept open to the passageway down which a continuous stream of military buffoons were coming and going at all hours. Not one took it on himself to salute me although they all looked in to see me there, and thought it a wonderful thing.

The toilet and common lavatory was at the end of the passageway, and can you imagine my fury and chagrin when I found I was to be escorted there by a grinning jackanapes of a sentry who then mounted guard immediately outside the door of that necessary office.

All that kept me sane was my writing. Johnston and Abbott came a-visiting to try to discourage me writing, or to intercept any mail I might forward. They already intercepted and confiscated all my official correspondence.

I was preparing an appeal to Admiral Pellew asking his assistance in quelling the rebellion. I took care to advise him to sail into Sydney Cove with his guns loaded and run out, and sent him a very fair map of the defences.

"There are only four guns at the entrance to the harbour," I wrote, " and a poor battery of fourteen guns near the town, twelve pounders. There are between six and seven hundred troops and officers under arms and in open rebellion." If

Pellew were still at the Cape then a frigate, a third-rater, could be here within three months. It was repugnant to think of Englishmen firing on Englishmen, but then it was equally repugnant to find Englishmen in open revolt against their Sovereign's appointed Governor. The letter I gave to Mary, and it was despatched by the end of the week in the *Albion*, which vessel was headed home via the Straits and thence to the Cape.

Another plan was exercising my mind — to obtain relief from my situation by a stratagem, by a finesse that would outwit the rebel villains. So as to conceal my plan it was necessary for Patterson to suggest an accommodation, not for me to initiate any discussion, nor to bargain.

Fortunately the *Admiral Gambier* was making ready to put to sea and they, all of them, were very assiduous to see me quit the Colony in her, and so revoke my appointment.

Seven days I sweated out in my prison, when I was summarily escorted to Johnston's offices and Mr Paterson was there to deal with me.

"This is a most unfitting confinement you find yourself in," he began severely, as if it were some quirk of my own choosing that I was held imprisoned. I said nothing, but waited, though indignation did fair to choke me.

"Knowing your impatience to seek redress for your current difficulties I have managed to obtain passages for you and your daughter, and up to three other members of your establishment you might think to accompany you, Mr Bligh, on the *Admiral Gambier*."

"That is very kind, very thoughtful indeed, but you will understand that I will have a great deal of preparation to do if I am to return in that vessel. I have several witnesses to secure, and very many depositions to take down, and much of my paperwork that I will certainly need when the rebels and their supporters are brought to trial."

This was a concept that brought him a great deal of uneasiness, and discomfort, and so it should, the drunken rogue.

"If I am to accomplish all this then I must not be restrained here, but must have my freedom to ready my effects." I could see him rehearsing in his mind how he was to break it to Johnston and Foveaux, and doubtless the detestable MacArthur, that he had succeeded in persuading the tyrant Bligh to desert his post, but that he had let the aforementioned Bligh loose as he wanted to gather sufficient evidence to have them hanged.

His eyes were inflamed and his hands shook, but not from emotion — he was, I judged, and common report supported it, he was in the later stages of alcohol poisoning. Not yet a drunkard, but the end of the road was looming close for him.

"I shall have to consider — we shall speak again. It may be we can reach an agreement. I shall return on the morrow, and we will settle it then over a glass, and a handshake."

One thought at a time seemed to be all his mind could accommodate, and yet in his younger days, before Hunter and King came out, he had been an active and vigorous officer. Though a very quarrelsome one, MacArthur once putting a bullet into him in a dispute. I would have wished to God it had been the other way round. In the happening, it was three days before he came again with a proposition. I can imagine what terrific disagreements and suspicions had been vented in the discussions between the disagreeable conspirators and principals in the Rebellion, each man trying to save his own skin now that retribution might be the order of the day. I can only tell you that I had a private visit from Captain Abbott, who told me in the greatest confidence that MacArthur would see me dead, for he dreaded me giving testimony in Britain. Abbott must have seen a chance to ingratiate himself with me, to have a leg in each camp as it were, but I received him coolly and sent him off, and he would not have been flattered had he had the benefit of the remarks about him that I committed to my journal that evening.

So there was much coming and going, to-ing and fro-ing, propositioning and counter-propositioning by the worried antagonists.

I was heartened by notes smuggled into me by Mary, and by Jubb, from the Reverend Henry Fulton, who was ever my supporter, detailing the great unrest and feeling for me right through the Colony, and by a message of support from

Marsden even. I had, of course, no intention whatever of leaving on the *Admiral Gambier*.

"There are some difficulties, I foresee," I looked solemn.

"Difficulties?"

"I am told MacArthur and Johnston propose to sail in the *Gambier* also, on their way to their trial and court martial?"

"They are travelling back, yes."

"And you see nothing wrong in their travelling in the restricted confinement of this ship together with the chief witness to their villainy and the subject of their mutiny and oppression. It is impossible, do you not see that?"

He chewed his lip in indecision, the ragged margin of his drooping moustache testifying to a life of chronic indecision.

"They must go on a later vessel," I said.

"I believe they will insist on taking their passage."

I believed this too. They would both want to run home to circulate their lying explanations before I reached home. I had no objection to travelling with them, on my terms. It would give me great pleasure do you see, to take them back to Portsmouth in manacles, and to hand them over as felons to the military and civil authorities.

The suggestion I was waiting for came.

"It may be possible for Captain Porteous to give you and your daughter passage home on the *Porpoise*. His orders are, I understand, to pursue the best interest of the Colony and to protect trade, so he could be persuaded that to convoy the *Gambier* home would not be inconsistent with those directions."

"It would not be a comfortable passage for my daughter." I didn't wish to appear over eager.

He looked worried, so I helped him along. "But it may prove to be the best solution to the difficulty if you cannot persuade the members of the other party to relinquish their passages."

"Naturally you will want to be back in Britain as soon as possible to prepare your defence."

I raised my eyebrows.

"When I have assembled the records and witnesses that the prosecution will require for the court martial of Johnston, and the trial of MacArthur, you may be sure that I shall waste no time in delivering my testimony to the appropriate authorities."

"Naturally there will have to be an inquiry, yes."

"An exhaustive inquiry. I should not be surprised if you and Foveaux are summoned home to testify as to the reasons for your reluctance to support and reinstate the King's appointed representative."

There was a fairly long silence while he examined the possibilities, then he took me aback by suddenly shouting at me with the utmost earnestness.

"We would of course want you to give us an oath."

"An oath?" I didn't follow him.

"Yes, an oath certainly. An oath that, if this passage is arranged for you, you will take your family and quit the Colony, and sail straight back to Britain. Will you agree to that?"

"Make an oath that I will sail straight back to Britain on the *Porpoise*? You are talking about *Porpoise*, are you?"

"Well I'm not promising that. It will depend on the circumstances, but I shall draw up a formal agreement."

I became a little concerned.

"I am not putting my name to any damned bill of goods that exonerates you or any of the rest of you."

"No, no, Captain Bligh, I was referring to a document in which you agree to our terms for your departure only. I must point out that my role will be seen as restoring order while despatching the protagonists in this squabble back to the authorities where the rights and wrongs of the case can be settled."

"I'm sure you are right. I wonder, would you arrange for a copy, a *résumé* will do, of the land grants in New South Wales of the last twelve months, to be made available to me?"

"What have the land grants to do with it?"

"Why, Sir, they will demonstrate to the Colonial Secretary that the business of the Colony is being carried on assiduously."

"I really believe, Bligh, that you will be lucky to leave these shores alive."

"Prepare your agreement, and I shall sign it, if it is how you describe it."

It came the next morning, brought in by Finucane and Abbott, two to witness my signature, you see. Patterson had already signed the agreement, and for his part he agreed that I should be freed of restraint and allowed to return to Government House, that I should be accompanied home by all such persons as I nominated as necessary, and that I should be allowed freedom of communication with my friends.

> *I, William Bligh, agree that, for my part, I shall undertake to embark on board the* Porpoise *on the 20th February inst., that I shall proceed to England with the utmost despatch, and that I shall neither remain at nor return to any part of this territory without His Majesty's Orders. I further agree that I shall not in any manner interfere with the government of this Colony, nor place an impediment in the outfitting and departure of the* Porpoise. *To the strict and unequivocal observance of these conditions I, William Bligh, pledge my honour as an Officer and a Gentleman.*

I carefully signed my name at the bottom. "You give your word, Bligh, as a gentleman?"

I looked him firmly in the eye. "I give you my word as a gentleman!"

Porpoise was swinging to her anchor in the lee of Garden Island and bobbing to a westerly which was tossing up a short sea, and a great expectant exultation gripped me as the government cutter closed with her.

"Mind your 'ead, Sir!" The gaff sail swung across, and the cutter beat down on the brig. She was businesslike but weathered — spars and rigging were scarce on this side of the globe. Her topsides were black and a yellow strake outlined her gun ports. The yards were crossed but there was no canvas showing above the furled topsails. Stains on her hull towards the head showed that the crew were careless with their slops, and indeed the water down her lee side showed evidence of a week's rubbish. The cutter was heading towards the larboard side where an entry port had been rigged.

"Starboard!" I snapped — the side used for naval officers. My authority as Governor might be questioned, but I was damned if I was going to suffer any question as to my undoubted primacy in the naval hierarchy.

The cutter luffed up at once, and just found enough way to squeeze in to starboard, hooking on with a clumsy scrape.

I took a deep breath and commenced the climb up the side battens. If I slipped here and got a ducking then my authority would be harmed beyond recovery. I took a firm grip on the man ropes and swung myself up. Then the deck was under my feet, and a boatswain's whistle was ringing in my ears. I looked up at the towering masts. The clouds were moving steadily in the upper sky, to the south, giving the masts an apparent motion. The deck was alive under my feet, and I pulled in a long draught of sea air. Five knots westerly backing south tonight and dirty weather blowing in. I didn't have to think about it. I was a creature of the sea, and I knew it.

Two sideboys stood afore a small line of marines and officers, Captain John Porteous was stepping forward to greet me.

"Welcome on board, Governor."

I saluted him, and then shook his hand.

"Captain Porteous."

"John Porteous, Governor."

"Bligh", I said, and stood to attention as at a sharp command a drum rattled, and my broad pennant climbed the main signal halyard. A twitch of the seaman's wrist broke the pennant out, and a loud bang marked a salute to it from the cannon in the waist.

I felt good. It was the first time I'd felt good for a year.

The officers and boatswain's mates were lined up, and I strode across to the First Lieutenant and stopped in front of him. He stiffened, and his eyes did not meet mine.

"Captain Porteous, I would be obliged if you would arrest this man, Lieutenant Kent, and hold him in close confinement while I prepare charges against him."

Kent's eyes snapped to mine now, and he was angry and defiant. I tried to stare him down, but he persisted so I moved away.

"Bos'n, I should be obliged if you would see my chest swung up."

Porteous had stepped aside with me.

"Kent, Sir, do you intend a close confinement in his cabin?"

"No mister, I do not." I encouraged no further questions, deeming it unnecessary. Mr Kent would grace the master-of-arms' cell. "Will you assemble the men aft. I wish to read my commission as Commodore, Chief of his Majesty Armed Forces on this station. Are the men all present?"

"Starbowlines are on shore leave until four bells, Governor."

"Very well, I shall proceed without them, but I require all shore leave cancelled. This ship must be held prepared to sail. What is your state of readiness?"

"Water butts are full, Sir, provisions for four weeks."

That was reasonable. Ships' biscuit they'd be well provided with, but casks of preserved meat were not to be had on this side of the ocean, so that ships sailing these waters were dependant on fresh fruit and vegetables, and usually carried a small menagerie of sheep and pigs and fowl to be butchered on the journey.

"What communications have you received from the rebels? Are you aware that my daughter and her lady will be joining us?"

He spoke carefully.

"I have a note signed by Colonel Patterson requesting me to receive your daughter, and yourself, and a small party, and to convey you to Britain. Colonel Patterson signs himself as 'Acting Governor.' I hold myself ready to serve you as my commanding officer."

"You show better sense than Lieutenant Kent."

I terminated the conversation, asking him to arrange for two chests of records to be brought aboard, and also two hoggets which I proposed to use to supplement our stores.

That day was taken up with arranging our berths and settling the ladies into their quarters. *Porpoise* had never been designed for the transport of ladies, nor of passengers at large if it came to that.

Porteous, good fellow, vacated his cabin to their comfort

and a screen was rigged across the maid servants bunk to protect my daughter's sensibilities. I was bunked in solitary splendour in the Master's cabin, but I fancy my berth was scarcely more commodious than Mr Kent's.

The next day, Tuesday, there was great traffic from ship to shore, and from shore to ship. Porteous was quite correctly wasting none of the opportunity to refill his stores, and cases of flour and oats were carried out in the ship's launch and hoisted aboard by a rope rove through a purchase on the main-yard end. The waist of the ship began to resemble Noah's ark more than one of His Majesty's men-o'-war. Fruit and greens were dreadfully hard to come by, but I had formed a convenient resolution that we should collect a supply of sour grass in Van Diemen's Land, this herb being very useful as an anti-scorbutic, although the men receive it very badly, and must be watched to see that they partake of it.

I had not broached my determination not to quit New South Wales to Porteous, but was busy with my agent, Coleson, who was rowed out. On him devolved the next stage of my re-instatement, the distribution of a manifesto, a proclamation publicly declaring that the New South Wales Corps was in a state of mutiny, and directing the free settlers to rally to the support of their appointed Governor. I also forbade any ship's captain, at his peril, to give passage out of the Colony to any of the persons connected with the Rebellion. I very well knew, as you will recall, that Johnston and MacArthur were planning to sail in the *Admiral Gambier*. Also covered by my proscription were Blaxland, Blaxcell, Atkins, Jamieson and Wentworth.

I waited in great anticipation for Coleson's return and at dusk he came out in a cutter. I had observed great activity at the barracks with detachments of men marching this way and that, and a congregation of gigs and pony traps suggested that my proclamation had been akin to poking a stick into an ant's nest. I had a lantern to my cabin and Coleson sitting at my table. Common courtesy dictated that I offered the man a drink before questioning him as to the day's events, but he looked doleful enough, and only revived a degree of liveliness when he was well into a jack of rum.

"Well Governor Bligh," he said, wiping his mouth, "Well you've put the town on its ear that's true enough."

"You put the proclamations out, without too much trouble."

"Aye, Fenwick took those to the Hunter, and Hawkesbury, and my men plastered the town. There wasn't an official building, nor wine-shop, nor foundry that didn't have one nailed to its door. I would consider that everyone in the Colony has read it by now."

"And how was it received?"

"Well enough, well enough." He thought. "Blaxland was near apoplectic. 'I told you,' he thundered at them, 'I told you not to trust him. Madmen, madmen to give him away. And now where are we at?' MacArthur was snarling, but he is on board the *Gambier* by now and will be off with the mornings light."

"Is Johnston aboard?"

"Aye, him too. The Hawkesbury district is up, and have bonfires lit."

He was right. I'd seen a glow on the northerly cloud bank.

"Foveaux is mortally afraid of a rising, I believe."

"What has he done?"

"The regiment are out with a picket on the great north road, and a gun too."

"A gun?"

"Yes, they swung one out of the barracks, and have sent it up the road with a bullock team. The guns at the quay are loaded and manned too. Begging your pardon, Sir, should we not be safer anchored on the north shore?"

"What! Fire on the Royal Navy?" They wouldn't have the stomach for it. Why man, if it came to that, *Porpoise* could flatten the town."

"Very likely you're right then. They had the regiment out tearing down the proclamations, and they had their own bonfire on the parade ground. Not as good a blaze as they ran at the Hawkesbury though, I would believe."

I felt exultant. My finesse in getting control of the ship had evened the balance dramatically. I could cruise the Harbour entrance for six months, or as long as it took for help to arrive, and I had them trapped like a fox in its hide.

"You've done very well. Now you had better leave as I need to consider my next moves. I will contact you when I need a further report on proceedings."

I had made his dismissal plain, but he sat there, twisting his hat around in his hands.

"Governor, I have dismissed the cutter. I had to come out after sunset, and dursn't return for they are looking for me."

"Are they, by God?"

"Smith, my clerk, tells me they have ransacked my office, and that charges have been laid against me for disturbing the peace. If I go back I will be arrested."

"Very well, we will put you ashore in Botany Bay."

He looked blank. "What can I do there?"

"Your brother still has his farm there. Will he not shelter you?"

"I beg your pardon, Sir, but most likely it is the first place they will look. There is a company marched out to patrol the coastal road as well."

It occurred to me that if I landed with fifty marines tonight I could occupy the barracks at my leisure. It was a tempting thought, but entailed obvious risks, and I was enjoying my freedom too much to hazard it on a venture like that. I despatched the guard from my door to acquaint Captain Porteous with my desire to confer with him.

It was still dark when a hand on my shoulder pulled me out of my slumbers.

"An hour to daybreak Sir," said a husky voice.

I come awake quickly, old habit reasserting itself, and pulled on my shirt and jacket. Harrads, the man assigned as my servant by Porteous, stood in the passageway outside the half open door sucking his teeth and grimacing at my sentry, a storm lantern in his hand. As I came on deck the first light of dawn was there, but towards the heads the dark sky was showing a hint of grey and the stars low on the horizon were becoming dim.

The wind was backing and there was a distinct chill in it. Porteous was with the officer of the deck, both dimly visible in the candlelight from the binnacle.

"Beat to quarters, Mr Jones", he said, having caught my

nod, and a marine drummer beat a roll as the boatswain's mates moved through the mess-decks with their calls shrilling. "General quarters, all hands to general quarters." All ships of the Royal Navy met the dawn with the ship's company standing to the guns and ready for action in time of war. It was as routine in Port Jackson as in the channel off Calais.

The sky was perceptibly lightening now in the east, and I could distinguish the seas running under our counter as cold grey chop with a yellowish spume beaming off the top. I drew my jacket about me, and quelled a shiver.

Topsails were shaken out, and the starboard watch were stamp and heave at the capstan. The anchor was left swinging ready to drop as we slowly gathered way against the seas, and beat up towards Circular Quay and the *Admiral Gambier*. The tide was near its flood and we moved with slow but steady menace under fore and main-topsails only. By the time we were off Farm Cove it was fully light and the ebb tide was running. It was a grey drizzly morning but the chill had dispersed and a mild warmth was promised. I trained a glass on the quay, and sure enough *Gambier* was singled up to a stern line and two cutters had towlines rigged to pull her off the shore and clear of the head land.

"Captain Bligh?"

"Now, if you please, Mr Porteous."

He gave the command, and the helmsmen pulled us to starboard. Slowly the masts circled against the sky, and the sprit traced an arc from Dames Point across to Kirribilli. As the larboard guns came to bear there was a muffled command from below and then a blinding flash and the deck shook to the blast of an eighteen pounder. The ball was lost as it crossed the *Gambier*'s bow but a cloud of dust and a fall of rock showed where it had ploughed into the sandstone cliff. There was a pause while the explosion rang in my ears, and the world was frozen still, then a thousand shrilling sea fowl took flight right around Circular Quay, filling the air with a frenzy of beating wings.

"Drop anchor, mister." The *Porpoise* had come up into the wind and lost way as her fore-topsail backed. There was a rattle and a roar as the cable splashed out and a quarter of a ton of iron clawed at the sandy bottom. She drifted back with the wind dead ahead, then snubbed up as the flukes bit deep. It was nicely done, I have lived with Captains who sailed over their anchors and fouled their cables. We had the *Gambier*, but the shore battery, even supposing they had the resolution, could not point a barrel at us.

To say there appeared to be considerable surprise on the *Admiral Gambier* was to understate it rather. One cutter had dropped its cable and was rowing urgently to the shore. Groups of figures, too small to distinguish separately, were dashing this way and that. A net of boxes being hoisted aboard by a derrick had dropped half on the quay and half in the water as the crew manning the derrick had sprung to take cover. The Master, or so I took it to be, was waving a loud hailer and flapping his arms like a demented semaphore as the topsails were let blow out.

To add to their discomfort, the ship had blown round on its single stern line and was chafing its quarter against the stone dock wall, as it struggled to leave the land.

Gradually, the situation was brought under control, another cable was carried ashore from the bow and she was winched back. The sails were furled the cutters returned to the shore.

"Send a boat across, Captain Porteous, please."

I sent a message across reinforcing my ban on any ship taking MacArthur or Johnston out of the Colony, and added, for good measure, that I would stop and search any vessel sailing towards the heads.

No answer was immediately forthcoming, but there was strenuous activity ashore with horsemen, and carriages, and pedestrians all plying back and forward in lively confusion.

I was pretty well satisfied with my mornings work, I can tell you.

We retired in good order to our former standing ground, in the lee of Garden Island, and it was thence that the Government cutter found us that evening with a communication from Patterson.

He had a great burden on his mind, the gist of which was that I had directly violated my parole, broken my word of honour in not departing from the Colony, and I was a thrice damned and forsworn liar!

"Mr Patterson," I wrote, "I hold the King's Commission and, so doing, I do not hold that any agreement made with a rebel can be considered binding."

Now we fell into a hiatus — the *Admiral Gambier* would not come out, and we could not go in — so at last I put the word about that we were retiring to the Derwent, to enlist the aid of the Lieutenant Governor, Collins.

Having spread this tale generously so that it would gain credence, *Porpoise* set topsails and gallants and with my pennant flying proudly we sailed down Port Jackson, and headed south.

Headed south but not too far. I was sure MacArthur and Johnston, seeing their opportunity, would set sail immediately. It kept me awake at night licking my lips, would you believe, to think of intercepting them and taking them home in chains. They would be excellent company for Kent.

We beat up and down the coast between Broken Bay and Port Stephens for ten days, but not a ship came out. Our communication with the shore had been stifled by Patterson's troops and constables, so we were completely in the dark as to their intentions, nor could we readily obtain any further stores.

At last, on March 17, we broke the stalemate. I set sail for Hobart.

* * * * *

"So, now's the moment," I said to myself.

I filled my glass, and with some effort I raised myself to my feet, and began what the interested audience took to be a toast to the happy affianced couple. This was not entirely my intention, but I used my opening remarks to put forward my proposition regarding the wine in the cellar. It was altogether too practical an idea for my poor Anne, who became very glum indeed, so that I winked at her to convey that it was just buffoonery, but it did not stop her lip quivering.

This was all to my purpose.

"Mrs Peebles," I said, smiling pleasantly to remove any taint of displeasure, "I wish to speak very closely to my daughters, and to Mr Bligh, of my plans for the coming year. I'm sure you will understand." She rose hastily.

"Indeed Admiral Bligh, I have a great deal to organise this day, with laundry not folded, and the tradesmen calling tomorrow for our yuletide orders. We must really consider engaging another junior to train. I know Armitage, who farms Henley Bottom has a younger daughter he would see in service."

I was staggered by her presumption.

"Thank you, Mrs Peebles, that will do now. It is something I have been giving some thought to — you may leave it with me."

She appeared inclined to continue the discussion, but Elizabeth exchanged a few quiet words with her, and she left us to our conversation.

"Mrs Peebles," said Jane, unhelpfully, "has been just splendid, Harriet. You have no idea how devotedly she nursed father when he was unwell. We did too, of course, but she was a great help to us."

I cleared my throat, the initiative appeared to be rapidly passing from me.

"I would wish to address a few remarks to you." An attentive hush fell over the family and Elizabeth came and sat down again next to Richard, and took his hand.

"It is particularly in my mind today that on such an occasion we all miss your mother, my very dear Bessie."

It was perfectly true. I did miss her — she would have sorted them all out in very short order. She would have sorted me out too, given the chance. She had been a very strong woman in all our tribulations and vicissitudes.

"Nobody could ever take Mrs Bligh's place." I paused to let this important point sink in.

"I am, of course, deeply gratified that Richard has expressed his desire for the hand of Elizabeth, and nothing will give me keener pleasure than to see them happily and securely joined in matrimony and settled in their own home. My gratitude to Elizabeth is heart felt. Since the death of your mother she has run this household for me, and organised my domestic details and arrangements like the most competent mistress in the world. It has been a burden and a strain for one so young, for this is a large house, and a great deal of the time I have been unable to give her the support she needed because of my ill health. In many ways it might have been easier for all of you if we had remained in London. You are all very isolated here on the downs, and separated from friends and acquaintances in the City."

I was now fairly into my stride, and they were listening attentively. I had the strongest feeling that Elizabeth was looking at me very carefully and suspiciously, but I refrained from catching her eye. I avoided it, in short, and pressed on.

"I am concerned, as I have said, that too much has been left on Elizabeth's shoulders, and for that reason I propose some staff changes. Firstly, a promotion. Frances, I propose to ask you to expand your role as my scribe, as the writer of my correspondence, into that of steward for my affairs. You have proved by your enterprise that you have a head for business, and I am sure you will not have any difficulty in handling the extra responsibilities."

Frances flushed, with surprise and pleasure I imagined.

"You will of course work in the beginning under my direct supervision, and I will retain control of the bank accounts, but I will certainly seek your assistance in most of the decision-making."

She was listening very carefully, and I saw her pleased flush diminish slightly as I qualified the scope of her duties.

I paused, and Elizabeth after staring at Frances had risen to her feet.

"Sit down Elizabeth. I have not finished."

She did not sit, but she remained silent.

"Jane —" she looked at me startled. "With Frances fully occupied you too will have your part to play. I envisage you taking over many of Elizabeth's duties in running the household." I did too, I saw them organised into two watches, with Jane the junior watch officer, Elizabeth first mate, and Frances the purser; or Captain's clerk. "Thus, when Elizabeth finally leaves our threshold, the transition will come easily." I drew breath.

Richard was looking a question at Elizabeth.

"You will be involved, Jane, in training some junior household staff, and indeed I shall expect you and Elizabeth to interview the girls and choose the best applicants."

"And Mrs Peebles, Father. Should she not be involved in choosing her assistants?"

"No — I shall come to that matter in a moment. Jane, I am afraid you will have no leisure for propagating poultry. The turkeys, I'm afraid, will have to go."

"But, Father..."

"Furthermore, Jane, I am disturbed by the time you waste in social intercourse with this person living on our boundary. With Mr Ffoulkes. You must see that his kindness and preferment may very well be greed to share in your endowment."

"My endowment?"

"Yes miss, your endowment. Like everyone else around here he sees me dead and buried, and your parcel of my inheritance coming to him. Don't pout at me miss, I won't have him whining and cadging around my coffin like a carrion crow. What else can he want with you but to get his hands on your money. Oh-ho — I've seen how the world turns, I see through Mr Ffoulkes."

"But Papa, he is our neighbour," she was distressed.

"I'll not have him set foot here, nor you there, do you hear me, not have it!"

"But Papa, he is the very soul of kindness to us all. He shows me no preferment."

"I'll take it more kindly in future if he keeps to his boundaries, and his blasted geese."

"And about Mrs Peebles." Elizabeth's voice was cold.

"Mrs Peebles must go, I shall give her her notice this very night."

"Dismiss Mrs Peebles!"

"But Papa, she has nursed you, she runs the house. Why, can you be serious?" They were all in it, clamouring at me together.

"Have you gone completely out of your mind?" — it was Elizabeth of course.

"Elizabeth!" Richard looked apprehensive.

"Elizabeth, you must not speak to Papa so."

"Thank you Harriet Maria, I shall handle her. No Elizabeth, I have not lost my head. You seem to be blind to the pretensions of the unfortunate woman — no, hear me out — the pretensions to take over the role of your blessed mother."

She looked at me. They all looked at me.

"She is the housekeeper. You pay her to run the house."

"She would take over the role of your mother both in the parlour and in the bedroom."

"You are out of your mind. She sat by you when you were ill and nursed you as a Christian soul, and went without her own sleep. How can you dream of rewarding her faithfulness in this ungrateful fashion?" Her voice was rising, I thought she might be about to give way to tears.

Anne was crying, but then Anne was often crying.

"She took advantage of my illness and weakness to make claims on my affections in a way that I had done nothing to encourage."

"I don't believe you."

"Well I believe you should look again in your mind at the way she has comported herself over these last two days. You do not, I trust, believe I have done anything to encourage her ridiculous pretensions?"

"She joined us at the table, but that was only when invited to do so by Harriet Maria."

"Think harder, look more closely and you will see I am correct. I intend to take this opportunity to reorganise the house. There is no reason we should be imposed upon by an overly-ambitious old woman, and a half-simple scullery maid. I shall give her a week's notice, although I don't believe I shall be able to give her a character. It would not be honest."

"You plan to give notice to Miss Evelyn too?"

"She is very little use, only to wash dishes and clean grates."

"Somebody has to wash dishes and clean grates."

"Well, I plan to hire two young active women. Until they are discovered and appointed I am afraid we shall have to manage as well as we can."

"Will you blacklead the grates, Father?"

"Elizabeth, I will not suffer your tiresome impertinence."

"Indeed, Father, it was not I who asked the question, it was Anne, and a perfectly innocent question. But let me ask also, are Jane and Frances to become maids and cleaners, cooks and dishwashers? Who is to direct their efforts?"

"Elizabeth, you will direct their efforts. I must ask this final favour of you, that your nuptials be postponed until the household is brought into order. I see no one to do this, and it is certain that your mother would have wished it so."

She has a very haughty temper, Elizabeth, when she does not get her own way, and she was letting it control her now. "You mean you did not ask Richard to lunch with us today to discuss a settlement, but to fob him off with this nonsense?"

"Indeed, I am sorry that you take it this way." I became piteous. "It seems likely enough that I shall not trouble you for too long. I just ask that you find some little pity for your father in his last months. Tregenza can do nothing for me."

I did in earnest begin to feel sorry for myself. There was a lump in my throat that threatened to unman me, but I took a resolute hold on my feelings.

"I ask you only to help us to re-establish the routine of the house for your sisters' sake. It will not be a long obligation to me, I promise you."

"And how long, or short, an obligation do you fancy it may take to re-establish the routine to the house?"

"If you will just bide for twelve months here with us, then we will undertake to manage thereafter."

"Twelve months!"

"Just twelve months."

"You expect Richard and me to wait another twelve months before we plan our wedding?"

"Please Elizabeth, I am not a well man." I had no sooner made this observation, than an intolerable weakness in my knees made my legs buckle, and I had to clutch at the table, knocking off a plate, to support myself. I fell back into my seat dismayed — I really was feeling quite ill.

"I don't believe there is anything serious the matter with you at all. You are recovered from the influenza and you have claimed that Dr Tregenza's restorative tonic has renewed your vigour. I believe you may live another ten years, Father, and I hope that you may, but you must not expect that I shall run your household for another ten years."

"I don't, I don't." It came out as a whisper, and she looked at me in surprise, then hardened herself.

"This is not the first time you have had an attack when you do not readily get your own way."

I could not stand up. She got angrier.

"I believe that this is a rigmarole about Mrs Peebles. Either you are mistaken in your convalescence by her kindness, or you have fabricated the whole affair to prevent me marrying Richard."

"Frances," I said. She came slowly forward. "Will you be so kind as to write a note giving Mrs Peebles seven days notice, and saying that her salary will be paid until the end of this month."

She did nothing just looked at me, and as my choler rose I could feel my head spinning. There was a ring of hostile eyes staring at me. At me, on my own threshold!

I banged my hand on the table but, although the hand knocked another plate down I heard no sound — my hearing seemed to be deserting me. My throat was aching again. Not hot and swollen as before but aching so I coughed to relieve it and coughed.

Elizabeth's voice, cold and businesslike, pierced the fogs of my hearing.

"We are being manipulated by his illness."

But Anne and Harriet Maria came to me in concern. And then I was supported, and a pure cold hell washed my brain and squeezed it with the mercilessness of hartshorn. Richard, I believe, half lifted, half dragged me to the settee, and quilts and pillows were tucked around me, and I was left alone.

It was a time to pull together the threads of my intentions, to plan the next steps in disciplining my household, but I slept.

When I woke I was confused and disorientated. I was not in my bed, I was not in my bedroom. The couch was hard, which persuaded me in my half wakened state that I was again on *Director*, or *Bounty*. Opening my eyes I recognised our dining-room in Kent, but for some time I could not recollect how I came to be sleeping there. I recognised the rug and the quilt, they were from Jane's room, and the bolsters were my own, from my own bedroom. My mouth was dry, but I refrained from calling. It was an instinct of caution to reconnoitre my position before revealing my presence.

I thought hard, and then I remembered. I had taken control of the situation, and although they might complain, as women do, there wasn't one of the household who would not benefit from my resolution.

The turkeys. I listened and all was silent. Mr Ffoulkes. It would be many a day before he would press his unwanted coach upon us again. And Mrs Peebles. She would have had her notice by now. I listened warily, but I could hear nothing.

What hour was it I wondered. Only a grey even light came through the panes, no shadow at all to give the time.

I could foresee an awkward meeting with Mrs Peebles. I would not shirk it, that has never been my way, but I was not looking forward to it with a great pleasure.

Elizabeth, now there I was on firmer ground. I knew that she would come around to do as I wished — she felt strongly the devolution of her mother's responsibilities for her sisters, and for me. It was disappointing for her, but there it was, her duty lay plain to hand, and I knew she would not shirk it. Besides, I felt the fervour to marry Richard was a passion that would be very quickly cooled once its object was obtained. With the best charity in the world I could see little in him that was lovable.

Steady, yes, stodgy even. At least in me she had a foeman worthy of her steel.

I have always liked to foster an image of myself as the crusty sea dog with an irascible temper and an astonishing fluency in cursing. I can imagine that those around me who really know me, recognise this pose, and smile to themselves all the while they pay lip-service to this tyrant, thus helping to fuel the myth.

This unhappily doesn't happen with everyone, some choosing to recognise the myth and ignore the man. They find it easier to shut me out with disapproval rather than join me in appreciating my secret humours.

This has two effects. One is that their stupidity makes me genuinely lose my composure and strike out at them. Then I sometimes try to overcompensate by excessive amiability, apportioning blame to myself when it is really their own damned stupid insensitivity which has caused the blasted conflict.

Anyhow, with Elizabeth I knew that I had a supporter. We might have our differences, but she would be saying — 'He may be crusty, very crusty, but you know that he cares for you.'

I wished she would come in. I wanted some brandy. I hoped Mrs Peebles might have already terminated her duties but I didn't choose to ring the bell and put it to the test.

A little self-congratulation crept into my thoughts as I pondered my plans for reorganisation.

A man makes his destiny what it is by coping, then by overcoming. It's too damned easy to lie down under adversity when facing it, outfacing it, can bring it down.

I got the best of the mutineers in Sydney, you know. I got the best of them in the end, by God I did and nearly had MacArthur too.

That I didn't bring him home in chains was due only to a vagary in the wind, you know, and his own consummate cowardice. The story of how I regained my freedom and got my ship back by finesse, and a stratagem, will give you as much pleasure to read as, you can imagine, it gave me at the time.

I suddenly thought of a decanter of brandy, which with a twin flask of oporto lived usually on the serving table in the corridor outside the parlour.

I could smell brandy fumes, rising like the ghost of long dead muscatels to strengthen and fortify me, and my mouth grew dry with the need of it.

I pulled back the quilt and swung my legs to the ground. I was surprised to find them bare and noticed now that I was arrayed in my nightshirt. This I could not fathom.

Concentrating furiously I pushed my left knee forward and transferred my weight to it. But it was weak. It was so weak that I had not the confidence to proceed, and I fell back on the settee. I rubbed my hand over my mouth and found to my surprise and distaste that I was unshaven, and had been so for some days. I looked around the room more closely, although my eyes seemed weak and would not focus. It seemed I must have been billeted here for some time, as various towels and basins suggested the toilet arrangements of a sick bay. There was my bedside bell on the table beside me and I took it and rang it with all the vigour I could muster.

Chapter Thirteen

A visit from Mr Hughes does me no good at all — Elizabeth announces her intention to marry — my instructions for the dismissal of Mrs Peebles are ignored — the last Mutiny — Anne alone remains loyal, and we take to the long boat together

The bell sounded smaller in the parlour than it did in my bedroom, diminished and tinny in its tinkling. I waited, but nobody came. Perhaps it had not been heard. My eyes were aching and my forehead felt flushed, I wanted a cold foment to bathe my forehead, and I wanted brandy.

There was a rattling against the window-pane and I turned to look out on a cloud of sleet falling on a sodden landscape. It was too early in the season for snow in Kent, but the lawns around the manor are poorly tended and great puddles form in the lower parts so that we stand in a lake of rainwater. The drains were blocked with fallen leaves and so the paths also were flooded. We badly required the service of an active handyman to keep the place up. There is a terrace outside the parlour windows, but the garden washing away from beneath it had caused a subsidence, and several yards of the stone balustrading had collapsed.

It was the season of water, and the season of decay — we frequently find toadstools growing from the damp corners of the ground floor passages, and westerlies blow storm-water under the door into our scullery. The previous tenants had given up on the struggle to use the cellars under the back part of the house.

Diversion drains, wet sumps and an abandoned sludge pump testified to the earnestness of their endeavours to pump it dry, but all our time they have held a foot of water and in the winter it deepens to two feet. It is a damp house.

As the manor house stands on a small rise, a mound, I have

considered the possibility of an excavation, a simple bricked pipe out on to the hillside to drain the cellars, but then if the foundations have been wet for centuries, to dry them out now would be likely to cause movement and cracks in the walls, and maybe bring the slates cascading around our ears.

I'd have tried it in my youth.

The greyness of the sky gave no clue to the hour of the day but I shivered at the malevolence of the season. It was intolerable to think there was another six months of chill, and rain, and mud and gloom before us.

I rang the bell again as loudly as I could, and then choked with impatience I threw it at the door.

Nobody came.

It was much later, or so I judged it, for the sky had darkened and the cold intensified. I lay huddled under my quilt for warmth, and believe I had dozed. There was a tumbler beside the bed, and a bottle. I thought that if it were the laudanum I might take a draught as it should warm me up.

I looked at it from the corner of my eye, I was having trouble turning my head, and nerved myself for the reaching out to secure it when footsteps came along the passage and stopped at the door, and it opened.

"Not before time," I said coldly, "it is a poor thing for a man to be left sick and alone in his own parlour," then I stopped. It was not Elizabeth; it was Mrs Peebles who entered, accompanied by Hughes, the district sawbones.

"Hughes?" I said in surprise.

"And how are we this afternoon, Admiral?" He employed the sycophantic ingratiating voice of a man humouring a child, the damned jackass.

I made no reply.

"It's Mr Hughes to see you, Mr Bligh."

"I'm not blind, Mrs Peebles." She left the room without further comment, but her lips had tightened. She could at best be called an ordinary-looking person, and that was probably being a bit charitable.

I had to put up with the blasted Hippocrates running through his panjandrum of tricks on my tired body. I hadn't the strength to dispute it with him, and he counted my pulse, and peered into my eyes with a lens, and palpated my chest, poked around my liver, and even looked up my blasted nostrils.

When I baulked at this, he said sombrely, "The inflammation of the membranes, Admiral, is the measure of the body's inner strength."

So I let him go on.

"Well, well, and how do we feel today?"

"I feel damned thirsty and rather neglected. If you wish to make some positive contribution to my health would you kindly ring for some brandy."

"I must caution you, Admiral, that brandy will inflame your liver. I have arranged a herbal draught that will give you more relief than ever the brandy could do."

He picked up the laudanum and poured me a thimbleful. I reached out for the flask, and poured myself a small glassful, and swallowed it.

"It is a potent hypnotic nostrum, you must take it in careful moderation, or you will harm yourself."

"Nonsense, man, do you think I don't recognise laudanum? It only causes problems with patients that are not familiar with it."

"And what degree of familiarity do you enjoy with it?"

"I'm not one of your opium addicts," I laughed, "if that is what you are suggesting. Although I do not believe that you can reach any degree of addiction by swallowing it, it is the most highly regarded of remedies, of panaceas I might say, in the East. It is only the benighted celestials who smoke its latex that fall into its grasp. I take what I need to relieve a little digestive pain that seizes me."

"And does it not cloud your faculties?"

"Never. In soothing the physical it promotes the cerebral. Indeed it sharpens my wits."

"What can you recall of the last two days? What can you tell me of my last visit."

He was looking at me steadily. I looked down, there was something wrong here.

"I can tell you nothing, I have been ill."

"Yes."

"I had an attack. I was improperly recovered from the bronchitis."

"Yes, well I can recommend the best thing for you is to rest completely. I see you are being cared for by splendidly efficient ladies, as we all might wish to be, but I suggest, Admiral, that you avoid putting any strain on your system. You should avoid exciting yourself or indeed I cannot answer for the consequences."

I hadn't asked him to, but the blasted fellow still hadn't finished.

"I will suggest to your housekeeper that you may commence a light diet. Sillabubs and custards will do you no harm, and some brown ale, if you wish, but no spirits. And, my dear Admiral, although it is true that habituation can lead to the safe ingestion of very large doses of opium, I suggest that if you do not intend to harm your reason then you should take your laudanum only when the pain becomes intense."

"I don't recall, Hughes, that I solicited your opinion at all. Will you send Miss Elizabeth in as you go out?"

"I am only a country doctor Bligh, not a Wimpole Street surgeon, but let me caution you. You can drink all the willow-bark extract in England without resolving in any particle the lump in your gut."

He went out, and I heard him talking for a considerable time. It was damned poor, I thought, for him to let professional pique cloud his medical judgement. You can say what you like about the dangers of laudanum, but it certainly eases pain, and elevates your spirits, and your buoyancy of spirits is a prime factor in achieving recovery.

Presently I heard the sounds of the front door closing and the rattle of his curricle. The door reopened, Elizabeth came in.

"Father," she came over to the settee, "and how are you feeling?"

271

"What is that damned fellow doing here? I won't have it — you can tell him not to come."

She gazed at me in dismay. "He's the doctor! It's Mr Hughes, you remember Mr Hughes?"

"I remember him as a fumbling incompetent that I wouldn't take a sick spaniel to."

"Well," she retorted with a flash of fire," he has been perfectly competent in the last two weeks in nursing you through a bout of pneumonia that threatened to carry you off. You may still feel wretched, but you mustn't be ungrateful."

"I dare say my strong constitution is what carried me through in spite of Hughes' misguided efforts."

She busied herself straightening the room, tossing and folding at my covers.

"Can I get you some broth, Father? Do you feel you could drink a little — it would be strengthening for you."

Beef tea, broth, chicken soup, they have a child-like trust, women do, in the virtue of these slops to cure any fever or illness.

"Brandy."

"Mr Hughes does not wish you to take spirits."

"Pneumonia?"

"Indeed yes — pneumonia."

"A complication of my bronchitis."

"Your lungs have been weakened by living in this damp house."

"Banks arranged the house lease for us."

"And can he not be gainsaid? Must we stay here until the next attack, or the next, carries you off?"

"I've not had pneumonia before."

"Well, you've had it now. Mr Hughes is concerned about the swelling in your liver. He thinks you exacerbate it with your willow-bark extract."

"But Tregenza has ordered it."

"And is the swelling subsiding?"

"Hughes is a fool."

There was a pause.

"Shall I fetch you some soup? Will you take it?"

"Why is Mrs Peebles here still? Has she not been given her notice?"

"We will talk about it in a little while, Father."

"No, we will talk of it now, Elizabeth."

"Father, we will talk of it tomorrow, Richard and I, if you think you will be strong enough."

"Richard! What have my domestic arrangements to do with Richard?"

She gave no reply, other than "Tomorrow," but busied herself fetching a dish of soup and a napkin and, more endearingly, a glass of brandy.

I drained it, and asked for another, and she fetched it for me, which worried me rather, but the glow it put upon things, the warmth and strength it gave my gut and my optimism banished all immediate concern. As dusk came in, Anne came beside me to share the evening.

"Anne, my dear, and how do you do?"

"Oh Papa, we have been so worried about you. Mr Hughes was here every day."

"You have had cause to be concerned then." It was an ambiguity that passed over her head.

"The doctor says this house is damp."

"It is. It has two feet of water in the bilge, but then so did the *Resolution*."

"Captain Cook's ship?"

"It was one of his ships, and he was one of its masters. I really can't fathom why all you hear is Captain Cook this, and Captain Cook that. I ran his ship for him on the last voyage, and do you know what my kitten?"

"What, Papa?"

"All the maps and charts that he put his name on — you'll have heard of them, they've been published. Well, I drew all those maps for him!"

"Papa, Mr Hughes says you are not to be excited, or he will not answer for the consequences." She was solemn as a codfish.

"Very well, then you read to me while I go to sleep!"

"I don't read very well — shall I fetch Frances?"

"No, no, I think your reading is the best in the world. Get one of your own books." She went and fetched her books. "Which will you have? 'Sly Squirrels' Tale', or 'Pilgrim's Progress'?"

"Why, whichever you choose to read."

Either would send me to sleep, I calculated, and so it proved. I dozed off as Christian, who seemed a timid fellow, struggled with Mr Worldly-Wiseman and the City of Destruction.

A wintry sun had peeped out next morning, and Frances came with Mrs Peebles to check on my condition, and offer me some breakfast. I had lately been drinking coffee with my meal, rather than seeing in the day with small ale, and it smelt so good this morning that I took two cups of it, with some bread, and some perfectly pellucid honey.

If Richard were coming I was eager to be dressed, not to impress him, you see, but a man feels unmanned to some degree if he doesn't have his britches on.

"Shall I ask Mrs Peebles to assist you, Father?"

"No, Frances, ask her to assemble some linen and my blue suit, and I shall contrive to fit myself into it." I could do with a shoulder, an arm to support me as I got the trousers over my thighs, but Frances was so uncomfortable about the performance that I had to dispense with her.

To my relief Elizabeth, the seasoned sickberth attendant, came to my assistance, so that presently a reasonable facsimile of an Admiral sat neatly in his parlour, being shaved by his daughter who possessed most of the skills of a gentleman's valet. Anne came in to watch. She was fascinated, and would like to try her skills at shaving. I am a fond parent, but not foolhardy, so I elected to have Elizabeth continue.

"But I must learn," said Miss Anne, "so I can shave you, Papa, when Elizabeth has married Richard, and left us." Innocent candour crumpled, and was silent under a blaze of anger from brown eyes. Brown eyes full of innocence as I looked up, and spoke to me of the weather, and of the reports from London, and of the fish for luncheon, a tench.

"And when is this marriage planned for?" I asked brutally.

"Why Father, you must wait until Richard comes, and he shall speak to you."

"You've practised him, have you?" It was a comment to myself really, but I would wager she had done so. We did not lunch all together. I did not feel up to it, candidly, and I settled for a piece of the fish and some custard in my parlour bedroom, where, when I had finished, and washed my hands and mouth, presently Elizabeth and Richard presented themselves before me.

"Sir," he said, after a short exchange of pleasantries and formalities had been induced and put aside.

"Elizabeth, my fiancée, and I have decided that it would be best for all if we proceeded with our marriage arrangements, and so we have. We have arranged for the wedding to be performed on the twelfth day of this December."

He gazed at me steadily. A hundred objections and questions struggled to my lips, but I could not readily decide which to voice first, and after a perceptible pause, he took heart to proceed.

"My father, your cousin, would like us to be married in the church at Plymouth by Mr Trestran, who is his kinsman by marriage, but Elizabeth has insisted, and I agree, that we shall be wed here at Leyborne by Mr Troubridge, as she is concerned about your health, and the difficulties attendant upon travel."

"Very thoughtful, I'm sure." It sounded petulant, and feeble, and as soon as I uttered it I regretted its inadequacy. There can be no question that Marcus Aurelius would have improved upon it. I rallied my resources, and tried again.

"And does Mr Troubridge not require banns, and the other formalities associated with an impending marriage?"

"The banns were read for the first time last Sunday." I have no time for lawyers, I turned to Elizabeth with some bitterness, stoically down-played.

"And you will leave me to battle through my last months alone. You cannot spare me a few months to keep my house in order?"

She looked unhappy, but to my surprise Richard put her gently to one side, and a little behind him, and took the answer upon himself. It occurred to me that I might have underestimated him to some extent.

"Admiral Bligh, Mr Hughes assures us that if you are sensible, and live quietly, then there is no reason to expect your early demise."

"And if I live a year, who will run this household?"

"Sir, during your time of illness, I took it upon myself to speak with your housekeeper, and inquire into your concerns about her attitude."

I was speechless. His effrontery was such that I did not know where to begin in demolishing it.

"I could find no fault in the performance of her duties, nor in her behaviour and recognition of her place, and so we have decided that for the present she should remain in her position, and so it has been arranged. I must say here that your daughters, Elizabeth of course, and Jane and Frances, were of the same mind as myself."

"I have ordered her dismissal. Do you argue with me in my own house?"

"It was agreed, we all felt, that you were not yourself, that your illness had depressed you, had altered your perceptions in making that decision, and that it was one you would regret when in full health and command of your faculties again."

"You coxcomb, you confounded rascal!" I was in a fair way to choke with chagrin and disbelief. "Do you tell me I am out of my mind, do you presume to act for me, you blackguard?"

"Father," said Jane, "You must not excite yourself. Mr Hughes will not answer for it."

"Mr Hughes be damned for a snivelling pox doctor, I tell you I will not have it."

I pulled myself from my chair to confront my antagonists, "I will not countenance any wedding this year, nor will I have you interfering with my domestic appointments, Elizabeth."

Again it was Richard who spoke. "The wedding will be on December the twelfth, and Elizabeth will be extremely upset if you do not attend. Please accept that we will not postpone it. As to your domestic arrangements, you must accept that a man who has been gravely ill for a greater part of the last six months cannot expect to exercise his judgement as he might if he were twenty years younger."

There was an interruption as Jane and Anne, and then Frances came in and stood with Elizabeth. I cleared my throat and said calmly enough.

"There is nothing wrong with my judgement. Do you seek to usurp my position as head of this household?"

"You must appreciate your situation, Sir. When Elizabeth has left your house to wed me, you will need Mrs Peebles to run your house."

"I will brook no opposition. Jane, Frances, you will manage my affairs."

Jane looked sulky. Frances, who had been fraying the end of her plaited hair, pushed it aside and standing up looked to Jane for support; then, facing Richard resolutely, said. "I believe Richard is right, Papa, you must not dismiss Mrs Peebles. Who else can run your house?" Mrs Peebles had organised her conspiracy well.

"Anne?" She burst into tears, and Elizabeth put her arms around her. "Don't fret her Father."

"Anne?" My voice was harsh, even to myself.

"Mrs Peebles is our friend," she whispered.

I steeled my heart against her.

I could feel the blood rising into my neck, and beyond, and beating behind my forehead.

"I will have Mrs Peebles packed up and out of Farningham by this time tomorrow, and Elizabeth if you fancy that I will be at Leyborne church to see you wed, this ..."

I paused. The pressure in my forehead was affecting my vision, so that now I saw two Richards, but not clearly, the images were overlapping and not focussed. I shook my head, but there was an ache in my eyes, especially in my left eye, an aching pressure, and I had a horrified feeling the eyeball might rupture with the pressure behind it and squirt out its contents in a jet of blood and watery humour. I shut both eyes and pushed my fists against them, but my face had no feeling, and there was a dull pain in my shoulder. I opened my eyes but the room was framed by a brown margin that was closing in and constricting my field of vision.

As I sank to my seat I heard Richard say to Elizabeth. "I believe you now, you predicted he would receive our news by declining back into illness."

It was a remark that I remembered and resented a little later, but at that time it conveyed nothing to me. I was struggling with my body. I could feel my jaw was clenched into a grimace but could do nothing to straighten it, I was concentrating on a pain in my lower gut that threatened to end in a disgraceful voiding of my bowels. I vaguely wondered if I was dying. I clenched my buttocks and felt my senses reeling.

Slowly I had my body back under control. It wasn't going to disgrace me, not this time.

Elizabeth came close, watching me intently.

"Richard, send the others out."

He glanced at her, then stared at me, then speaking quietly he ushered everyone out of the room, and came over to her.

"You had better send Jackson to fetch Mr Hughes back." She took a rug and folded it around me.

"He's not — you don't think he is just…"

"He is ill, I think he has had a seizure."

Richard looked at me hard, then went out quickly.

Elizabeth took a flannel and smoothed it, cool and moist over my forehead, then she poured a tumbler of water and held it to my mouth. My mouth was dry. I took a sip, but to my surprise and distress I could not hold it in my mouth, and it ran from my lips and down my chin, and dripped on the front of my uniform coat.

Patiently she dried it, and cautiously held the tumbler to my mouth again.

I took a more cautious sip and sucked it noisily back into my throat. She had pinched my lip against the rim of the glass tumbler, and I turned my head aside.

Richard came back in, and Elizabeth turned to him with a question.

"Jackson has sent to your neighbour, Mr Ffoulkes, to send a man for the doctor, and Ffoulkes himself is coming across directly, I understand, to see if there is aught else he can do to assist."

"You will stay Richard?"

"I will stay until morning. You and I and Frances will need to consider assuming the management of your fathers' business affairs while he is incapacitated."

"You spoke of this last night."

"I believe we should see his attorney's, Grimes & Struthers, in Bond Street. It may be expedient for you and Frances to apply now to the Courts for power of attorney."

I tried to speak, to voice protest, but when I put tongue to words they came out laboured and ran together. I wanted to say to her "You rob me of my authority as your father, Elizabeth, you band your sisters together against me. Have I deserved this of you? Is this the fruit of the love I have shown you? Does love of your Richard poison and desiccate your affection for me?"

I could not make it intelligible, she leant towards me and frowned, then wiping saliva from my lips she said. "Don't try to talk Father, just lie still and rest until the doctor arrives."

Tears of frustration pricked my eyes.

"This is a mutiny, Elizabeth. Don't you think I can recognise a mutiny?"

If she understood she gave no sign, but settled me back on the cushions. She rose and went quietly out of the room, and presently Mrs Peebles came in to close the shutters.

Anne came to me with the dusk, and kneeling by the bed put her cheek against me.

"Anne, are you not part of the mutiny?"

It was still garbled, but she understood me. There was a bond between us, an understanding that did not always require words.

"Papa, Papa, I'm always with you." She clasped her arms behind me and rocked me like a child.

"It's mutiny Anne, my baby, it's damned mutiny."

"It's all right, Papa, everything will be all right."

"They won't beat me, Anne, I'm a survivor — they forget that."

She was crooning a soothing lullaby.

"I persist, I just persist, until I triumph. They'd forgotten that. I'm the one man who knows what to do about mutiny."

"Hush, Papa."

"But it's lonely in the boat, where are the others?" The pain of it made me shiver.

"Papa, I'm here with you."

"It's a long way Anne." It was getting dark and cold, and spray was coming in over the bow.

"It's all right, Papa, as long as we're together."

"Five thousand miles, but we just take it a wave at a time. Steer through this one and the next one." The sea was getting up and we were thrown against each other, so that she put an arm out to support me.

"We can do it together."

"It's all right Papa, I'm here."

And she sat close as the night came down on us.

Epilogue

The Gentleman's Magazine
December 1817

Marriages —

Richard Bligh, Esq., of Lincoln's Inn to Elizabeth, third daughter of Vice Admiral Bligh of Farningham House, Kent.

Deaths—

Vice Admiral William Bligh, of Farningham House, Kent. December 7th, 1817, aged 64 years.

Vice Admiral Bligh was survived by six daughters. His remains are deposited in the family vault at the Parish church of St. Mary, Lambeth.

The monument proclaims:

Sacred
To the memory of
William Bligh, Esq. F.R.S.
Vice Admiral of the Blue

The celebrated navigator who first transplanted the breadfruit tree from Otaheite to the West Indies.
Bravely fought the battles of his country;
and died beloved, respected and lamented,
on the seventh day of December, 1817
Aged 64.

The Historical Record

The Family

Bligh, Elizabeth, called 'Betsy' by Wm. Bligh, born as Elizabeth Betham, met Bligh on the Isle of Man and they married there in 1781. She died in 1812.

Bligh, Harriet Maria, Mary, Anne, Elizabeth, Frances and **Jane,** daughters of William and Elizabeth Bligh.

> Elizabeth married Richard Bligh.
>
> Harriet Maria married Henry Barker.
>
> Mary married John Putland (d. 1808), then married Maurice O'Connell.

Bligh, Richard, nephew of Wm. Bligh, was fiancé of Bligh's daughter Elizabeth and later married her.

Bligh, William: William Bligh was born in 1754 and entered the Royal Navy at the age of seven years and nine months as a Captain's servant on H.M.S. *Monmouth*. This was to serve as his nursery into the navy, and into adult life.

Following this he was for some years at Plymouth Free Grammar School before returning to the navy as a midshipman. Distinction in this capacity on several ships led to his appointment in 1776 as Master of H.M.S. *Resolution* on Cook's last, and fatal, voyage. Much of Cook's mapping on this voyage was undoubtedly done by the young Bligh.

When *Resolution* was paid off in England in 1780 Bligh made a trip to the Isle of Man, where he met three families who were to be involved in his future — the Bethams, the Christians and the Heywoods. In 1781 he married Elizabeth Betham at Douglas on the Isle of Man.

In 1787 he was appointed as commander of the *Bounty*, charged with bringing breadfruit from Tahiti (then known as Otaheite) to the West Indies, where they were to be introduced as a crop.

After the joys of Tahiti the crew mutinied, and Bligh was set adrift in an open boat with eighteen others. By superb seamanship he brought them through native attack, storm, and starvation over 4000 miles to Timor. Weathering the social perils of Timor, Bligh and his diminished crew made their way home.

Meanwhile the mutineers led by Fletcher Christian sailed back to Tahiti, where they took on a cargo of native wives and sailed in search of a new home. A search for them by H.M.S. *Pandora* failed to find the ringleaders but they were later found on Pitcairn Island.

In Britain's continuing Napoleonic wars Bligh commanded H.M.S. *Director*, which was involved in the great naval mutiny at the Nore in 1797. Later he led this ship into his first naval action at the battle of Camperdown. In 1801 he commanded H.M.S. *Glatton* at Copenhagen where she played a major role.

In 1804 while in command of H.M.S. *Warrior* on blockade duty he was brought to a court martial by his second officer, a Lieutenant Frazier, on charges of bad language and tyranny. He was acquitted.

He was appointed Governor of New South Wales, sailing thither in 1806. He clashed with MacArthur and the New South Wales Corps in a dispute which ended with the Rum Rebellion. He was held by the rebels for a year until gaining freedom by what he described as a 'finesse': he blockaded Port Jackson in the naval ship H.M.S. *Porpoise*, which had been intended to carry him to Britain.

On the arrival of his successor, Lachlan Macquarie, he sailed home to England and to the trial of the leaders of the insurrection.

He was made a Rear Admiral in 1811, and a Vice Admiral in 1812.

Campbell, Duncan, uncle to Elizabeth Betham. Bligh entered his merchant service, sailing ships to the West Indies between 1783 and 1787. It was in this service that Fletcher Christian first served under him.

Putland, Lieutenant John, husband of Mary Bligh, voyaged with Bligh as his lieutenant to New South Wales but died there two weeks before the rebellion.

Family friends and acquaintances

Banks, Sir Joseph, Bligh's lifelong friend and patron, is best remembered as botanist on Cook's first voyage. The banksia is named after him. He met Bligh when Cook was fitting out *Resolution* for his (Cook's) last voyage. Banks was also Bligh's sponsor in his election to a Fellowship of the Royal Society.

Barnes, the apothecary in Farningham.

Hughes, the doctor of medicine in Farningham.

Jackson, gardener, groom, handyman in Bligh's household. He had served under Bligh on the *Glatton*.

Tregenza, Mr Adrian, physician and surgeon in London.

Troubridge, the Reverend James, Vicar of St. Stephens, Lower Farningham.

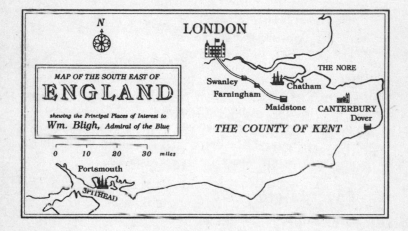

The Warrior *court martial (1804)*

Cosway, Mr J.S.R., Bligh's counsel, who acted as Deputy Judge Advocate.

Cotton, Vice Admiral Sir Charles, President of the Court.

Frazier, Lieut. John. Frazier claimed to have injured his leg in an accident. Bligh discounted the seriousness of the injury, and insisted that Frazier keep his watches. When he refused he was court-martialled at Bligh's instigation for "contumacy and disobedience of his commanding officer". Following his acquittal he, in his turn, charged Bligh with using abusive and tyrannical language both to him and to other members of the crew. He acted as prosecutor. Bligh was admonished by the court and told to be more correct in his language. Bligh returned to command of the *Warrior*. Frazier was dismissed from the Navy.

Witnesses for the prosecution:

Amplett, John, marine.

Boyack, Alexander, third lieutenant.

Cock, Henry, master's mate.

Knowles, Samuel, midshipman.

Quade, Charles, surgeon's mate.

Witnesses for the defence:

Johnston, George, first lieutenant, led the defence.

Numerous others, who were so staunch in his defence that the smallest of suspicions persists that they had been coached in their testimony. The same suspicion also clings to the witnesses who appeared for the prosecution.

The Bounty *Mutiny (1789)*

In the immediate aftermath of the Mutiny the mutineers returned in the *Bounty* to Tahiti where they were joined by their Tahitian female companions and some natives who elected to join them in an attempt at establishing a colony where they could live without discovery. The Island of Toobouai was chosen because the inhabitants were known to be very fierce, which discouraged visitors.

There were many disagreements between the sailors and the natives leading to skirmishes and death. Eventually the settlement was abandoned. They returned to Tahiti where several members of the crew elected to stay. Fletcher Christian and eight other mutineers, together with their female companions and some natives, sailed in search of another refuge. Eventually they found Pitcairn where the *Bounty* was burnt and sunk. There was much jealousy and fighting amongst the group and their numbers dwindled because of accident and murder. John Adams (Alexander Smith) was the sole survivor when the island was rediscovered.

Two of the group who stayed on Tahiti, **Charles Churchill** and **Matthew Thompson**, were killed by natives. The remaining 14 were apprehended by H.M.S. *Pandora*, commanded by Captain Edward Edwards in 1791. H.M.S. *Pandora* had been despatched in 1790 with orders to search the South Pacific for the *Bounty* mutineers. Edwards also found evidence of the *Bounty*'s subsequent voyages, including its abortive landing on Toobouai. However, he failed to find Pitcairn Island, which had been incorrectly located on the Admiralty charts of the period.

Finally abandoning the search, Edward set sail for home, but was wrecked in Torres Strait. Four of the mutineers were among those drowned in this wreck. The ten survivors were brought to trial in Britain, on charges of mutiny, in 1792.

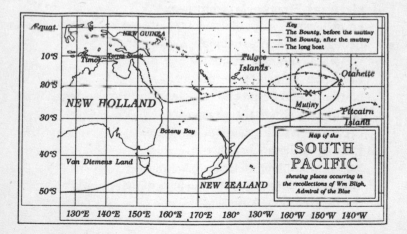

The fate of the crew of the Bounty

Those who died on Pitcairn:
William Brown, Fletcher Christian, Isaac Martin, William Martin, William McKoy, John Mills, Matthew Quintal, John Williams, Edward Young and the last survivor, John Adams (Alexander Smith).

Those who were murdered on Tahiti:
Charles Churchill and Matthew Thompson.

Those who died in the wreck of the Pandora:
George Stewart, John Sumner, Richard Skinner and Henry Hillbrant.

Those who were court-martialled and hanged:
Thomas Ellison, Thomas Burkitt and Jonathon Millward.

Those who were court-martialled and acquitted:
Charles Norman, Josiah Coleman, Thomas McIntosh, Michael Byrne, Peter Heywood, James Morrison, Willam Musprat.

Those who undertook the voyage in the launch with Bligh were:
Cole, William, Boatswain.
Elphinstone, William, Master's Mate.
Fryer, John, Master. He should occupy a special place in any classification, as neither party wanted him.
Hall, Thomas, A.B.
Hallett, Jonathon, Midshipman.
Hayward, Thomas, Midshipman.
Lamb, Robert, A.B.
Lebogue, Lawrence, Sailmaker.
Ledward, Thomas, Surgeon.
Linkletter, Peter, Quartermaster.
Nelson, David, Botanist. He died shortly after reaching Timor.
Norton, Jonathon, Quartermaster.
Peckover, William, Gunner.
Purcell, William, Carpenter.
Samuels, Captain's Clerk.
Simpson, George, Quartermaster's Mate.
Smith, Jonathon, A.B.
Tinkler, Robert, A.B.

The Mutiny at the Nore (May 1797)

Bligh was appointed in 1796 to command H.M.S. *Director*, a fourth-rate ship of 64 guns. This was his first important naval command. *Director* was part of the Channel Fleet under **Admiral Duncan**, which fleet was engaged in blockading the Dutch fleet in the Texel. During 1797 the British nation was rocked by a series of naval mutinies which threatened the security of the island. The first major outbreak was at Spithead, and **Lord Howe** was despatched to quell this with a proclamation of pardon for all involved should they return to duty, and several concessions which addressed some of the mutineers' demands.

Within a week the much more serious Mutiny at the Nore broke out. Duncan's fleet was crippled, only his flagship *Venerable* and the *Adamant* remaining loyal. The dissident crews each elected two delegates to a committee with **Richard Parker** being elected president. Bligh was the last commander of the North Sea fleet to be turned off his ship. The Mutiny was not contained until the Thames estuary was virtually blocked by the removal of navigation marks, and the dissident ships were surrounded by shore batteries armed with furnaces for heating shot. Supplies of food were kept from the mutineers, and Duncan was put on alert to attack them with such loyal ships as could be mustered.

Bligh was ordered to make a tour of the ships urging the crews to return to their duty. For his efforts he was formally thanked by the Admiralty.

It may be significant to point out that following the Mutiny the officers of whose brutality the crews had complained were removed from their ships. The list contained over one hundred names, but that of William Bligh was not among them.

The Battle of Camperdown (October 1797)

De Winter, Admiral, commanded the Dutch fleet and flew his flag on the *Vrijheid*.

Duncan, Admiral Alan. Commander of the blockading British fleet. His flag was on H.M.S. *Venerable*.

Onslow, Vice Admiral Sir Richard. The second in command flew his flag on H.M.S. *Monarch*.

Williamson, John, Captain of H.M.S. *Agincourt*, whose ship was alleged to have stayed outside the action, was court-martialled for cowardice after the battle, and was dismissed from the service.

Officers on Director *included:*

Birch, Second Officer.

Clarke, Surgeon.

Eldridge, Midshipman on the signal lines.

Foote, Lieutenant, Third Officer.

Ireland, Gunnery Officer.

McTaggart, First Officer.

Roscow, Fourth Officer.

The Battle of Copenhagen (1801)

Foley, Thomas, Nelson's Flag Captain on the *Elephant*.

Graves, Rear Admiral Sir Thomas, supported Nelson's efforts, and in particular his turning a blind eye to Hyde Parker's signal to disengage at the height of the conflict.

Hardy, Lieutenant on the *Elephant*, had been with Nelson on the frigate *Minerva* at St. Vincent, and was to be his Flag Captain at Trafalgar.

Nelson, Vice Admiral Horatio, second in charge, impatient at what he saw as Hyde Parker's dilatory approach forced the resolution of the dispute by leading a column of ships up the Strait of Copenhagen.

Parker, Admiral Sir Hyde, in command of the British fleet sent to the Baltic to compel Denmark and Sweden by force, if necessary, to abandon their policy of 'Armed Neutrality' which was excluding British ships from trade in that sea.

Riou, Captain Edward, commander of the *Amazon*, was cut in halves by a roundshot. He had been a midshipman on Cook's *Resolution* when Bligh was Master.

Events in New South Wales

Atkins, Richard, Magistrate, sometime Judge Advocate, notorious for his frequent inebriation.

Crossley, George. Attorney, forger, and freed convict was the only source of knowledge of legal procedure available to Atkins.

Gore, William, was the Provost Marshal.

Jubb, George, Bligh's steward.

King, P.G., Governor. In charge of the Colony until Bligh replaced him.

Lewisham, Charles. A convicted forger who served Bligh as secretary in the Colony.

Oakes, Francis, Chief Constable at Parramatta.

Short, Captain Joseph, was commander of *Porpoise* during the voyage of the convoy bringing Bligh to his Governorship. There was heated dispute as to who was in overall command of the convoy. Short was sent home to a court martial, but was cleared. His wife died on the voyage back to Britain.

Members of NSW Regiment:

Abbott, Capt. Edward, was second in command of the Regiment.

Finucan, Lieut. Bligh was imprisoned in his quarters for 7 days.

Foveaux, Lt. Col. Joseph. He was Johnston's senior, and on his arrival from England pronounced himself to be the Lt. Governor, replacing Johnston.

Johnston, Lt. Col. George, was in command, and assumed the position of Lt. Governor on Bligh's deposition.

Paterson, Lt. Col. William, was Foveaux's senior and the Lt. Governor of the Colony under Bligh. He had been endeavouring to start a settlement at Port Dalrymple, on the Tamar estuary in northern Tasmania. He tardily returned to Sydney almost twelve months after the insurrection, and assumed control.

Piper, Capt. John.

Settlers:

Blaxland, Gregory, together with his brother John, Garnham Blaxcell, Simeon Lord, James Badgery, James Mileham, Nicholas Bayly, and Thomas Jamison all signed the petition to Johnston to arrest Bligh.

Campbell, Robert. An honest and disinterested friend to Bligh, and a reliable witness to the events.

Kent, Lieut. W., was commander of H.M.S. *Porpoise* at the time of the insurrection.

MacArthur, John, sometime Captain in the New South Wales Regiment, landholder and entrepreneur. (His name is generally spelt thus by Bligh, as McArthur by the man himself, and as Macarthur in modern accounts.)

Macquarie, Lachlan, Governor of New South Wales sent out to relieve Bligh.

Porteous, Capt. John, in command of *Porpoise* when Bligh joined that vessel ostensibly to leave the Colony.

Some notes on the rum trade in NSW (from 1790 to 1808)

In 1789 the British Government decided to raise a regiment for service in the settlement of New South Wales, and eventually a full regiment of ten companies arrived in the Colony to take over the military duties hitherto carried out by marines.

The officers and men quickly rose to dominate the affairs of the settlement, and during the years up to 1795 martial law prevailed with the commanding officer of the regiment acting as Governor.

Property and power became vested in the officer corps, with generous land grants being given to each of the officers for their 'services to the community', and so were established the large estates of such men as John MacArthur.

The officers also commanded a monopoly of all spirits arriving in the Colony, which they disposed of at enormous profit in barter with the struggling settlers. The system worked like this: the Government, which was controlled by the officers, claimed a monopoly on all spirits arriving at the port, which spirit, mainly rum, was purchased by the officers at very favourable

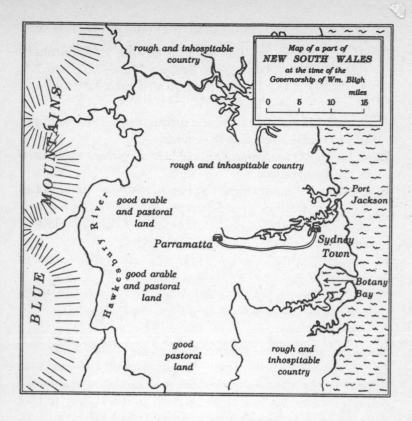

Map of a part of
NEW SOUTH WALES
at the time of the
Governorship of Wm. Bligh
miles
0   5   10   15

rough and inhospitable
country

MOUNTAINS

rough and inhospitable country

Port
Jackson

good arable
and pastoral
land

Hawkesbury River

Parramatta

Sydney
Town

BLUE

good arable
and pastoral
land

Botany
Bay

good
pastoral
land

rough and
inhospitable
country

terms. The rum was sold at an exorbitant profit through grog-shops or shanties, or was carried through the country by agents who bartered it in exchange for the farmer's stock, or crops, or produce. By 1806 rum had become the only currency and the officer corps was battening on the whole community which was kept in great poverty and distress.

Governors Hunter and King made efforts before Bligh to curb the privileges and depredations of the Corps but were largely unsuccessful as this same regiment was the only force in the Colony available to back up the civil administration.

Bligh posed a much sterner threat to them, instituting a cash society by ordering that the soldiers be paid in cash, and running the Government stores so that farmers could obtain reasonably priced goods in exchange for their produce. Bligh had brought with him specific instructions to stop the trade in rum, and he also banned the distillation of spirits. It was an attempt by MacArthur to import an illegal still that led to his arrest and trial. This trial was to become the flashpoint of the insurrection of the New South Wales Corps and the arrest of the Governor on January 26th, 1808.

Abacus Books now offers an exciting range of quality titles by both established and new authors. All of the books in this series are available from:

Little, Brown and Company (UK),
P.O. Box 11,
Falmouth,
Cornwall TR10 9EN.

Alternatively you may fax your order to the above address. Fax No. 01326 317444.

Payments can be made as follows: cheque, postal order (payable to Little, Brown and Company) or by credit cards, Visa/Access. Do not send cash or currency. UK customers and B.F.P.O.: please send a cheque or postal order (no currency) and allow £1.00 for postage and packing for the first book, plus 50p for the second book, plus 30p for each additional book up to a maximum charge of £3.00 (7 books plus).

Overseas customers including Ireland please allow £2.00 for postage and packing for the first book, plus £1.00 for the second book, plus 50p for each additional book.

NAME (Block Letters) ....

....

ADDRESS ....

....

....

☐ I enclose my remittance for ....

☐ I wish to pay by Access/Visa Card

Number ☐☐☐☐☐☐☐☐☐☐☐☐☐☐☐☐

Card Expiry Date ☐☐☐☐